DESTINED LOVERS

DESTINED LOVERS

FATE COMPELS THEM

C.A. CLEARY

Published by C.A. Cleary

ISBN: 978-1-7376195-0-5

Editor: Makenna Albert / OnTheSamePageediting.com

Cover design, illustration & interior formatting:
Mark Thomas / Coverness.com

I dedicate this book to my son, CJ,
for always inspiring me to be the best role model I can be.

You are my muse.

"Did my heart love till now?

Forswear it, sight!

For I ne'er saw true beauty till this night."

-Shakespeare "Romeo & Juliet"

Chapter One

"You need to calm down." Collin followed me into my office, stopping the door a moment before it slammed into his face.

I flung a stack of papers off my desk and stormed toward the large floor-to-ceiling windows overlooking the city.

"They're *fools!*" I growled.

"Caleb, they're afraid," Collin countered.

I sighed and pinched the bridge of my nose. Tearing my fingers through my jet-black hair, I faced my brother. "We're at a crossroads, Collin. You know that as well as I do. Our ancestors watched as humans evolved, believing their strength would somehow benefit us, and instead we've endured decades of mass killings. Hunting groups tracking down our settlements, slaughtering our kind...our parents. We've been hiding too long. We once numbered in the thousands. Our entire race is living in fear of extinction. It's...unbearable! We must preserve our line. Even if it means mating with...*humans.*" I shuddered.

"And you really believe that the creation of Dhampyres are the solution?" Collin's golden eyes scanned my face.

Truthfully, the idea of the half-vampire, half-human creatures made my stomach churn. "What choice do we have?"

"You look tired. Have you lost weight? You seem slimmer than usual."

"I haven't eaten in a few days." I shook my head. "Don't try to change the subject. The world needs all of us, mortals and immortals. The balance must be maintained. Tharaat knows this as well as any of us, but he's being stubborn. The light and darkness are necessary."

"Humans have always feared the dark. We haven't always been civilized. There was danger in the dark," Collin added.

"True." I couldn't argue that. "But some of the most beautiful things can be found in its depths. We aren't inherently evil, Collin. We need them to see we are not as naïve as we once were, when we let our curse, our thirst for blood, rule our actions. But we have overcome those urges. Humans have nothing to fear from us now."

"In a perfect world, it would be easy to expect them to take our word, but humans are weaker and fear what they cannot control. It won't be easy."

"Nothing about this is easy. Even suggesting we mate with *them*...I don't know how Father let this happen. He had to see this. Whole families were being killed."

"I don't think he, or anyone on the Council, could have anticipated the impact on our future offspring."

"Perhaps. I still don't understand why they are born such monsters. Our bloodlust has always been strong, but we've been able to maintain control. The offspring being born are abominations." I slumped into my chair, my cerulean eyes shuttering from fatigue.

Collin watched with a discerning eye. "I need a drink, want one?"

I could only imagine what I looked like. Broad shoulders bent forward, head in my hands. The responsibility of taking our father's seat on the Tribunal, as well as becoming head of the Vampire Council, was starting to show.

Collin headed to the cabinet against the far wall and poured us both a double shot of whiskey.

"I'm tired of hunting them down, aren't you, brother? Vampires shouldn't kill vampires." I rubbed at my face.

"I agree. You need to give the other Tribunal members time. Let them process what you're suggesting."

"Vampires don't have time, ironic as that sounds. If we are going to do this, we need to start now. I've done what I can. I've already met with all the members of the Council, and they're in agreement. The last step is to persuade the members of the Tribunal to follow in our footsteps."

The Tribunal comprised of myself as the highest-ranking vampire, along with Tharaat, the Elder of the Fae; Angus, the King Alpha of the werewolves; Fiona, the Grand High Priestess of witches; and Kaan, the Lord of dragons. My father helped establish it centuries ago for the purpose of maintaining peace among the immortal races. Meeting every five years, we typically alternated between each member's domain to discuss items of concern with the ever-changing world.

"Angus, Fiona, and Kaan are on board. It's just that stupid faerie…" I shook my head. Collin chuckled.

"He will never agree to what you're suggesting, and you know that, Caleb. The Fae barely leave their forest. Heck, I'm surprised Elder Tharaat agreed to join the Tribunal."

"If they refuse, the Fae will die off." Humans believed they had eliminated vampires and turned to the Fae for the past several years. "They won't last long. We don't need his consent for the rest of us to move forward, but…" I gazed out the window. "I don't know what impact the extinction of the Fae will have on the world."

Collin exhaled. "They've been removed for so long, and while they are among the strongest magical creatures, they aren't the only ones who help maintain balance."

"The world will be much darker without them, but I do not think it will perish."

"What will you say when you go back in there?"

"I will disband the Tribunal meeting. The best course of action now is for each leader to work with their individual councils to do what they feel is right for their people. We will move forward with the plan the Council has approved. It won't break any of the Tribunal Peace laws, so there shouldn't be any problems. I only hope the others will follow and do what's necessary to save themselves."

Collin nodded. "I'll go speak with the other heads of households and get them started on next steps. I'll give them one month to find humans willing to join us that suit our cause."

"Do they understand what we are asking of them and why?"

"Yes. I've gone over your plan as you laid it out. Thankfully, there are several human families working and residing in our community that don't despise us and have kept our secret. If all goes well, we will have eight human couples chosen to start reliable human bloodlines. They will contract with the Council to present their children when they come of age to all unmated vampires."

"And they know that each of them must come willingly, no coercion or false promises of immortality? They were satisfied with bestowing the gift of immortality to their mate once they have offspring if they choose?"

"They are aware and know the penalty if they disobey. No one complained."

"Good. No one is to be turned," I ordered. "It is not our place to play Creator. We are giving up too many of our traditions, and we will not go against our own laws."

"So why not bring *all* of the humans in the community together and match them to our unmated vampires?"

"We need to maintain control to ensure this plan works. Not every human will want to join with a vampire, and I won't force any of our kind to choose a mate either. It slows the recovery process down, but I prefer these gatherings to be a way for our kind to mingle with humans safely and find matches naturally. Our bloodlines will become diluted over time, it's unavoidable, but this way, it's not as quick. Many of the Council members have questioned if we should be taking mates, or if we should merely have them bear our offspring."

Collin chuckled, his golden eyes sparkling with mischief. "Sounds like the ideal loophole for a certain vampire."

"Don't start with me, Collin. I have enough to worry about. Finding a mate is not on my list of things to do."

"It should be. Why shoulder this burden alone?"

I hissed, bearing my fangs.

Collin raised his hands. "On that note, the others are waiting for you. You should get back to them and let them know what we're doing. Our town is about to have a growth spurt."

"Are we ready?" I turned to face my brother.

"Of course." Collin smiled and left me.

I collected the millions of thoughts filling my head as I headed back to the meeting room.

I know the Council will be expecting me to set an example but the idea of mating, least of all with a human and for life, makes my teeth itch. I'll find a way to avoid it altogether. I have no desire to sire offspring or enter a committed relationship with anyone. I don't have time in my life for such folly. Fate be damned. I will never...NEVER take a human as my eternal mate.

My brow furrowed. Vampires didn't often show their emotions, and the world mistook that as meaning we didn't have any. However, it was far from the truth. Vampires were truly passionate beings. My solution numbed me to my core, but we had little choice. I didn't fully despise humans—they are my food source after all. I simply hadn't met a human I wanted to spend much time with, least of all eternity.

Once I was seated again, I explained my plan and looked to each of my guests for their reactions.

"Caleb, you are suggesting we taint our bloodlines with those disgusting, idiotic creatures." Tharaat's green eyes held a look of distaste reinforcing his words.

"It's the only way to ensure immortals remain a part of this world. I'm not thrilled at the idea of mixing pure vampire bloodlines with those heathens either Tharaat, but unless someone can produce a better plan, I don't see any of us has much of a choice."

Angus laughed. "You're all making too much of this. Werewolves have been mating with humans for years. Would you prefer mating with us, Tharaat?"

Tharaat's porcelain skin paled. "You can't be serious!"

Angus upturned his nose. "Of course not. We can't stand the smell of faeries."

"Like you dogs smell any better?"

"Say that again…" Angus said. Standing at his full height of seven feet, he dwarfed the elder Fae. He flexed his arms, showing the network of veins beneath the skin.

"That's enough you two. Remember Angus, after you turn your mate, they can still have pups," Fiona said. The lithe witch squared her shoulders, firmly letting them know she would not tolerate any mischief. "We have also mated with humans in the past and have had no problems with the offspring produced by those unions. Some of our most powerful priestesses are of mixed blood."

"That's fine for all of you." Kaan's deep voice rumbled over the members at the table. "I am the last of my kind, and I am not able to mate with humans. Bearing a dragon offspring is not something the human body can survive."

"So, find a human to impregnate, let them bear you a child, and then replace them." Angus plopped back into his seat and drank from the stein before him.

Kaan's coal-colored eyes glared at him. "You're a barbarian."

"Angus, human females can't carry a dragon offspring to term. Both the baby and mother die." Fiona winced. "Forgive him, Kaan. Angus is more beast than human."

The werewolf snuffed. "Well, you are, my dear." She squeezed his hand.

"Only you could get away with saying such things to me. Anyone else would be staring at their still beating heart as I ate it before them."

"And my point is made."

"Back to business," I continued. "While the others are already ahead of us, Tharaat, it remains the vampires and the Fae that must change. I've already given my instructions to the Council, and Collin is moving forward with the other pureblood families. We will form a system that works best for our community and mingle with humans to ensure the continuance of our race. Whether I like it or not is irrelevant. Dhampyres will be our salvation. I suggest you find yours."

Tharaat stood. "You can do as you wish. The Fae will not sully themselves in such sordid affairs as mixing with…*humans*."

"Even if it means the ultimate extinction of your kind?" Fiona raised one of her brows.

"Yes. If the Fae are not meant to remain of this world, then we will face the end of our time with grace and dignity." With his final words, he waved his hand and vanished.

Angus growled. "I hate when he does that. Would it kill him to use the door like everyone else? Why does he always have to show off?"

"The man is a fool."

"It's his choice, Caleb. Personally, I don't think they will be missed." Angus finished off the ale in his stein and stood as well. "If there's nothing else to discuss, I'm going for a run and then back to my castle."

I waved him away, smirking as I watched the behemoth werewolf stoop through the doorway.

"I too must make my departure." Fiona stood, her blonde hair falling over her shoulders and down her back like a waterfall. "The covens are meeting tonight, and my presence is required. Caleb, I wish you and the Council good fortune as you start down this new path. And thank you for being such a gracious host as always. Kaan, don't be a stranger." She blew him a kiss.

"Safe travels," we said in unison.

"Well old friend…" Kaan started once she left. "Do you think your plan is wise?"

"I don't see that we have much choice. We've tried everything else."

"Why not make more vampires? You have the ability."

"It is not our way…and more disagreeable than mating with a human."

"This can't be easy for you and the other purebloods."

"We face extinction, Kaan."

"Because of the same humans you now wish to bring into your community."

"The irony is not lost on me, my friend. The Council and I have come up with some exceedingly high standards for the selected humans, and I've instructed that each human who forms a contract with the Council comes willingly, knowing what we are asking of them and their descendants."

"So you're hoping for a mutually beneficial agreement between the two?"

I nodded.

"But what about love?"

"Hopefully those that find mates will find love as well."

"And you?" Fire seemed to simmer behind his eyes as Kaan searched mine. "Why do you continue to shut yourself away? A vampire's life is too long to live alone."

"I have no use for such frivolous exploits. I am content with my books."

"I must say, you continue to surprise me. I've known you for centuries, Caleb. We've fought side by side against formidable hunters. I've never known you to be afraid of anything and yet..."

"Love doesn't scare me." My fangs elongated at the accusation.

"If you say so. Don't get worked up." Kaan stood. "I wish you luck, my friend. I envy you. Humans are not as bad as you think. Most of them are kind and peaceful beings who see the wonders of this world that we have long since become blind to. Give them a chance. You never know, you may find—"

"Never." I cut in. "I will never take a human as my eternal mate."

Kaan chuckled. "One thing I've learned in all my years is to never say never. Be grateful you have the opportunity. Take it from this old dragon, loneliness is not something to which we are immune."

I met his gaze, noting the sadness lying within them. "I am sorry, my friend."

"Ahh...do not pity me. I have plenty of company in my cave and forest with all the creatures that need my protection. They are my children now."

Kaan departed, leaving me in the Council chamber with nothing but my thoughts and his advice.

Chapter Two

"Tharaat, you're telling us that their best solution is suggesting we mate with humans?" a gaunt looking man sitting at the Fae Council's table asked.

"Never!" several other members shouted in unison.

"I hear you, my brethren, and I agree. We have never mixed with another race and we will not start now."

The members nodded.

"We will find another way to survive. Our war with the humans is not over. We will be victorious."

I found I didn't share in my fellow Council members' opinions. We were dying too fast to win the war humanity had waged against us. The only way to keep the Fae from disappearing from the world was to mate with a human. I left the chamber in search of our mage. Shatale would know what to do.

*

"If the council catches you, they will kill you, Taniel."

"I know, but what choice do we have? The Fae cannot vanish from this world. Even if only one remains…"

"But the bloodline will be diluted."

"Will it matter?"

"The world won't be the same, but even a single drop of Fae blood will keep the balance."

"Then I will find a human female of age and mate with her."

"If that is your wish."

Noticing the solemn look on Shatale's face, I took her wrinkled hand in mine. "Why do you look so sad? We have discussed this often, knowing how blind Tharaat and the others are to the threat that truly faces us."

"I wanted so much more for you, Taniel. Love, a wife...a family."

"We all have our cross to bear in these times. Do not mourn for me. I am happy doing my part."

"There is no guarantee that your line will continue after your child is born," she added.

"Is there a way to ensure it?"

"There is a spell that might help, but it is not without its complications."

"Complications?"

"It's tricky. A modified love spell of sorts. Only the female descendants will inherit the Fae gene, and they will be driven to find their mate, much like the werewolves. It can make their lives difficult until they find him."

"What do you mean?"

"If I'm right, her Fae blood will act much like a pheromone, drawing unmated men to her until she finds the one meant for her. She will find all others unacceptable. For protection, this knowledge must be passed down through the generations."

I shook my head. "The risk of discovery is too great. This must remain secret. The first generations who carry our blood must never be made aware of it. If they ever let it slip, especially while the Fae still walk the earth, they would be killed without question."

Shatale sighed. "We have no way of knowing how this will impact future descendants. However, that is your choice. Keep your secret and pray your plan works. When will you go?"

"Tonight. I must find a female and return before the Council reconvenes."

"You'll have three lunar cycles. Here, wear this." She placed a talisman around my neck. "It will help you locate a female that is strong and ready and will shield you from the guards. Be quick and return safely."

I nodded and left the mage's hut, praying to the earth goddess that the Fae would live on in my descendants.

After changing into the latest human fashion, I tied my long silver white hair back into a neat gentleman's ponytail, making sure it covered the tips of my ears. Wearing the talisman Shatale gave me, I slipped from the forest undetected, putting miles between me and the Fae community.

In a local restaurant one morning weeks later, one of the waitresses caught my attention. Her hair was as dark as night, contrasting her bright porcelain skin. She was cashing out a customer at the counter. Her smile lit up my whole world. How could a human be so beautiful? She grabbed a pot of coffee and approached my table.

"Can I top off your cup?" she asked. Her blue eyes sparkled in the overhead lights.

"Please." I smiled at her and inhaled her aroma—jasmine. I spotted her employee nametag. "You have a beautiful name, Corrina."

She glanced down at her apron. "Oh, thank you."

"Is it a family name?"

"Yes, it's my grandmother's middle name on my mother's side."

I watched intently as the pupils of her eyes dilated and her nostrils flared as she breathed in my Fae scent.

"You seem familiar. Have we met before?" she asked.

I laughed. "Isn't that supposed to be my line?"

Corrina giggled. "I suppose it is. Listen, my shift ends in an hour. There's a motion picture playing at the theater this afternoon. Would you like to go with me?"

"I would love to."

"It's a date then." She glanced over her shoulder. "I better get back to work before the boss yells at me."

Corrina's boldness was due to the effect Fae pheromones have on humans, but seeing how it enhanced her bravery made me realize she was the perfect choice.

"By the way…" she asked, turning once again. "What's your name?"

"Taniel."

She smiled brightly before returning to the counter.

Shatale, I've found my human. Now let's pray our plan works.

*

The plan didn't go as smoothly as I'd hoped. Two months later, Corrina learned her fate. She would be married to another human to assist the Vampire Council's idea. Their descendants would be the first to attend the monthly *Legăturas* and mingle with the unmated vampires.

"I know we haven't been together very long, but I'm beginning to fall in love with you, Taniel. I don't want to marry someone I don't know," Corrina cried. "My father is forcing me."

"I care very deeply for you too, Corrina, but we cannot stay together. You know why I came here. I must return to the Fae. I can't take you with me. But I never imagined I would find…love. We will always be a part of each other, but it is not our destiny to be together for long."

She shook her head. "I don't understand."

"You will. Your true mate is waiting for you at the *Legătura*. He will make you happier than I ever could. You will feel a love for him like you've never known, and he will return that love, I promise. I have the gift of sight and can see another's future when I touch them. I have seen your future and it is full of happiness."

"I believe you, but a part of me doesn't want to accept it. Is there no way we can be together?"

I sighed. "My people are dying. Soon the Fae will leave this world. I came because I have a duty, a responsibility to ensure that at least one Fae remains— even a half-blood." I pressed my hand to her lower belly.

Corrina's eyes widened. "What are you saying?"

"You are with child, Corrina. My child…*our* child. She will be the start in ensuring we do not disappear forever. Her children will carry the fate of the Fae, but she must never know of her true lineage. You must keep our affair secret."

"How? How can I do that with a child growing inside of me?"

"You will be married soon. Consummate that marriage and no one will suspect your husband is not the father. Fae are born smaller than humans. They will merely think she came early."

"And you're sure it's a girl?"

"Yes." I kissed Corrina's forehead. "And she will be healthy and strong and beautiful, like her mother."

Corrina placed her hand over mine. "I will take good care of her. I promise."

"I know you will. That is one reason I chose you."

"And the other?"

"Because I love you." I kissed Corrina one last time and held her close.

"I'll never forget you," she whispered between tears.

"Nor I you. Be well, my love, and do not fear. I have seen all I told you. Live well and long."

With my final words, I departed.

CHAPTER THREE

I sat in Shatale's cottage, a small ornate box in my lap.

"Taniel, is this really your wish?"

"Shatale, it is the only way. The day will come when my secret must be revealed. Who better to tell my story than myself?"

"You will be gone from this world before the sun sets." She sighed, sorrow filling her heart.

I leaned forward and held the old mage's hand. "We all have our time. Mine has come. You know this must be done." She nodded, biting back tears. "You are the only one I can trust, Shatale. Once the spell has been cast, you must ensure the box makes it to Corrina with my letter. Promise me you will make this happen."

"I promise. I will do as you ask. A mother never wishes to outlive her children, and no mother could ever be prouder than I am of you, my son."

I hugged my mother. Words were not enough to thank her for all the love and support she had given me.

As was our tradition, I placed my forehead against hers and pushed all the love in my heart through our connection. Shatale's eyes filled with tears. Her shoulders shook lightly. Smiling, she cupped my face in her hands and kissed each cheek. "Let us begin."

Shatale assisted me, lending her magic with mine as I infused the talisman she had given me with my memories, knowledge, and finally…my life force. The lapis pendent had been carved into the shape of a lotus. One day, when the world was ready, when the one chosen to bring forth the light was made whole, the box would reveal itself and all would be restored.

The spell complete, I sealed it and gave it to my mother.

"My time here is done. Thank you, Mother. Now I must rest." I laid back on the bed. At peace, I smiled.

"Sleep, my son. Your destiny is complete." Shatale stroked my hair from my brow. "I love you."

My mother rose from her seat to leave the forest she had lived in her entire life one last time. She would fulfill her promise. Closing my eyes, I took my leave from the world.

*

"May I help you?" I asked, opening my front door.

The woman on the stoop smiled. "I can see why my son was so fond of you, my dear."

"Your son?" I clenched the doorframe. "Taniel?"

"Yes, child. He asked me to bring this to you. You must keep it safe and hidden from the world. Can you do that for him?"

I nodded, taking the ornate blue box she held out. "Would you like to come in?"

"Thank you for your offer, child, but I cannot stay. My time has come to leave this world. My last task is now complete."

"Is Taniel all right?" I had a foreboding feeling in the pit of my stomach.

"He wrote this for you." She handed me a letter. "It explains everything. Be well, my daughter, and know that my son loved you more than anything in this world."

"Will you tell him that—"

She cupped my cheek. "He knows, Corrina."

"Is he already…" I couldn't finish my sentence. Her red-rimmed irises answered me without words. My eyes stung. "May I ask your name?"

"My name is Shatale."

I nodded. "Thank you."

With a wave, she walked away and faded into the sunset.

I closed the door once she was out of sight and went to the library. My husband wouldn't be home from work for hours. Sitting on the couch, I opened the letter.

My dearest Corrina,

When you read this, I will already be gone from this world. While our time together was brief, know that I loved you with all my heart. Even though I can't be there, I will be watching over you and our daughter from the heavens.

Inside this box is a precious gift that must be guarded and kept safe until the one destined to receive it is called. Below is the incantation that will open the box. If there is anything you wish to place inside, it will be kept safe. I'm sorry I can't be with you. Know that you live in my heart for all eternity.

Be well and happy, my love.

– Taniel

Tears fell down my cheeks. Despite the sadness, my heart felt warm. I pulled out my journal and wrote the incantation on the last page, then folded Taniel's letter and placed it inside the box. There was a hidden cabinet behind the loose panel in the far corner of the library. I opened the panel and placed the box inside, wedging a potted plant in front of the section on the wall. My husband rarely visited the library. The box would be safe.

Chapter Four

E very month, the same thing happened.

Black sedans lined our quiet street, one parked in front of each house with a child who had turned eighteen. I watched from our front porch as happy young adults left their families, some with big smiles, some with eyes full of tears...but it was the parents that caught my attention. They hugged their children, giving them smiles of reassurance, kisses of love and pride. I envied those kids. Not for where they were going, but for what they had in their lives. Something I would never experience...love.

I had been taught about these special gatherings called *Legăturas*, or "The Bonding," how the offspring of the families contracted with the Vampire Council would congregate at the community's clubhouse and present themselves before unmated vampires. All to prevent vampires from going extinct. It'd been this way for a century.

"Victoria!" My mother's screech could be heard through the storm door.

"Coming, Mother." I gathered up my notebook and bottle of water and headed inside. Time for my afternoon lessons.

"What were you doing outside?"

"Watching the neighbors leave for the *Legătura*."

She glanced out the window and nodded. "Good. That will be you someday.

If we are lucky and you learn your place, you might be chosen and bring honor to your father and I." She turned on her heel and entered the library, my classroom for all my daily lessons. In the mornings, I had a regular academic tutor homeschooling me.

"Can we go to the clubhouse and see it decorated for the party?"

"No. The clubhouse is no place for children like you. I've explained that a hundred times. Why do you insist on asking me?"

"I'm curious about the vampires." The questions I had bottled up started pouring out. "What are they like? What do they look like? Do their eyes glow? Can you see their fangs?"

"*Enough!*" My mother placed her palms over her ears. "Must you ask so many questions? Take your seat and don't speak unless I say so."

"Yes, Mother." I hung my head and sat at my makeshift desk.

She sighed deeply. "Vampires don't look any different than us, apart from their height. They are tall. The difference is how you feel when you're in their presence. Their power overwhelms you. Every cell in your body will scream out—"

"In fear?" I interrupted.

She pinned me with a dark glare, but continued. "Sometimes, but not always. You will know when a vampire means you harm, though by then, it's usually too late."

These were the kindest words my mother ever spoke to me. Something in her expression told me to remain quiet now. Her eyes looked as though they were filled with longing and sadness. *Is it because she wasn't chosen?* My mother always prided herself on being a Starling. I never heard her introduce herself by anything other than *Cynthia Starling*, and she always introduced my father as *Edgar Starling*.

I hated being a Starling. The kids at school had bullied me for my name. I had no friends, and my parents...Well, beyond providing the very basic needs to survive, they barely acknowledged my existence.

"*Victoria!* Pay attention," she barked, breaking me from my reverie. "A vampire only loses their control for blood in two situations, when?"

"Either when they are starving, or when they are near their mates and lust overcomes them."

"Correct. Now what does this tell you?"

"To keep my mate fed," I answered, instinctually robotic.

"Correct. A vampire who feeds off their mate is quickly satisfied and never drinks enough to kill them. Therefore, you must make yourself stand out so that you are chosen as a mate and not a blood servant."

"Blood servant?" My voice faltered, making my mother smirk. *What is that?*

"Yes, Victoria, if you are diligent in your studies and somehow become beautiful enough, perhaps you will bring us the highest honor and be chosen by a pureblood to birth his offspring, instead of being merely his dinner."

I knew vampires survived on blood, but it was never explained how they obtained what they needed. *Were some humans chosen as meals?*

My mother continued. "As you know, your father and I never found vampire mates. My mother before me didn't either. We were lucky that they allowed us to marry other humans. A blood servant's only purpose is to be food. I assume they die eventually if they aren't drained the first night."

That answered that question...but I have so many more. Cringing, I obediently wrote my notes. I didn't really need them. I remembered everything I was ever told. I could even remember whole textbooks once I read them. The doctor told my parents I had an eidetic memory. I can recall past scenes with "eerie accuracy"—at least that's how my father described it. My mother smiled watching me write down her words of wisdom, assuming they had some importance to me.

"Do you think a pureblood will take me as his mate?" I shivered.

My mother sighed. "I am not hopeful. You are too plain. However, he would only need you as a birthmother. Perhaps, if the timing were right, you might have a chance."

I shuddered again. I wasn't completely afraid of vampires, but not knowing my fate was more than my young mind could handle.

"Now let's continue our review..."

I could recite my mother's speech verbatim as she droned on about the history of the Tribunal and how humans became involved with vampires.

The main immortal races all had a seat on the Tribunal in addition to their own councils, all except the Fae. They had been extinct for almost a century. My mother never spoke of them, feeling they were irrelevant to my education now that they were dead.

"The eldest vampire from each of the sixteen pureblood houses composes the Vampire Council. You should study your notes and memorize their family names and status in the community, so you know who to mingle with when your time comes, and who to avoid."

I nodded. Would it matter? My mother believed I was unworthy of being chosen, which meant I would become a blood servant—food for the vampire I served.

I feared that was my destiny.

My mother's voice faded as I stared out the window. All the sedans had pulled away and the street outside our home was empty once again.

"What about the *Legăturas*?" I interrupted again. She turned sharp on her heel, nostrils flaring. What I pictured of the *Legăturas*—like a large animal auction—scared me more. What happened to all of them? "Are we paraded on a stage while the vampires yell out bids until there's a winner?"

"You are such a simpleton. It's not an auction, it's a lavish party. Unmated vampires and humans mingle, there's food and cocktails, even dancing—all for the purpose of getting to know one another before the pairing decisions are made. Therefore, you must work harder to be perfect. Vampires are a refined and elegant race. They cling to their traditions. While they have learned to embrace change, they have high standards. The most powerful families are given first pick of who they wish to invite into their families. You will only have this one night to make a proper impression. If you weren't a Starling, I doubt you'd even be noticed. However, there is a chance."

"Do they ever change their minds?"

"I've never known it to happen. Vampires mate for life, and once they have offspring, they have the option to bestow the gift of immortality on their mates."

"Does that mean they turn their mates into vampires?"

"No, that practice has been forbidden for centuries, and only a pureblood has the power to turn a human. Both vampires and Dhampyres have the ability, through a special incantation, to bestow the gift of immortality on a human, but they must go through the mating ceremony first."

"Can they force immortality on you?"

My mother sighed. "No, just as the human must accept becoming the vampire's mate, they must also choose to give up their mortality. Must you ask so many questions?"

I had reached my mother's limit for the day. Too many questions weren't tolerated, but I couldn't help being curious.

"What happens to the humans that don't get chosen for anything?" My ten-year-old mind started imagining horrible things as I asked her.

"Who knows. Most likely, they become slaves to the vampire families, I suppose." She shrugged. "Serving as maids, cooks, caregivers to the young. I've never cared to learn more. Your father and I were exceptions. We had a higher purpose. Being from two of the most prominent families, we were paired to ensure the continuance of the Starling line. Unfortunately, we weren't blessed with a son." Her nose scrunched. "Merely cursed with a girl."

My mother could be so cold. "Do they kill them?"

"Possibly, or as I mentioned, they become blood servants and vampires use them for food until the human's body can no longer provide."

"I don't want to do this!" I sobbed, tears falling freely down my cheeks.

My mother's hand flew across my cheek, making my head snap to the side.

"*This is your only purpose*! You were made to meet the obligation your father and I have as the last descendant of the Starling bloodline. If you can't carry on the Starling name, you will at least do what's necessary to secure a prestigious assignment. You will fulfil your obligation and you will do so without complaint!"

"Go easy on her, Cynthia." My father stepped into the room, not even glancing in my direction. "After all, she's just learning about her true purpose. You can't fault her stupidity."

All hope of being saved from my mother's wrath went out the window with his words.

"To think I had to carry her inside me for nine months, enduring the sickness and ungodly food cravings and hours of painful labor..." My mother glared down at me. "The least she could do is be grateful for the honor she will bring us."

"She will learn in time, my dear, as you are an excellent teacher." He kissed her cheek. "Don't take too long. We do have dinner tonight with the Worthers."

"Ah yes, delightful. I do enjoy their company...and their money." My mother giggled softly. "Now," she snapped at me, all delight gone. "I expect you will clean your face before you go to bed tonight, and you will not leave your room until you are sent for in the morning. Am I understood?"

"Y-yes, Mother." *This is the last time I will ever show emotion in front of my parents.*

She took my chin in her fingers and raised my eyes to hers. "Be grateful for what little beauty you've been given. It will serve you well in the *Legătura* when your time comes. The most prestigious bloodlines will look to you first since you are a Starling. Hopefully, it will be enough to ensure your survival. You must remember your place—*your life is not yours.* You are nothing but what they will tell you to be."

"What if I'm not chosen?" I whispered.

"It matters not to me. You won't be returned to us." She paused. "And even if you were, we would never take you back and be disgraced."

With that, she stood, turned off the light to the library, and ushered me toward the stairs.

I spent hours staring at my ceiling that night, praying for a way out. Even if it meant death.

Chapter Five

"What's wrong Victoria?" my tutor asked me one morning.

I winced. "My head hurts. May I go find Anton and take some aspirin?"

"Be quick," he sighed.

As I passed by him, he pulled me into his arms. I pushed against his chest as he tried to wrangle me into his lap.

"Don't be difficult. You're a beautiful girl, Victoria. Indulge me…"

Before I could scream, my mind filled with images of my tutor walking along a sunny street. Other men buzzed around him wearing hard plastic hats on their heads. I heard screaming, then my vision blurred into black.

Anton must have come in during my episode because I blinked and found myself staring up at his concerned face.

"Victoria, are you all right? What happened?"

I shook my head. "I d-don't know." I huddled on the floor, arms wrapped around my legs. My eyes shifted to my tutor in the corner. He stared back at me. Eyes wide, face pale.

"She must have had a seizure."

"No, Anton, it wasn't a seizure." Tears blurred my vision. I shook my head violently.

"Mr. and Mrs. Starling, you must come quickly!" Anton yelled out into the hallway.

My parents arrived, Mother frowning at the scene before her, Father looking on with disinterest.

"What did she do this time?" he asked my tutor.

I spoke first. "I-I didn't do anything. I had a headache and was heading to the kitchen to ask Anton for some medicine when he grabbed me." I pointed an accusatory finger at my now shaking tutor.

"I-I did no such thing." He glanced from me to my parents. "She walked by and lost her balance and then started shaking and mumbling to herself."

"I saw your...your death," I blurted out. "*You're going to die.*" My body trembled as I sobbed.

"What?" Anton seemed horrified.

"Victoria, we don't tolerate lies in this house." My mother's voice was flat and cold.

"I'm not lying. When he grabbed me, I saw him walking down a street around a bunch of other people wearing thick plastic hats and screaming. Then he was crushed."

"Ex-xcuse me?" My tutor's face was even paler than before. "What are you saying?"

"I'm saying I saw your death. Something is going to fall on you and crush you. Why won't any of you listen to me?"

"That's enough of this folly, Victoria. Things don't just fall out of the sky. If this is your idea of a joke, it isn't funny." My mother turned to my tutor. "I'm so sorry for this. She's usually very studious."

He straightened his jacket. "She's very bright for her age, but she's too mischievous for me. I don't think this is going to work out." He packed his bag and left the house.

"Another one, Victoria?" My father's hard tone cut through me. "We are running out of options for tutors in this town. Perhaps we should consider sending you to a boarding school until you are eighteen." He turned and left the room.

"Anton, make sure she cleans up in here and give her something to eat. Then send her to her room." My mother gave me one last angry glance and turned on her heel.

"Anton, you believe me, don't you?"

He didn't reply. I watched as he began picking my books off the floor.

*

A few days later, my mother screamed for my father to join her in the foyer.

"Edgar! EDGAR!"

"What is it, Cynthia? And must you yell?"

"Look at this!" She shoved the local paper in his hands.

I joined them, sneaking a peek at the front page. A story about a local teacher who had been walking through a small construction area in town and crushed by a pallet of bricks. Killing him instantly.

I gasped. Finally noticing me, my parents looked to each other and then to me. I couldn't decipher the look in their eyes. Perhaps a mixture of fear and opportunity. They took me to the local doctor who told them I suffered from migraines. Then they carted me off to a psychiatrist, who diagnosed me with nothing more than an overactive imagination. Not satisfied, they brought me to a small shop in town run by a woman who claimed to be psychic. She told my parents that I had a gift. The gift of sight. It's a rare power that many claim to have, but few actually do. And lucky me, I was one of them.

"So, you're saying that she can see someone's future?"

"Yes, it seems that physical contact brings on the visions. Since she hasn't had many, it's hard to say how powerful her gift is…It would need to be tested."

"Tested?" I asked.

"Yes, dear. You would need to touch random people. Write down what you see and wait to learn if it comes true."

"Can I shut it off?"

She laughed. "No, my dear. Once your gift manifests, your only option is to learn control over it. It will never fade. If you nurture it, it will grow stronger. It can be a blessing and a curse."

It's definitely a curse.

After that day, my parents began testing my gift. Desperate to learn if it was real, they took me out of the house to local restaurants and ordered me to touch our waiter or the hostess, anyone I could get close to without raising suspicions. Each time I had a vision, the seizures lessoned. I would tell them about the images, and each time, they would come true. Disgust curdled in my gut—it was horrible seeing these people's demise and being powerless to help. Occasionally, glimpses of happiness and good fortune would come, but not often.

Satisfied my gift was real, my parents decided to exploit me for their personal gain. They began holding exclusive parties where their friends could arrange for a personal reading of their future.

It wasn't long before I could control the images.

"This is wonderful!" my mother exclaimed. "Now you can limit what you tell them."

"Why would I do that?"

"You are so naive." She sighed. "If you only tell them a portion of what you see, then they will have to come back for another reading to learn more. We'll make double the profit."

"Brilliant as always, my dear," my father remarked from behind his newspaper.

I was feeling brave that day. "What if I don't want to do this anymore?"

"Then you can go hungry," she sneered.

They never asked me how I felt about these parties or how they affected me. They didn't care. All that mattered to them was the exorbitant fees they were able to charge their guests and how popular it made them. But the visions left me drained, exhausted. Every night, I would return to bed haunted by their deaths, a hollow numbness in my soul, leading to plagues of nightmares.

I started searching for a way to shield myself. After an exhaustive online hunt, I read how some seers used meditation to clear their minds and release their inner tension. Each night I would follow an online guided meditation until I could successfully do it alone. The visions still left me tired and with a headache by the end of the night, but guarding against the soul-sucking exhaustion had become easier. The nightmares faded.

*

The first time I met a vampire, I was almost sixteen. She arrived unexpectedly, much to my parents' dismay. They seemed flustered that she was attending their party. It never occurred to me that they never informed the Council of my gift.

She was the most beautiful woman I had ever seen, and the power emanating off her body was spellbinding. Her golden hair and green eyes reminded me of the sun hovering above a summer meadow. When she smiled at me, I felt... safe. It was not what I expected.

"How unusual," she remarked, bending down. Her eyes met mine. I never considered myself short at five and a half feet, but she towered over me. "You do not fear me, little one, do you?"

"No, mistress. You're very beautiful. I like your smile." I blushed. I worried I had over spoken. My mother's glare confirmed my fear.

But the woman before me laughed as soft as a whisper, no malice in her voice. "I mean you no harm, child, and thank you for your compliment. It warms my heart. I must say that you are quite stunning yourself, little one. You have the most beautiful eyes I've ever seen."

"Thank you." I spoke so softly I feared she didn't hear me. I knew she was only being polite. My mother never missed an opportunity to remind me of my plain features, how little hope they had for a reputable vampire family to choose me during the *Legătura*, how disappointed I made them. My mother, never shy in her contempt toward me, often called my eyes unsettling. But I loved their deep blue-violet color and the specks of gold in them.

"Now tell me, child, I hear that you see visions of people's futures. Is that true?"

I nodded. "Sometimes. It doesn't happen with everyone, and I can't compel them. I think it only happens when something is about to happen because it never takes long for the things I see to come true."

My mother pinched my shoulder, feeling I had revealed too much.

The beautiful vampire growled at my mother, her eyes glowing. "Do not harm the child for answering my questions. She spoke plainly and truthfully. Never speak otherwise." She directed the last comment to me, then turned her attention toward the room behind her. "Would you mind if we went into your library with a friend of mine? I'd like to know if you can see his future."

I met her gaze. "I don't mind."

"What is your name, little one?"

"Victoria."

"A lovely name for a charming young lady." She turned to my mother. "We meet with Victoria alone."

Her words left no room for argument, much to my mother's anguish, but she simply nodded and walked away. With an elegant sweep of her hand, she led me into our library. Waiting for us was a handsome young man with sandy brown hair and eyes the color of warm chocolate. He smiled as we entered. They kissed and the woman introduced me.

"Darling, this is Victoria. She's the child I told you about." Sadness flickered in her eyes, but it lasted only a moment.

The man sat down in a chair and beckoned me over. I was hesitant.

"Why do you hesitate, child? I will not harm you." He spoke softly.

"I'm sorry, most…most men act odd when they're near me for too long." I choked the words out.

The woman looked between the man and I, a concerned look in her eyes.

"Surely your parents protect you?" he asked.

I shrugged and made no comment. I didn't know why I told the truth to these two individuals. I didn't know them, nor did I owe them anything, but I couldn't bring myself to lie. They looked at me with such kindness, and the woman had scolded my mother for hurting me. Her partner showed no interest in me other than what I might be able to tell him about his future. The feeling of safety was both foreign and overwhelming.

The vampire gently placed her delicate hand on my head and looked deep into my eyes. "One day soon, you will be free from your pain. I too have the sight, and I can see that your future will one day be full of happiness."

I gazed into her eyes, holding onto her every word. "If you have the sight, why do you wish for me to tell your partner's future?"

"Once those of us with the sight are mated, we can no longer see their future. I assume it's nature's way of protecting us." She smiled, but I could tell she was worried.

I took his strong hand in mine. Closing my eyes, I let my mind clear and my body relax.

"You're sick?" I gasped, my eyes opening wide. *He's human.*

"Yes," he confirmed.

I stared into his eyes. "You are receiving treatments at the hospital?"

He nodded.

Closing my eyes, I pushed further, deepening the connection. "You're going to get dreadfully ill from the treatments. Your mate's powers will help ease your discomfort, but it can't cure your illness." My eyes opened again and met the woman's.

"Sadly, no. I am a Dhampyre—only a pureblood has the power to fully restore a human's health."

I nodded in understanding. I searched further, and then smiled. I released his hand, breaking our connection. "You will survive. It won't be easy. There will be days you will be close to death and you will feel pain, but in the end the treatments will cure you. The cancer will go away. You can then become immortal but not before that…You must wait and be patient. If you are not, if either of you cave, you will live a miserable existence wishing for death every moment of every day until your mind descends into madness."

The room was silent for a moment.

"I'm s-sorry. I couldn't stop," I whispered. "You needed to know everything. You've both looked at me with such kindness. Kindness I've never known. I couldn't keep any of it back. Please don't be angry with me." I wrapped my arms around my body, trying to still the tremors of fear.

The woman hugged me so tightly I thought I would cry. "Oh, child, there is nothing to forgive. You have given us hope and a sensible warning. I could never be mad at you." She turned to her mate, kissing him deeply, which made him blush. "Do you hear that, darling? We only have to be patient and see this through."

"Thank you, Victoria. Thank you for telling us all you saw and meeting with us this night. We will never forget you." He smiled.

"Yes, Victoria. I know that your family is one of the bloodlines chosen for the *Legătura*. When your time comes, I promise I will be there for you. My name is Serena, and this is Greggory. You always have a friend in us."

I smiled at them. "Take care. And Greggory, I'm very sorry for what's to come."

"You're very kind, Victoria, thank you." With that, they turned to leave.

"Serena!" I called. "I don't know if I have the right to ask you this, but will you keep my gift a secret from the Vampire Council?"

She looked at me for a long moment, then nodded her head. They left without a word to either of my parents.

My mother came rushing into the library, eager to know what had happened.

"Nothing," I lied to her. "I held his hand, but nothing came. No visions."

"What did they want?" she pried. "Did they pay you anything?"

"I'm not sure." I continued the lie, taking satisfaction in keeping this one secret from her. "No, they didn't give me anything—they left. I believe she's about to bestow immortality on her mate and wanted to know if anything would happen to him beforehand. I saw nothing and they seemed happy."

"Or they think you're a fake. Let's hope they don't tell the Council." She looked torn between believing me and rage. She was biting on one of her manicured nails, the new diamond ring my father gave her that night sparkling menacingly. I had to always watch my mother's hands, never knowing if or when they would strike. Until that night, I had never lied to her.

She caught me staring at her hand and smiled wickedly. "You're done for the night. There's no one else here who wants to pay to see you, so I suggest you make yourself scarce and go to your room." She turned on her heel, her exorbitant dress rustling over the hardwood floors, and left me.

It was good the conversation didn't continue. A fuzziness dimmed my vision. I had pushed myself to see Greggory's future, forcing the connection and holding on to it for dear life, pulling the visions toward me as quickly as I could. In the past, I let the visions come to me at their will and never sought to see more. *I didn't know I could do that...It's exhausting.* My head was pounding.

I stopped in the kitchen first to grab a can of soda before heading to my closet-sized room upstairs. Downing a pain killer and the entire can of soda, I took a quick shower, changed into my pajamas, and passed out on my small bed.

I dreamed of Serena and Greggory that night. Though I felt great sadness at the pain he was about to endure, it would all be worth it in the end. I smiled in my sleep.

I never stopped wondering about them.

Chapter Six

I entered the Council's headquarters that morning thinking it would be an easy day. I passed on my position as head of the Council to my brother earlier that year but still liked to stay informed. If I was being honest with myself, it was hard to give up that control.

"You know I can handle this," Collin said, following me into my office.

"I know." I sipped my coffee. "Old habits...."

"Hmmm."

"Anything I should be aware of?" I set down the paper I was reading.

"I've asked the Starlings to meet with me. I'm heading over to the clubhouse—care to join me?"

I hissed. "And endure those insufferable humans? I'll pass. Why are you meeting with them anyway? Edgar and Cynthia are greedy, boorish people. He has to be the laziest human I've ever known. Even his position as chairman of Starling Enterprise is a façade. It's all his grandfather's work anyway."

Collin pinched the bridge of his nose. "I hate them as much as you do. However, there are rumors about the parties they've been holding every weekend for the past two years. I'm sure it's nothing of concern, but I want to hear their side."

"What are the rumors?"

"Seems they provide 'entertainment' at these gatherings and charge their guests a fee."

"How unsavory. What sort of entertainment?" I could only imagine given what I knew of them.

Collin shrugged. "That's been a little difficult to determine. I don't know how the Starling bloodline has fallen into such disgrace. They were once the most noble, most respected, of all the human houses associated with the Council."

"It's true…Poor choices were made in their pairings. I blame Victor Starling. He was too controlling, too narrow-minded when approving matches for his sons."

"And now there is only one remaining heir."

I sighed. "How old is she now?"

"Only sixteen—she won't be presented for another two years."

"Have you seen her?" I leaned forward in my chair before I could stop myself.

Collin smiled. "Why do you ask? Finally interested in taking a human mate?"

"Never." My eyes glowed in warning. "I'm merely staying informed of a once prominent human household."

Collin laughed. "If you say so, brother. And, no, I haven't seen her. In truth, I'm not sure anyone has since she was a young child. At least, no one seems willing to speak of her. The Starlings never bring her to the clubhouse, or any community events. From what I can gather, she doesn't go into town."

"Why is that? Is there something wrong with her?"

"I suppose I can ask them at lunch. My understanding is she was bullied at school and her parents chose to homeschool her. They've never held any parties for her as far as I know, and they rarely talk about her. It's almost as if they don't even have a child." Collin's brow furrowed in distaste.

"What, no coming-of-age party? She's sixteen! Her introduction to our world should've happened at the annual ball last month."

Collin shook his head. "She didn't attend. And you would've known if you had been there."

"You know I never go to those things. Too many—"

"Humans. Yes, I know."

I returned to reading the paper. "Enjoy your lunch date."

"Thanks," Collin scoffed, aiming for the door.

"What's her name?" I blurted out before I could bite down on my tongue.

"Victoria." Collin smiled slyly as he closed the door behind him.

Hmm…named after her great grandfather.

*

My parents were called to meet with the head of the Vampire Council that afternoon. They discussed their summons in the hallway.

"What does he want to see us for?" my mother whispered.

"I don't know, Cynthia. He didn't give an explanation. His message said to meet him at the clubhouse restaurant today at noon."

"Didn't you call him back?"

"*Of course I did.*"

"You don't need to snap at me, Edgar."

My father huffed. "I'm sorry, darling. I'm worried it's because we didn't present Victoria at the annual ball. I told you it was a mistake to withhold her. You know it's when children are introduced to the vampire families."

She dismissed this with a wave of her hand. "She's a Starling. She doesn't need to be introduced. That ball is drivel anyway so the children won't find the *Legăturas* as intimidating. Besides, if they see how plain she is and those… eyes…no one will want her. We only have two more years." My mother tapped a long nail on her teeth. "Maybe we should consult a plastic surgeon."

"Cynthia."

"I'm just thinking out loud—but it's an option. I don't care if she finds her *Legătura* intimidating; she'll get over it. Why didn't you ask what he wanted when you called him back?"

"I am *not* questioning the head of the Council. He said to meet him so I gave him the only answer I could." My father fumbled with the collar of his jacket. "Now we need to leave. We are running late."

The front door slammed shut, but their argument still carried on through it.

*

"What do you mean they're dead?" I exclaimed.

Anton asked me to join him in the study to give me the news that my parents had been killed in a car crash on their way to the clubhouse restaurant.

"It seems your father lost control of the car as they rounded the bend on the main road. The car jumped the barrier and plummeted over the cliff." He paused. "The authorities are combing through the explosion wreckage."

Anton seemed sad. I wasn't surprised. My parents had been kind to him over the years. And though we weren't close, I saw more of him than my own parents. I always kept a distance between us to avoid the odd behavior, like what happened to the many staff members over the years if they stayed near me for too long. I didn't want Anton to be fired too. He always had my best interests in mind.

"I'm sorry, Miss Victoria." He turned to leave the study. "Is there anything I can do for you?"

I sat still, shock steeling my body. If only they had hugged me before they left, maybe I could have seen it coming. Maybe I could have warned them. I knew I should be feeling sadness, loss, even guilt, but I felt...*free*!

"If you could speak with the authorities and arrange the funeral, I would appreciate it. Tell them I'm too consumed with grief." I had something more important to concentrate on now—escape.

"As you wish." Anton nodded and left me alone.

I took a few breaths, quickly forming a plan in my mind. I called my parents' attorney first to give him the news.

"I'm so sorry, Miss Starling. I know this must be a complete shock and an incredibly sad time for you. If there's anything I can do, please don't hesitate to let me know."

"I would like you to pull their estate plan and let me know what directions they left for their holdings." I needed to act fast, or my plan would fail. I wasn't sure I could pull it off.

Being homeschooled had the advantage of an enhanced education. I had completed my high school education earlier that year and was attending online college courses. My parent's financial holdings had also been a lesson in my afternoon studies—it was the only time I had ever spent with my father.

"There's plenty of time for that, Miss Starling. Right now you need to concentrate on letting things settle and mourning the loss of your parents. After their funeral we can meet—"

"NO. I don't wish to wait…" I interrupted. "I want to know about all of their assets and what they wanted done with everything in the event of their deaths."

Silence.

"If you're worried about money, Miss Starling, I can assure you…"

"Please Mr. Anderson, I need the distraction," I pleaded. "Anton is handling the funeral arrangements. I need something to concentrate on during this time." The change in my tone had him agreeing.

"All right, I'll pull the documents and look them over tonight. Why don't you come to my office tomorrow morning and we will go over everything?"

"Thank you, Mr. Anderson, I'll be by around ten o'clock if that works."

"Yes, that's fine. I'll see you then. And Miss Starling, try to get some rest tonight."

"Thank you, I will."

I hung up the phone and padded down to the kitchen for a cup of tea. Anton wasn't there so I assumed he was in the library making the arrangements for the funeral. I wasn't going to attend. If there were no complications from my meeting with Mr. Anderson tomorrow, I was selling everything and disappearing. I didn't know where I was going to go. I just needed to run. Over the years I had fantasized about running away, researching different locations on the oversized atlas in our library, but without money, it would be impossible. My parents withheld all the funds from the parties. Now I would take it all and use it to live a life where I was in control.

Let the world think that I died with my parents. With luck, I would be long gone before the Vampire Council came to pay their respects. Why would they care about one girl anyway?

You are nothing.

My mother's words echoed in my head. Right, I was nothing to them, to the community. Surely I was nothing to the Council.

I took my cup of tea and returned to the study, pulling out a local business directory and selecting the first real estate agent listed. I made an appointment for her to come see the house at one the next day. Looking around me, I took a mental inventory. Was there anything I wanted? No.

I hated everything in the house, even the house itself. Everywhere I looked reminded me of how unloved I had been. How I was nothing but a tool to my parents. If I wanted to break free, now would be my only chance—before the Council stepped in as my guardian.

I closed my eyes.

Is it truly over...Am I finally free?

*

The next morning, I gathered the information I thought I would need. My parents helped me open a joint bank account the year before with my father—not that there was much in it. I grabbed a bank slip with the account information. I wouldn't keep it much longer—just long enough.

My meeting with Mr. Anderson went more smoothly than I had anticipated. They left everything to me: the house and all their monetary holdings. A fully funded trust had been set up in Anton's name, so I wouldn't need to worry about him. Mr. Anderson assured me he would work directly with Anton. He would be set for the remainder of his life, which made me happy.

"Sell off everything," I instructed Mr. Anderson.

"What?" He almost choked on his coffee. "Miss Starling, your monetary assets are making money. I would recommend that you keep your holdings and draw off them for any funds you may need."

"No. As custodian, you can liquidate everything, correct?"

"Yes, but..."

"Here's the banking information. Please deposit the funds into this account."

My skin tingled as I looked into his eyes and gave my instructions. I shook it off, dismissing it as nerves.

He looked at the paper and hesitated. "Al-all right."

"Mr. Anderson, if anything comes up after you've completed this transaction, please donate it to a local children's home. I want nothing more than what we discussed today."

"Wait!" He stared at me a moment. "Are you sure this is what you want?"

"Yes. I won't remain here. There's nothing here but pain."

"What if that could be changed?" He stood from his chair.

Oh, no.

"Miss Starling, I know your parents were never kind to you. I'm sorry. I will follow your instructions if you make me a promise."

"What is it?" I stood to leave. Familiar warning bells clanged in my head. Even the air in the room shifted.

"Now that you're on your own, you're a beautiful young woman. You can start living a fuller life…a happier life." His eyes gleamed. It was all too familiar. "Know that if I can provide for you in any way, I would be more than happy…" He started to round the desk between us.

"Thank you, Mr. Anderson." I cut him off and headed for the door, only stopping once I opened it. "Please do as I instructed."

I stepped out into the lobby and closed the door behind me. Through the glass, I saw Mr. Anderson shake his head, as if confused. He muttered something to himself while gathering the papers together on his desk.

*

I didn't attend my parent's funeral the following week. While Anton headed to the funeral home, I packed up one of my parent's cars and drove out of town. Anton had taught me how to drive after I begged him for months. I smiled as I remembered how patient he had been with me.

A single tear fell down my cheeks as I thought of my parents. As the authorities expected, there weren't any discernable remains. The fire from the explosion had burned too hot for much to survive. Their coffins would be buried empty today. Although they had never been kind, I hoped their deaths had been quick.

The house and its contents sold much faster than I expected. I never met with the buyers, asking Mr. Anderson to close the sale as quickly as he could. If my absence at the funeral caused a commotion, I didn't care. I drove out of town and never looked back.

*

I stood stoically off to the side under a large oak tree. Guests nodded respectfully toward me but didn't approach. Their confused thoughts bounced around in my head.

Lord Carrington never attends the funerals of the human families. Why is he here? Was he friends with the Starlings?

I found their curiosity amusing. They were all dying to know, but no one was brave enough to approach me. I liked it that way. In truth, I had no feelings toward the Starlings. I had come for one reason and one reason only—Victoria Starling.

My interest in the sheltered Starling girl had peaked since my conversation with Collin. Since that day, my dreams had been haunted by a raven-haired beauty with blue-violet eyes.

Could it be Victoria? I was here to confirm it wasn't her. *Why would I dream about this human girl? Where is she? This is ridiculous...I've wasted enough time.*

I turned and strode back to my car.

"Take me to the office," I ordered my driver.

Chapter Seven

"What do you mean she's disappeared?" I paced behind my desk. "She's a human, the last of the Starling bloodline. She couldn't have just disappeared."

"I'm sorry, Collin. We've searched but can't find her." Darin stood on the other side of the desk. My temper was flaring. I knew this wasn't Darin's fault. As my right-hand man, I relied on him, but it also meant he always caught the brunt of my outbursts. Though this kid was lucky I was nothing like my brother.

"What about the Starling estate?" I asked. "Hasn't she been living there?"

"Apparently it's been empty since their funeral."

"That was two years ago!"

"Victoria had her attorney sell it and all her parents' holdings after they died. She took the funds and…poof."

I stopped. "Poof?"

Darin shrugged. "That's the best explanation. It's like she dropped off the face of the planet. No money trail, nothing under her name, no pictures even."

"Wait…no pictures? How's that even possible?"

"The only recent portraits are of the Starlings themselves. There was one photo of Victoria in her room, but it was of her as a child."

"What about the family butler?" I shook my head. The Starlings were a miserable pair of humans. I was the reason they were headed to the clubhouse the day they died. I had dreaded my meeting with them and wished them no ill will—but even I didn't mourn their passing.

"We spoke with him. He says she met with the family attorney the day after her parents drove off the cliff. He hasn't seen or heard from her since the funeral. She took nothing from the home either. No clothes or mementos."

"How did she get out of town?"

"One of the cars from their garage is missing. We think she took it and drove off."

"Have you traced the car?"

"Yes. We found it not far at a used car lot. The dealership didn't even have it logged in their inventory. I think she dropped it there and bought a new one with cash."

"Clever girl." I frowned. "I can't believe we haven't noticed that she's been gone."

"I'm not surprised, Collin. No one really saw her while her parents were alive. Those that did have been afraid to go near the house. No one in the community checked in on her. Many feel the Council may have had something to do with the Starlings' death."

"Why in all the heavens would we do that?" I growled.

"Because of whatever they were doing at those parties of theirs." Darin sighed. It broke his heart when he thought about it.

"No one would tell you?"

Darin shook his head. "I could force someone if you want me to."

"No. It would undo all our years of work to build trust with the humans. Did Anton at least give you a description?"

"Yes, the last time he saw her, she was sixteen years old. She would be around eighteen or nineteen now. I don't know if she would change much in that time..."

"And?" I was losing my patience. I should've insisted the Council take over her guardianship and place someone in the house, not just buy the estate.

Victoria was still a minor in school at the time. I assumed she would be scared and remain in her family home until her eighteenth birthday. Everyone felt if the Council owned the home, she'd feel safer, and we would simply collect her when it was her time for the *Legătura*. It was becoming clear I had underestimated this human and what her parents had put her through. *A mistake I will not make again when I finally find her. I want to meet this clever human female.*

"He said she is about five and a half feet, lean but curvy. He believes her hair is raven black, but he admits she always wore it up, so it could be dark brown." Darin paused.

"What is it?"

"He said it's her eyes that make her stand out. He has never seen anyone with the same color."

I motioned for him to continue.

"They are the deepest blue-violet he has ever seen, almost unnatural, with specks of gold, reminding him of lapis."

Why does that sound familiar? I frowned.

"What I don't understand is why our trackers can't find her. I pulled the scent marker in the Starling file, but so far, they can't pick up her familial blood scent. We have nothing recent of hers to capture it either."

"It's a problem, that's for sure," I agreed. "I don't know of any case where our trackers haven't been able to scent someone out. We've had humans go missing before, kids wander, but have always found them."

"There's not much in her room, but I can have them try to pull her scent from her clothes."

"Have you spoken with the attorney or the real estate agent?"

Darin shook his head. "The real estate agent died last year, so that's a dead end. All we have are the sale documents in our files. We went to the attorney's office yesterday, but his secretary says he's away on vacation until tomorrow. I already have an appointment with him in the afternoon."

"Good, good." Remembering something, I made my way toward the office door. "I need to talk with Serena. Is she here yet?"

"Yes, I saw her in her office."

"Thank you, Darin. Keep me posted on what you learn from the attorney."

"Excuse me for asking Collin, but what is the urgency for this girl? There are enough humans from the other bloodlines. We have more than we need for the *Legătura* next week."

I sighed. "Call it a matter of pride. In all our history, we've never lost touch with anyone from the human bloodlines. She was due for the upcoming *Legătura*. I can cover for her absence and say we have enough, but she's the last of the Starlings. The families are whispering. I haven't been the head of the Council for very long. I don't need this hanging over me."

Darin nodded in understanding. "And if we can't find her?"

"I don't know, Darin…I don't know."

The door clicked shut behind me as I sought out Serena's office. She worked for the Council, overseeing and organizing all Council events including the monthly *Legăturas*. I needed to let her know Victoria wouldn't be present, and one of the details Darin gave me about her was bothering me.

"Ah, good morning, Collin." Serena looked up from her paperwork, a smile on her face.

"Good morning. How are the preparations for this month's event coming along?"

"Everything is all set. We have more vampires and Dhampyres hoping to find a mate than the past few months, so each human should find a suitable match." She beamed.

"You always have enjoyed a good love story," I mused. "Even when you were little, you would beg me to read them to you."

"It's your fault for indulging me. Besides, I live one, and maybe it's my human side, but I like seeing people fall in love."

"Speaking of Greggory, how is the ol' boy doing these days?"

"He's fabulous! He wanted me to pass along his thanks for lining up that job for him. I think he's still on cloud nine."

"It's the least I can do after all he's been through. I really was sure we were going to lose him."

"I told you not to worry about that, didn't I?" Serena started to busy herself.

"Yes, you did." I walked around to the back of the desk and leaned against it, tapping my fingers against my chin. "About that…what was it you told us? You had an exceptionally reliable source that confirmed it was going to get much worse before it became better, but Greggory would survive without a doubt."

Serena nodded. "Hmmm, yes, that sounds about right. Why do you ask?"

"You found this seer girl in our community, and she was able to confirm that he would be fine." Serena was also a seer from her human half. Her power wasn't very strong, nor did she have control over it. I couldn't remember the last time she had a vision.

"Yes, so?" Serena shrugged, keeping her eyes on the papers before her.

"Remind me what she looked like." I leaned down, turning Serena's chair so she faced me. "I seem to remember you were quite taken with her. A real beauty—inside and out—I believe is what you told us." My eyes glowed, letting her know I wouldn't let this go.

"Don't glow your eyes at me like I'm some weak-minded human you can make do your bidding." She slapped me away. "I have work to do. Besides, it was so long ago I don't remember."

"Liar." I turned her around again. "You may be able to hide your thoughts from me, but you're not telling me the truth. I can smell it."

Serena sighed. "I promised I would never reveal who she was to the Council."

"Why would you do that, Serena?"

"Her parents used her, Collin. They were cruel to her." Serena's eyes filled with unshed tears. "I touched her that night and could feel the pain her gift caused her. So much misery night after night…She was exhausted. I think she feared what would happen to her if the Council learned of her."

"What do you mean her parents were cruel to her?"

"They used her, held parties with their human friends, charged fees to have her do readings every night. There was no love in that house, Collin." Serena stared out the window. Pieces of a long-forgotten puzzle were starting to click into place. *Could it be?* "Greggory and I often talked about taking her away and raising her as our own, but with his illness, we didn't think it would be fair. Maybe we should have done it anyway."

I shook my head. "You know the Council would never have allowed it. Taking what isn't ours without consent is forbidden."

"She would have consented."

"But her parents wouldn't have." I stood. "This girl, did she have deep blue-violet eyes?"

"Like lapis," Serena finished, staring at Collin.

"It was Victoria Starling, wasn't it?"

Serena hung her head and nodded. "Yes."

"Take my hand, Serena. I need to see what she looks like."

"Why?" I could smell the alarm spiking in her blood, making it run colder than usual.

"She's missing, and there are no recent pictures of her in the Starling estate. She ran off the day her parents were buried, and we can't find her."

"How is that possible?"

"I don't know, but we need to find her."

Serena took my hand and opened her mind. "I'm worried, Collin. If only we had gone to see Victoria, asked her to stay with us, she would be safe. But now Victoria is out in the world…alone."

"We will find her, I promise."

So that's what they were charging their guests for at their weekly gatherings. My brow furrowed in disgust. The world was truly a better place without the Starlings. *I need to talk to Caleb.*

*

A knock on the door to my study interrupted my reading.

"Come in, Collin. No need to lurk outside my door. I can smell your distress from here."

"Must you always show off?" Collin grumbled, entering the dark room.

"Since when do you knock?"

"Complaining?" He arched a brow, then squinted. "For all that is good in

45

this world, can you turn on a light or open a curtain in here? It's depressing."

"I can see just fine."

"That's hardly the point. We aren't going to burst into flames from a little sunlight despite what they show in the movies."

I hissed when Collin threw open the curtains to the large window, illuminating the room. The darkness offered quiet and peace. In the light, there was too much assaulting my senses.

The study served both as my office and my library. Two wrought iron spiral staircases loomed in the far corners, giving access to each level. Books lined the walls, three stories high, some old first editions and some brand new.

"Is this what you came here for, to bombard my senses with sunlight and idle chatter?"

"Don't be so grumpy." Collin threw himself down in the broad leather chair on the opposite side of the large mahogany desk. "What are you reading?"

"I'm not grumpy. You're the one sulking." I closed the book and placed it on my desk. "*The Principia.*"

"Newton's book? What a snooze."

I leaned back, folding my hands together. "Let me guess. You've lost something…or should I say someone? Someone precious?"

Collin laid his head back and growled. He could never hide anything from me.

"You're an insufferable know-it-all. And don't think I don't know about all the connections you have at headquarters keeping you informed of everything."

I chuckled. "Do you want my help?"

"No." Collin glared. "…Maybe."

"Now who's grumpy?"

"Caleb, she's disappeared. Even the trackers can't scent her."

"That isn't possible. She's human. Have them pull the blood marker from her father's file."

"I've already done that…and there's no trail."

"They aren't trying hard enough then," I insisted. "Have they gone to the family home?"

"Once the Council bought it, she fled. It's been empty all this time. She had all her parents' assets liquidated. The family butler hasn't heard from her, the real estate agent who sold the house is dead, and Darin's speaking with the attorney tomorrow." Collin snatched a paperweight off my desk and twirled it around in his hands. "She's extremely clever for one so young."

"You sound impressed."

"Maybe a little. Aren't you?"

"How did we not know about this? Her running, I mean."

"I have no idea. It's…well, frankly, it's embarrassing. We dropped the ball on watching her. I think we even made it easier for her when we bought the estate."

"There's nothing to be done about it now. Let's wait for what the attorney says. I'm sure he knows how to find her. She was a minor when they died, so he had to be helping her."

"She's the seer that helped Serena and Greggory."

"Really?" I sat forward. After the funeral, I had forced myself to stop thinking about the Starling girl. Serena hadn't told us much about the person who had seen Greggory's future, but the story had intrigued me nonetheless. Human seers were rare, and those that could see with as much detail as this one, to my knowledge, had never existed. The only seers I had known were Fae, and they chose extinction over evolution. And people thought vampires were arrogant.

"Yes, can you believe it? Talk about a small world. Darin got a description of Miss Starling from Anton, and when he mentioned the color of her eyes, I knew there was a connection. I spoke with Serena this morning and she confirmed it."

"The color of her eyes?"

"Yes, remember? Serena said they were unusual—like nothing she had ever seen."

"Not really. So what color are they?"

"Deep blue-violet, with golden flecks—like lapis, she said."

My heart thumped. A rush of warmth flooded my body. It took all my strength to keep my hands from shaking. *Could Victoria be the woman in my dreams? Why would I dream of her?* I shook my head and returned my attention back to my brother.

"Something bothering you? You look like you're about to be sick."

"It's nothing. I'm fine. Are you sure the butler isn't hiding her?"

Collin shook his head. "Darin might be half human, but even he can smell a lie. I trust the butler has no idea where she is. She didn't even go to her parents' funeral."

"I know. I was there."

Collin cocked his head to the side, setting the paperweight back on the desk.

"I was curious." I shrugged. "She's the last of the Starling line, once the most prestigious human bloodline in existence until it started breeding disagreeable humans. Even desperate vampires were unwilling to take them for mates. I wanted to see the last of them."

Collin chuckled. "Scoping out the merchandise. That's not like you."

"Shut it, Collin! Don't be so crass. I'm still the highest-ranking vampire, and I will not be disrespected even by you."

"Okay, okay, sorry. I meant no disrespect. I'm just shocked. You've never shown interest in humans before other than to make sure we had enough numbers for the upcoming *Legăturas.*"

"I *still* have no interest in humans."

"If you say so." Collin shrugged. "Anyway, that's not the reason I came. I need advice on damage control if we can't find her. This isn't how I anticipated starting off my time as head of the Council. We've never had a human run away before now. Any suggestions?"

"Simple." I grinned. "Find her."

Collin rolled his eyes. "Thanks."

As he stood to leave, I stopped him. "Collin, if the attorney is no help, let me know. There will be a way to save face with the other Council members."

He smiled. "Thanks. I appreciate it. Now go outside and get a tan or something."

Collin ducked as the paperweight he had been playing with whizzed by his head. He shut the door, his carefree whistle carrying through the halls of the manor until he left. *What are you planning now?*

"One of these days, brother, I won't miss." I chuckled.

*

I waited in the lobby of Mr. Anderson's office. A sturdy man in a brown suit walked in carrying a worn briefcase and a coffee.

"Are you my one o'clock?"

"I am." I stood and shook his hand.

"Come on in and have a seat. How can I help you, Mr...?"

"Digsby."

"Mr. Digsby, what can I do for you today?"

"Please, call me Darin. I'd like to ask you about one of your clients, Miss Victoria Starling."

Mr. Anderson's eyes glazed a moment. "Oh yes, Edgar and Cynthia's girl. Such a shame for her to lose her parents so young. How is she doing these days?"

"Well, she left town after they passed away. No one has heard from her or knows where she is. It's a lot to ask, but this is Council business. It's important that we speak with her. I was hoping you might have a current phone number."

"I would be glad to help, although I don't usually give out client information. You say this is for the Council?"

"Yes. I wouldn't ask if it weren't important. Do you need a formal written request from Lord Carrington?"

"Uh, no, I don't think we need to bother him." He seemed flustered. Anyone would be around Caleb. "Any information we have would be in her file. Let me grab it."

I breathed a sigh of relief. Maybe I would finally have good news for Collin.

*

"What do you mean nothing?" I raked my hand through my hair.

"I'm sorry Collin, but there wasn't anything in the attorney's records. Even he seemed very confused. There were only his notes to liquidate the Starling holdings and deposit them into a bank account."

"Did you at least get that information?"

Darin hung his head. "It wasn't there either. Seems the attorney didn't keep it."

"This is unbelievable!" I slammed my hand against the wall.

"Mr. Anderson doesn't recall liquidating the assets. There aren't any signed papers. She was a minor at the time, and he was the custodian. There should've been forms with his signature showing what he did with the funds."

"Wait…he liquidated everything and gave a sixteen-year-old the cash? Then destroyed the paper trail?"

"It appears that way, but he doesn't remember doing any of it."

"I need to talk to Caleb."

Chapter Eight

"TORI! Over here!" A short red-haired girl propped herself up at the bar and frantically waved her hands to grab my attention.

I smiled and maneuvered my way through the crowd.

"I wasn't sure if you would come tonight."

"Hey, Cassie." I hugged my friend. "I figured if I didn't, you'd send Stephen to drag me from my apartment."

"You're damn right she would have, and I would have gladly obliged." Stephen laughed.

For the past five years, I had been working in a nearby restaurant as an entree chef. That's where I met Cassie and Stephen. Stephen bused tables and helped with deliveries and Cassie was a hostess. We were normally joined by another waitress friend from the restaurant, Tanya, but she had a family birthday party to attend that night.

"Tanya is so bummed she can't be here tonight to help us celebrate," Cassie pouted.

"It's okay. Family comes first. It's nice they want her so involved." I sighed. I missed my friend but envied her as well. How wonderful it must be to have such a loving family, one that misses you and wants to include you in everything. "We're going to meet for lunch on Sunday. You guys should join us if you can."

"I can't. I have to help my grandfather fix his fence." Stephen grinned. "If I don't do it, the old guy is bound to try and make the repairs himself."

Cassie and I laughed. We had met his grandfather before, and his resolve wasn't surprising. Even at eighty years old, Mr. Humphrey refused to let time slow him down.

"You should probably stay over at his house tomorrow night," I suggested. "Otherwise he'll be up and working before you get there."

"Probably a good idea," he agreed.

"So, Tori, are you excited about tomorrow night? It's your first night working as a head chef." Cassie beamed at me. She knew I had worked hard to gain the trust of the kitchen staff and the owners in the hopes of obtaining the position.

I nodded. "Yes, and a bit nervous too. Saturday nights are our busiest. I'm not sure why Mr. Calet wanted it to be my first night."

"He has full faith in you...just like we do." Stephen's broad grin was infectious.

After the death of my parents, I started using the name Tori Langley. Finding someone to create a fake identity hadn't been easy, but I learned almost anything is possible if you have enough cash and ask the right questions. Each night I went to bed praying that it was enough, that the Council wouldn't find me. I found an apartment not far from the center of town and secured a job at Chez Calet's working initially as a waitress and later transferring into the kitchen.

Cassie and I became fast friends. It was hard not to, with her exuberant charm and outgoing nature. We would go out after work for drinks and shopping on the weekends. She had even stayed over at my apartment a few times watching movies and hanging out. I never imagined I would ever be this happy. This was probably the happiness Serena had foretold for my future. I didn't regret running—not for a single moment.

During one of our girls' nights, Cassie asked me what I thought of Stephen.

"He's handsome and friendly." I shrugged.

"Handsome? He's *gorgeous*, an absolute dream. That sunshine blond hair? Those blue eyes? And he's so sweet. Like how he goes over to his grandfather's house every day to make sure he has enough food and clean clothes or just anything he needs. I mean, how many people do that?" Cassie's eyes had glazed over at that point.

I giggled. "So you're saying you like him?"

"I'm so in love I don't know what to do with myself." Cassie sighed, hanging her head.

"Why does that make you sad? Have you told him?"

"Oh goodness no…What if he doesn't feel the same?"

"But what if he does?" I looked at her over my glass of wine. "You know, some guy's fear being rejected."

"It's not that simple, Tori." Cassie shook her head. "If he doesn't feel the same way and I say something, it will make things so awkward at work. I really love my job at Calet's."

"I think you can find out without having to give him a full confession." I put my glass down. "Maybe I can help." I took her hand in a subtle gesture of support. "Why don't you practice with me?"

I looked in her eyes and squeezed her hands. Cassie didn't know about my gift. No one did…and no one ever would if I could help it.

"Don't be silly, Tori. But I appreciate the offer." She squeezed my hands, then pulled away.

I didn't see anything that night. I even tried reading Stephen one afternoon when he was helping me stack boxes. When I lost my balance on the ladder, he steadied me. I took the opportunity to put my hand on his shoulder. Visions of him and his grandfather filled my mind, but nothing about Cassie.

"Well, what should we have to toast your promotion?" She shoved a drink menu into my hands, interrupting my thoughts. "I know you don't like champagne."

I wrinkled my nose. "I don't like how it tickles."

Stephen laughed. "Usually that's what girls love about it."

"That's why I like it." Cassie giggled.

Stephen smiled down at the little redhead and tucked a lock of hair behind her ear. "Exactly."

Their look lingered for much longer than usual and I smiled.

Are they finally realizing how they feel about each other?

I was surprised when I didn't get a creepy vibe from Stephen after being so close to him. Stephen didn't act the way most guys did toward me—a genuine relief. I managed to keep a distance between us. I knew how Cassie felt about him, and I didn't want to lose my best friend…my first friend. Some of the kitchen staff had tried to corner me, but Stephen always glared at them, and with his bulk and height, it had been enough to keep them at bay.

"Well, I'm in the mood for a Cosmopolitan." I signaled to the bartender to place my order.

"Mmm, that sounds good." Cassie ordered one too.

Stephen frowned. "That's a chick drink. I'll take a whiskey straight."

The bartender nodded and went to make our drinks.

"It's crowded in here tonight." I scanned the people around us.

"I hear tonight's cover band is one of the best," Stephen added. "That's probably why. I know I'm looking forward to hearing them."

"I hope you're ready to dance till you can't stand. Once they start, I'm not leaving the dance floor, and you two are going to keep me company." Cassie poked both of us.

"Of course. You'll get crushed out there if I'm not with you." Stephen laughed.

"Hey, I'm not *that* short," Cassie pouted.

"Yes, you are…" I squeezed her tight. "But we love you anyway."

We finished our drinks, and the cover band began to play. Cassie grabbed our hands and dragged us onto the dance floor. Cassie and Stephen danced much closer to one another than usual, and even seemed to get lost in their own little world during some of the slow songs. They made a great couple. Part of me envied them. I hadn't met anyone that I wanted to be with. The way guys reacted around me annoyed me more than anything, but sometimes the missing piece twinged my heart.

We danced until the band finished their set and then left the bar and headed home. Cassie and Stephen dropped me off at my apartment. I went upstairs, slipped out of my dress, and decided to take a quick shower before going to bed. Tomorrow was a big day, and I needed to make sure I was well rested.

The menu had been set, the kitchen stocked. I knew each staff member having worked with them for years and had no doubts in their ability to handle the busy Saturday night schedule. I was ready for this next step, but that didn't stop the doubt from creeping into my mind.

You are nothing, my mother's words whispered.

"I can do this." I fell into a deep but fitful sleep.

My dreams had always been filled with images from the past, or nightmares about the Council finding me. What would they do if they did? Would I be punished? Or simply dragged back to the community?

That night, a new image visited me. I dreamed of a tall vampire with hair as dark as mine and eyes of deep cerulean blue. They shifted between disgust and contempt to loving and tender. I couldn't discern his features, but a strange attraction pulled me to him. The feeling terrified me, reminding me of where I came from, what I was born to do. Yet I wanted to run to this stranger, wanted him to hold me and never let go. In my dream, it felt like he was there for me, to claim me, but when I was close enough to touch him, he pushed me back so hard it sent me reeling.

I woke up with a cry, tears streaming down my cheeks, and covered in sweat.

*

My phone rang the next morning before my alarm.

"He loves me!" Cassie screamed through the phone.

I winced and held the phone away from my ear until the noise subsided. "Who loves you?"

"Who do you think?"

"Mr. Calet?" I teased.

"TORI!"

I laughed. "Okay, okay…Why don't you come over and tell me all about it? We can walk to the restaurant from my place."

Cassie arrived shortly after we hung up with her work clothes in hand and an impossibly wide grin. I was afraid her face might split in two.

"So, tell me everything." I dropped down on the couch.

"Well..." Cassie then talked nonstop, recounting every detail of the conversation she had with Stephen as he walked her home the night before. "And that's when he told me that he is in love with me and has been for a while now, but he was too scared to say anything." Cassie had a faraway, dreamy look on her face.

I suppressed a laugh. "Did he kiss you?"

Cassie blushed so hard that her face turned as red as a pepper. "Y-yes...and more."

"More?" I almost spit out my coffee.

Cassie nodded and colored even more. "He ended up staying the night."

"Wow...okay. You can spare me those details."

"Are you sure?" Cassie wiggled her eyebrows.

"Positive. I will say, it's about time. I was beginning to think we'd all be in nursing homes before you two finally confessed to each other."

She slapped my arm, and smiled. "Tori, you don't think it will be awkward at work? Or when the three of us go out?"

"Not at all. I'm sure the Calets already know how you feel about each other. The rest of us aren't blind, Cassie. We all see it."

"Tori, I know you'll find yourself a good guy one of these days."

"Where did that come from?"

Cassie shrugged. "I worry now that Stephen and I are going to be a real couple, you'll get that lonely look more often now."

I tensed. "What lonely look?"

"Sometimes it flashes in your eyes when we're at the club and you see a couple being all cute together. Or when the Calets are being nice to all of us at the restaurant. Even Stephen notices it when he talks about his grandfather."

Sighing, I looked out the living room window.

"What makes you get that look, Tori?"

"My family wasn't particularly close. I sometimes find myself wondering how my childhood would have been different if..." I trailed off. The vision of that tall, dark, and handsome someone from my dreams flashed in my mind. "Anyway, it's all in the past. If I'm meant to find love, I will, but you know I'm focused on my career right now."

Cassie nodded. "Yes, but you've reached your goal. You're head chef...Don't you think you should start looking for that special someone?"

I laughed. "Cassie, I haven't even worked my first night yet. I hardly think it's time to check that goal off my bucket list."

"I suppose you're right. I don't want you losing sight of that side of life. It's easy to get consumed by work, especially in your position. Most head chefs don't have much of a social life once they make it and especially if the restaurant starts doing well. I know you love your job and cooking, but don't forget about love."

"Okay." I smiled.

"Promise me."

"I promise." Cassie left no room for compromise once she made you promise something. Her positive attitude was contagious—it's why I loved her so much.

*

The next day, I met with Tanya at a café not far from my apartment.

"Hey, we missed you Friday night. How was the birthday party?"

"It was great. I haven't seen many of the people there in a while. The house was full—and loud." Tanya looked pale and tired.

"Are you okay?"

"I didn't get much sleep after helping my mom put the house back together again. I'm so glad I don't work today and the restaurant is closed tomorrow."

I nodded. It was a great time to recharge.

"If you're not feeling up to this, we can just get a cup of coffee so you can head home to rest."

"No, I really want to catch up with you. I need to eat something before I crash for the night anyway. So tell me, how did last night go?" Tanya leaned forward. "Was it what you expected?"

"Yes, and so much more. We were so busy, but everyone did a great job.

We really missed you out on the floor. A couple of your regulars came by and asked for you."

Tanya smiled. "That's what I love the most about Calet's—the regulars who come in every Saturday night. They're like extended family."

"That's true."

"Did Joshua work last night?" Tanya asked, sipping her coffee.

"Yes."

"You don't like him, do you, Tori?"

"It's not that I don't like him…more like I don't know him, Tanya. He does make me a bit uneasy for some reason."

She frowned. "I don't think you're being fair."

"I'm sorry, Tanya. I didn't mean to upset you. I know you like him, and if he's good to you, then I'm happy for you. Really, I am. But I get the feeling he doesn't want to be friends with me."

"I'll talk with him. I'm sure that's not the case. Besides if he's going to date me, then he should try to get along with my friends, right?"

Tanya really likes this guy.

"I'd like that." I wasn't hopeful. Joshua wanted to transfer into the kitchen. Maybe if he did, that would give me the chance to get to know him better…for my friend's sake.

*

"We want to thank all of you for your dedication and hard work over the past year. Without everyone, Chez Calet's would not be the popular restaurant it is today. Our wait and bus staff are the best in the city, we have the most beautiful and gracious hostess, and our kitchen staff can't be beat. Tori, I don't know what Mr. Calet and I would do without you. Making you head chef was the best decision we ever made." Mrs. Calet and her husband had exclusively opened the restaurant for the staff to celebrate the restaurant's recent upgrade to four stars.

I never dreamed I could be this happy. I have everything I've always wanted.

"I can't thank you enough for giving me this opportunity. It's been an incredible year. I want to thank everyone for all your support. I couldn't have done it without you. Let's raise our glasses to Mr. and Mrs. Calet for being the best bosses any of us could ever hope for." I smiled. "Salute!"

"SALUTE!" Everyone at the table toasted.

I glanced around the long table. They weren't related to me by blood, but they were family. For the first time in my life, I felt loved. My eyes met Stephen's.

Oh. No.

His eyes flashed, a look I had hoped I would never see. It was gone in an instant. My heart sank.

*

"She's great, isn't she, Joshua?" Stephen whispered.

I simply kept the fake smile plastered on my face and nodded, going along with Tanya's request to try and get to know her friends. I still didn't like them, especially Tori. When her eyes met Stephen's, an odd look crossed her face.

Hmm…I wonder what's going on between those two. And can I use it to get rid of her?

Chapter Nine

T ime was passing quickly. I had never been so busy in my entire life. Cassie, Stephen, and I still managed to make time for each other on my nights off. Unfortunately, Tanya no longer joined us. She spent most of her time with Joshua, and despite our best efforts, none of us could get any closer to him.

Over the past year, I had kept a slight distance between Stephen and I, and thankfully, he didn't act any differently toward me. I dismissed the look I saw that night at the restaurant as a fluke. Cassie moved into Stephen's apartment earlier that year, and they were planning on getting married in a few months. Mr. Calet offered them the restaurant to use for their wedding reception, his gift to them. I would oversee the menu and the preparations, even though I wouldn't be working in the kitchen that day since Cassie asked me to be her maid of honor.

Cassie called that morning like she always did.

"Where shall we go for lunch today?"

"I wish I could, but we have a big shipment arriving today. I need to be at the restaurant early to get everything organized."

"Do you need help?"

"Tanya and Joshua are coming in to help me, so I should be fine. Why don't you spend some time with Stephen? I know you two haven't seen each other much with him at his grandfather's."

Cassie sighed. "I would love that, but he has to go back again today. There's still something wrong with the sink in his kitchen. The house is getting old and really needs a lot of repairs."

"You know he'll never sell it, Cass. Mr. Humphrey was born in that house..."

"And he's going to die in that house," we said in unison, quoting the old man.

"You really have to love him, though. I hope I'm as lively at his age."

"True." Cassie laughed. "Well, I'll let you get going."

"Do something fun for yourself today."

After hanging up, I arrived at the restaurant as the delivery truck was pulling in out back. I propped open the back door and told the driver and his assistant where to unload everything. I looked at the time on my watch. *Tanya and Joshua must be running late.*

She was acting strange lately, probably something to do with Joshua. It wasn't affecting our work at the restaurant, but there was a distance growing that saddened me. I kept my promise to Tanya and really tried to be friends with Joshua. We all did. He was so closed off and didn't seem interested in spending time with us outside of the restaurant. Even after he transferred into the kitchen, it was difficult to get to know him. He was an excellent cook and great with the kitchen staff. He had the potential to become a head chef, which is what I believe he wanted. However, like most guys I ran into, he always had this yearning look in his eyes when he gazed at me. I kept my distance as much as I could because it made Tanya upset.

I still hadn't figured out why men looked at me that way. *It's unnerving. I don't consider myself any prettier than Cassie or Tanya.* In fact, I felt quite ordinary around them, but it always starts out the same. I would meet a guy and they're fine at first. Then after an hour of being near me, a dark gleam fills their eyes and they become aggressively seductive. The change in their personalities frightened me. I would get a tightness in my chest that made me want to escape every time.

While I pondered this, they had offloaded all the supplies. I was in the middle of logging everything in the restaurant's inventory database when a familiar voice crept up behind me.

"Need help?"

"Stephen, what are you doing here? Is Cassie with you?"

"Cassie went to have her nails done. She's going to come later at the normal time. I was done early at my grandfather's, and she told me I should check in on you."

"Well, I'm glad you're here. There's no way I can get all of this unpacked and put away before dinner time."

"You're alone." Stephen's eyes flashed.

My chest tightened. "At the moment, but Tanya and Joshua should be here any minute. They said they would come to help out."

"Great, then we should have this all taken care of in a jiffy." His eyes returned to normal.

Breathe, Victoria. Everything will be fine.

"If you don't mind doing cold storage for me, I'll take care of the other boxes."

"Sure thing, boss." Stephen gave me one of his wide grins.

I need to distance myself.

I turned and headed to the far side of the kitchen to continue logging in the items we received and put them away. My hands were shaking. I was glad we were working in separate areas. Hopefully the distance would cool whatever feelings were brewing in Stephen.

I finished my tasks and headed back to check in with him. He was almost done unpacking the boxes.

"I forget how fast you are at this…" I searched his eyes. They looked normal.

"I've got a system."

"Well, it's a good one. Anything I can help you with?"

Stephen stood and brought the box cutter to me. "If you could open up those last three boxes, I'll unpack them."

"Sure." My fingers grazed his hand as I took the box cutter from him. His eyes darkened in desire. He slammed my back against the wall, his hands trapping my wrists above my head.

No…no…NO!

Wedging his knee between my legs, he leaned in close, sniffing the nape of my neck. Chills traveled down my spine. My heart thumped.

"Stephen, stop!"

He didn't react. He was acting as if he couldn't hear me.

Meeting his gaze, I raised my voice. "STEPHEN, STOP!"

"No."

I turned my head. Was he possessed? He leaned in and kissed my neck, trailing his tongue along my jaw.

I shuddered. *This can't be happening.* I writhed and twisted trying to break free, but it was no use. He was too strong.

"Stephen, think of Cassie. You love her. You're getting married. You don't want me… This isn't you. *You need to stop,*" I pleaded, trying to break the spell he seemed to be under.

I heard a gasp followed by an evil chuckle. Tanya and Joshua had arrived.

Stephen's eyes cleared. He blinked at me as he took in our position.

"I told you she was bad news." Joshua snickered.

"What happened?" Stephen blinked. "Tori?"

I scurried away from him, trying to put as much distance between us as possible.

"How could you, Stephen? And Tori? Cassie is your best friend. Why would you do this to her?" Tanya's glare cut through my soul.

"We didn't…" I stumbled. What could I say? "Nothing happened."

"Didn't look like nothing." Joshua's venomous words stung my ears. "Sorry we interrupted your little fling."

"There's no fling. I'm not interested in Tori like that…I don't know what happened," Stephen stammered. "Tori…what happened?"

"I don't know." I looked at him. "You'll think I'm crazy, but it happens sometimes when guys get near me…It wasn't your fault. You didn't know what you were doing."

"Wow, aren't we full of ourselves," Tanya sneered. "What are you, some siren that men can't keep their hands off of?"

"No...No, I'm not. But i-it's...this isn't the first time." Tears welled in my eyes. My world was crashing down around me. What would Cassie say? How would I explain this to her?

"Come on Tanya, let's go get something to eat before the restaurant opens. They obviously don't need our help." Joshua turned to leave. "Sorry we interrupted you."

"Wait a minute!" I stopped them. "Where have you two been? You were supposed to be here hours ago."

Joshua stepped closer. "Well lucky for you we weren't...or should I say unlucky for you." He winked and led Tanya out the way they came.

I turned to Stephen. "You need to go to Cassie. You need to tell her before Tanya calls her. Blame me. Tell her it was my fault. Tell her I tried to seduce you."

"But...but you didn't. Did you?"

"No..." I hung my head. "You and Cassie belong together. I won't let this ruin what you have. I'm sorry I don't have an explanation for you. I will take the blame." I met Stephen's eyes. "I know how this sounds. Please believe me when I tell you this is not what I wanted. I love you and Cassie, you're my family, but I won't be the reason why you two aren't together. Please go. Now. Tell her...tell her you were pushing me away, trying to make me stop. That's what they saw. You were defending yourself from me."

Stephen sighed. "But..."

"No buts, Stephen. We don't have a choice. It's the only way. Please, if you truly love Cassie, do it!" A plan formed in the back of my mind, even as my heart broke. "I'll finish up here and go talk with Mr. Calet. I'll tell him that I've always had a crush on you, and I lost control. She may never forgive me even if I begged for it, and I may lose my position here, but there's no other way."

I turned away from him. He left without another word, his footsteps echoing on the kitchen tile. Tears fell freely down my cheeks.

"Please, please let Cassie be understanding. Let her blame me...let her be happy with the man she loves. This is my fault, not his!" I whispered.

Why does this keep happening to me?

＊

"I have to say, I'm very surprised and disappointed in you, Tori." Mr. Calet frowned at me from across his desk. "I'm not sure what to do."

"Please believe me, Mr. Calet, it was a moment of weakness. It will never happen again. I expect that Cassie and Stephen will never forgive me, but I'm hoping we can still all work together. I'll do my job the same as I've always done. I can get someone else from the kitchen staff to man deliveries." I hung my head. "I understand if you need to let me go. I'll stay on until you find a replacement if that's what you decide. I don't want to make your life or theirs any more difficult than I already have with my actions."

It pained me to lie to the man who had given me so much, but how could I explain something even I didn't understand?

Mr. Calet sighed. "Cassie and Stephen have been with me since we opened. I don't want to lose you as my head chef, Tori, but I don't think I have a choice. Is there anyone on your current staff that you feel is ready to step up? I know Joshua has been working toward it, but is he ready?"

My heart sank. I knew that Joshua coveted my position. His attitude that afternoon was probably an indication that he saw this as an opportunity. *I'm surprised he wasn't here before me.*

A knock at Mr. Calet's door made us both jump.

"Come in," Mr. Calet called. Joshua poked his head in.

"Mr. Calet, are you in? Do you have a moment?" His voice fell as he noticed me. Several emotions flashed across his face.

He's so transparent.

"Joshua, come in." I stood. "Mr. Calet and I were just talking about you."

"Really?" Joshua hesitated, but stepped into the office and closed the door.

"Yes, I was telling him how hard you've worked this past year and that you're ready to take over as head chef. After the events earlier this afternoon, I've decided to hand in my resignation and recommend you as my replacement."

"Tori?" Mr. Calet looked at me.

"Mr. Calet, you're right. This is for the best." A familiar tingle crawled over my arms. The gentle man nodded. I turned to Joshua. "You know this weekend's menu. Do you think you can handle it, or do you need me to shadow?"

Joshua stood silently. The stunned look on his face almost made me laugh and I would've had I not been close to vomiting.

"I can handle it, but if it will make Mr. Calet feel better, I don't mind if you shadow me this evening."

I nodded. "Then that is what I will do. Mr. Calet, I suggest that we don't tell the staff anything. I'll inform the kitchen that I'm shadowing this evening as part of Joshua's training. Tomorrow, you can tell them I resigned and announce Joshua as your new head chef."

"Don't you want to say goodbye?" Mr. Calet's voice hitched at the last word.

"After tonight, I expect none of them will want to talk to me."

"All right Tori, it's your choice. This is not how I expected my day to go when I woke up this morning...I hope we all can survive this."

"I'm very sorry, Mr. Calet." I turned back to Joshua. "Let's head down to the kitchen and go over everything for tonight's menu."

Joshua wasted no time after leaving Mr. Calet's office. "You surprise me, Tori."

"How so?" I really wasn't in the mood for his taunting.

"I never expected you to be the type to go after another girl's man. I had assumed it was Stephen who cornered you, so why are you taking the blame?"

"Listen, you're getting what you want. You'll be head chef after tonight and I'll be gone. Let's not complicate it by trying to get your twisted mind to comprehend things that are clearly beyond you."

"Tsk, such a sharp tongue, Tori." He pushed in front of me. "I deserve this position, but make no mistake, this is not how I wanted to get it."

I folded my arms. "Oh really? And why were you coming to talk to Mr. Calet? Just going to talk about the weather I suppose..." I met his steely glare. "Don't play your games with me, Joshua." I shoved past him. "And don't play them with Tanya either. She may not consider herself my friend anymore, but I care about her. If your feelings aren't sincere, let her go. Now let's get to work."

We reviewed that night's menu in-depth. If I hadn't despised him so much, I would have been grateful to have him as part of my kitchen staff. Joshua would certainly keep Calet's a distinctive and unique experience. The restaurant would continue its success. I clung to that positivity like a lifeline.

Everyone is replaceable. My mother's words echoed in my mind.

You are nothing.

*

Once the staff arrived, I informed them of our plan for the evening. I was about to wrap up my prepared speech and set them to work when the kitchen doors flew open.

Cassie, looking like a cheetah on the hunt, stormed up to me and resoundingly slapped me across the face. My head snapped to the side. My cheek heated and burned instantly. I could picture the red handprint probably starting to form. Everyone in the kitchen gasped.

"Y-you…you bitch! You were my friend…my best friend! You were going to be my maid of honor. Stay away from him and stay away from me!"

"Cassie, please not now." Stephen gently tugged at her elbow.

"NO! She deserves this!" Cassie turned toward me, fire in her eyes. "Don't speak to me. Don't even look my way. If you ever touch him again…I'll…I'll kill you!"

Cassie marched out of the kitchen. Stephen glanced warily my way before following after her into the main dining room. The sadness in his eyes tore at my heart. I lost the two most important people in my life. I placed a hand on my flaming cheek and winced. The kitchen was silent. Only Joshua stood watching with a wide grin of amusement.

"All right, show's over. Back to work everyone. We have food to prepare." I left the kitchen to splash cold water on my face. Cassie's words split my heart into pieces, but I found comfort in knowing that they were still together.

I'm used to being alone.

I thought I found my place in the world. A life filled with love and friendship. I should have known it was too good to last.

You are nothing.

"Never again," I whispered to the image in the mirror. "I will never open my heart to anyone again...I'm not meant to find happiness in this world."

The dinner rush passed by in a blur. Leaving the restaurant for the last time that night, I thanked the Calet's.

"I appreciate the chance you gave me all those years ago. I've genuinely loved being a part of this family. I can't take back what happened, and I hope in time everyone will forgive me. Joshua is an excellent cook. He will do well."

"Tori, are you sure you won't stay?" Mrs. Calet pulled me into a hug.

"I wish I could, but...it's better for everyone if I leave."

Mr. Calet shook his head. "I still don't believe your story. It's not like you to do something like this, but if you won't tell us the truth..." He sighed. "I'll miss you, little girl. Please take care of yourself. And if you ever need anything, don't hesitate to come back."

Mr. Calet hugged me tight and kissed the top of my head.

"Thank you" was all I could manage to say before turning my back on the only caring family I had ever known.

My dreams were haunted that night by visions of Cassie's angry outburst. I even dreamed of the dark-haired man again. My eyes were red-rimmed and puffy when I woke the next morning. I pulled out my suitcase and began packing the few personal belongings I owned. The furniture would stay since it wasn't mine.

Later that afternoon, I called an apartment listing in a city two hours away. They had a furnished one-bedroom available. I was able to rent it out over the phone, on the condition I meet with the manager in the morning to sign the lease and hand over the first month's rent and deposit. I would drive there that night and stay in a hotel. With all the restaurants nearby, I was sure I'd be able to find a job. The Calets said they would give me a good reference despite what happened.

I would start over, a new life…if that's what you could call it.

*

An unnerving feeling nagged at me in the pit of my stomach. I pushed away from my office desk, staring out the window, until someone knocked on the door.

"Come in," I responded absently.

"Are you all right?" Greggory rounded the desk, concern in his eyes.

"Oh Greggory, it's you…Just lost in thought I guess."

"Serena?"

I sighed. "I was thinking about Victoria. Do you think she's okay?"

Greggory knew the girl never seemed to be far from my thoughts. She had given us the most precious gift…hope. And I had instantly fallen in love with the girl. "I like to think so. They still haven't found her, have they?"

I shook my head. "No. And perhaps that's a good thing, but I have a very bad feeling right now."

Greggory hugged his wife close. "I'm sure she's fine."

"I hope so."

Chapter Ten

L
ife had been relatively quiet since I left Chez Calet's. I was now working as the manager and head chef of a local steak house, Tangi's. I never expected to fill my previous role so quickly, but the owner and former head chef, Nicholas, had been in an accident that left him unable to stand for long periods of time and desperately needed help.

We instantly connected during my interview. He explained that he only used produce acquired locally each week. It had been hard to find a chef that wanted the challenge of an ever-changing menu—running a kitchen was hard enough. I loved the challenge. Adapting the recipes and coming up with new dishes depending on the ingredients we obtained gave me a sense of control and accomplishment I had never known. The only constant item on the menu was the steaks, Tangi's trademark. The cuts of meat just melted in your mouth.

"Tori, *ma chérie*, why do you always seem so sad?"

"What do you mean, Nicholas? I'm not sad, I'm concentrating."

"No, no, I know sadness when I see it. The eyes become dull. I know what we will do—we will find you friends!" he announced.

"Nicholas, you worry too much. I have friends here at the restaurant."

"Ah, you are *friendly*, yes, but you are not *friends*." He wiggled a finger at me.

"You never go out after work."

"That's because I'm exhausted. You work me too hard."

"If I were thirty years younger, I would take you out on the town. Such a beautiful woman should be spoiled and made to smile every day," he teased.

"You make yourself sound like an old man past his prime. Any woman would be proud to be on your arm." I winked.

His deep belly laugh could vibrate the walls. "Tori, you flatter me. I am old." He sighed. "But in my prime, I was a wonder to behold and broke many… many hearts."

"You're too sweet to break hearts. Although I'm sure lots of women pined over you."

"You see right through me. Therefore, you are the only one I can trust my beloved kitchen to."

"Remember your promise. When I came on board, you and I agreed you would find a backup chef I can train."

"Ah…*ma chérie*…you would never leave me. *Voudriez-vous*?"

"Don't sweet talk me. You know it's the right thing to do. You were lucky you found me when you got hurt. If I get sick, or something happens to me, you would have to close. So enough stalling."

I was keeping my distance from the restaurant staff, making no friends, I never knew when I might have to pick up and leave. I wasn't going to have a repeat of what happened at Calet's. I had grown fond of Nicholas and refused to leave him in a situation where he would have to hire someone on the fly or close. Tangi's was his life, and even though he could retire comfortably, it was the spark that made his life worth living.

"You win, *ma chérie*. I will put together the advertisement for you to review. You'll have to help me hire someone."

"Good." I smiled. "Now get out of my kitchen, old man. I have work to do, and you have an ad to write."

"Your kitchen indeed," Nicholas grumbled as he retreated to his office.

*

After a month of interviews, Nicholas and I hired Thomas. He wasn't as creative as Nicholas wanted, but he fit well with Tangi's atmosphere. His expertise and skills made him an excellent chef and a fast learner.

Although we worked side by side every day, he didn't show any interest in me. He did have an eye for one of the bus boys in the restaurant. I would smile each time I caught him staring at Sean. Thomas's ears would turn red, and he would promptly look away.

"You should ask him out," I suggested while we were restocking the pantry.

"No, I can't do that…"

"Why not?"

"What if he doesn't like…me?"

I nodded, and then sighed. *Seems like only yesterday I had the same conversation with Cassie.*

"Tori, are you ok?"

"Yes. I was thinking about what you said. I can imagine it would make things uncomfortable if he didn't share your feelings. But if you don't try, can you live with never knowing?"

"I have no idea what to say to him. Even if he likes guys, he may not like me."

"Talk to him about everyday stuff then. If he's interested, you'll find out eventually."

Thomas nodded.

Surprising us both, Sean poked his head into the pantry. "Oh, there you are." He winked at Thomas and then continued. "Thomas, come find me when Tori's done with you. I have something I want to ask you."

"Uh-huh. Yeah…sure," Thomas stammered.

"Great. I'll be in the main dining room."

Thomas stood as still as a statue, staring at the spot Sean had just occupied.

"Earth to Thomas…" I chimed in his ear, waving my hand before his eyes.

"Do you think he heard us?"

"Probably not—but he really seems eager to talk with you." The wide grin on his face said it all. "I think you've found your answer."

Thomas didn't stop talking the next day after his date with Sean. Every time he dropped off dishes in the kitchen, he made sure to catch Thomas's eye and wink at him.

"It was such a great date. We had so much fun. We never ran out of things to talk about. He's such a great kisser. Did you know that he's from the town next to mine? We lived so close but never ran into each other once our whole lives. We probably were at the same football games together and never met, not once. Can you believe it? Oh, and did I say how dreamy his kisses are—"

"Thomas!"

"Yes Tori?"

"Breathe…" I laughed and rubbed his back.

A blush stained his cheeks. "Oh…sorry. Am I talking too much?"

"Yes," Craig muttered from across the prep station.

"Be nice." I pointed a finger at him. "He's excited and he has every right to be. Remember when you met Abby last year? You talked so fast you passed out," I gently reminded him.

"He did?" Thomas asked.

"I did not!" Craig huffed.

"You most certainly did," Maddie added, walking into the kitchen to pick up her order. "If Nicholas hadn't caught you, you would have split your head open on the floor and bloodied up the entire kitchen." She bumped her hip into his.

"Easy, sharp knife in hand." Craig's face turned ten shades of red, causing the entire kitchen to burst into laughter.

Maddie grinned and stuck her tongue out at him.

"All right, let's not lose our concentration. We have a dining room full of hungry people. Stay focused everyone." Even though the staff bantered with each other while working, it never really slowed them down.

As I made my rounds through the kitchen making sure everyone was on task, I noticed Maddie missed one of the dishes for table seven. I grabbed it from under the heat lamps and headed out the kitchen door. I rarely left the kitchen unless someone important asked to speak with me directly, usually a food critic or a political patron, but the thought of someone being served a lukewarm meal gave me hives.

We had been busier than usual due to a convention at one of the local corporations. I hadn't been as careful with keeping my jacket clean. I was a mess. My body swayed when I approached the table.

Vampires!

I recognized the feeling in my very core. My stomach churned from the power emanating off their bodies. *What are they doing here?*

Maddie hadn't stopped talking about the guests at this table from the moment they were seated, telling the entire kitchen about the stunningly handsome and well-dressed men.

"Maybe one of them will find my phone number slipped into their pocket before they leave." She winked at Thomas.

"Don't let Nicholas hear you talk like that. Now get back out there," I had warned, ushering her out of the kitchen.

They were handsome, no denying that, but a menacing aura swarmed about them. *Purebloods?*

I wondered if they had Maddie and the entire restaurant charmed. No one else seemed to be aware of who sat amongst them. There were four at the table, but one of them stood out from the others.

Even though he was seated, I could tell he was taller than the average human man. His broad shoulders seemed to stretch the seams of his sport coat, and his chestnut hair and cinnamon brown eyes sparkled despite the low lighting. I picked up what he was saying to his comrades as I came closer.

"I think the business concepts they discussed could really be useful when dealing with our foreign offices." He took a sip from his wine glass and glanced in my direction.

Of course. I sighed. It was his dinner I held in my hand. There was no way for me to avoid meeting his gaze.

"Sir, you ordered the ribeye cooked rare, with the side of parmesan risotto and grilled asparagus?"

"Ye…" His voice trailed off as he looked into my eyes. "Yes…I did. Thank you."

I placed the dish before him and turned to leave. "Haven't you grown into a pretty little thing." He seemed amused as he stared into my eyes.

"Excuse me, sir?" *Does he know who I am?*

"Forgive me. I seem to have forgotten my manners." He looked me over, preventing me from leaving. "By chance, are you the head chef?"

"I am."

"Did you prepare this dish?" He was staring at me as if he couldn't believe what stood before him. I was used to this reaction. Besides my presence affecting men sometimes, my eye color attracted attention too. *This feels different.*

"I didn't prepare your meal personally, no sir, but I assure you my entire staff is well trained. You won't find a better steak within a hundred miles."

"Really? Well, I look forward to eating it." He grinned with delight.

"Very well, sir. Enjoy your evening." I kept my eyes down and once again turned to leave. *I need to get out of here.*

"Oh, I definitely will. Before you go, may I ask your name?" He now had an even wider smile on his face.

I searched his eyes for that familiar glazed look, but it wasn't there. Instead, he looked like a man who had just won the lottery or…perhaps a cat about to eat a canary.

"Tori."

"Tori." He smoothly rolled my name across his tongue. "Thank you, Tori, for bringing me my meal. I'm sure we will meet again…very soon." With a wink, my world crumbled once again.

Oh no! He knows. I could see it in his eyes and feel it in the pit of my stomach. *I need to run.*

I hastened back to the kitchen and found Thomas.

"Thomas, I have to go. I'm suddenly not feeling very well. Can you manage the last hour of the night without me and close? Maddie and Sean are on closing tonight too, so you'll have help."

"Are you okay, Tori?" he asked, looking concerned.

"Y-yes, I'll be okay. I need to go home and rest. Please, can you do this for me?"

"Of course, go, I've got this. I was trained by the best, you know." He winked at me.

"Thomas…" I paused, knowing I would never see him again. I gave him a quick hug. "You're a fantastic chef. Don't ever forget that…I really enjoy working with you."

Thomas frowned. "Tori, you're not dying, are you?"

I shook my head. "I just wanted to tell you."

"Of course, we're friends, right?"

"Right…and thanks." I smiled at him as I grabbed my purse and ran out the back door, flooring the gas pedal all the way home.

I burst into my apartment and locked the door behind me. I had no idea where I was going, but the destination didn't matter. I just needed to pack quickly and hit the road, or I'd never get away. I refused to be someone's slave.

Panic wormed around in my gut. With shaky hands, I tore off my jacket, threw on a sweatshirt, and pulled out a suitcase. *Forget it, I'll buy new clothes.*

I grabbed a duffel bag instead, tossing in the only picture I had of Cassie and I from my dresser and my favorite book, *The Iliad*. There wasn't anything else that I cared about, or that I couldn't replace.

Zipping up the bag, I headed back out to the living room, taking one last good look around at the life quickly slipping through my fingertips. I threw open my front door—and ran smack into the solid, well-muscled chest of the vampire from the restaurant. The impact made me bounce backwards. If he hadn't grabbed my arm, I would've landed on my back side. Those golden eyes were *glowing* down at me. He was much taller than I had first assumed. Power vibrated off him, making even my bones stir. He reached up and took my bag. My head danced with a certain lightness while my vision blurred.

"Hello, Victoria. I've been looking for you for a very, very long time," he purred.

My mind screamed. I had my own life. I was in control. Was I going to lose it all now?

"H-How did you find me?"

"We followed you."

"Let me go." I tried to pull my arm from his grasp.

He looked down at me. "I can't do that, Victoria." Leaving little room for argument, he motioned for me to head down the stairs.

Thoughts tumbled through my head. Could I make a run for it once we exited the building? He would be much faster than me and no doubt his men were waiting outside, but I had to try. As we made our way down the stairs, he released my arm. I couldn't allow myself to be auctioned off to the highest bidder. Bile stung my throat as I thought of what my mother had said. *You are too plain. You most likely will become a blood servant.*

NO!

I opened the front door of the building and turned to run, but I wasn't fast enough. He grabbed my wrist, yanking me backwards.

"Don't make me chase you, princess. I already missed out on that glorious meal and I get cranky when I run on an empty stomach."

I pulled on his grip only once before he led me to a black SUV parked outside the front door. *Why are the cars always black?*

One of the men with chocolate brown hair and matching eyes from the restaurant sat in the far back seat. My captor opened the door and motioned for me to slide in, then joined me and closed the door. The locks clicked into place. I pulled on the handle to my door, but it didn't open.

"You won't be able to escape, princess."

A man with white hair sat in the passenger seat, and a dark-haired man was driving. Neither turned to look at me. No, I certainly wouldn't be able to with all these vampires.

As the car pulled away from the curb, my captor made introductions. "Victoria, the man behind you is Darin Digsby. He's my right-hand man. The grumpy looking dudes in the front are Bastian and Blake Boylston. They may not look like it, but they're twins and my top guards. You can't run away from us, so please don't try. I fear it will only end with you getting hurt. Guys, this is Victoria Starling. She is my special guest and is to be treated in accordance. Clear?"

They all nodded.

"Hi Victoria, it's nice to finally meet you." Darin extended his hand over the seat. His large eyes and broad smile reminded me of an eager puppy.

I stared at him, then carefully shook his hand. *I probably shouldn't be rude to a vampire who could tear me apart in seconds.*

"Why would I want to do that?" Darin looked hurt. I frowned. "Sorry, your thoughts are just really loud right now." He leaned back into his seat.

"Y-you can hear my thoughts?"

"We aren't going to hurt you, Victoria," the man next to me confirmed. *Right.* "You have my word."

"Then what do you want with me?"

"Surely you were told about your duties growing up. You missed your first *Legătura*. I have to say, I'm impressed you were able to avoid detection for so long. We've never had a human run away, never mind remain invisible to us for ten years. How did you manage it?" He looked me up and down.

I frowned. "Please don't do that."

"What?" He cocked his head to the side.

"Look at me like I'm a side of prime beef."

He chuckled as his cell phone rang. "Excuse me a moment. Yes?" The voice on the other end spoke quickly. "Yes, I have her. We'll be there in three hours. Make sure everything is ready. Tell Mrs. Gallagher to meet us at the front door. Oh, and have her call my brother and remind him of his obligation."

The voice on the other end spoke again before he hung up. He turned his attention back to me. "Sorry about that, Victoria. Lots of last-minute details that need my attention."

"Last-minute details?"

"Why yes, for your own special *Legătura*, of course."

"Tonight?" I croaked.

"I see no reason to wait. And with your extraordinary escape skills, the sooner the better."

I tore my gaze away and stared out the window as tears streamed down my cheeks. *This can't be happening.*

He handed me a white handkerchief. "There's no reason to cry."

"Says the vampire that gets to make his own decisions about his life," I sneered. The men in front seat stiffened. *Go ahead. I don't care if you get angry with me.*

"Is being mated to a vampire that horrid of an idea to you? It's what you were born for—"

"Don't talk to me about what I was *born* for…You don't know me! You don't know anything about my life! *You don't know what they put me through!*" I swallowed down my tears. Years of pent-up rage rose up instead. "I have the right to choose! I'm not just some…some item you pick off the shelf at a convenience store because you like the look of me! Mate? Not everyone is chosen as a mate, so don't sugarcoat it like some fairytale ending. Becoming a mate is not the only reason for the *Legătura*. I am not some stranger's property or a *food source*…I'm a person! I deserve to decide how I live! I will not become a slave."

I turned back to the window, huddling as close to the door as I could. Sobs racked my trembling body as I pulled my knees into my chest. I couldn't hold back, couldn't stop the trembling. Exhaustion eventually took over. I slumped weakly against the window.

*

The intensity of Victoria's emotions vibrating throughout the car made the hair on my arms stand. Her rant left her weak and spent. She was huddled so tightly against the door I feared her body would meld with it as she slept.

"Can you feel that?" I whispered. Each of them nodded. Her sadness and fear left a sour taste in my mouth.

Darin looked at me. "I'm not sure whose heart is more broken, hers or mine."

The two stoic vampires in the front seat even turned to look at the passed-out human with worried expressions. I met each of their gazes. Darin's human side always made him more sensitive than the other half-breeds, but the reaction from the Boylston twins surprised me.

Darin leaned back into his seat and stared out the window. I could read the expression on his face. If he had been able to, he would save Victoria from her fate, but it was not within his power.

My brow furrowed. "Did she say *food source*?"

"She did." Darin sighed.

"And *slave*?"

"Yep."

"What in the hell did her useless parents tell her?" I growled.

*

When did I pass out?

I woke as the SUV turned off the highway. I was surprised the vampire hadn't killed me on the spot for my outburst.

Maybe I should have fought harder to escape. I may have gotten hurt, but if I had managed to get away, it would have been worth it. Now it was too late. I had no idea what awaited me, but I would surely be paraded in front of who knows how many vampires, given to the highest bidder, and used for…what? Food, probably.

I had been born and raised without choice. Told repeatedly that my life was never mine. It had been a blessing when my parents died. I had good memories mixed with bad, but I had known freedom.

How can I ever go back? It will be my death.

"Let's hope it isn't. It would be such a shame to never see such a beautiful goddess again." The tall vampire was staring at me.

"Get out of my head," I snapped.

He chuckled. "Don't think so loudly."

"Does nothing irritate you?"

"Not being able to find you for ten years has caused me to have a few sleepless nights."

"Good. Why not go another ten years…or even a hundred? We could even make a wager on how long it will take."

"I like you." He slapped his hand on his thigh. "You've got grit. If my brother doesn't take you, maybe I'll keep you for myself."

"May the heavens strike me down now and save me from such a tragic fate."

"Hey, I'm a good-looking guy. I could grow on you."

I scowled. "Like a fungus."

The dangerous looking vampire with white hair looked back and growled at me.

"Easy, Frosty..." I put my hands up.

"Frosty...hear that, Bastian? I think we found you a nickname."

Bastian didn't say anything and his face remained blank, but you could tell he wasn't thrilled. Even Darin chuckled, earning him a menacing glare.

"Sorry." Darin smiled.

"So, who are you anyway?" I asked him. "Why have *you* been looking for me personally?"

"I'm Collin Carrington, second eldest of House Carrington and head of the Vampire Council."

I frowned. "I thought the head of the Council was named Caleb?"

"Good memory, princess. That's my brother. He passed the position to me right before you disappeared ten years ago."

"Lucky you," I jabbed. Collin didn't react. "You said *if* your brother doesn't take me. What does that mean?"

"Well, my goddess, there won't be many in attendance tonight. As the eldest unmated pureblood, Caleb has the first right to decide if he wants you or not. My dear friend and I have convinced him to claim you—at least, I hope we have him convinced."

That doesn't sound too assuring.

"Wait...wants me?" My heart pattered in my chest. "Wants me for what?"

Collin shrugged. "I have my aspirations."

"Aspirations? You're a very odd vampire, you know that?" I crossed my arms and glared back at Frosty, who once again glanced over his shoulder and growled. I stuck my tongue out at him.

"And you are one very unique human, Victoria." Collin smiled. "Not many humans in our community object to the *Legăturas*, and I can guarantee you I've never met a human brave enough, or should I say foolish enough, to stick their tongue out at a pureblood vampire, least of all Frosty."

"There's a first for everything," I grumbled.

Collin laughed even harder. "You, my dear, are exactly what my brother needs."

CHAPTER ELEVEN

W e pulled up to the largest mansion I had ever seen.

"Whose house is this?" I asked.

"This is the clubhouse. Haven't you ever been here?" Darin asked from his spot behind me.

I shook my head. "No. My parents never brought me. They told me it was for adults only and no place for children." Collin and Darin exchanged a confused look. "I'm assuming that was a lie?"

"I'm sorry, Victoria. There are lots of family activities and kid-friendly programs offered here at the clubhouse." Collin's eyes held a sadness close to pity.

"What did your parents tell you about our community?" Darin asked.

"Not much really. They were more focused on teaching me my place and purpose...and how I could make their bank account grow." I shrugged, looking back out the window. "Doesn't matter now. What's done is done."

"I think I might cry." Darin sighed.

I changed the subject. "What happens now?"

"I'll let someone else explain that to you."

"Who?"

"It's a surprise." Collin winked at me as he opened his door.

"Great, this night is just full of them."

"Oh, I think you'll like this one, trust me."

"Trust? You?" My thoughts were cut off by a familiar voice.

"Victoria?! You're finally home."

Serena came running down the front steps. I couldn't believe my eyes. I didn't remember my body moving, but I found myself scrambling out of the car and dashing up the walkway toward her.

"Serena? Serena is that you?" I threw myself into her open arms. We held on to each other and collapsed to our knees.

"Oh my darling Victoria. Look how grown you are! You're a woman now." Serena cupped my cheeks in her hands and gazed into my eyes. "I've been so worried about you." She kissed my forehead.

I couldn't speak through my tears, so I just stared at her. She pulled me to her once again.

"Let's get you inside and have a nice hot cup of tea."

"Serena, there's not a lot of time," Collin warned.

She casually waved off his comment. "Give the girl a break. You've ripped her away from her life, and she's just spent the last three hours in the car with you lot. There's always time for tea and catching up. I will not rush her."

"Serena!"

"Go do what you do best, Collin...Stall." Serena ushered me into the clubhouse and to a private drawing room off the front entryway. "Now, I've bought us some time." Serena placed a hot cup of tea in my hands. "How are you, little one?"

I shook my head. "I don't want to do this...I'm scared. I want to go back to my life."

"I know darling, and if it were in my power, I would whisk you away, but..." Serena hung her head. "It's not something I can do."

The door inched open behind me. "Is she here?" A deep voice full of anticipation echoed in the room.

"Greggory?" I jumped from my chair, almost spilling my tea.

"Victoria…Oh my, little one, look at you. You're all grown up." Greggory pulled me into a tight embrace.

I looked up at him, his face blurry through my unshed tears. "You're all better now?"

He nodded. "Yes, everything you said came true. It was rough going for a long time, but I've been cancer free for eight years."

"I'm happy for you. I'm glad my visions were right." I hugged him again. "I've missed you both."

"We've missed you too."

I searched Greggory's eyes. Even though his arms were around me, he still didn't get that flame of desire like my tutor and Stephen and countless other men. *What made him different?*

"How are you? I'm sure this is coming as a big shock to you." He sat on the couch next to his wife.

"Honestly, I've been better." I returned to my chair. "Even though I tried, I knew I wouldn't escape my fate forever. Although I don't know why they are in such a rush to pass me off."

"Well sweetie, you are a bit of a…" Serena paused.

"Flight risk," Greggory finished, a sheepish smile on his face.

I laughed. "I guess I am. I hoped they would stop caring."

"You're the last of a very important human bloodline, Victoria. They won't ever forget about you."

I sighed. "Collin told me that his brother has first choice to claim me tonight. Am I going to end up being his blood servant?"

Greggory laughed. "Blood servant? Where did you hear such nonsense?"

"My mother told me I'm not pretty enough to be chosen as a mate and would most likely be a servant to a vampire family."

His laughter died off. Serena and Greggory looked at each other.

"Princess, she lied to you." He placed a calming hand on my shoulder.

Just like with everything else it seems. "I suppose that's a relief. So, Caleb… what's he like?" Serena sighed. I slumped in my chair. "That good?"

She leaned forward and placed her hand on my knee. "I told you long ago you would find happiness and I still believe that. Caleb is…well, he's closed himself off, especially to humans. Deep down, he's a good man, a good vampire. I've known him all my life and he won't treat you poorly."

"That's not giving me a lot of hope for a life of happiness, Serena."

"Give him a chance," she pleaded.

"If he even chooses me." I sipped my tea.

Greggory turned to Serena. "You need to speak with him before Collin comes to get her. The Moriat family is here."

"Malcolm?" Serena gasped.

Greggory nodded.

I sat up. "Who is he?"

"No one you want even looking in your direction." Serena scowled. "He's arrogant, a narcissist, and unstable. He puts on a good show of being the perfect gentleman, but he's not the nicest vampire."

My body started to shake as tears filled my eyes and fell down my cheeks. Would that be my fate?

"Don't worry, sweetie. I promised you I would take care of you and I will. Let's get you cleaned up and I'll go talk with Caleb."

Serena brought me to an adjoining chamber, complete with a full luxury bath and dressing room.

"It's already been a long night for you. Take a hot shower, fix your hair and makeup, and I'll be back to help you get dressed. And Victoria, I'm sure I don't have to say this, but this room will be guarded."

"Don't look sad, Serena. I would've been disappointed in Collin if he didn't post guards."

She smiled and blew me a kiss before closing the door behind her.

I took a deep breath, peeling off my clothes and trying to prepare myself. I was at a *Legătura*. A private one. Just for me. I knew two vampires who would be there, but how many more would be staring at me, scrutinizing me, trying to decide if I was worthy of their houses? My nightmares were coming true.

You are nothing.

I tried to let go of my fears as I stepped into the hot shower, letting the water flow over my head and body. *Maybe it will all be okay.*

*

I stepped out of the private room and immediately went in search of Caleb. I had personally dragged him out of his office and drove him to the clubhouse. He was staring at the night sky on the second-floor balcony when I found him.

"She's here?" He glanced at me as I joined him.

"Yes, finally. She's all grown up, beautiful…" I sighed. "But she's terrified."

Caleb remained silent.

"Can't this be put off? Let her adjust to what's to come?"

He turned. "You know the other Council members would never approve that…and I can't say I blame them. What if she runs again?"

"Is it so important for the last Starling to be claimed?" He frowned. "Okay…" I resigned. "At least promise me you'll be the one to claim her."

"Why would I want to do that? I have no use for a human in my house."

"Caleb Carrington, stop giving me a hard time and promise me you will. This isn't a normal *Legătura* where the attendees mingle and get to know one another before matches are made. You can't let that beast get his hands on her."

"What beast?"

"Malcolm. You know what he's like. Evil incarnate." I shuddered. "And if the rumors are true…he'll hurt her. I promised her I would keep her safe. I promised her a life of happiness."

"Why would you make such a foolish promise to this child?"

"Don't be cold, it's not who you really are." I grabbed his hand. "Please Caleb, please promise me that you will keep her safe…for me. You don't have to house her at your manor. She can live with Greggory and I once everything is settled. But you're the only one Malcolm won't challenge."

Caleb relented. "I will do as you ask. Now go back to her."

"Thank you. You won't regret this, I promise you." I stood on my tiptoes and kissed his cheek.

"We'll see," he muttered, not convinced.

*

Why am I agreeing so easily to Serena's request?

A strange sensation formed inside my chest the moment Collin arrived with Victoria. We were on separate floors of the clubhouse, but I could feel her presence and an overwhelming urge in the pit of my stomach to find her. My self-restraint was being tested.

I spent years trying to deny that Victoria was the woman who had haunted my dreams, but I knew it was her when Serena brought her in. Tonight, that vision of beauty and desire was here, and based on a promise, I would be claiming her as my own. My chest tightened with excitement and disdain. The conflicting emotions were irritating.

I'll do as Serena asked and immediately send her away. I have no need for a mate. Nothing will change my mind—certainly not this human.

*

I dried my hair, pinning it up in a loose twist and curling the thin tendrils that now framed my face. Putting the finishing touches on my makeup, I began feeling a queasiness in my stomach. The hot shower had done little to quell my turbulent emotions. At first, I thought it was my desire to fling open the front doors and run away as fast as possible, hoping I could get past the guards and far enough from the grounds before the others realized I was gone.

No, I don't want to run. I want to go to the upper level. Why?

I tried to shake off the feeling and still my quivering hands.

"You're absolutely stunning, little one." Serena returned and stood behind me, smiling at me in the mirror.

"Thank you," I whispered.

"Come, I have the perfect dress for you."

I followed Serena into the dressing room. It was huge, much larger than my apartment, and was lined with clothing on one side and floor-to-ceiling shelves of shoes on the other.

"This one is perfect for you." Serena held out a navy-blue gown.

I took off my robe and stepped into it. The sweetheart neckline was low, but not immodest, and the thin straps slipped easily over my shoulders. The fabric in front gathered across my waist, pulling to one side. It collected just over my hip and a small oval sapphire surrounded by smaller diamonds fastened the silk in place. The skirt flowed to the floor, pooling behind me. A side slit made walking in the dress easier but showed off more of my thigh than I wanted given my situation.

"It's a bit…revealing, don't you think?"

"It's perfect." She ignored my concern, handing me a pair of heels that matched the color of the dress perfectly. "Here, these should fit you."

Once I had everything on and Serena zipped up the back of my gown, she turned me around, looking over every inch of me. I blushed beneath her careful scrutiny.

"Oh sweetie, you are an absolute vision. He's not going to be able to keep his eyes of you."

"Who?" I panicked. *Malcolm? That mean vampire? I don't want him looking at me!*

"Caleb, of course." Serena winked at me. "He promised me he would claim you, but after he sees you in this dress, the promise won't matter."

I didn't know if I should melt into the floor or run screaming from the room. This couldn't be happening to me. It was all too fast.

"I'm not ready for this…" I shook my head and stepped back. "This has to be a nightmare. I need to wake up."

"It's not a nightmare…It is happening and happening now!"

Collin stood in the doorway gesturing dramatically with his hands.

"Ugh! Go away…" I sighed.

"It's nice to see you again too, my beautiful goddess. You know what? I think I've changed my mind. I may have to fight my brother to keep you." He stepped closer. His mischievous eyes didn't hold the same type of uncontrolled lust I had seen in so many men, but he was clearly enjoying the view.

"You couldn't handle me," I shot back at him. It was a silly thing to say, but I didn't want him to think he managed to fluster me.

Collin laughed.

"Don't you dare mess this up, Collin Carrington, do you hear me?" Serena shook her finger at him.

"Wouldn't dream of it, little sis…" He offered his arm to me. "Shall we?"

"I don't seem to have a choice." I took his arm.

"Not this time. I'm sorry."

"Don't be. This is my fate."

Collin's eyes seamed sad for a moment. I couldn't blame them for moving fast. As much as I loved seeing Serena and Greggory, given the chance, I would have run and never stopped.

He led me from the room and down the hall. I glanced briefly at the landing on the second floor, but it was empty. Stopping before a large set of mahogany double doors, I involuntarily stepped back.

Collin squeezed my hand. "You'll be okay, Victoria. I promise."

"What about Malcolm Moriat?"

"You don't need to worry. I outrank him. If Caleb backs out of his promise and doesn't claim you, then I will. I like you, and I like joking with you, but I won't let anyone harm you. Trust me."

Before I could respond, the doors slowly swung open. Red velvet and dark-paneled walls lavishly decorated the room. Waiters carried trays of drinks and canapés. There weren't many people mingling around the high-top tables, but it felt like I had a hundred eyes on me.

A butler dressed in an ornate suit announced our arrival. I didn't have the presence of mind to look at him closer, but at first glance, he didn't appear to be human. "Master Collin Carrington and the human offering, Miss Victoria Starling."

I winced. "Great choice of words."

Collin suppressed a chuckle. "My apologies."

The room gasped at the announcement of my name. *Was I a surprise?* As Collin led me into the center of the room, a warmth of desire spread through my body. The intensity of it made me shudder.

"Don't be afraid, Victoria. I have to leave you here, but you'll be fine."

It wasn't fear that made my body shake. I glanced around the room, searching for the source. My eyes stopped when they reached the far back wall. I could feel him. He was shrouded in shadows, but I knew it was a pureblood vampire. The desire streamed from him.

Who is he? The power emanating from him was both terrifying and intoxicating. I couldn't see them, but I knew I was looking straight into his eyes. I licked my lips and tried to swallow. My mouth suddenly dry. Fire licked my body. *What is this feeling?*

*

Occasionally I would attend the *Legăturas*, even though I never participated in them. After all, it was my plan that created these gatherings. The events had changed over the years, much to my pleasure. They were more relaxed and allowed the attendees to get to know one another. *I should thank Serena.* It was all her doing. Normally, I would order a drink from the bar and take up my usual place in the back of the room. Leaning against the wall, I would watch as unmated vampires and Dhampyres mingled with the humans presented, making connections and often selecting mates. I barely noticed the humans walking around the room.

Tonight's event would be different, more closely resembling the *Legăturas* of the past. When the doors opened, I prepared myself. I promised Serena I would claim Victoria, and I intended to keep that promise no matter how distasteful I found it. *With luck, she won't be anything like her useless parents.*

Collin's head appeared. Standing six and a half feet tall, it was hard to miss him, even amongst other vampires.

The butler announced them. "Master Collin Carrington and the human offering, Miss Victoria Starling." I winced.

Nothing could have prepared me for when Victoria came into view. In all the years I lived, no one had left me breathless before. Serena was a genius when it came to fashion, so I wasn't surprised that Victoria looked stunning. Had the wall not supported me, my knees might've given out.

The dark navy-blue dress clung to her curves, showing off her hourglass figure. The slit in the side of the dress gave a glimpse of her long, shapely legs, and the tendrils of hair curling around her face and cascading down her delicate neck made my mouth water. But it was her eyes that captivated me the most. Stunning deep blue-violet.

What is this feeling?

When Collin left her in the center of the room, my body pulled away from the wall. That's when her gaze fell on me. The lights weren't on in this area of the room—I knew I was concealed in darkness—but somehow, she had spotted me and stared directly into my eyes. I forced myself to lean back against the wall, pinning myself there. All the while, her gaze never left me. Heat bloomed in my core while a foreign tension twisted my stomach. Her individual scent fluttered toward me. Like the forest after a thunderstorm mixed with the faint scent of jasmine.

Despite the terror I could smell radiating from her, Victoria impressed me. She stood tall, her chin raised in defiance as her eyes scanned the room, memorizing every detail. The faces of the people gathered at the tables, the drinks in their hands, curiosity in their gossip. Her heart was pounding but she carried herself calmly and with reserved confidence. Victoria was a conundrum of emotions.

I didn't need the promise I made to Serena.

I want her.

*

"Welcome to tonight's *Legătura*," Collin's voice boomed. "I want to thank each of you for coming on such short notice and promise we won't take up too much of your time." Collin stepped over to me. "Tonight, we have one human guest, Miss Victoria Starling. In accordance with tradition and law, the highest-ranking unmated pureblood in attendance will have the first right to take this human as his mate or reject her."

Reject. My stomach fell at the word. I didn't know which vampire was Caleb. Honestly, I hadn't been able to tear my eyes away from the figure still hidden in the shadows.

"Caleb, brother, would you like to step out from your favorite resting place and give us your choice?"

Silence fell across the room as every head turned in the same direction as my gaze. My heart was pounding in my chest. I feared it was going to burst out and land with a thud on the floor.

The corners of Collin's mouth tipped up. "Remind me to teach you how to shield your thoughts when this is over. You're thinking very loudly right now." My cheeks warmed.

A tall, well-built man with a stern expression stepped from the shadows. He wore a black suit, with a crimson vest and matching tie. A touch of silver tipped his midnight black hair. I gasped.

It's not possible.

The man from my dream. He stopped shy of the light, just enough out of the shadows so he could be seen. I couldn't read the expression on his face. *Longing? Disdain?*

Caleb didn't speak. Merely nodded his head once. His deep cerulean eyes locked with mine. The brief connection made my entire body tingle...It was captivating. This beautiful, terrifying vampire had claimed me in so many ways with a single glance and without a word.

"There you have it, folks. Caleb Carrington is executing his first rights to claim this human as his own. Victoria Starling, you are now and for always will be tied to Caleb Carrington and the Carrington bloodline. This concludes..."

Wait...what? That's it?

I thought I was going to pass out right there. This vampire didn't utter a word. No introductions and it's done! If I could revive my mother and kill her again for all her lies, I would.

"A moment please..." An opulent man with snowy skin, hair the color of sunshine, and eyes of an almost colorless blue stepped forward.

Once my eyes locked with his, I couldn't look away...He was stunning. His cold, chiseled beauty was enchanting, but he radiated such malice that I shivered. It seemed as if the temperature in the room dropped below freezing. I wanted to shrink into the shadows. My body shuddered against my will.

Don't lose it now, Victoria.

The man continued. "Caleb, it's well known that you have never desired taking a human as your mate, and now you expect all of us here to let you simply take something so precious as the last of the Starling bloodline without contest?"

"Yes," Caleb responded calmly, his voice quiet and full of warning.

Ah…so he can speak.

The man's hesitation was almost imperceptible. I would have missed it if I hadn't seen the corners of Caleb's mouth turn up in an amused grin.

"I would like to claim the girl for myself," he continued. "My family has long waited for a human worthy to carry out our bloodline. As a Starling, she is valuable, and I find her appearance…acceptable. The Moriats would have no objections to me taking her as my mate."

The air in the room was so thick with tension I could taste it. *The Moriats? Oh no, this must be Malcolm then. Please go away, you crazy vampire.* I prayed to whatever deity was listening that I would not find myself in the middle of a war between two purebloods.

Wait…did he say acceptable?

That stung.

Caleb casually stepped forward. His gaze never left Malcolm's face as he stalked toward the center of the room where I stood in the spotlight. I looked from one vampire to the other, like a rabbit caught between two hungry wolves.

"Thou know'st 'tis common all that lives must die." Thank you, Shakespeare, but maybe not now!

*

I almost chuckled at all the thoughts racing through Victoria's mind, each one battling against the other and keeping her frozen in place. She wasn't wrong wishing to not be in the middle of a fight, but putting Malcolm back in his place would be a simple task and one that would bring me great pleasure.

"Are you challenging me?" I asked, taking my place by Victoria's side. My icy tone was not lost on either of them.

Malcolm took a step back. "Lord Carrington...no. It's just...I—"

I smiled, waiting for him to continue. Malice roiled in my gaze, my body language, enough for Malcolm to physically flinch beneath me. Even Victoria shrunk beside me.

"Which is it?"

"Forgive my boldness. I withdraw, with my most sincere and humble apologies." Malcolm backed away, but a look lingered in his eyes. One I knew too well. I feared this was far from over.

I smiled, still standing next to Victoria, and glanced at Collin with a look that told him to hurry it along. Victoria was on the verge of fainting. The tension in her body was vibrating so fiercely I was amazed she still stayed upright.

Collin continued, "As I was saying, this concludes this evening's *Legătura*. Thank you all for coming."

*

Caleb offered me his arm. My brain had ceased functioning properly the minute he stood next to me. I merely stared at him, not comprehending what he wanted me to do.

"Sweetness, take my arm. It is time for us to depart."

His voice was soothing. My heart thumped in my chest with each syllable.

Did he just call me sweetness?

"Sweetness?" I repeated back, staring at him. *Curse my stupid brain, what is wrong with me?*

I couldn't feel my body, couldn't form a complete thought. It wouldn't obey.

Gently, Caleb took my hand and linked my arm with his. I let him lead me from the room. We stepped back out into the large hallway where the air was much cooler. I didn't realize how warm I had been.

And then my body swayed, my vision clouding over. I had the brief sensation of falling.

*

"Well, would you look at that?" I nudged Serena as we watched Caleb scoop Victoria up into his arms and carry her outside to the limousine waiting to take them to the manor. We exchanged a hopeful look with Greggory.

"Collin, do you think…?" Serena left her question hanging in the air.

"If anyone can break through those walls, I believe Victoria can." I smiled. "She's a brave girl. If we hadn't had a plan, she'd be going home with me tonight."

"At least she's back where she belongs and Malcolm didn't get his hands on her." Serena sighed.

I scoffed. "That fool is going to regret his actions tonight. Caleb was playing nice, but there's no way he will let that go."

Greggory snorted. "It's hard to feel sorry for him."

Chapter Twelve

I cradled Victoria in my lap as the limousine pulled away from the clubhouse. My manor was more than half an hour away. I assumed she would wake up before we arrived, but I didn't want to let her go. Gazing down at her delicate features, I brushed a stray hair from her forehead and tucked it behind her ear.

"What is this feeling you're giving me, Miss Starling?" I sighed.

I don't know how long I held her before she started to stir in my arms.

*

I could feel my body again—and realized I wasn't alone. I was in someone's lap. Strong arms were wrapped around me, holding me in place. The scent of cedar and cinnamon enveloped me and soothed my senses.

I slowly opened my eyes and nearly screamed as I looked up into Caleb's solemn face. He was more handsome than any man had a right to be. His almond-shaped eyes held no emotion as they stared into mine. His jaw was regal and strong, but I stopped when I took in his full…inviting lips.

What are you thinking, Victoria? Snap out of it.

I blinked and shook my head. I smiled weakly. "Um…you can let go of me now. I don't think I'm in danger of fainting again."

Caleb opened his arms, letting me slip out of them and onto the seat next to him. I inched over to the other side of the car.

"Thank you," I whispered.

"For?" His gaze remained on me.

I shifted. "For catching me and for not letting that other vampire claim me. Serena told me he's...not very nice."

Caleb chuckled softly. "That's an understatement."

I frowned. *Is he making fun of me?* "Maybe, but anyway, thank you."

"There is no need. I was merely fulfilling a promise I made to Serena. When things settle down, you will go live with her and Greggory."

"Oh?" There was a time that would have made me the happiest person alive, but in the moment, it left me feeling empty inside. "I won't be staying with you?"

"No."

"But back there you said you were claiming me as your..." Before I could finish, Caleb loomed over me. His long fingers wrapped around my chin, bringing my face within an inch of his.

"*I know what I said.* I have no need for a mate and even less use for a human. Let them babysit you if they wish...I have no desire." He let me go and slid back to his seat.

Shocked and angry, I lashed out. "I'm not a child. I don't need to be babysat. If you don't want me, why not return me back to my home? To my *life!*"

"You are the last of the Starlings. You have a contract to fulfill."

"I didn't sign a contract," I shot back.

"Your ancestors did—it's binding. You managed to stay hidden for quite a long time. It's impressive, but that is done. You will remain here."

"Why? If you aren't taking me as a mate, what does it matter where I live or die? I'm the last of the Starlings and will be the last, so let me go!"

The growl that issued from between Caleb's teeth made me pull back.

Did I go too far? Please don't kill me. I closed my eyes and waited.

When he spoke again, I barely heard him. "You will do as you're told. Your life..."

"Is not mine," I answered. My head hung low. How many times had my mother uttered those same words to me? I had tasted freedom, if only for a short while. I turned and stared out the window.

What will life be like now?

I often dreamed of living with Serena and Greggory when I was young, but that dream never included being tied to the most powerful, and apparently the grumpiest, living vampire.

*

I was going to say, "Your life is here now." What have her parents told her? What did she mean her life wasn't hers? Why did she think I was going to kill her?

I closed my eyes, taking a deep breath to calm myself, but instead it filled my senses with her scent.

Why did I growl at her?

I frowned. I had never felt such conflict. I never wanted a mate, especially not a human, but things changed when I saw Victoria. Holding her in my lap felt right, like the scattered pieces of my long life finally clicked into place. Yet here I was, pushing her away with my cruel words. Promising to send her away as soon as I could.

Maybe she was right. Maybe I should let her go back to her old life. In truth, I might have, except now that Malcolm Moriat had his eye on her, there was no place safer for her than in my mansion. Serena and Greggory could protect her, even Collin could if needed, but to be truly safe, I would have to keep her with me. Malcolm was arrogant but not so foolish to take what was mine. It would mean his death.

Tensions between our families had been growing for decades. I had managed to keep the peace until Malcolm's father had been killed twenty years ago. Now in charge of the family, Malcolm felt he had become my equal. One day soon, I would have to correct that ill-gotten sense of importance. Now with Victoria, that day was coming much faster.

*

I must have dozed off because my body jerked when we turned onto the gravel road leading to Caleb's mansion. I rubbed at my eyes trying to get them to focus on the sight before me. The manor we were pulling up to was even larger than the clubhouse.

Is that even possible? Why would one vampire need a house that big anyway?

The limousine pulled into a circular driveway and stopped before the front steps. Caleb ducked out and then extended his hand for me. I accepted it and let him help me from the car. Glancing at the front of the house, I had to crane my neck to see up to the very top.

"Welcome to Carrington Manor." Caleb led me up the steps to the front door, which opened on its own—or so I thought until we stepped inside, and I saw a butler closing it behind us.

He doesn't look human. His eyes were all black, and tiny horns sprouted from his forehead.

"He's a demon," Caleb explained.

"Oh." I met his gaze. "Please don't do that."

"What?"

"Read my thoughts."

"Then you should learn to think more quietly."

"Until I do, please stop. Your brother did the same thing and it's very rude." The butler snickered.

"Talin, shall I make it your job to teach this human how to think quietly, or perhaps to not think at all?" He ignored the glare I aimed at him.

"Forgive me, Master Caleb." Talin bowed.

"Talin, it's very nice to meet you. I'm Victoria." I held my hand out to him.

Talin looked at me like I spoke in a language he didn't understand before taking my hand and pressing it lightly to his lips.

"The pleasure is mine, mistress."

I followed his timid gaze to Caleb, who was looking at me with an odd expression. "I'm sorry, was I not supposed to introduce myself?"

"Most humans are terrified when in the presence of a demon." Caleb was still staring at me.

"Well, Talin seems so polite and kind."

He snickered. "Thank you, mistress."

"Talin, I want you to show Miss Victoria to her chambers and around the mansion."

He bowed. "Yes, my lord."

"You won't be showing me?" I asked as Caleb turned to leave.

"No. I suspect we won't be seeing much of each other. Talin can see to your needs and introduce you to the rest of the staff. Talin, I'll be in my study." Caleb turned and strode off to the far end of the mansion.

It wasn't until I heard the opening and closing of heavy doors that I turned to my guide. "I'm sorry. I don't mean to be a burden to you."

Talin looked taken aback. "Not at all, mistress. This is my job, to do as the master commands. Would you like to see your room?"

"Yes please, although I don't have any clothes to change into. I'm also a bit hungry."

Talin nodded. "I'll have Galia come see you. She can outfit you with clothes from her closet—you're about the same size. Once you've changed, she can show you to the kitchen. I'll meet you there. In the morning, she can take you shopping if you'd like."

"Thank you, Talin. I appreciate your help."

"Forgive me mistress, but you aren't like any other human I've ever encountered. Are you not afraid of me?"

"Should I be?" I was beginning to second guess myself.

"No." He shook his head. "As Master Caleb mentioned, it's unusual for a human to be unafraid. Not all demons are like the ones that work here at the manor."

"What do you mean?"

"The demons here on this estate have chosen to live a more human-like lifestyle. We work, get paid wages, have families, and don't go around feeding on human souls."

Feed on what? "I see. Are there y demons who choose to live like you?" I asked as Talin led me up the large staircase.

"More and more are changing their ways every day, but many still live to cause chaos and destruction." Talin seemed incredibly sad.

"I'm sorry, Talin. That seems to cause you pain." I paused. "How many demons are working here on the estate?"

"Ten live and work here daily. We have another twenty that come once or twice a week to work on the landscaping or any maintenance that might be needed in the mansion. But they have homes and families off-site."

"I'm looking forward to meeting them."

Talin smiled. "Mistress, this is your room." He opened the double doors, leading to an elegantly decorated sitting area of soft purple and white. A long couch and three ornate chairs surrounded a wide-faced fireplace.

"Oh…it's beautiful!" I couldn't believe what I was seeing.

It's enormous too!

Nearby, another set of glass-paneled doors led out to a large balcony overlooking a garden that seemed to stretch forever. Up the small landing was the largest canopy bed I had ever seen, with more pillows than five people would ever need.

"If there's anything you need, please pull this braided cord and either Galia or I will come." Talin gestured to the white cord hanging from the ceiling by the front door.

"Thank you, Talin. I'll see you downstairs shortly."

With a bow, Talin left the room.

Chapter Thirteen

It had been a few months since my *Legătura*, and I hadn't seen Caleb except in passing. I spent my days getting to know Talin, Galia, and the other demons that worked in the manor and the estate's expansive gardens.

I quickly settled into a routine. Most days, I met with Serena and Greggory for lunch at the clubhouse or shopping in town. Caleb had given me leave to buy anything I needed since I came with nothing. I felt guilty using his money, so I asked Greggory to help me establish an account in my real name at a local bank and transfer the funds I still had under my alias.

"I'm surprised you have so much of your parents' money left." Greggory smiled. "Considering you were so young when you left. Most teenagers would have gone on a spending spree."

"I've been working all these years too. Even while I finished school, I was a waitress. I never had to touch the money from my parents' holdings."

"Would you like to go back to your old house?" he asked me. "It's still owned by the Council and no one is living in it."

I shook my head. "It can burn down for all I care. I never want to see that place again."

Serena and Greggory exchanged guilty glances. Her voice was soft when she spoke. "I'm sorry we never came back, sweetie."

"It's all right, Serena. I know you couldn't. You had to take care of Greggory, and my parents never would've let you near me anyway. Once they were gone, I left. If you had come, then the Council would have known I was gone much sooner." I smiled. "You did me a favor by staying away."

"It broke our hearts, you know," Greggory admitted.

I squeezed his hand and smiled. "We are all together again now."

"How's Caleb been treating you?"

"I don't see him, so I guess okay."

"He isn't spending any time with you?" Serena huffed.

"No. He's always in his study."

"Have you tried talking to him?" she encouraged.

"A couple times. He's polite but always curt. I've been cooking for the demons working in the manor and was thinking of asking him to have dinner with me one night. I know he doesn't need to eat, but I can't think of anything else."

"I think that's a grand idea." Greggory beamed. "We humans always say the way to a man's heart is through his stomach."

Serena laughed. "I know it's the way to *your* heart."

"What can I say? I love food."

I laughed. "Well, I'm not trying to make my way into his heart. I would just like us to get along since we're living in the same house and all. Do you know if there's anything he enjoys eating?"

"Honestly, sweetie, I've known Caleb all my life, and I don't think I've ever seen him eat actual food. I'm sorry." Serena tried to smile.

I sighed. "I'll make my favorites and go from there."

*

I stopped at the market on the way back to the manor. I would make my favorite rib roast with grilled asparagus and roasted potatoes. Once I unloaded the groceries, I decided to seek out Caleb and invite him to dinner.

Knocking on his study door, I waited patiently.

"Come in."

Here goes nothing.

I cracked the door open. "Caleb?"

"Yes, Victoria."

The room was pitch dark. Not a ray of sunshine escaped through the long heavy drapes shielding the window. No lamps were turned on. For a moment, I thought maybe he wasn't in the study at all and somewhere else nearby.

"Don't stand there in the doorway. Come in and close the door."

"Oh. It's so dark I didn't know if you were really in here." I stepped through and closed the door behind me. I leaned back against it, hoping my eyes would adjust and I could make out my surroundings. No such luck. "Um, I wanted to ask if you would consider joining me for dinner tonight. I know you don't need to eat human food, but I was at the market today and there was a beautiful rib roast and it's too much for me to eat on my own…so I thought you might share it with me."

I waited. And waited. The silence seemed to stretch forever.

"Fine," he eventually answered.

"Great, dinner will be ready at six. I'll have the dining room table set." Silence. "Okay…I guess I'll go now. See you at dinner."

I slipped out again, rubbing my eyes against the sudden brightness in the hall. *Now I need to make sure that this meal turns out perfectly.*

*

As I cooked, Talin was kind enough to answer many of the questions I had about life with a vampire. He explained to me what my mother told me was a cruel lie.

"Vampires don't keep blood servants. They haven't bitten humans in over a century."

"So how do they get the blood they need to survive?"

"When the Council reached out to the humans living in our community to form contracts with them for the *Legăturas*, several families actually stepped forward and agreed to be blood donors. Every week they visit a facility run by the community hospital to donate blood. It was the foundation for how humans and vampires could coexist."

"That's so much more civilized than what my mother told me. Why would she lie?"

"It sounds like she wanted to scare you, mistress. I'm very sorry."

I sighed. "Thank you for explaining it to me."

"My pleasure, mistress."

"Talin, when you set the table tonight, please make sure to have Caleb's nightly decanter of blood at his place setting."

"Are you sure you're okay with that, mistress? Watching him drink blood, I mean?"

"Yes, I'm fine with it. Since you explained how it works, it no longer scares me. Besides, he needs it to live, and I don't know if he will like the meal I've prepared. I'd rather him not go hungry."

Talin merely nodded and made his way to the dining room. I grabbed the serving cart and followed him.

I heard Caleb enter as I was laying out the platters of food on the table. As expected, he was there promptly at six o'clock. I smiled as I watched him inspect the table.

"I really hope you like everything. If you don't, it's okay. I won't be offended. I had Talin bring your decanter just in case."

He looked at the carafe on the corner of the table next to his place setting. "It doesn't bother you?"

"Not at all. Please sit, let's eat."

*

I took in the elaborate meal set on the table. Eating human food had never interested me. I never understood the twins' obsession with it. Having tried it centuries ago, I found it bland, but the smell of spices wafting off the table were making my mouth water in anticipation.

I hadn't spent much time with Victoria since she arrived. Collin told me she was the head chef at a prominent restaurant when he found her, and Talin reported that she had begun to cook dinner for the demons working in the manor, even learning how to make some of their favorite meals. She told him it was the least she could do since they took care of the house and were helping her learn the layout of the manor and surrounding town. Talin had raved about her cooking, which was why I agreed to have dinner with her.

Everything looks and smells enticing.

Victoria filled my dinner plate and set it before me. The roast was cooked to perfection. The first bite melted in my mouth. I'm not sure if it was the look on my face or if I made a sound, but when I opened my eyes, Victoria was staring at me.

"You like it?"

"Mm, yes, it's…" I swallowed my bite before finishing. "Delicious!"

"Then I will cook more for you if you like." Her delighted response sent waves of heat through me, something I had never felt before. It was disarming, to say the least.

"That would be…acceptable." She seemed so eager I couldn't say no. My own enthusiasm caught me off guard.

Victoria hesitated. "Oh, okay. Is there anything you'd like to have…I mean… would prefer?" Uncertainty laced her voice.

"Surprise me." I smiled.

"Challenge accepted." Her eyes lit up, and the most beautiful smile graced her lips.

*

Over the next few months, she surprised me every night with something new until I found my favorites. She would make those more often but still tried to create a new recipe at least once a week. There wasn't one meal that I didn't like.

However, I was finding there was one meal that I longed for, craving so strongly it made my blood boil and my body ache.

I wanted her.

I wanted to claim her, taste the sweetness of her life force. I wanted to join us, forming a bond that would last for all time. I hadn't marked her. Refused, even, to claim her, holding to my vow of never taking a human mate, but I would not send her away. *She's mine.*

Each night, I asked Victoria to walk in the gardens with me. *I want to know everything about her.*

"Join me for a walk, Victoria."

"As soon as I clear the dishes."

"Talin can take care of that..."

"No." Victoria stood, shaking her head and began piling together the dishes to carry to the kitchen. "He does enough already. The least I can do is clear the table."

"Leave it, Victoria," I hissed. *Just do what you're told.*

She stood straight and met my gaze. "If you can't wait, then go ahead without me." She gathered up the plates and walked off toward the kitchen.

Who does he think he is, ordering me around like that?

I turned and stormed out onto the terrace. Her loud thoughts tested my patience.

A few moments later, she joined me.

"I don't like being ignored, Victoria," I growled.

"Neither do I." She glared back. "And yet, here we are."

How do you like it, Caleb?

She really needed to learn how to shield her thoughts. Though she had a point, I was not used to being spoken to in such a way. She had no fear of me.

My eyes glowed in warning. "You can be so insufferable."

"I'm insufferable? You're the one who's intolerable. Always locked away in that library of yours." Her eyes met mine. Fierce and unwavering. "It's a wonder how you endure my existence."

Tears welled in her eyes despite the effort she was making to hold them back.

"Let us walk." I gestured toward the path before us.

Victoria hesitated before joining me by my side. I searched for something to say to cool both our tempers. Glancing over at her, I noticed her hair was up in its typical twist. It always looked so soft and shiny, and I wondered what it would feel like between my fingers.

I can't touch it when you wear it like that. I suddenly felt irritated at the lack of access.

"Why do you never wear your hair loose?" My tone was much sharper than I intended.

"That's an odd question." Victoria seemed to think for a moment. "I guess it's out of habit. Always working in a kitchen, you must wear your hair back. If I'm being honest, I've always worn it up since it started getting long."

"Why?"

Victoria sighed. "Since I was a young girl, people—men mostly—have looked at me funny. I felt like they were taking something away from me that didn't belong to them. If I pinned my hair up and hid it, I could keep it for myself. I couldn't stop them from staring, so I kept the few things I could."

"What were the other things you kept to yourself?" I pressed.

Victoria took a deep breath, blushing slightly. "My heart and my body."

What? I couldn't keep the next questions from escaping my lips. "You've never loved? Never lain with anyone?"

"What kind of question is that?! What kind of woman do you think I am?" Victoria blushed, then fury filled her eyes. "No, I've never been loved or loved anyone. What do you care?"

She turned her back on me. I didn't mean to insult her. I had only been shocked. I was all too familiar with the human world and how promiscuous women were these days. At her age, I assumed she would have had some experience.

"I didn't mean to offend you, Victoria. I was…surprised."

Looking at her back, I couldn't help but notice the elegant curve of her neck, the few loose tendrils of hair gracefully framing her ears and delicate jawline. A longing deep inside my chest nearly set me on fire and teased at my patience. My hand reached out, desperate to feel the warmth of her skin. I pulled back. I didn't know if I wanted to throw her over my shoulder or kiss her senseless.

"It's okay," she whispered.

"Are you…are you happy here?"

Victoria looked up in my eyes. "I suppose. Are you happy that I'm here?"

"It matters little to me," I lied.

"Then why have you not sent me away?"

I breathed in deep, her scent wrapping around me. "I promised Serena I'd let you stay here...and you intrigue me."

She seemed to struggle with her response. I loved watching her emotions and thoughts reveal themselves in her features. She was so honest, so pure, easy to read. A smile threatened her pink lips. *I intrigue him. That's good...right?* Then her brow furrowed. *Oh...like what Mother and Father used to do to me.*

"I mean to say that I find you interesting. You're unlike all the other humans I've ever known. You're brave in the face of fear and honest."

"So I'm entertainment?"

I smiled. "Well, I do find our times together entertaining."

Victoria huffed. *Just like they did.* Memories flooded her mind. Irritation, but mostly pain, clouded her eyes. Her brow creased in anger. "Maybe I should charge a fee."

"Victoria." My eyes softened. "I'm not your parents. You're safe here."

Am I? She nodded. "I admit, I do enjoy our times together, even though they are brief and only when you aren't grumpy."

"Grumpy?"

"Yes, grumpy. I suppose it's from centuries of being alone. Of course, it could be old age too." She giggled softly.

"Old age?" I scoffed. "You think I'm old?" I feigned being hurt. *Can't argue with her. I am old.*

"I don't think it...I know it." She winked at me. "Sometimes I wonder if you think you would wither into dust if you let yourself relax and enjoy the world around you. Just because you've borne witness to centuries of evolution doesn't mean you've seen it all."

How idiotic and highly insightful. I smiled despite myself. "Victoria." I watched her from the corner of my eye. "What was your life like before coming here?"

She hesitated for a moment, stopping to glance up at me. Her eyes darkened. "It was nothing."

"Surely that's not the case. You worked…had friends? Or do you simply not wish to share it with me?"

"Why do you want to know?" Victoria's tone was harsh.

I growled. *Why must she question me?* If she were anyone else, they would no longer be standing. "Tell me," I insisted.

Victoria sighed, plucking a cluster of jasmine growing on the edge of the path. We stopped at one of the many shallow pools scattered throughout the garden. I often saw her during the day seated on a blanket by this same pool. I assumed it was her favorite since her beloved flower, jasmine, surrounded it. The full moon reflected off its clear waters and lit the garden around us. "My life was nothing before I ran away," she began quietly. "I was born, cared for in the most basic manner. I had no friends, no family…no love."

"Your parents never loved you?" I wasn't sure why I pressed her.

"My parents barely acknowledged my existence except to educate me. When they learned that I'm a seer…" She stopped then, glancing at me to no doubt watch for my shocked reaction.

I nodded instead. "I know. Serena told me."

"Once they learned what my gift could do, I became a prop at their parties. Entertainment for their guests and a way to make money. There was never love. They never wanted me. I barely satisfied their contract with the Council in their minds because I wasn't a boy. That was all."

My inner beast roared. Rage like I'd never known boiled in my veins as I listened to the pain in her voice. Only centuries of experience kept me from uprooting every plant, tree, and stone that surrounded us. I had never cared for Edgar or Cynthia Starling. Edgar was a brainless puppet who did what anyone told him, and Cynthia was manipulative and selfish—they were both great disappointments to their families.

"Our family butler was the only one that ever showed any concern for me, and that wasn't much to speak about," Victoria continued. "Anton was a good man, but we weren't close. He at least convinced my parents that I *should* be educated. He argued if the vampire families found me crude, they wouldn't accept me and I would be considered unworthy. He warned that the Council would take their disappointment out on them. My father feared the Council, so he agreed and hired private tutors. I had so many it was like a revolving door."

"Why so many?"

"Any time one of my professors showed any sort of…affection, they were replaced."

"Affection?" *I don't like the way that sounds.*

Victoria hung her head, refusing to meet my gaze. "Many of my tutors were men. When I became a teenager, something changed. If I spent too much time near them or made contact of any kind, their interest in my education became…less focused on academics."

I clenched my fists instinctually as thoughts of another man daring to touch her filled my mind. *She's mine.*

She deftly changed the topic. "I sometimes helped Anton in the kitchen. I found I loved to cook. Before my sixteenth birthday, I convinced my parents to let me enroll at an online college early. I think they were shocked when I passed the entrance exam and started classes. A few months later, they were dead."

"That's when you decided to disappear?" The picture she painted of her life angered me.

"Yes." She nodded. "I sold the house I guess to the Council, but I didn't know that at the time. Sold off their assets too and then ran. I obtained a fake ID, found an apartment and a job working at a nearby restaurant, and continued my online classes. My life was simple: work, school, sleep. I kept to myself at first but then I made friends for the first time in my life. The owners of the restaurant were like family. I was happy…but it didn't last."

"What happened?"

"The same thing that always happens." She shrugged. "I was close friends with the hostess and one of the bus boys—we went out after work, met for lunches. One day I was accepting in a huge order at the restaurant. Stephen came in to help me…Things were going well until they weren't. He pinned me against the wall, a faraway lustful look in his eye. He looked like he was being forced to do something he couldn't control, and he must've been since he was in love with my best friend. Two of our coworkers walked in and assumed the worst. I took the blame so that Cassie and Stephen could be happy. I moved and began working in a restaurant called Tangi's. That's where Collin found me."

I reached forward and ran a finger down her cheek. "I'm sorry. I hope that you can find happiness here."

Victoria smiled.

We continued our walk back to the manor in silence. I wanted to press her more on the mysterious effect she had on men, but her eyes held so much pain I couldn't bear to make her continue. Was she having the same impact on me?

Is that the reason for my lustful thoughts?

*

From that night forward Caleb and I would have dinner together and then walk around the gardens. Our conversations mostly revolved around our thoughts on books and things happening in the world. Caleb read several newspapers from around the world each morning. When I showed interest, he said he would leave them in the kitchen for me when he was done.

I had never been one to stay current on worldly affairs, but it gave us something to talk about during our walks. I enjoyed listening to the point of view of someone who had lived through so much history.

"Caleb, can I ask you a question?"

"Seems to me you just did."

I wrinkled my nose at him. "Very funny. I mean a personal question."

"You may do as you wish, but I reserve the right not to respond."

"Can you just say yes like a normal person? So contrary..." I huffed. I knew he was teasing me.

"Ask your question, Victoria. I will answer."

"How old are you?" I glanced sideways at him, not sure if my question made him uncomfortable.

He sighed. "I'll be four hundred fifty this summer."

"Oh, isn't that a milestone like when humans reach fifty years old? We should have a party!" I smiled, starting to feel excited.

Caleb looked at me like he would an overexuberant puppy. "We most certainly will not!"

I was going to talk with Serena and Collin about this no matter what he said. "What's it like, living for that long?"

Caleb thought about his answer for some time. "I'm not sure I can put it into words. Each day is much like the last. Time passes, but you don't necessarily feel it. It's when you lose those around you that marks its passage or when you look back on the major changes in the world. It can be exciting and fun, and it can be very lonely."

I linked my arm through his. "I'm sorry."

"For what?"

"For the times you've felt lonely. I haven't lived as long as you, but I know what loneliness feels like. I wouldn't wish it on anyone."

Caleb patted my hand in understanding but didn't unlink our arms as we continued walking.

"I knew your parents," he started. I remained silent. "I admit, I wasn't very fond of them. If I had known…"

"What could you have done? Threatened them? Taken me from them? Even I know that vampires aren't allowed, by your own laws, to take what doesn't belong to you. There's nothing you could have done, Caleb. There's nothing anyone could have done."

"Perhaps."

"Thank you though." I smiled up at him. "Your words mean a lot to me."

We stopped walking and stared into each other's eyes. Caleb reached forward and trailed his long fingers down my cheek. They were so warm.

I was happy living in the manor with him, but I couldn't tell him. He made it clear he didn't want me as his mate. There would be no point in confessing my growing love for him if he would never reciprocate. Once again, I felt like I wasn't meant for happiness. We were growing familiar with each other, but a vast distance still sprawled between us. Yet my heart fluttered during tender moments shared on our walks.

I closed my eyes, savoring his touch. Sparks danced behind my eyelids. His musky scent of cedar and cinnamon filled my senses, beguiling me. My body yearned to be in his arms. I wanted to beg him to claim me.

Is this the charm of a vampire? I had never felt this way before about anyone.

What do his lips taste like? Would it feel good having his hands roam my body, feel his breath on my skin...feel his fangs? I shook my head. What was I thinking?

I opened my eyes and was stunned by the desire burning in Caleb's eyes. Though fear gripped me at first, it wasn't like the other times. It was deep and strong. They seemed darker than usual—if that was possible. Could he know what I was just thinking?

*

My fingertips tingled as I grazed Victoria's cheek. She had closed her eyes and leaned into my touch. My heart thumped.

I want to kiss her. Pick her up in my arms and love her until the sun rises over the horizon.

I could sense Victoria's thoughts as I gazed at her peaceful face. My chest felt tight, my body warm. The scent of desire wafting in the air around her made the beast inside me come alive.

If I stay, I'll claim her right here in the garden.

I let my hand drop. The sudden loss of warmth in my fingers hurt. I stormed off toward the house, leaving her there in the dark.

*

The cold night seeped in. I shivered. My arms wrapped around my body as I watched Caleb walk away. My heart cracked.

CHAPTER FOURTEEN

"Talin, do you think she's the one?" Galia asked me as we made our way down the hallway.

"If anyone can break down the walls around Master Caleb's heart, it will be her."

"She is quite unique, isn't she?" Galia agreed.

"Yes. The other day she was in the kitchen taking stock of the pantry and making a list. She's cooking a birthday dinner for Master Caleb tonight." I was still in shock about it.

"What?"

"He told her this year is his four hundred fiftieth birthday. She's invited Master Collin and a few of the others over for a dinner to celebrate. She's cooking the entire meal and making a birthday cake for him."

"Did you warn her that might not be a good idea?"

"I did, but she said she was willing to take the risk."

Galia shook her head. "She helped me take down the drapes in the living area and told me to have them cleaned and put away. She's ordered new ones that aren't so dark and gloomy. They arrived this morning. I'm headed there now to help her put them up."

"Master has given her leave to make any changes she wishes, with the exception of his study and sleeping quarters."

She sighed. "He's still not spending enough time with her, is he?"

"Outside their nightly dinners and walks in the garden, I don't believe they see each other. She brought him tea in his study the other day and they briefly discussed some of the books he has. She asked him if he was interested in playing a game of chess, but when she opened the curtains, he got angry and threw her out."

"Again? He's so impossible at times."

"Don't let him hear you say that," I warned. "Now, Victoria is waiting for you. I'm off to bring the master his tea." I indicated the tray I carried with tea and biscuits. "I'll see you later this evening."

Galia disappeared down the hallway. I entered the study. Master Caleb was on the upper level, pacing and muttering to himself.

"Maybe I should ask her to take a walk with me this afternoon. Or perhaps we could take tea on the terrace." I cleared my throat. "Oh Talin, my apologies. I didn't hear you enter. I'll be right down."

"No need to rush, master. I brought your afternoon tea."

"Thank you."

"Forgive me master, but you seem to be troubled by something this afternoon. Is there anything I can do to assist you?"

"Talin, what is your impression of Victoria?"

I stifled a smile. "I find her to be a lovely young lady. Mistress Victoria has a way of making you feel at ease around her, and she has the most beautiful smile, don't you agree?"

"Hmm...yes, it is quite enchanting, isn't it?" He nodded absently.

"I also find it very pleasing to speak with her. She seems to be quite knowledgeable about a multitude of subjects, especially for one so young."

"I agree. I've never met anyone like her before...She is quite unique."

"Yes, master. Her presence here has had an uplifting impact on the entire staff. She's adjusting well to living at the manor, although I sometimes find her to be a little sad."

Caleb frowned. "Sad, really?"

"We are all so busy that I fear she is lonely at times. Master Collin and the others stop by for lunch each week, but I do not believe it is enough."

His brow furrowed. "Do they? Maybe I should consider spending more time with her."

"I think the mistress would like that very much. She often asks about you, and I think it would be beneficial for you as well, master."

"Really?"

"Yes." I watched the expression on Caleb's face change from delight to obstinate resignation and sighed. *So close...* "Would you like me to invite Mistress Victoria to have tea with you?"

"No. I have no need or desire for her company."

"Very well, master." I bowed and took my leave.

Someday soon you will need to cease this stubborn reluctance.

*

It had been six months since I arrived at Carrington Manor and Caleb's birthday was that night. The food for the dinner party was all prepped. I was sitting in the living area reading a book I borrowed from Caleb's study to kill time. Galia and I had finished hanging up the new drapes earlier that morning, and now that they were in place, they looked even better than I imagined. I was nervous about Caleb seeing them, although he rarely came out of his study. I doubted he would ever see them during the daytime.

As I finished my tea, my eyes drooped so I leaned back to rest. I must have fallen asleep because when I opened my eyes, the room was cast in the orange and red hues of dusk. A tall figure stood on the other side of the couch, staring out the floor-to-ceiling window.

"Caleb?" My voice was still heavy from sleep. He turned his head slightly but remained silent. I stood and went to his side. "Do you like them?" I chewed on my bottom lip and twisted my hands together as I waited for his answer.

Caleb looked them over, his expression giving nothing away. Finally, he nodded. "Yes." He turned and walked out of the room.

I suppose I should be happy...He didn't tear them off the wall.

Caleb had given me permission to make changes in the house, but there really wasn't much I wanted to do other than update the window treatments with brighter fabrics to allow for more light. For some reason, Caleb preferred the dark. I had learned that sunlight didn't affect vampires, something my mother also never shared with me. However, his reaction left me bewildered. I followed him to his study, opening the door without knocking.

"If you don't like them, I'll take them down." I stayed by the door.

"They're fine, Victoria. I'm never in that room anyway," he responded from somewhere in the darkness.

"Why do you prefer the dark?"

"I just do."

"But if sunlight doesn't hurt you…"

"I find it more calming. In the light, there's too much to see."

"Isn't that the point…to see all the beautiful, wonderful things that are in this world?"

Caleb growled. "Why do you insist on having these meaningless conversations with me?"

The tips of his fangs descended past his upper lip, stark white in the black, but it didn't deter me. "Why are you so cranky? If we're going to be living in the same house, I want to get to know you."

"I have no desire to get to know you, *human*. You're loud, smelly, entirely too happy, and…and you're always in the way."

"In the way? In the way of what exactly, your self-imposed isolation? Why are you always mean, ill-tempered, and entirely too grumpy? You know what, you deserve to be alone." Before I turned and stormed out of his study, he growled at me. "Don't you dare growl at me…you big…meany." I stuck my tongue out at him, slamming the door shut before he could say anything back.

Loud? Smelly? I almost went back to yell at him more. A single tear fell down my cheek. *My heart hurts. He doesn't deserve tonight, but I can't cancel now.*

*

Big meany? My eyes widened. *Did she stick her tongue out at me? Did I tell her she smelled?*

I shook my head at my idiocy.

I normally would've been furious, but I found her to be irresistibly adorable. *No, no, I'm not going down that rabbit hole.* The only reason I let her make changes to the décor was to keep her busy and away from me. I could always change it back once I sent her away—though I couldn't bring myself to let her go. Truth was, I liked what she had been doing. Talin was right: the atmosphere in the manor felt lighter since she arrived. Even the demons that worked on my estate had fallen in love with her. They talked about her in the hallways or outside when they thought I wasn't around. Everyone seemed... happier.

They all wondered if she would be the one to finally win my heart, break down the frozen walls that encased it. Little did they know I was already head over heels for her. I couldn't bring myself to admit it, not to her, not to anyone—especially not to myself. It tormented me each night hearing her soft breaths as she slept in her room. Her distinct smell even lingered in the halls.

It called to me.

I wanted to break down her doors and claim her as my own...but that part of me, that stubborn pride, refused to let go of my past convictions of never mating with a human. The distraction of her scent was too much. I had taken to sleeping in my study each night to avoid it. Denying myself was making me very irritable. Already blessed with a short fuse, I felt ready to explode.

*

I arrived as planned. It was my job to get Caleb out of the house while Victoria finished preparing for the birthday celebration that evening. I tried warning her that Caleb wasn't fond of surprises and even less fond of his birthday, but she insisted on moving forward. When she had looked up at me with those beautiful pools of blue-violet, I couldn't say no. *I'm so weak.*

Darin, the twins, and I were already wound around her finger, even if we refused to admit it.

"Caleb, are you hiding in here?" I opened the door to the study.

"I'm not hiding."

"Yes you are, and you're definitely sulking. What's wrong?"

"Nothing."

"Liar. Out with it. I'm your brother, and we don't keep secrets."

Caleb arched an eyebrow. "We don't?"

"Not when I'm the one wanting to know what's going on." I grinned. *Truth is, that little goddess you've been ignoring already told me about your little spat.*

"Victoria and I..."

"Stop right there...I've heard enough. Come on, put on your jacket and let's go!"

"What? Go where?"

"Women problems require alcohol."

He scowled. "Collin, I'm not going drinking with you."

"Yes you are, or I'm going to drag Victoria in here and we can talk about it together."

"Don't you dare!"

"VICTORIA?" I yelled out into the hallway. I probably didn't need to shout so loud—she was waiting around the corner for my cue—but we had to keep up appearances for Caleb.

She smartly waited a few seconds before poking her head in. "Yes Collin, why are you shouting?"

"Collin and I are going to head out for a bit," Caleb said quickly, grabbing his jacket and pulling me toward the front door.

You're too easy, brother.

"Oh, okay...Will you be back for dinner?" Victoria asked innocently.

"I promise I'll have him back on time." I winked at her.

"Have fun!" Victoria waved as we walked out the front door.

Oh, don't worry, princess...I'm going to enjoy this!

*

Well, that was easy. Time to get cooking.

The cake and the hors d'oeuvres were done. All that remained was to prepare the main course.

Serena, Greggory, and the twins would be arriving soon to help put up the modest decorations I had hidden in the dining room. Everyone had incessantly warned me that this was a bad idea, so I kept them simple. A few streamers and special flower arrangements for the table would be enough. Darin was picking up the wine and champagne for me and would hopefully arrive before Collin brought Caleb back to the house.

I laid out the last of the hors d'oeuvre trays on the long buffet. Darin arrived with the drinks, and the room looked splendid. Everything was going according to plan.

"Great job everyone. Thank you so much for agreeing to help me."

"You know, we're mostly here to protect you when Caleb goes into a rage." Blake winked at me.

"Oh, ye of little faith…" I punched his arm.

"Why do you always have to resort to violence?" He pouted and rubbed his arm.

"As if I could hurt you through the twenty layers of muscle."

"Even I have to agree with Blake. I think you're putting your life on the line with this stunt. Caleb hates surprises." Serena had a worried look on her face.

"Serena, I thought you'd have my back on this," I whined.

"Oh sweetie, I do have your back. I'll do what I can to give you a head start, but when I say run, don't hesitate."

"You're all a bunch of party poopers."

"Well, I'm on your side, little one. I can't wait to see the look on his face." Greggory chuckled, popping a stuffed mushroom into his mouth.

"Hey! No eating before the guest of honor arrives."

At that moment, the front door opened and Collin's boisterous laughter filled the entryway.

"Okay, it's showtime," I whispered and walked toward the doorway that connected the main hall with the dining room. As Caleb and Collin hung up their jackets, I started to have second thoughts. Would Caleb be angry with me? We hadn't spoken since our spat. *Too late to worry about it now.*

I smiled as Caleb approached. "I know you said you didn't want to have a party, but I planned a special dinner to celebrate your birthday. I hope you like it. Happy birthday, Caleb!" I stepped aside so he could enter the room.

At first, everyone was silent. I made a small gesture with my hand and they all said, "Happy birthday!"

Caleb's face turned red. *Oh, they were right. I'm never going to see another sunrise.*

He looked at me, to the table, and back at everyone standing nearby waiting for his reaction. When he turned to me again, he said, "You planned all of this?"

I nodded. "And I cooked everything too. Dinner will be ready in about an hour."

"Thank you," Caleb whispered and walked into the room to greet our guests, who all had stunned expressions on their faces.

My eyes met Collin's. I smiled up at him.

"Good job, beautiful."

"What did you say to him while you were gone?"

Collin winked. "It's a secret."

"He's going to wait until everyone is gone before he kills me, isn't he?" I whispered.

"Maybe...we'll have to wait and see." He ruffled my hair.

*

Greggory's laughter filled the room.

"It's not that funny," Serena pouted.

"Sweetheart, I'm sorry. I'm picturing you all dolled up in a pretty pink dress covered in mud."

"You have no idea how much trouble I was in because of those two." She pointed an accusatory finger at Caleb and Collin. Both were trying their best to look innocent.

"I don't remember you objecting to our little adventure when we suggested it." Collin's eyes twinkled.

"You promised I wouldn't get dirty."

"How were we supposed to know you'd fall into the river?"

"You made me walk across a moss-covered log. What did you think would happen?"

"That you'd make it across," Caleb replied smugly.

Greggory snorted again. Serena crossed her arms and huffed. "My mother was furious. I was grounded for a week. I still haven't forgiven you."

Caleb laughed, almost choking on his wine. "I think seventy years is a bit long to hold a grudge."

"And it will be another seventy years if you keep laughing like that, Caleb Carrington." Serena's eyes narrowed before she broke into her own fit of laughter.

"Come to think of it, wasn't that the first time you wore a dress?" Blake asked.

"What? Really?" Greggory seemed shocked and looked to his wife.

"Yes, our little fashionista used to be quite the tomboy when she was younger." Blake winked.

"What do you expect? I was surrounded by these brutes. There weren't any other girls to play with, so it was either keep up with them or be alone."

I must have made a sound because everyone turned to look at me. Surrounded by everyone at the table, it felt like I had found a family...my family. The warmth of happiness was countered by a sting of pain. Something about Serena's last comment struck at my heart. Tears were building in the corners of my eyes.

"If you'll excuse me a moment." I stood from my seat.

"Victoria, are you all right?" Caleb asked from the head of the table.

"Yes, I'm fine. It's time for dessert. Serena, will you help me in the kitchen?"

"Sure." She glanced from me to Caleb before joining me. Once we were in the kitchen, she stopped me. "Victoria, are you okay?"

"I am. It just felt like...well, like family in there. I guess I got a little overwhelmed."

Serena hugged me. "We are your family, little one."

I nodded and hugged her back. "I think Caleb is enjoying himself tonight."

"Are you worried he's only acting and is going to exact his revenge when we all leave?"

"The thought had crossed my mind." I giggled.

"I think you're safe."

I pulled the cake out of the fridge and placed three candles on it, one large four, five, and zero.

"Oh, you didn't!" Serena covered her mouth.

I grinned wide. "Of course I did. It was this or the large number balloons. I figured this was less ostentatious."

"I take it back. He may kill you after we all leave."

"If he does, it's been great seeing you again." I winked, lit the candles, and headed back to the dining room.

As I made my way to the table, I started singing "Happy Birthday," and everyone joined in. The song was broken with laughter as they noticed the numbered candles on the cake. Collin had to duck out for two verses to get it under control.

I placed the cake in front of Caleb and leaned in close, kissing his cheek. "Happy birthday, old man. I hope this has been a birthday you'll remember for the rest of your life."

Caleb stood so quickly I stepped back, a moment of fear flooding my mind. *Goodbye everyone.* Before I could register what was happening, Caleb pulled me into his arms and kissed me soundly on the lips. I thought I heard gasps and snickers, but I wasn't sure since all my senses were engulfed by the warmth of Caleb's lips on mine. I wrapped my arms around his neck and pulled him closer.

Then he was gone, only a gust of wind announcing his exit. The candles flickered and died out.

I stared at the others around the table, feeling warm, confused, and very embarrassed. "W-who wants cake?" I asked, grabbing the knife and cutting perfect slices for everyone.

Collin squeezed my arm. "I don't think he's going to kill you."

I glared at him and shoved a plate into his hands. "Maybe not tonight, but he's definitely going to be the death of me. Go eat your cake."

"As my goddess commands." He bowed his head as he walked away.

After everyone finished their dessert and left for the night, Serena helped me clean the dining room. Caleb didn't return from wherever he went, most likely his study. It was where he always retreated.

She and Greggory bid me good night and headed home.

I made a cup of coffee, placed it on a tray along with a slice of cake, and made my way to his hideout. I knocked before opening the door, but didn't wait to be invited in. I was tired from the day and confused by Caleb's actions.

Although it was dark, I had become accustomed to moving around the room and knew there was nothing blocking my path between the door and his desk. I placed the tray down and turned back. "I hope you enjoyed your birthday dinner. Happy birthday, Caleb. Good night."

I closed the door behind me and retired to my room.

*

I reached forward and pulled the tray across the desk.

"Thank you, Victoria, for a very unexpected evening."

CHAPTER FIFTEEN

It was almost time for my weekly lunch with Collin, Darin, and the twins. I was in the kitchen when Darin arrived.

"Victoria are you in here?" he asked as he poked his head in.

"Yep, come on in. I'm almost done cooking lunch."

"Smells wonderful!" He breathed in deep. "What did you make?"

"Your favorite, lasagna. I thought we could eat on the terrace. Why don't you take the plates and silverware and set the table?" Darin grabbed the stack of items from the island. "Where are Collin and the boys?"

Darin chuckled. "Running late as usual, but they're on their way."

I turned around. "What's so funny?"

"I don't think I'll ever get used to you calling Blake and Bastian *the boys*."

I smiled, "it irritates them and it's fun."

"Only you would feel that way about them, Victoria."

"They are entirely too serious. Well, at least Frosty is."

"You have no idea." Darin chuckled and headed toward the terrace.

Collin, Blake, and Bastian arrived famished as always. It didn't take them long to polish off the entire meal. After lunch, the twins started telling stories from their childhood. More accurately, Blake brought up the embarrassing ones about his brother.

"Wait, Bastian, you actually got stuck?" I couldn't hold back my laughter.

"He sure did," Blake confirmed. "Took me two hours to get him out."

Bastian crossed his arms and growled. His ears were a bright red, which only made me laugh harder.

"I-I'm sorry, Bastian." I took a deep breath. "But you have to admit, that's pretty funny."

Bastian glanced sideways at me, the corners of his mouth turning slightly upwards. "I was only ten at the time," he defended.

"And I bet you were adorable," I teased.

Collin choked on his iced tea. Laughing, he slapped a hand on Bastian's shoulder. "Hear that, Frosty? She thinks you're adorable."

Bastian slapped his friend's hand away, grumbling under his breath.

"Now, Collin, be nice," I chided him.

"C'mon Victoria—calling Bastian adorable?" Darin smiled and patted my arm. "I don't think anyone would use that term for him."

"I'm sure when he was little, he *was* adorable." Another wink in Bastian's direction made his entire face turn red. The table erupted in laughter.

*

When I opened the front door, I was met with the most wonderful sound— Victoria's laughter. Warmth bloomed in my chest while a smile formed on my lips. Then I saw them.

She was sitting with Collin and the others on the terrace. *They* were the reason she was laughing uncontrollably. My chest tightened. My smile faded. Darin placed his hand on her arm, and an uncontrollable fire raged through my body.

Everything blurred, my rational thoughts rendered obsolete. A loss of restraint I had never experienced in my long life.

She's mine.

*

128

Caleb stormed onto the terrace. His hand wrapped around Darin's neck, lifting him from his chair.

"Caleb?" *When did he get home, and why is he choking Darin?*

Everyone at the table jumped to their feet, eyes wide in surprise.

"Do you dare to touch what's *mine*?" The deep growl issuing through his clenched teeth held the threat of death.

Darin's face was turning red, confusion and terror gleaming in his eyes. His fingers clawed at Caleb's.

"Brother, he meant nothing by it. Put him down!" Collin tried to soothe his brother's rage.

"No." Caleb lifted Darin higher. "This fledgling needs to learn."

"Caleb." I took a deep breath and laid my hand on his arm. "Please…you're hurting him."

"That's the point, Victoria." Caleb glared at me. His eyes glowed red. "Do you have concern for your lover's life?"

"My what?" I stammered. "D-Darin isn't my l-lover…"

"No, he's mine!" Bastian growled beside Caleb, his eyes glowing and fangs bared. "Caleb, put him down. *Now!*"

"That's right, he's…wait, what?" Collin looked between Bastian and Darin, who was now turning a dangerous shade of purple.

I need to stop this, or they are all going to kill each other. Despite the fear I felt inside, I gently placed my hand over his, squeezing it lightly. Caleb's grip loosened, but not enough.

"Caleb, listen to me. Darin and I are not lovers. Do as Bastian says—release him." I stared intently into Caleb's eyes. An intense rage burned in them, one I had never seen before. My hands trembled against my will.

Caleb released Darin. Bastian caught him before he collapsed to the ground. Darin gasped, trying to fill his lungs with air, bruises already appearing on his neck. The glow nor the rage had left Caleb's eyes. He grabbed my wrist and dragged me into the house and up the stairs. I could barely stay on my feet.

Why is he so enraged?

Halting, he spun me around, slamming my back against the wall next to my bedroom door. His long fingers wrapped around my neck. He forced his knee between my legs, trapping me in a cage of strong limbs.

"You are *mine!*" he hissed into my ear.

Are those his fangs?

I met his gaze. "I am not your property." After all the times he told me he didn't want me as a mate, how dare he? "I am a person with feelings, not some toy you can take off a shelf whenever you get bored."

His grip tightened, but not enough to cut off my breath. I was either very brave, or very foolish.

"Naïve human. All of you—your mind, your body, your life—*it all belongs to me*. Never forget that."

"No. You're wrong…I'm not your slave." Tears flowed down my cheeks.

"What was that, my sweet?" He was dangerous right now, but I refused to back down.

"You're wrong…" I gasped as his grip tightened again, but I continued. "You may be able to take my life, but my mind, my body, belong to me. You cannot have what I do not choose to give you."

Caleb leaned in. "Shall we test that theory?"

"Don't you *dare!*" I challenged, trying to push him away and failing. *When will I learn to keep my mouth shut?*

He turned my head, exposing my neck.

"Caleb…please," I begged.

"I can and will take of you what I want, when I want. Learn your place. You…are…*mine!*"

He sank his fangs into my neck. I winced at the initial pain. An arousing warmth I'd never known filled my body. I leaned into him, my fingers digging into his shoulders and pulling him closer as he drank. All the fear melted away, replaced by a longing deep inside me—I didn't want it to end.

I moaned.

*

My anger subsided the minute Victoria's blood trickled down my throat.

What am I doing? It's so sweet, so enchanting. I've never...

The heat inside my body was proof of my burning desire. I needed to claim her, place my mark on her. My breath deepened. All I had to do was say the incantation and it would be done. She would be fully mine. No one would take her from me.

"Why?" Victoria whispered. "Why do you hate me?"

I don't hate you. I love you.

Her eyes were unfocused, lids hanging heavy. I withdrew my fangs, licking at the puncture marks on her perfect skin. Victoria sighed, pulling me closer. The influence of the bite had consumed her.

"I try so hard...I know I'm not good enough...never good enough." Her voice grew weaker.

You're perfect. You're everything I've ever wanted but never dreamed I could find. My pride kept me silent. *I'm sorry.*

"You're a monster. I hate you."

No, please.

She lost consciousness. My heart cracked wide open. She had every reason to feel that way about me.

I lifted her in my arms and carried her into her room. Laying her on the bed, I pulled a blanket over her shoulders and kissed her forehead. I stood listening to her shallow breathing until the color returned to her cheeks. Only when I was sure she would recover on her own did I leave her to lock myself away in my study.

Collin was already there waiting for me. "Where is she?"

"She's fine. She's asleep in her room." I went to open the door, but he grabbed my arm.

"Don't you dare brush this off. What the hell was that, Caleb? You nearly killed Darin. If Blake hadn't dragged his brother out of here, your head would be lying on the floor next to you right now."

I met his steely gaze. "Release me."

"Not happening, brother, not until you answer my question. What did you do to Victoria? Do I need to take her to the hospital?"

"No, I said she's fine."

Collin waited.

"Where's Darin?" I asked.

"They took him to the hospital. He's bruised but he'll survive."

I nodded.

"Let's go. You're staying with me for now. I'm not letting you lock yourself away in that study, and I don't trust you to be in the same house with Victoria right now. You and I both know what this is, and until you face it, you're a danger to her."

My heart thumped. He was right.

"I need to tell Talin before we go."

"Send him a message. He'll know what to do. We are leaving...*now.*"

CHAPTER SIXTEEN

I woke in my room to the sound of birds chirping. Sitting up, I winced at the sunlight streaming through the sheer curtains and tried to sort through my memories. Lunch on the terrace, Caleb storming in, strangling Darin, and…oh!

"That son of a bitch bit me!" I rubbed at my neck, the puncture wound already healed and gone. He had bitten me in a fit of rage. *Why?* "What did I say to him?" I remembered arguing and pleading with him. Then…

Oh no…

I told him I hated him, called him a monster. My heart sank.

I rubbed my temples. Wait…did Bastian reveal that he and Darin are lovers? My mind was a mess of thoughts ricocheting in my brain. I needed to talk to someone. I picked up my cell phone and sent a message to Serena.

Are you available?

> *Victoria, you're awake?*

Serena, he bit me! That jerk actually bit me!

> *Calm down, Victoria.*

How can I be calm? He. Bit. Me. Why would he do that?

> *I'll be right there. Give me an hour and I'll explain everything.*

Okay. See you soon.

Tossing my phone on the bed, I decided to take a hot shower before heading downstairs. I was still fuming when I left my bedroom. Descending the stairs two at a time, I went to the library and threw open the doors.

"CALEB!" No answer.

I stormed through the house, checking the living room and terrace and even the gardens, but he wasn't here. Was he already at his office? It didn't occur to me to check his bedroom until I was downstairs. My stomach growled. I needed to eat instead. I made my way to the kitchen to make a cup of tea and ran into Talin and Galia.

"Good morning, mistress," they greeted.

"Good morning."

"Are you hungry?" Talin poured me a cup of coffee.

"I'm famished, but you don't have to cook for me."

"Nonsense, I'll have it ready in two shakes of my tail."

I tilted my head. "You have a tail?"

"I do." He snickered in his usual playful way. "You can only see it when I'm in my full demon form."

"You surprise me every day, Talin." I smiled.

"How are you feeling?" Galia asked, placing a palm on my forehead.

"A little tired still, like I've run a marathon. How long have I been asleep?"

She sighed. "Two days."

"Two days?!" I nearly choked on my coffee. "Caleb isn't here, is he?"

The two demons looked at each other. "Master left after he…" Galia looked to Talin for help.

"Bit me." I finished her sentence.

"He hasn't returned." Talin set a plate before me. "But don't worry about him right now. You need to concentrate on building up your strength. This will make you feel better."

Talin made me my favorite eggs with a side of sausage and cinnamon raisin toast with butter. I didn't realize how hungry I was until I started eating. The two demons smiled as they watched me.

Serena arrived as I was finishing up breakfast.

"Where is he, Serena?"

"He's staying with Collin for now. Collin feels it's best until he finds a way to control his feelings."

"His feelings?"

"Little one, it was the bloodlust that made him act that way."

"That's not possible. I know he's been eating. Talin brings him a decanter of blood every night."

Serena smiled. "It's not that kind of bloodlust, little one."

"Then...oh...*OH*!" I shook my head. "No, that's not possible either. We haven't spent any time together and we aren't mated. He's made it very clear he has no desire for me. There's no way it's because of that."

"Victoria, a vampire doesn't need to be mated to feel bloodlust for someone. They only need to desire that person. And, unfortunately, if they let that desire go unanswered for too long, they tend to be a bit...aggressive when they lose control."

"He was a little more than a *bit* aggressive." I gazed into my coffee cup. "Are you saying Caleb desires me? To be his mate, or just...?"

"All I know is Collin said Caleb is a wreck. He's beating himself up over what he did to you."

Tears filled my eyes. "I told him I hated him."

"Do you?" she asked me softly.

"No, but I'm not sure I believe he has feelings for me."

"If he didn't, he wouldn't feel an ounce of guilt for what he did and he wouldn't have left the manor. Think about it, Victoria, with how he kissed you at his party. Your walks in the gardens. Your nightly dinner routine. I'd say that's more than just desire. I'd say that's *love*."

"He's told me repeatedly he doesn't want a mate, especially a human one. How could he love me?" *Dare I hope he shares my feelings for him?*

"Victoria, give him time. He's stubborn, and always has been. Do you know why he's never taken a mate?"

"He's never told me."

"No real reason. He simply decided one day when he was young that he didn't have the need or the time for such foolishness." She rolled her eyes. "Now he's too prideful to admit it was a silly vow and refuses to abandon it. It's the most ridiculous thing I've ever seen."

"Serena, what if it was my fault and not Caleb's?"

"What do you mean? How could this be your fault? You didn't do anything wrong having them over for lunch. They've been here before."

I shook my head. "That's not what I mean…There's something wrong with *me*. Since I became a teenager, if I spend too much time around a man, something happens to them."

Serena laughed. "Well you are a beautiful girl, Victoria. It's only natural men would find you attractive."

"No, it's not a 'finding me pretty' reaction. It's like they become…obsessed, but they don't know it."

Serena frowned. "Is that what you meant the first time you met Greggory and I? What happens?"

"Yes." I nodded. "Their eyes get a strange look, and it's like they can't control their actions. They want to be near me, to touch me."

"Has anyone ever hurt you?"

"I've never let anyone get close enough. Mostly they try to kiss me."

"Did Caleb have that look?"

"No, but his eyes were glowing, so it's hard to say. It doesn't seem to happen with vampires. Collin is always giving me funny looks, but I know he's teasing me, and I don't see it in Darin or the boys. So far, it's only happened with other humans, though Greggory seems unaffected." I paused. "I've never understood why it happens, but it's the reason I moved after I ran away and why I chose not to make any friends." My heart broke remembering Cassie and Stephen and everyone at Tangi's who had been so nice to me. And Nicholas…I never had the chance to tell him goodbye.

Her eyes were filled with concern as she patted my leg. "There's someone at Council headquarters who I can speak with that may have the answer you need."

After talking with Serena, I no longer felt angry. *Could Caleb have feelings for me? Was his behavior due to the bloodlust?*

The events of that day haunted me. I needed to stay busy, so I went in search of Galia. I'd help her with the house chores while I waited for Caleb to come home.

CHAPTER SEVENTEEN

Caleb still wasn't home, and Galia and Talin probably needed a break from my restless energy. I messaged Serena and Blake and invited them over to work on my training. Serena was helping me learn to control my visions, and Blake was trying to teach me how to block my thoughts from others, something I was finding increasingly difficult and against my nature.

"I can't do this." I paced on the terrace.

"Yes, you can, little one. You just need to concentrate. Now try again."

I took a deep breath and formed the image in my mind of the first time I met Serena.

"Do you have it?" Serena asked from next to me. I nodded. "Okay Blake, take her hand." Blake did as he was told. "Now Victoria, imagine sending that image to Blake's mind."

My hands trembled with the effort, but Blake squeezed them.

You can do this, princess, his voice whispered in my head.

Not now Blake, I can't block thoughts and send them at the same time.

I took a deep breath and pictured the memory again. The more I tried to form it into a concrete image, the more my mind wandered. I frowned.

"What's the matter, princess?" Blake asked.

"Every time I try to think of something, all I can see is Caleb and the look he had that afternoon on the terrace. He was so…dangerous."

Blake sighed. "Bloodlust can be a vile thing Victoria, especially when a pureblood tries to ignore it. Believe me, Caleb didn't mean to harm you. I know that doesn't excuse his behavior toward you or Darin, but until he stops denying how he's feeling inside, he has to stay away."

I nodded. I still wasn't sure I believed him or Serena when they told me that Caleb had feelings for me, but I wasn't going to argue with them. "Okay, let's try this again." I closed my eyes and recalled the memory of that night in the library. I pictured the image floating from my mind to Blake's, as if being sent over a wire.

Blake flinched.

"What do you see?" Serena asked.

"You…and Greggory in a dark library. You look younger, Serena."

She punched his arm, causing him to pull his hands from mine. The connection broke apart. I sunk to my knees, sweat beading on my forehead.

"I did it." I smiled. When I looked up, they were also smiling at me.

"I knew you could." Blake winked at me. "You're getting better at your lessons to block your thoughts too."

"Let's not get ahead of ourselves. Help me up." Blake grabbed my hand and lifted my dead weight effortlessly. "I need a nap."

"With a bit more practice, you won't get so tired. At least you didn't pass out this time." Serena winked.

I laughed despite the exhaustion. "True."

Talin brought out a pitcher of lemonade and poured us all tall glasses.

"Thank you, Talin."

"You're welcome, mistress. Will you be wrapping up for the day?"

"Ye—"

"Nope." Blake cut me off. "She still has work to do with me."

"What? Blake, I'm tired."

"Perfect time to work on guarding your thoughts. If you can do it when you're exhausted, it will be easier when you're not."

You're a beast! I glared at him.

Blake laughed. "And don't you forget it, princess. Now let's get to work."

"That's my cue to leave." Serena stood and hugged me.

I sighed. "Traitor."

"I love you, sweetie, but Blake's lessons make my skin crawl."

"Oh come on, Serena. I'm not that bad a tutor. You used to love our training afternoons."

"I was young and naïve. Now I'm wiser. Be nice." With a wave, she left us.

*

"Blake, it's been three hours. Can't we take a break?" I rubbed my temples. The mental exercises didn't seem to be doing anything other than create a nasty headache.

"Keep me out and I'll let you rest."

"You're relentless." *I hate you right now,* I shot toward him for good measure.

Blake frowned. "Is that what you were thinking?"

"What?" I stared at him. "No, it wasn't." *I was thinking that I hate you right now. I want to go to bed.*

Blake's face was serious as he stared hard into my eyes. "What are you thinking right now, princess? The truth."

"That I hate you right now and want to go to bed."

"That wasn't very nice," he pouted with a mischievous smirk.

"You really didn't know what I was thinking?"

Blake shook his head. "Nope, no clue. I only knew that your words didn't match your thoughts."

"I did it?" I jumped to my feet. "I did it!" Blake laughed as I pulled him from his seat and spun us around.

"Yes you did, princess. I knew you could." He laughed and pulled me into a tight embrace to stop the spinning. "Ready to call it a night?"

"Are you crazy? No way. Let's do more." I was too excited to sleep now.

"I thought you were tired."

"I was, but not anymore." I smiled.

"All right, but on one condition."

"What's that?"

"You have to cook me dinner." He winked.

"Deal."

Chapter Eighteen

"**B**rother, it's been ten days. You need to go home!" I placed a cup of coffee before Caleb, who was sitting at the kitchen counter looking like he had slept in the same outfit for a week. *Actually, that might be accurate.* "And for goodness' sake, clean yourself up and change your clothes." I wrinkled my nose. "You stink."

I had never seen Caleb look this…broken before. It was a bit unnerving.

"I can't, not while she's there. You were right. I'm a danger to her."

I sighed. "You can't avoid her for the rest of her life. You've done enough of that already. You've locked yourself in your study for centuries, waiting for the right person to fall into your lap, and by some miracle that's happened. Don't turn your back on this gift. Stop fighting it."

Caleb ran his fingers through his greasy hair. "She said she hates me."

I smiled behind my coffee cup. *I shouldn't be enjoying this, but watching this human girl melt the walls around your stoic, anti-mate heart is very entertaining.*

"You know she doesn't mean it. Anyone with eyes can see how she looks at you. She may not even realize it, but the last thing she feels for you is hate." Caleb stared at me in disbelief. "Don't tell me you haven't noticed? You're losing your touch, brother."

"Collin, I attacked her. I didn't just bite her. I told her she was my property, mine to do with as I please, basically confirming all the lies her parents told her about us. I was a barbarian, a *monster*, as she said."

"Did you mean any of it?"

"Of course not!"

"Then explain to her it was the bloodlust. You've seen what it can do to the best of us when we *aren't* denying ourselves. Stop ignoring your feelings for her and it won't happen again. You know this. Besides, if she does hate you—and with the way you've been playing hot and cold with her it wouldn't be surprising—then change her mind. Honestly the two of you just need to..."

"Don't finish that sentence," Caleb warned.

My expression turned serious. "It was amusing at first, watching the two of you dance around your feelings, but now it's pathetic. If you're not careful, it could be dangerous...for Victoria." I put my cup down. "Listen, it's time for you to come out from the rock you've been living under for centuries. By the grace of the universe, Victoria was born for you. She's so damn perfect it's frightening. After the life she's led, she needs someone to show her what she's truly worth. If you won't do it, then give her to me."

Caleb stood and growled deep. I didn't flinch. *That's it, brother. Let's do this.*

"Don't let that beautiful goddess waste away believing what her useless parents told her. She's extraordinary, and she deserves to be loved and loved well. If you won't do it, then I will."

Here it comes.

Caleb threw himself at me, pinning me against the far kitchen wall. "She's *mine!*" he hissed.

I winked. "Then stop wasting your time playing with me and go tell *her!*"

Caleb shoved me away. "You're infuriating, you know that?"

I rolled my shoulders. "So, you've been telling me for centuries, but I'm not wrong."

Caleb turned and stormed up the stairs to the guest quarters.

All right goddess, it's up to you now.

*

I sat at the kitchen window seat waiting that morning like all mornings for the past week, hoping Caleb would return. I was about to give up again when I saw Caleb's car pull up to the house. It was almost impossible to remain seated. Every fiber in my body wanted to run out to greet him.

He entered the kitchen. I smiled and tried to remain calm. "Welcome home."

He jumped at the sound of my voice.

"Would you like a cup of tea? I was about to get a refill." I stood and made my way to the stove.

"Sure." Caleb's voice was measured.

His scent drifted over from across the kitchen island. His hair was damp. He must've just showered.

"I'm making a roasted chicken for dinner tonight. Would you like to join me?"

Caleb looked at me with wonder. "Are you sure?"

"Of course, it's one of your favorites." I handed him his cup. "I was hoping you would come back today so we could have it together."

"Thank you." He glanced down. "Listen Victoria, about…" Caleb paused as if he didn't know what to say next. It was endearing seeing him struggle to find the right words. Maybe Serena was right. Maybe he did care more than he was willing to admit.

"Caleb, I'm not angry." I tilted my head back so our eyes met and smiled.

"You should be."

"Yes, but I'm not. Not anymore." I laid my hand on his arm.

I thought my words would bring him relief, but his brow furrowed at my touch. With a curt nod, he turned and left the kitchen without another word.

"And…he's off again," I whispered, shaking my head. I set about prepping everything for dinner. Maybe our conversation later tonight would be better after he had a chance to settle back in here at home.

*

In my study, I paced before the cold hearth.

Dammit! Why did her touch feel so electrifying? Things were going well and then I fled like a coward.

You fool. You're a pureblood vampire, one of the most dangerous living creatures, and you're acting like a scared schoolboy.

I stopped and gripped the stone mantle. Bracing myself I took a deep breath. *What am I doing?*

*

Conversation was light during dinner, mostly about the book I was reading. After we had finished eating and I cleared the table, Caleb asked if we could go for a walk in the garden.

"The night is clear, and the moon is full. Shall we take a walk in the gardens?"

"I'd love to."

The massive garden stretched out behind the manor with its many reflecting pools. Summer's last fireflies danced on the ripples. The air was cooler than I expected but not freezing. The full moon was high and lit the grounds like it was mid-day.

"Shall we?" Caleb offered me his hand. Slipping my hand in his, I noticed how much larger his was and delighted in its warmth. He laced his fingers through mine, pressing them briefly to his lips before linking our arms.

That's new.

"It's a beautiful night. So many stars are visible." I gazed up at the sky.

"Do you know a lot about the stars?"

"A bit. I took an astronomy class in college. It's been a while. Let's see…" I looked around. "Well, there's Cassiopeia and Perseus." I pointed at the two constellations. "So that means Pegasus is…there."

Caleb chuckled. As we continued to walk, he pointed out a few more that I had forgotten. We talked about the legends behind each constellation.

"Your knowledge of Greek mythology is impressive," he commented.

I blushed at his compliment. This was the most time we had spent together in a while, and I was really enjoying myself. "If I had known it would impress you, I would've brought the subject up sooner." I giggled. "I've always been fascinated by it. All mythologies, really."

"I have many books on the subject in the library I think you'd enjoy. I can recommend some you've probably never heard of if you're interested."

"Really?"

"Yes, I have the only copies—since I wrote them."

I almost laughed at how proud he seemed. "Now it's my turn to be impressed. Maybe I shouldn't touch them. If they are that rare, I wouldn't want them to get ruined."

"Nonsense." Caleb frowned. "Why would you ruin them? Besides, books are meant to be read, not collect dust."

"If you're sure. I would like that very much, but I won't remove them from the library. Let me know when you won't be there and I'll read them then."

Caleb stopped walking. "Why would you only read them while I'm not there?"

"I know you like to keep the library dark, and I don't want to disturb you. It's not a problem. I can work around your schedule."

"Don't be silly. You won't be disturbing me."

"But last time I opened the curtains…"

"I know what happened last time!" Caleb snapped before taking a deep breath. "I deeply regret my actions and promise that will not happen again. Come to the library whenever you want to read."

"Are you sure?"

"Victoria!" Caleb's voice was strained.

"All right. Thank you."

We toured the rest of the gardens before the cool breeze drove us in. Back in the house, he walked me to the bottom of the stairs and brought my hand to his lips.

"I enjoyed our evening together. It's late. You should retire for the night. I still have some work to do."

"Thank you, Caleb. I enjoyed tonight as well. Don't work too late." I turned and climbed the stairs.

"Victoria?" Caleb called when I was halfway up.

"Yes?"

"The annual ball is next month. We will be attending. Have Serena help you find a suitable gown." He turned and headed into his study.

Wait. The annual ball? Collin told me that Caleb never attends.

"Sure, I'd love to go with you..." I grumbled to absolutely no one. "It would've been nice to be asked properly." Sighing, I went up the rest of the stairs and entered my bedroom.

*

In my study, I let out a deep breath. I enjoyed our walk, but it took all my willpower not to pull her into my arms and kiss her senseless. *Can I do this?* The memory of her sweet blood left my mind reeling. When she discussed Greek mythologies, I never wanted her to stop. The sound of her voice and her innocent viewpoint left me enchanted. I knew she was intelligent beyond her years. She had told me she entered college early through online courses, but I never figured she was so well read. How...invigorating.

These feelings were all new to me. I didn't mean to be so abrupt when telling her about the annual ball. I should've asked her properly, but I lost all good sense when it came to her.

Victoria, how can you ever forgive me?

Chapter Nineteen

Serena and I had been searching for two weeks for the perfect gowns without success. That afternoon, we were at one of the dress shops in town scrutinizing their newest arrivals.

"There are so many new gowns this week, so why is this so difficult?" I sighed.

"You're overthinking it, Victoria." Serena smiled. "What about this one?"

I shook my head. "Too revealing." I held up a champagne-colored gown. "This one?"

"How old are you...ninety?"

"Serena, it's not that bad. The color is beautiful."

"I agree, but it looks like something my great grandmother wore in the 1800s."

I laughed. "Okay, you have a point."

"Listen Victoria, if you want to break through those walls around Caleb's heart, you're going to have to appeal to his inner desires." I blinked at her. "You need to show a little skin, darling."

"Serena..." My cheeks warmed.

"You know I'm right. You're a beautiful woman with a gorgeous figure. Flaunt it a little." She wiggled her hips and eyebrows.

"You're incorrigible, you know that?" I giggled. "But I suppose you have a point." I pulled a midnight blue gown from the rack and held it up.

She gasped. "That's it!" Serena exclaimed.

"You think so?"

"Yes, now go try it on to make sure it fits." She ushered me toward the dressing room. "I'm going to try this green one."

"Oh, that's the perfect color for you. It will really make your eyes pop."

*

The day of the annual ball arrived. I insisted on doing my own hair and makeup, much to Serena's disappointment. Not that I didn't enjoy going to the salon, but I had a look in my mind and I didn't trust anyone to get it right. This was my first official outing with Caleb since I was brought back, and I wanted to look perfect.

The annual ball was a big event for our modest community of vampire and human families. The entire community would be there, both young and old. Even Talin and Galia were attending. I recently learned they were mated to each other and was thrilled they would join the festivities. My mother had lied to me about so many things.

I slipped the dress on first. The full-length skirt of my midnight blue gown cascaded to the floor in deep undulations. Tiny dark blue crystals were sewn in amongst its folds, giving it a sparkle effect like the night sky. The sweetheart neckline accentuated the fullness of my bosom, while thin straps ensured it stayed in place. Decorative chiffon cap sleeves draped off my shoulders, and two pleated chiffon panels sewn to the back flowed out behind me, brushing the floor. I opted for opera-length white gloves and simple silver dangle earrings as my only accents. I chose to buy the dress because I knew it was Caleb's favorite color and it made me feel like an absolute princess. I only hoped my prince was waiting for me downstairs.

I curled my hair and swept it to the side in a loose twist, held by a jewel-studded comb. It still allowed for several large curls to tumble over my shoulder. I applied a light smokey eye, just enough to highlight the blue-violet color. A light gloss on my lips was the final touch.

"Victoria, are you ready?" Serena knocked and entered my room. She and Greggory had come early, along with Collin, Darin, and the twins. We were heading to the clubhouse together. She was an absolute vision in her dark green gown. The natural glow of her clear green eyes sparkled brightly. "If you don't come down soon, Caleb is going to wear a hole in the floor. He hasn't stopped pacing...*oh my!*" Serena stopped as I came out of my dressing area. "You look *gorgeous!*" she squealed.

"Serena!" I put my finger to my lips. "Not so loud."

"Oh, little one, I'm sorry, but you're absolutely stunning. Caleb is going to lose his mind when he sees you."

"Do you think so?" I asked, twirling for her.

"If he doesn't, we'll have to check his pulse because it means he's dead." She winked. "My dear, are you ready to poke that hornets' nest?" I looked at her quizzically. "He's not going to be able to keep his eyes...or his hands off you."

"Oh...maybe I should change?" I stepped back.

"DON'T YOU DARE!" She leapt forward and tugged on my arm, pulling me away from my closet. Serena dragged me out into the hall but kept me out of sight of the landing below. "Okay, I'm going to go down, but don't come to the stairs until I'm next to Greggory. I want nothing to block you from his view."

"Serena!"

"Victoria...I don't want to get knocked over if he decides to scoop you up and carry you off to his bedchamber. This. Is. Perfect. Ready?"

"Ready as I'll ever be." I smoothed the front of my gown. After waiting a few moments, I stepped forward and could see Serena standing next to her husband. I slowly approached the top of the stairs.

The twins were having a conversation with Darin while Bastian retied his lover's askew bowtie. Now that they had announced their relationship, it was nice to see how openly Bastian doated on him. But the man who caught my eye was the tall, stunningly handsome vampire pacing beyond them. Caleb was wearing a black tuxedo with a white vest and matching tie. His dark hair was styled as usual, long on top and short on the sides and back, except he flipped his bangs over to one side, shielding his eyes. He took my breath away.

Here goes nothing.

I sighed and started my descent. Serena looked up and winked at me. I took the first few steps before Greggory noticed and smiled. He hit Collin's arm and gestured my way.

"Holy..." Collin gasped. At a loss for words, he let out a low whistle.

Collin's response caught the attention of Darin and the twins. Blake choked on whatever he was drinking and went into a coughing fit.

"Why are you all making so much noise...?" Caleb snapped and stopped pacing, his words dying on his tongue as he followed their gazes.

My heart pounded in my chest. I stopped when his eyes met mine. How could he manage to look more gorgeous facing me? A burning heat rose in my cheeks. *What must I look like?*

Caleb rushed forward, taking the remaining steps two at a time to reach me. "Victoria, you..." His eyes glowed while his nostrils flared in desire. His warm breath tickled my cheeks.

"Yes?" I could barely breathe.

"You're...beautiful." He sighed, taking in every detail.

I gazed into his eyes, seeing them darken with desire as he appraised me. All the tension between us vanished. Serena was right. I had indeed started something. *Go, Team Victoria!*

"You look very handsome tonight, Caleb," I complimented him, trying to keep my voice measured and calm. I stroked my hand behind one of his lapels, pressing the backs of my fingers against his chest. His muscles felt warm and firm. He drew in a deep breath at my touch, a low growl rumbling in his throat.

"Um, maybe we...um...thank you." He offered his arm, then let out a deep breath to start over. "We should get going."

Collin winked at me as I walked by. "Good job, goddess. You've got my big bro tongue-tied."

"Shh...." I hissed at him. "Don't be fresh."

Collin held up his hands in surrender.

We left the manor and piled into the black sedans waiting to take us to the ball. Caleb didn't take his eyes off me, but had remained silent since we entered the car. I glanced over at him, noticing he seemed upset.

"Is everything okay?"

He frowned. "No."

"No?" My heart sank. "Oh, did I do something wrong? Is it my dress?"

"Yes…I mean no. You misunderstand me. You're an absolute vision. I'm not sure I want anyone else to see you in that dress."

I smiled. I would never doubt Serena again. *Lord Carrington, could you be any cuter?*

"I suppose I don't have to wear it, but walking into the ball in only my underwear and heels might cause a commotion, especially since I'm not wearing a bra."

"Victoria!" Caleb drew in a breath.

His neck and ears flushed red as the vision formed in his mind. *I am definitely playing with fire. Serena would be proud.*

"I'm only joking, Caleb. Stop frowning and smile." I reached over and smoothed the wrinkle between his brows with my fingers. He caught my hand and brought it to his lips, nipping each fingertip through the fabric of my gloves. Waves of pleasure lapped through my body. I gasped. Pulling me across the seat and practically into his lap, he wrapped his other arm around my waist and nuzzled his nose into the crook of my neck, inhaling.

"You smell…delightful," he hummed.

My eyes closed, heat rising in my chest. His heart beat wildly beneath my hand on his chest. "So do you."

We pulled away far enough to look into each other's eyes. His breath brushed my lips. It tasted as exhilarating as he smelled…cinnamon with a hint of mint.

He sighed. "Victoria, what are you doing to me?"

"I could ask you the same," I breathed, leaning in closer. I wanted him to kiss me, wanted him to tell the driver to take us home.

Before either of us could move, we arrived at the clubhouse and the driver opened the sedan door. Caleb growled at the interruption.

"What terrible timing," I pouted.

The spell broken, I tried to catch my breath. *What is happening between us?*

*

"What happened to you?" Blake asked, joining me before the main steps that led into the clubhouse.

"Nothing, what do you mean?" I looked up at his cheeky grin.

"Your neck, ears, and cheeks are as red as a cooked lobster."

"Oh." I covered my ears with my hands. "It was hot in the car."

"I bet it was." Collin wiggled his eyebrows at me. I promptly punched him in the arm. "Ouch!"

"There's that violent streak of hers." Blake winked.

Serena came to my rescue and ushered them away. "All right you two, that's enough teasing. You might want to put some distance between you and Victoria before Caleb rearranges your body parts."

Blake chuckled. "Agreed. I prefer my insides to stay inside."

I stepped over to Caleb and took his offered hand.

"Everything all right?" he asked, his own cheeks finally regaining a normal color.

"Yes, all good." I smiled. "The boys are just being fresh."

"Did you straighten them out?"

"Of course." I winked.

He chuckled and led me inside. The clubhouse ballroom was enormous. A full wall of windows lined the back of the room and the largest chandeliers I had ever seen hung from the vaulted ceiling. Hints of red offset the silver and white decorations. Despite the thick crowd of residents, I saw Talin and Galia seated at one of the side tables and waved at them.

Children ran between the groups of adults, but no one seemed to mind. I smiled as two little boys and a young girl hurried by, talking about the dessert table. Then I thought of my parents and how they always told me I wasn't allowed to attend events held in our community.

"You look sad, sweetness. Is the ball not what you expected?" Caleb squeezed my hand.

"It's beautiful, just old memories coming to haunt." I sighed. "I'll be okay."

Caleb put his long slender fingers under my chin, raising my eyes to his. "No tears tonight, Victoria, only smiles. They can't hurt you anymore if you don't allow them."

I smiled. "You're right."

As we mingled, many of the guests greeted me warmly, either asking how I was adjusting or introducing themselves. Some of them whispered about the infamous Carrington bachelor claiming the last Starling, but I ignored them. I turned my attention to the couples on the dance floor. They all looked so elegant in their formal wear, waltzing in perfect harmony.

"Would you honor me with a dance, sweetness?" Caleb bowed his head and motioned toward the middle of the room.

"It would be my pleasure." I curtsied and giggled.

I followed him to the dance floor where Caleb effortlessly led us in among the other dancing couples. Dancing like this, it felt like we were gliding across the floor, a scene out of a romantic novel. A twinge of regret tightened my chest as I remembered Cassie and I taking dance lessons one summer.

"You're an exceptional dancer, my dear," Caleb whispered in my ear, breaking my thoughts.

"That's because I have a wonderful partner." I winked.

He laughed. "I can't take all the credit."

Couples nearby stared in awe. I smiled, glancing around. "Be careful, Caleb. You may give them the wrong impression."

He raised his eyebrows. "And what impression might that be?"

"That you're really not an old, grumpy vampire."

He feigned a shocked expression. "Old? Grumpy?"

"Yep, old *and* grumpy," I teased. "Oh, and ill-tempered and prideful… and…"

"I see." Caleb quickly dipped me backwards, low to the ground, and whipped me back up in a twirl, taking my breath away.

I gasped. "You win."

"Anything else?" he challenged.

"And…handsome, intelligent, dangerous…" I breathed.

"Much better."

We smiled, finding joy in our playful banter. After several dances, we meandered over to the bar. Caleb ordered us both a glass of red wine.

"Having fun, Victoria?" Collin joined us, stealing my glass and draining it. My pout made him smile.

"Very much so, but I fear I've been teasing your brother a bit too much tonight."

"Really? Tell me more, my sweet goddess." He leaned in.

"She called me old, grumpy, and ill-tempered," Caleb sulked.

He grinned at his brother. "That's not teasing, that's just telling the truth. We can't have our Victoria telling lies, now can we?"

"*Our?*" Caleb's tone was stern and held a note of warning.

"Yep. I found her, so she's part mine." Collin wrapped an arm around my waist. "And now it's my turn to spin her around the dance floor. Come Victoria, let me show you how a couple should dance at this event." Before Caleb or I could protest, Collin lifted me off my feet and pulled me to the dance floor.

I lightly punched his arm. "You're going to start a war, Collin."

"He'll get over it." Collin chuckled. "He knows I'm harmless."

"Like a viper," I teased.

He chuckled. "You may be right, my goddess. I still haven't decided if I'm going to let him keep you or steal you away." I glanced up at the impossibly tall man twirling me around the floor. He winked at me and we both laughed. "Seriously, are you two getting any closer to sealing the deal?"

"Collin!" I gasped. "Honestly, you're incorrigible. Is that all you think about?"

"If I had a beautiful goddess like you living under my roof, we would never see the light of day until I made sure you were loved so completely you'd never want to leave my bed."

"I never know if you're being a tease or if a part of you is being serious."

"And that's why this is so much fun." He laughed.

I sighed and shook my head. "You're impossible."

Collin twirled me around so quickly I had to cling to him to not lose my balance. This type of teasing from him was becoming normal. I knew he was only playing, and in his heart, he wanted nothing more than to see Caleb and I mated.

And I want that too.

When the song ended, we rejoined Caleb at the bar. He wrapped his arm around my waist and pulled me close. There was no place I'd rather be than at his side. This closeness was a sudden change, but I wasn't going to complain. We had avoided each other—and our feelings—for long enough. *I'm not going to deny them any longer.*

"There you are!" Darin and the twins joined us. "Sorry to bother you, boss, but Greggory says he needs to have a quick word with all of us."

"What about?" Collin asked.

Caleb arched his brow in curiosity.

Blake glanced at me. "He has the information you were asking for and it can't wait. He wants your opinion too, Caleb."

"Will you be all right, Victoria?" Caleb asked.

"Of course, go take care of business. I'll mingle and try to find Talin and Galia."

"All right, don't leave the ballroom. I'll be back soon." He kissed the top of my head.

Collin and Caleb followed the others out of the ballroom, and I started my search.

*

Circling the dance floor twice, I was unable to find them or Serena. I wondered if they had gone outside for some fresh air. *It is a bit warm in here.* I promised Caleb I wouldn't leave the ballroom, but I wouldn't be gone long. Before I got far, someone grabbed my hand and pulled me back.

I turned with a smile. "Caleb, you're back already?"

"No, my pet."

My smile faded as I looked up into the cold blue eyes of Malcolm Moriat. I shivered.

"Malcolm? Please let go of my hand."

"I can't do that, my pet. I've been waiting all night to get my hands on you, and now that I have you, I don't feel like letting go."

I looked around for someone to help me as he pulled me onto the dance floor. All eyes followed us, but no one stepped in.

"Malcolm, you're causing a scene."

"Oh, I certainly hope so. Let them all see to whom you truly belong." He leaned in and pressed his lips to my ear, wrapping a long muscular arm around my waist.

"Stop!" I pushed against him. "He'll kill you for this."

"He's welcome to try, my pet..."

"I'm not your pet. Now let go of me." I struggled against him, but he was too strong.

"I can smell your fear." He leaned closer and sniffed the air. "I want you to fear me. The way it tastes..." He licked his lips. I shuddered in revulsion. It would've been erotic had it been anyone other than the psycho vampire grasping me. "I shall enjoy drinking from you, my pet."

"I'm sorry to disappoint you, but that will never happen. I will *never* choose you, Malcolm."

Malcolm leaned back and laughed. Mocking me. "My sweet pet, my delectable naïve peach, your choice doesn't matter. You are already mine because I say so."

I pushed on his chest, glancing around the room. *Caleb, where are you?*

"You can't take me away from Caleb without my permission. And I'll never choose you!"

He leaned in close, his cold fingers grabbing my chin and snapping my head to the side. His fangs lightly grated the goosebumps along my neck. *Would he bite me right here on the dance floor?*

"Let me enlighten you, my dear. That rule only applies if the vampire recites the mating incantation and the human bears their mate's mark." He smiled as my body stiffened, realization sinking in. "Tell me, my pet, has he given you his mark? I don't see it, but perhaps you have it covered up?" I gasped. "No, I didn't think so. All I need to do, my sweet flower, is utter those special words, mark you, and drink of your delicious nectar right here in front of everyone, and there's nothing that pretentious Carrington could do about it."

Fear gripped my heart. My voice failed me. My only thoughts were of Caleb. An evil chuckle vibrated in his throat as he kissed my neck.

"Malcolm, don't…" I croaked. A single tear fell from my eye.

"I'm not going to claim you tonight, my pet. No, I want that Carrington fool to understand that I can take you whenever I wish and he's powerless to stop me. Think about what I've said. Keep building that fear in your heart. I'm sure you've heard rumors of what an evil vampire I am—believe them! The rules mean *nothing* to me. When your fear reaches its peak, I'll claim you and sink my fangs in deep, relishing in the glorious taste. Then you'll be mine… forever!" He released me and disappeared. I was left shaking in the middle of the dance floor alone.

Ignoring the stares and whispers, I bolted from the ballroom and down the front steps of the clubhouse. I didn't stop until I reached the massive fountain in the center of the large circular driveway. I collapsed to my knees, violent sobs racking my body. I tried to breathe but choked on the cool evening air.

*

"What have you found out, Greggory?" Caleb asked once I closed the door to the meeting room.

"Collin, your suspicions are correct. Malcolm hasn't given up on Victoria. He's telling those close to him that he intends to persuade her to leave Caleb and be with him."

I sighed. "Did you learn how he plans to do that?"

"Brother, I don't think we need to worry about Victoria being persuaded to leave me."

"Perhaps not, but that doesn't mean he won't take her by force. She's still unmarked." Caleb winced at that.

"I don't know if he has a set plan," Greggory continued. "I spoke with Allister directly. He's the one that overheard one of Malcolm's bodyguards boasting about how the Moriat house was finally going to be victorious."

"Until we know more, there's not much we can do but keep an eye on him and his men." I looked to Caleb. "Unless you want to take care of him tonight?"

He shook his head. "I wish I could, but I won't risk a war between our houses. He has to be a bigger fool than we thought if he truly intends to fight me."

"I would call Malcolm a lot of things. Wise is not one of them. We should head back before we are missed. Besides, I think I need another dance with *our* beautiful goddess." Caleb's dark eyes glared at me.

*

Returning to the ballroom, I looked for Victoria, but she was nowhere in sight. The other guests stared and whispered as I walked past. I was used to it, so I paid it no attention until Allister Aspen, one of the other older pureblood vampires and my lifelong friend, approached us.

"She's not here. She ran outside a moment ago."

"What? Why?" I frowned.

Allister sighed. "Malcolm grabbed her, pulled her onto the dance floor, and made a spectacle out of them."

My hands clenched into fists. "I'm going to kill him."

"You may have to," Allister agreed. "I won't say I'd be sad if you do. Listen Caleb, I don't know what he said to her, but he's still planning to claim her. She's still unmarked, yes?" I nodded. "You need to decide, my friend. I'm not telling you what to do, but she looked terrified the entire time. If he takes her…he will hurt her. And when he's had his fun and gets bored, he'll kill her."

Allister knew my conflicted feelings for Victoria. He didn't tell me this information lightly.

"Which way did she go?" Collin asked.

Allister nodded toward the front doors, then glanced over my shoulder at Greggory. "I found Serena and sent her outside. Hopefully she is with Victoria right now." Turning back to me, he added, "If you need anything, don't hesitate."

I nodded. "Thank you, Allister."

"My house is yours."

Once outside, we found Serena cradling a sobbing Victoria on a bench by the front entrance fountain. Serena's eyes were filled with pain, anger, and fear.

When Victoria saw me, she threw herself into my arms. Her body shook violently, deep sobs issuing from her chest. I held her tight. My heart breaking with every whimper. My resolve to kill Malcolm deepening with every tremor.

When her breathing had slowed, I gently asked, "What happened, sweetness?" I wiped away her tears with my thumbs.

She shook her head, still unable to speak.

Serena laid her hand on Victoria's shoulder. "Show him, little one. You can do it. Just like we practiced."

She looked up at Serena. With tears glistening in her eyes, she nodded.

"Caleb, take Victoria's hand and look into her eyes. Clear your mind and relax. Let her in," Serena instructed, "Victoria, breathe and concentrate. Recall what happened as if you were watching it from a far."

I hissed as the image of Malcolm grabbing her hand took shape in my mind.

"Do not react to what you see—not yet. If she feels your emotions, the connection will break. Stay calm and focused."

I nodded and watched her memories unfold in my mind. She looked terrified. How dare he touch her and make her afraid! I wanted to find that slimy vampire and rip him apart, but I had to remain calm and detached for Victoria's sake. She was reliving it for me, so I could see what he had done to her. I never should've left her alone.

One thing was clear. I was going to kill Malcolm Moriat…and soon.

Chapter Twenty

It had been a month since the annual ball and my encounter with Malcolm. Caleb's demeanor toward me had changed after that night. He was more distant, grumpier—if that was even possible. He had erected the walls around his heart again and was avoiding me. No matter what I did, I couldn't break through. Even though we ate dinner together every night, we might as well have been miles apart. We no longer took our nightly walks through the garden.

I don't understand him. I miss him terribly.

I barely left the manor and was running out of things to do. When I woke that morning, I decided to work on the flower beds surrounding the back terrace. I headed to Caleb's study to make sure he didn't object. In truth, it was more an excuse to talk to him.

I'll just march into his study and tell him. What's the worst that could happen? I knocked on the thick wood door.

"Come in."

"Caleb?"

"Victoria, can I help you with something?"

I looked around, letting my eyes adjust to the darkness. I could hear him and heavens help me I could smell him, that luxurious scent of cinnamon and cedar, but I couldn't see him. "Where are you?"

"I'm up here," Caleb called from the second floor of his study.

"Oh." With hands extended, I felt my way up the staircase. I knew his study well, but it was still too dark for me to see clearly. "What are you reading? How can you see anything up here?" Keeping my hands out, I used the railing as a guide, trying not to tumble over it to my death until—*bmphf*. I bumped right into the solid wall of Caleb's back. "I'm so sorry."

Caleb sighed, catching and balancing me back on my feet. "What do you need, Victoria?"

There's that tone. Why is he being so short with me? The ride to the annual ball was still fresh in my mind, and after my hands roamed his muscular back, I wanted to say a cold shower but thought better of it. He hadn't been in a jovial mood for weeks.

"I wanted to ask if I could work on the flowerbeds that line the back terrace."

"You don't need my permission. Tell Talin what you want, and he'll have the landscapers do it."

"But I want to do it myself."

Caleb turned to face me. "Are you pouting?"

"Would you believe me if I said no?"

Caleb chuckled. "No, because I can see you."

"You laughed." I leaned in close, trying to see his face. "Are you smiling?"

"Maybe."

"You haven't smiled since—" I caught myself before I said it. "It would make me very happy if you are."

"Then no…I'm not smiling," he teased.

"Liar." I lightly punched his arm. *He must be in a good mood. I don't want it to end. Could we go back to how we were that night?*

"Are you calling one of the most dangerous vampires alive a liar?" He tried to sound angry, but I could tell he was amused.

"I am," I quipped. "So, can I? Please, please, please…."

"Yes, yes, if you'll stop that incessant begging."

"Thank you." Reaching up, I wrapped my arms around his neck, stood on my tiptoes, and kissed his cheek. "I promise you're going to love it." I practically skipped down the stairs and out into the main hallway to look for Talin.

*

I stood in shock for what must have been an hour.

I had been avoiding her. Victoria was a distraction. I *needed* to deal with Moriat before moving forward with her—to keep her safe, I told myself. I was meeting with Collin and the others that night to discuss the situation. Putting distance between us was tearing me apart inside, and with one kiss, she tore down the walls...again. I enjoyed our tête-à-tête, that was true. Even when she had bumped into me in the dark, I wasn't irritated. If I was being honest, I longed for her touch and the electric shocks that coursed through my skin whenever she was near. The warmth from her lips still lingered on my cheek. I craved more.

Shaking my head, I went back to reading, desperately trying to make myself forget the alluring feel of her body against mine. Since the ride to the annual ball, I was finding it increasingly difficult to stay away from her.

Allister's warning constantly ran through my mind. My friend was right. As an unmarked human, Malcolm could steal Victoria and claim her, not giving her a choice. I should've whisked her home that night and marked her, but she had been so traumatized it would have been selfish timing. I wasn't going to force Victoria. Being my mate had to be her choice. I needed her to come to me willingly.

I was still adjusting to the vision Victoria shared with me. Not just what took place, but every feeling she had as Malcolm threatened her as well. She had chosen me. She told him she would never choose him. My heart soared. The beast inside me growled with pride. Yet I couldn't bring myself to claim her. *I'm being stubborn. I love her. Damn my pride.*

She was trying so hard to break through to me again. Taking care of Malcolm Moriat first was merely a pathetic excuse. Deep down, I was afraid of the feelings Victoria elicited in my heart. I had never given myself so completely to anyone in my long life. *Loving her makes me feel complete...and weak.*

Later that evening as the sun was starting to set, I found Victoria out on the back terrace, hair pulled back into a messy bun, an apron tied around her that I assumed had once been white but was now covered in potting soil. She was up to her elbows in one of the planters.

"Victoria?"

"Hmm? Oh, Caleb, hello." She stood, using the back of her hand to wipe a stray hair from her brow.

I laughed at the sight of her. She was positively glowing and completely filthy.

"What's so funny?" She looked at me with a confused expression on her face.

"You're covered in soil."

She glanced down at herself and giggled. "I guess so."

"Here." I gently ran the back of my fingers down her cheek. She instantly blushed. *She is so enchanting.* "You had some dirt there."

"Huh…" Victoria's eyes seemed to glaze over as my fingers wiped away the smudge. "Hmmm…"

"You okay?"

Victoria blinked. "Yes…thank you." She shook the dirt off her apron and peeled off her glove, absently rubbing her cheek.

"I have to go to a meeting this evening. I'll be out of the house until late. Don't let anyone in and don't go out. If you need anything, ask Talin."

Victoria frowned. "Since when am I a prisoner?"

"You're not. I would like you to stay in tonight…Actually, for the foreseeable future, I would like to ask that you not go out alone."

"Sounds like I'm a prisoner with yard privileges. At least tell me why." I could see she wasn't going to let this go.

"Victoria, please do as you're told."

Her neck, cheeks, and ears turned red in anger. "Don't treat me like I'm a child. You promised you wouldn't do that anymore."

I sighed. "Victoria…"

"Caleb?" She crossed her arms, her tiny foot tapping on the stone terrace.

"If I promise that I will tell you soon, will you let this go for now? Trust me, please, and do as I ask."

"You always say that, and then you never tell me anything. I don't understand. I'm trying to have a life here with you…uh…with everyone…but I won't be locked away or treated like a child who can't make her own decisions."

Before I could stop myself, I wrapped my arm around her waist, not caring if my suit got stained. I hooked my finger under her chin and brought her face up to meet mine. "This time, I promise I will tell you, but not yet."

"When?" She searched my eyes. Her warm hands pressed against my chest.

"Soon." I brushed my lips on her forehead, then let her go.

She resigned. "All right, I trust you. Even though you're still being infuriatingly vague." She added, "I'll leave a plate of food out for you."

I waved, not looking back, still processing what was happening between us.

*

I watched Caleb head back into the house, my fingers tracing my brow. I could still feel the warmth of his lips. The kiss had been fleeting, almost imperceptible, yet my forehead was hot to the touch. In moments, my entire body was inflamed with an intense heat I had never experienced before.

Caleb.

My body tensed as the vision struck. I was no longer looking at the back of the manor. Images flashed before my eyes, so quickly I couldn't decipher them. Two men fighting…blood. So much blood. Theirs? Mine? They threw punches, talon-like nails tearing flesh, baring fangs. No, not men. It was two vampires! Were they fighting over me?

The images faded, leaving me empty. I shivered. My world went dark as I collapsed onto the cold stone terrace.

Chapter Twenty-One

The smile on my face didn't fade even as I headed to my meeting. I had something to look forward to when I returned home: one of Victoria's meals.

I entered the Council's headquarters and made my way to the large meeting room on the second floor. Collin, Greggory, Darin, and the Boylston twins were already there.

"I'm glad you all came," I started.

"Just so you know, Serena is furious that you won't let her be here," Greggory informed me.

"I know how much she loves Victoria and wants to protect her. I need her focused on being Victoria's friend. Her support will be what Victoria needs the most until we deal with this problem."

"Got it." Greggory gave two thumbs up. "She's the distraction. I'm sure that will go over well." He sighed. Knowing her, she would do what I asked, but she wouldn't be happy about not being on the front lines.

"Problem? Is that what we're calling that lunatic?" Collin laughed, changing the subject. "I keep telling you rip his head off, bro. Problem solved."

Bastian and Blake smiled in agreement. "Or let me do it," Blake added. "I want to see the look on his face."

"You know it's not that simple. Until he makes a threatening move on her, I have no reason to go after him, despite what he says to people. It would start a clan war, and that wouldn't be good for anyone."

"Then mark her already! Make Victoria your mate and this all goes away. He wouldn't dare touch her." Collin glared at me. "She loves you, you love her. What are you waiting for?"

I growled, gripping the edges of the table so hard a crack ruptured down the middle.

"Good grief, Caleb, I just had this replaced from the last time you were in this room."

"If you weren't family, I'd rip that loose tongue of yours out."

Collin held up his hands in resignation. "Pride is going to be the end of you one day, Caleb. Don't let it be the end of Victoria."

I was about to leap across the table when I realized he was right. Taking a deep breath, I started over and changed the subject. "What is Malcolm saying?"

Darin cleared his throat, almost afraid to speak amidst the sibling rivalry. "He's been telling everyone that you lied at Victoria's *Legătura*, that you never intended to take her as your mate. She's merely a prisoner in your home—a slave. He claims he's been seeing her when she leaves the mansion and that they are in love. He intends to challenge you for her."

Rage, quick and hot, built inside of me. "It's one thing for him to make claims against me but to tarnish her...."

"I suggest we have Bastian or Blake accompany Victoria whenever she leaves the manor." Greggory leaned forward in his seat. "Any one of you can protect her, but they are the best."

Collin laughed. "Hear that, Frosty? You and your brother are going to babysit our beautiful goddess." The twins glared at him. "Oh, come on, you two fell in love with her the instant she stepped into that SUV."

Bastian sighed. "True."

"Frosty?" I questioned.

"That's Bastian's nickname. Victoria gave it to him the night we found her. She even stuck her tongue out at him when he growled at her."

I chuckled. "Why doesn't that surprise me? Bastian, Blake, from tonight forward, you'll be Victoria's bodyguards whenever she leaves the house. I also want you to watch over her while she roams the estate. She likes to walk in the gardens, and I can't always be with her. Wherever she goes, one of you goes…got it?"

"You got it, boss. It will be our pleasure." Blake winked. Bastian elbowed him, shooting a glance at Caleb. "Sorry, Caleb. We'll keep her safe."

"In the meantime, I am going to have a friendly chat with Malcolm tomorrow."

"Friendly?" Greggory raised an eyebrow.

"Yes, as friendly as I can be to tell him to stop talking about my…about Victoria."

Collin and Greggory stole a glimpse at each other.

"I have to applaud you, Caleb." Greggory stood. "If another man was making claims about stealing my woman, I'd rip their heart out and feed it to them."

"She's not…."

"Yes, yes, she's not your woman, as you always say." Collin waved a dismissive hand and stood as well. "Keep telling yourself that, bro…though I don't expect you or anyone else is going to believe you."

As I was about to respond the door to the conference room flew open and Talin burst through.

"My lord, you have to come back to the manor…Mistress Victoria…" He bent over, trying to catch his breath.

My heart stopped, the blood in my veins running cold. "What about Victoria?"

"She collapsed in the garden."

I was out of the room and running toward the manor using my vampire speed before anyone said anything.

*

When I woke, I was laying on the sofa in the living area and Galia was pressing a cold cloth to my forehead. I blinked and tried to sit up.

"Mistress Victoria, you must lie down."

"What happened?"

"We found you passed out on the terrace. Talin carried you in here and went off to get Master Caleb. Please you must rest, mistress."

I leaned back. "I'll be all right, Galia. I know you're worried, but it's only a headache."

The front door slammed open with a bang and pounding footsteps raced into the hall.

"*Victoria!*" Caleb's voice boomed.

"In here, master!" Galia called to him.

Caleb entered the living area and flew to my side. He cupped my face in his hands and searched my eyes. "What happened? Are you okay? Did someone attack you?"

"Slow down, Caleb." I pressed my palms to my temples.

Caleb looked to Galia, who shook her head and shrugged. "What happened?" he asked me in a softer voice.

"I had a vision after you left, and I must have passed out." I closed my eyes, trying to will away the throbbing in my head.

"You have a headache?" I nodded. "Galia, could you get her something for the pain?'

Galia nodded and left the room.

More footsteps strode into the house. Soon the living room was full. Collin, Greggory, and Darin stood off by the fireplace. Serena sat on the opposite side from Caleb. Bastian and Blake stayed in the hall but were facing the room and watching me with worried expressions. Talin was in the kitchen making snacks and brewing tea.

"Please everyone, you don't have to stay here. It's only a headache. It will go away."

"Victoria, what did you see?" Serena asked. "Caleb was the last one to touch you, but he was gone when you had your vision, right?"

I nodded, then winced at the spark of pain.

"Have you ever had a vision without being in contact with someone before?" she asked, concerned, looking to Caleb.

"No. They only come when I have physical contact with someone."

"Sweetness." Caleb laid a freshly cooled compress on my forehead. "Do you remember what you saw?"

Everyone in the room smiled at his term of endearment.

I tried to concentrate. "It's a bit hazy. There were two figures fighting, and there was so much blood everywhere, but I don't think it was theirs."

"Whose blood, then?" Serena asked.

I opened my eyes and looked at her. "I think...I think it was mine."

Caleb growled. Blake and Bastian tensed, their eyes glowing from across the room.

"Caleb?"

He hung his head. "Could you see who they were?"

"No, but they were vampires. I saw fangs." I placed my hand over his. "Caleb, what aren't you telling me?"

Caleb sighed. "Malcolm has been making claims that the two of you are secret lovers and meeting outside the manor. He says he's going to...he's going to take you and mark you as his mate."

"He's insane!" I stood so fast my world instantly began to spin. *Bad idea.*

Caleb caught me before I could fall forward. He pulled me down onto the couch, his arms around me.

"He's lying. I haven't seen him since that night...I swear." I looked up into Caleb's eyes, searching for the bloodlust, but it wasn't there. *Please believe me. I would never betray you. I...I love you.* Oh, how I wanted to say those words out loud.

"I know, sweetness. He's saying these things to provoke me into starting a clan war. Although I do believe he intends to try and take you."

"Is that why you asked me not to leave the manor?"

"Yes." Caleb nodded. "From now on, Bastian or Blake will be with you everywhere you go."

"All right."

Caleb pulled me close and kissed the top of my head. "No argument?" he asked, surprised.

"No argument." Leaning into his embrace, I wrapped my arms around his waist, finding comfort in his warmth. I laid my head against his chest and closed my eyes. My visitors started to shuffle out, but I barely noticed as I held on to him. Without moving, I whispered, "I won't ever leave you, Caleb."

"I know."

*

We had been laying quietly for several hours when Caleb spoke. "Victoria, are you awake?"

"Yes." I shifted in his arms.

"I know this is long overdue, and I don't even know how long I've wanted to say these words…I love you."

I thought my heart would stop. Caleb's eyes were warm, and a goofy smile was plastered on his face. I pushed myself up and placed a soft kiss on his lips.

"I love you, Caleb Carrington, with all my heart."

Pressing my forehead to the inside of his neck he tightened his arms around me and laid us down on the long couch.

I must have fallen asleep shortly after because I woke the next morning in the same clothes in my bed, a throw blanket tucked over my shoulders.

Chapter Twenty-Two

I was euphoric from Caleb's confession. A happy tune hummed in my throat as I went about my day until aching doubts filled my mind. *It's been three days…Why hasn't Caleb asked me to be his mate? Maybe he doesn't love me enough? How does love work between a vampire and a human?*

I was driving myself insane. I repotted all the plants in the garden and organized the pantry three times, much to Talin's dismay. He was so frustrated with me that he finally kicked me out of the manor.

"Mistress Victoria, I think you need to go to the clubhouse and have lunch with Miss Serena."

"Am I driving you crazy, Talin?"

"Just slightly…" His cheeks blushed.

"I'm so sorry, Talin. I'll get out of your way. You're right, going to the clubhouse will be good for me." I ran upstairs, grabbed my purse and a light sweater, and called Serena. Once I was downstairs, I found Blake and asked him to drive me to the clubhouse.

"I'm at your disposal, princess." He winked.

"Always so cheeky, Blake. I think you've been hanging out with Collin too long."

"He does have a way of rubbing off on those around him."

"Not in a good way," I teased. "Oh, we need to swing by and pick up Serena. She's not in her office today."

"Your chariot awaits." He held the front door open for me. I punched him lightly on the arm as I passed by. "I'm going to log a complaint," he pouted, rubbing his arm.

"Aww...you big baby. How about I make you an apple pie later this afternoon, just for you?"

"Really?" Blake's eyes lit up.

I laughed. "You're so easy."

*

At Council headquarters, I gathered with Collin, Greggory, Darin, and Bastian in the large conference room.

"I may have an idea how to prevent a clan war with the Moriats," I started.

"Does it still allow you to rip Malcolm's head off?" Collin asked.

"I'm hopeful."

"Let's hear it, Caleb!" Greggory leaned forward.

"As you know, I was never able to have that *conversation* with him. After Victoria's vision, I felt we needed to find a better solution. Malcolm's brother Malikai is back...I'm meeting with him tomorrow to discuss his brother's actions."

"Oh, this is going to be good. Malikai despises his brother more than we do." Darin chuckled.

I nodded. "Yes, that's what I'm counting on. He's much more levelheaded than Malcolm, but as second born, he can't take over the Moriat clan."

"Sounds like you're going to make him an offer?" Bastian cracked his knuckles.

"I'm going to present my dilemma and ask if he has an agreeable solution that will benefit both bloodlines and prevent further retaliation."

"The civilized assassination approach." Collin leaned back and grinned. "I'm liking this plan."

"Where do you come up with these crazy ideas?" Sighing, I pinched the bridge of my nose. "You're incorrigible." *And exhausting.*

"So you and Victoria keep telling me."

"Speaking of Victoria, how is she?" Greggory asked.

"She's doing wonderfully. We confessed our love for each other that night after you all left the manor."

Collin clapped his hands and jumped to his feet. "About time! This calls for a celebration. Now that she's marked, Malcolm wouldn't dare touch her."

"Wait, Collin…" Greggory frowned, eyeing me. "Caleb why are you meeting with Malikai if you've marked her?" I shifted, stilling my features.

"You did mark her, right, brother?"

"No, not yet."

"W-What…" Collin stuttered. "W-Why the hell not?"

Silence. The one that spoke up next shocked me.

"Caleb, do you know something about Victoria that we don't? Or are you simply a fool?" Bastian's quiet voice held every note of seriousness. Everyone in the room drew in a breath. Darin's face visibly paled.

My eyes glowed in warning. "Bastian." *Careful, old friend.*

"You've been locked away in your study for centuries. By some miracle of fate, a woman seemingly born for you lands in your lap and confesses her love for you. You love her, and you haven't marked her yet? I'd say that is the purest definition of stupidity. What the hell are you waiting for?"

"I don't know." I sighed, running a hand through my hair. *He's right.*

Bastian kept going. "Collin, he obviously doesn't want her, so why don't you go over there and take her? This imbecile doesn't deserve her." It was the most he had ever said in our meetings, possibly his entire life.

"Bastian, enough," Darin warned his lover.

"Am I wrong?"

"That's not the point."

"Well, Caleb, what is the point?" Bastian's hard eyes turned to me. "Are you hearing me?"

Don't push it, Bastian. "If you were anyone else…"

"You'd rip my heart out and eat it while I watched…but you know what

I'm saying makes sense. The love of your life is in danger from an evil son of a bitch who wants to mark her as his, torture her, and drain her dry, and you're sitting here with your head up your ass instead of doing the one thing that can keep her safe."

"*Enough!*" I stood, eyes alight with my growing anger. My patience was waning.

Bastian stood too, his own eyes glowing in response. "Go home, Caleb! Stop letting some ill-conceived notion that you're better off alone haunt you because you're not! Claim your mate before she's stolen from you, or worse…*killed.*"

I growled, slamming my fist on the table and splitting it in two. I stormed out of the room.

*

I sighed, gesturing to the broken table. "You're paying for this."

Bastian smiled. "Don't worry, Collin. If he goes home and claims Victoria, it will be worth it."

"That was a big risk you took, my friend." I shook my head. "I've teased him myself to push him to action—with no luck. Even I know better than to call him stupid."

Greggory let out a shaky breath. "I think Victoria is rubbing off on you, Bastian."

"You had my back."

"Against Caleb when he's angry? Oh no…you were on your own. I like breathing and my heart right where it is."

The slap resounded through the room before any of us had noticed Darin stalking over to Bastian.

He rubbed the back of his head. "Hey, what was that for?"

"The next time you're going to put your life on the line, you better warn me. I almost had a heart attack." Then he stormed from the room as well.

"Looks like you have some damage control of your own to do." Greggory winked.

Bastian grumbled, "He can be so sensitive."

"You better go after him."

Bastian stood and left the room.

I smiled. "They are so cute together."

"Don't let him hear you say that. He'll rearrange your face." We laughed, knowing it was true.

*

I found Darin in his office. He was looking out the window, his arms crossed in front of him and his back to the door. *He's angry.*

"Hey," I whispered as I came up behind him.

"Hmph." Darin shrugged.

"Listen…"

"No, you listen. Do you know how dangerous that stunt was?" Darin only turned his face to the side, keeping his back to me. "It's one thing for Collin to go off on his brother and play against his feelings, but the rest of us…Even as a pureblood, Bastian, you are no match for Caleb. He could have killed you."

Why are you so cute when you're lecturing me? I sighed, pressing my chin on his firm shoulder. Darin wasn't that much shorter than me. I wrapped my arms around his slender waist. "I don't suppose you'll accept a simple apology?"

Darin wiggled as if in protest. "Well it would be a start, but I'm very mad at you right now."

"Look at me, Darin." I hooked a finger under his chin, turning his body around. Keeping him in my arms, I gazed into his eyes. "I know that I scared you. I'm sorry, but it had to be done. Caleb has been stubborn for too long, and he wasn't going to do anything until he was pushed and pushed hard. He and Victoria belong together."

"I know but…"

"No buts, Darin. This is for Victoria's safety. If Caleb doesn't mark Victoria, she's in danger. Malcolm will take her, and he will kill her when he's done. Even all our best efforts may not keep her safe. Marking her is the best way to protect her. Even if Malcolm is stupid enough to take her, Caleb can track her through the mark. Without it…well, I don't want to think about what could happen. I'm sorry. Please don't be mad at me."

"I don't know what I would do if I ever lost you." I wiped away the single tear that formed in the corner of Darin's eye.

How did I get this lucky? "And I don't know what I would do without you. I love you."

"I love you."

Tightening my grip around Darin's waist, I pulled him close. I wasn't completely forgiven...but I could remedy that. I placed my hand behind his head and kissed him deeply. He melted into my embrace and moaned. Pressing his hands to my chest, he gripped my shirt as our tongues explored each other's mouths.

I broke us apart reluctantly. Catching my breath, I held out my hand. "Let's finish this at home, shall we?"

Darin, unable to speak, merely nodded.

*

Serena was pouring over her paperwork in our combined home office when I arrived.

"Welcome home, darling, how was the meeting?" she asked as I sat down on the couch.

"Very interesting."

"Oh...do tell!" Serena joined me. I told her everything that happened at the meeting earlier that night. She gasped. "He didn't!"

"Yep, sat there with the coolest expression I've ever seen and chastised Caleb for being stubborn."

"And he really asked Caleb if he was stupid?"

"Gave us all mini heart attacks. Especially Darin. I imagine Bastian is getting an earful right now."

Serena giggled. "Probably, but Darin won't stay mad long. He's too in love with Bastian not to forgive him."

"Bastian has quite the soft spot for Darin, doesn't he? I don't know how we all missed their relationship."

"He's always been a private person."

I nodded. "Yes, I'm sure he'll do whatever it takes to make up for scaring Darin. It's nice to see that he has a softer inside than he lets on."

"Don't let your guard down too much."

"He's pretty worried about Victoria, that's obvious."

"We all are," Serena admitted. "Speaking of Victoria, I want you to look at something I received from Stuart."

"Stuart Schwartz from archives? What does he have to do with Victoria?"

"Remember when Caleb bit Victoria and she thought that it might have been her fault and not the bloodlust?" I nodded. "I asked Stuart to look through the archives to see if he could find any records of that happening with another human."

"And?"

"Here, look at what he sent me. He reached out to Felix in human studies, and there was a case about ninety years ago where a female from one of the original human families experienced something similar. But once she went to her *Legătura* and was mated to another human, the issue stopped."

"It doesn't say what caused it."

"I noticed that too, so I asked Stuart. He said there's only two situations in which this could happen...Victoria is either Fae, or she produces such a strong pheromone that human males overreact to it."

I chuckled at the first reason. "She can't be Fae."

"I agree. Victoria is a seer, so we already know that she's a rare human. It only makes sense that she could be producing a strong pheromone that human men can't ignore if they are around it for a long period of time."

"Why doesn't it affect vampires? None of the others have had that kind of reaction to her."

"Vampires aren't as susceptible to human pheromones. And you weren't affected because we were mated when we first met her."

"I would have said it was because you are the most beautiful and perfect woman in all the world to me." I nuzzled her neck.

"Greggory..." Serena giggled.

"It's true." I nibbled on her ear. "I think I need to show my beautiful, perfect wife how I'm feeling right now."

"It's the middle of the day!"

Ignoring her protest, I scooped Serena up in my arms and carried her off to our bedchamber.

CHAPTER TWENTY-THREE

I entered the house and immediately went in search of Victoria. Bastian was right. I was being foolish. It was time for us to stop denying how we felt about each other. *I'm not holding back any longer.*

I didn't know how one tiny human could manage to break through the walls I placed around my heart for centuries, but with one look, she had me hooked and completely under her spell.

Perfect. She's home.

I followed her scent to the dining hall. Victoria was arranging flowers in one of the large vases in the center of the buffet. Her hair was twisted and pinned up at the back of her head, but it looked like it was starting to come undone. Her short baby pink dress stopped mid-thigh, showing off her shapely legs, and heavens help me she was barefoot. I stopped a moment and watched her place the flowers in the vase, humming to herself as she chose the perfect location for each bloom. I leaned against the doorway, taking in every movement, every glorious note of her captivating voice.

My reverie broke when, without turning, she asked, "How long are you going to stand there?" She glanced over her shoulder.

"You knew I was here?"

"Mmhmm."

"How?"

"I heard you come in. And I can smell you."

"Wait…I smell?"

She laughed. "No, you don't *smell,* silly, but you do have a scent that's your own."

"A good one, I hope." I straightened and stepped into the room.

"Very good. Actually…it's quite…*sexy.*"

Is she flirting with me?

"Sexy you say?" I wrapped my arms around her waist from behind and pressed my nose to her neck. "You know, you have your own scent too."

She giggled as my breath tickled her. "Do I?" She tilted her head to the side, giving me more access.

"Yes. It's very…*distracting.*" My lips grazed her skin.

Victoria turned and faced me, wrapping her hands behind my neck. "And what is the reason for all this *affection*?"

"Are you complaining?"

She shook her head. "Never. I want to learn what I did to earn this wonderful reaction so I can do it again…and again." Victoria pressed her lips against mine as she spoke. "I've missed you."

Her eyes were filled with desire and love. *Why can't I breathe?*

"I love you." I captured her bottom lip between my teeth.

She moaned. "I love you too."

"Victoria?"

"Hmm?" Her eyelids hung heavy. Pressed so close to each other, I could feel her pounding heart and quick breaths.

"I want you." She pulled back slightly, shocked at my forwardness. "I want all of you," I continued. "Right now. I want to carry you up to my chambers and love you. I want to mark you."

Please say yes. Tell me you want me.

I held my breath, waiting for her response. She searched my eyes as if expecting me to say this was all a joke. I didn't break from her gaze.

"Caleb…you do? You *really* do?"

"Yes, sweetness."

"I want all of you too. I want to be yours and only yours." Her fingers traced my jawline and caressed my cheek. The fire that simple touch set off in me was enough.

I scooped Victoria into my arms. Using my enhanced speed, I carried her up the stairs to my bedchamber.

*

My mind was reeling from Caleb's confession as we entered his room. *If I'm dreaming, I hope I never wake up.* This was the first time I had been inside his bedchamber. The walls were a deep blue, and the long sheer curtains let in enough light that the room wasn't completely shrouded in darkness. A settee and matching chairs of a dusky blue offset the rich mahogany furniture. A furry ivory rug covered the floor before the fireplace.

Once inside the room, he closed the door with his foot and set me down not far from his four-poster bed. It was all happening so fast that I hadn't been nervous until I stared at the high mattress behind me. I was inexperienced, and now I was in the bedroom of the man—the vampire—I loved with all my heart. *What if I'm not good enough?*

I chewed on my bottom lip. Sensing my fears and doubts, Caleb kept one arm wrapped around my waist and raised my chin with his other hand.

"You're beautiful and perfect." He brushed his lips against mine. The taste of cinnamon and mint made my mouth tingle. Our kiss began soft at first, then became greedy as we wrapped our arms around each other. His tongue flicked out as he nipped at my bottom lip, begging me to give him entry. A warmth bloomed in my belly as our tongues found their own special dance, exploring each other's mouths. Our breathing quickened. It was if my body knew instinctively what to do.

Without thought, my hands pulled away from behind his neck and found the buttons of his shirt. I undid each one until I reached his waist. Slowly, I pulled out the fabric tucked into his jeans and undid the remaining two buttons. I trailed my hands up his stomach and chest, feeling the firm defined muscles. *He's gorgeous.*

Running my hands across his shoulders, I pushed his shirt from his body. He let it fall to the ground. Wanting to trace all of him, I slid my hands up and down his shoulders and arms. *I want to drive him crazy.*

Caleb shuddered at my light touch. "Victoria!" His voice was deep and husky.

I deepened our kiss, leaning my body into his. The tiny buds of my breasts hardened, and a warmth in my groin made it hard to hold still. A deep growl rumbled in Caleb's throat. He was holding back, letting me drive the pace.

"Unzip my dress..." I whispered between kisses.

Caleb's eyes glowed and darkened with desire. His long fingers trailed up my back from my hips, sending a wave of goosebumps down my spine. Finding the top of the zipper, he slowly pulled it down. He hooked a finger under each thin strap, then did away with them. His touch made my skin tingle. Electrifying shivers shook me, and I moaned. My dress fell to the floor. I stood before him in my bra and panties. His hands rested on my hips as he examined every inch of exposed skin.

I reached behind me and undid the hooks to my bra, letting it drop to the floor as well. Caleb's nostrils flared while his fingertips dug into my flesh.

Not taking my eyes from him, I reached forward to his belt buckle and quickly undid it, then the button and zipper of his jeans. He was already aroused, his erection threatening the limits of his boxers. All I wanted to do was free him from the confinements of his clothes. I wanted all of him with such ferocity it surprised me. *Easy, Victoria. Don't rush.*

I brushed my fingertips on the inside of his waistband, inching his jeans over his hips, grazing the skin just above the edging of his underwear. Caleb drew in a sharp breath. His eyes closed for a moment as his head tilted back. He was struggling with maintaining control. *Good.* I wanted to push him to his limits, wanted him to step over the edge and claim me without restraint.

As he shook his jeans to the floor and stepped from them, I moved to his boxers. I pushed my fingers behind the elastic band just above his firm cheeks. Leaning in, I placed light kisses on his chest, flicking his hot skin with my tongue and nipping his flesh. All the while, I inched the material down slowly. Making my way to the front, I gazed up into Caleb's dark eyes as I continued my assault on his chest. My fingertips grazed his lower abdomen, freeing his sex from its confines. I traced a finger around the tip, making him twitch.

"Fuck," he groaned. "Victoria…I can't…"

I smiled and inched his boxers down until they fell to the floor. Trailing my hands up his sides, feeling his muscles tighten against them, I licked his neck stopping at his ear. I sucked the soft spot behind his earlobe. He twitched against my abdomen.

"Don't hold back, Caleb. Claim me…now!"

His grip on my hips tightened as he lifted me from the floor. My legs wrapped around his waist. Dropping me on the bed, he pulled my underwear off in one motion. If they ripped, I didn't notice. I was laying before him, splayed out on his bed completely naked.

"You're so beautiful!" Caleb's eyes took in everything. He placed urgent kisses on the flesh just above the mound of my breasts as he cupped them with his long fingers. His hot tongue trailed down to the waiting bud, flicking it in short, quick strokes before he took it with his teeth. My spine arched off the bed. I threw my head back as my hands buried themselves in his hair.

"Ngh…Mmfp," I moaned, unable to speak.

"If you keep making those delightful sounds, I'm not going to be able to hold back. You taste so sweet." His hands massaged my breasts as he played with one and then the other before his tongue traced a line down the center to my belly button. He nipped and kissed the tender flesh, leaving several love bites. He continued his descent, kissing, nipping, and sucking on the skin above my hip bone. The ticklish sting made my hips buck.

He pinned me to the bed as he lowered himself between my legs. The flick of his tongue sent waves of pleasure through me.

"Mngh…ooh." My head tossed side to side with each touch. I was so sensitive to him.

I could feel him smile briefly before his tongue found that sweet spot, circling it, his lips sucking in the sensitive flesh. I writhed and twitched at his skilled stimulation. My hands dug into the duvet as his fingers caressed my inner thigh, inching toward my core. A sound I never thought I could make escaped my lips as his fingers more urgently claimed my inner warmth.

"Call my name, sweetness."

My vision blurred as I reached a body-racking climax. Pushing myself up, I screamed his name as my body shook with pleasure. "*Caleb!*" As the final wave passed over me, I collapsed back, out of breath and feeling dizzy.

"Good girl." He hummed, trailing sweet kisses up my stomach and chest, claiming my mouth with an unrequited hunger. I released the bed cover to grip his shoulders, my eyes misty with pleasure.

"Are you ready for me, sweetness?"

"Yes," I breathed. "Please Caleb, hurry."

"How can I deny such a delightful request?" His hands lifted my hips as he pushed into me, slowly but deeply, filling me so completely that an intense bolt of pleasure coursed through me. I barely felt the pain. Slowly, I moved my hips, matching his rhythm, amazed at how our bodies came together to fit like pieces of a puzzle.

His breath was faster now. I looked up into his eyes. Desire and an intense love I never thought I'd see gazed back at me.

"Victoria, will you be mine? Will you be my mate?"

"Yes, Caleb, for now and for always."

His fangs elongated, and a second set of smaller fangs descended next to his canines. The mating mark was different than a regular vampire bite. This one would leave a mark distinctive to Caleb.

His eyes glowed as he whispered the incantation that would bind us together. It was in a language I didn't understand, an ancient language used only by vampires, but I knew its translation. I had read it in one of the books in my parents' library.

"*In love, in life, the unbreakable bond is made. Consent of the heart has bound us together until death.*"

With the final word, Caleb sank his teeth into the soft flesh in the crook of my neck. The pinch lasted only a moment. I barely felt it as Caleb lifted me up onto his thighs and quickened his pace, our hips rocking faster as we built our pleasure. He drank greedily from me and lapped at the wound with his tongue. A powerful warmth filled my body.

Caleb's arms wrapped around me as he thrust harder. A moan issued from his lips. My fingers dug into his tense shoulders, pulling him closer as my core tightened, building to its own release. In moments, we were calling each other's names before collapsing onto the bed.

Caleb kissed me tenderly. I could taste the remnants of blood, my blood, on his lips and found it strikingly luscious. I must have chuckled.

"What is it, sweetness?" He pulled me up into his arms and settled us onto the pillows and under the thick covers.

"I can taste my blood on your lips."

"What?" His hand went to his mouth.

"It's okay. It doesn't bother me. I think I like it, knowing that it's from you marking me."

He drew me in close. "You're mine now. I'm never going to let you go."

"That works out well," I teased, "because you're stuck with me. I don't plan on going anywhere."

He kissed my forehead.

"Caleb?"

"Yes, sweetness?"

I hesitated. "No regrets? I mean, I know it's too late now—well, sort of—but am I truly what you want?"

He raised my chin so my eyes met his. "Why are you having doubts, Victoria? Is what just happened not proof enough?" He didn't look angry, but his tone conveyed his concern.

"I just…am I good enough for you? Will you tire of me?"

Caleb turned, placing himself above me and brushed the stray hair from my face. "You are perfect. I love you more than words can ever convey. It's my fault for not telling you before now. I will never tire of you, and if you do not tire of me, I intend to spend an eternity with you."

"Oh…Caleb…" My eyes filled with tears.

He laid back down and pulled me into his arms. We kissed, letting our love flow between us, finally falling asleep in each other's arms.

Chapter Twenty-Four

I stopped by Caleb's house early the next morning. If I timed this perfectly, I could give him and Victoria a special wake-up call.

"Master Collin, you're here early. I don't believe the master is up. Shall I...?"

"Nope. I'll let him know that I'm here."

"But Master Collin, he's still in his room. I'm about to bring up his and Miss Victoria's breakfast...Please let me announce you're here! He'll be angry if you barge in..."

"Probably, but he'll get over it." Ignoring his warning, I winked and bounded up the stairs two at a time. Without knocking, I opened the bedchamber door.

"Shh...Talin, Victoria's still—"

"Aww, I was hoping to surprise both of you..." I glanced over at the bed. "I guess I'll have to settle for irritating you instead."

*

I turned from the window to find Collin standing in the doorway, a punch worthy grin on his face. Thankfully, Victoria was bundled up under the covers, and all he could see was her peacefully sleeping face and one tiny foot peeking out from under the blankets.

"What the hell are you doing here? And why are you in my room?" I hissed at him.

"I thought I'd stop by to make sure everything went well last night. You left in such a hurry."

"Get out. Go tell Talin to bring us coffee in my study. I'll meet you there in a minute." I pushed him out the door and closed it, locking it in the process. "Honestly, I'm going to kill him one of these days."

Victoria stirred. "Caleb?"

I went over to the bed and sat on the edge. Leaning over, I placed a kiss on her forehead. "It's still early, sweetness. Sleep a little longer."

"Hmm, come back to bed and keep me warm," she purred.

I am assuredly going to kill my brother.

"I have something I need to take care of, then I'll be right back. Don't go anywhere."

She smiled. "I promise, I'm not moving from this spot."

Kissing her again, I hurried down to my study. The quicker I dealt with my pest of a brother, the sooner I'd be back in Victoria's arms. I slammed the door open.

"Alright, Collin, out with it and make it fast."

"Why the rush, brother? Have something you need to get back to?" Collin teased.

"Collin, I swear if you don't get to the point, I'll rip your head off as practice for Malcolm."

"All right. First, I'm glad to see that you and Victoria are moving things forward. Please tell me you marked her."

"I did…Is that all?"

"Not quite. Although that makes me incredibly happy, it means I can avoid continuing the lecture that Bastian started last night…"

"Collin!"

He chuckled. "Okay, the last thing is I want to go with you when you meet with Malikai."

"Why?"

"Because I'm head of the Council now and I want to be there."

"It's because you're head of the Council that you *shouldn't* be there…and you know it."

Collin frowned. "At least tell me when and where you are meeting with him. And promise me you'll bring one of the twins with you."

"Are you worried about me, brother?"

"Obviously." Collin stood. "I don't trust the Moriats. Even if Malikai despises his brother and wants him removed as head of the house, they are still blood."

"I can handle Malikai, but if it will make you go away, I'll tell you the details of the meeting once I know them. I'm to call Malakai later this afternoon. Good enough?"

"Yes. Now get back up to that beautiful goddess laying in your bed and stop playing with me." He smiled and with a wave left the study.

*

I was enjoying the warmth of laying in Caleb's bed. The pillows, sheets, and blankets all held his scent. I felt surrounded by him. *All that's missing are his strong arms wrapped around me and his succulent lips on mine.*

When I heard Collin come into the room, I wanted to sit up and scream at him for taking away my beloved. Caleb had promised to come back, so I waited…and waited. Finally, the door opened slowly, and I knew it was him sneaking back in, trying not to wake me. I laid still, pretending to be asleep as he disrobed and slid under the covers. Feeling his arms snake out toward me, I rolled over and turned my back on him.

"Sweetness, are you awake?" He continued to close the gap between us.

"Nope, I'm asleep. Leave me alone." With a huff, I tried to sound miffed.

"I'm afraid I can't do that, my love." Caleb gently pulled the hair away from my neck and started showering me with kisses, nipping the sensitive flesh. My skin heated beneath the course of his warm tongue.

I wriggled, trying to deny him access, but he clutched me.

"You can't get away from me, sweetness," he purred.

"You left me," I pouted.

"Only a moment." He trailed kisses across my shoulder, down my arm to my fingertips, nibbling them. "I'm back now."

"Hmph." I glanced at him out of the corner of my eye, a slight smile turning up the corners of my mouth.

"How should I apologize?"

"Why don't you surprise me?" I turned to face him, wrapping my arms around his neck, and planted my own kisses behind his ear.

"Challenge accepted," he growled.

We spent the remainder of the morning tangled in each other's arms, kissing, laughing, and showing our love for each other in more passionate ways than I could count. Our love making was only interrupted by the sound of my stomach growling.

"You need to eat."

"I'm fine. Keep kissing me."

"Victoria, you haven't had anything since dinner last night. I'll ring Talin and have him bring you lunch. I have calls to make and you need to work with Galia to move your belongings."

I sat up. "Move my belongings? To where?"

"To here, of course. Did you think you would keep your own bedchamber now that we are mated?"

"Honestly, I didn't think of it. Are you sure you want me to move in here to your room?"

"Without question. I want to be with you every night and wake up with you every morning." Caleb leaned over and captured my lips in a kiss before heading into the shower.

I giggled. "Want company?"

"Of course."

After we showered, I put on one of Caleb's robes and headed to my room to finish dressing. I told him not to ring Talin, that I would make my own lunch. Caleb told me he had several business calls to make and was going to meet with the second oldest son of the Moriat house to discuss our concerns about Malcolm.

"Is that a good idea?"

"Malikai despises his brother. If anyone can help us defuse this situation peacefully, it will be him. I'm not sure how much he's willing to help, but I must at least talk with him."

"You're bringing Collin with you, right?"

Caleb shook his head. "No. As head of the Council, he can't be involved in this mess, especially in any back-door discussions. I'll ask one of the twins to come with me."

"Take Bastian," I requested.

Caleb looked at me. "Why him?"

"I'm not sure. Maybe it's silly, but I feel like he's the one you should take along."

"All right."

"You will be careful, won't you, Caleb?"

"Yes. I'll be home tonight." Caleb kissed my head and headed out to go to his office at Council headquarters.

After dressing, I went down to the kitchen and made myself a sandwich. Sitting at the kitchen counter, I pulled out my phone.

Collin, have a moment?

Is my beautiful goddess texting me? I was sure she'd be too tired to move her precious fingers.

I was going to invite you over for dinner tonight but now...maybe I'll ask Serena and Greggory over instead.

I'm only teasing...

I know, silly, so was I...Can you come?

Of course. Everything okay?

Caleb told me about his meeting with Malikai and I don't want to be alone.

You're worried?

Aren't you?

Caleb can handle himself. Malikai and Caleb have a mutual understanding. I'm sure it will be fine.

If you say so...

I do. I'll tell Serena.

Okay. See you tonight.

I'm counting the hours, my sweet goddess.

*

After putting my phone back in my pocket, I smiled. "Seems you know your mate well. She asked if I would come over for dinner. I need to invite Serena and Greggory too."

Caleb smiled. "I didn't think she'd want to be alone."

"She's worried."

"I know, but she shouldn't be."

"It's only natural since she loves you. I admit, I'm a little jealous, brother."

"You'll find a mate. Why not try again with Celeste?"

I snorted and grinned. "Very funny. I'm not exactly her type. I've been lecturing you so much lately that I stopped looking, but there are so many beauties out there. How should I choose?"

Caleb slapped my shoulder. "I'm sure Victoria and Serena would love to play matchmaker for you."

"Oh no! Don't you dare." I shuddered. "I don't need their help."

Caleb laughed and headed out to his meeting with the second eldest Moriat brother.

*

"Ah, my darling baby brother. What brings you back to our sleepy little community?"

"You know why I'm here, Malcolm. You aren't the only one with a network of little birds keeping you informed."

"And what have your little spies whispered in your ears this time?" I lounged in the chair opposite him.

"I hear Caleb has finally found a mate." Malikai sipped at his cup of tea, not meeting my icy stare.

"She's not *his* mate," I hissed. "She belongs to *me*."

Malikai smiled behind his cup. "Are you sure about that? What's so special about this human? Or is it simply that she's with Caleb that makes you want her?"

"He doesn't deserve a beauty like Victoria." I paused, recalling how enchanting she looked at the annual ball. "She has the most *alluring* scent."

Malikai placed his cup on the table and folded his hands in his lap. "You want to play with her?"

I giggled. "Oh, yes. I really do."

"Malcolm…"

"*You* do not have the right to finish that sentence." I stood. "It's more than just wanting to play with her. This is an opportunity to bring Carrington to his knees."

"Brother, please listen to me. The past needs to stay in the past. We both know that Grandfather was not the savviest businessman. Friendship and business rarely result in a happy ending. The Carringtons lost large sums of money over his schemes. They had every right to be angry, but our fathers found a way to smooth over the past transgressions and find peace. Are you looking to start a clan war, Malcolm?" he asked.

"What if I am? It's time those Carringtons learned they are no better than the rest of us."

"The Carringtons are one of the original vampire houses and the strongest bloodline still living. They *are* better than the rest of us, but Caleb and his brother have never prevented our family from prospering. Why do you continue to carry such hatred toward them?"

"You're weak, Malikai. You never wanted our family to have more than what we do. You have no ambition, no drive. It's good you are second born."

"You go too far." Malikai's eyes glowed in warning.

"Let us not fight amongst ourselves. We should have a common goal—bring the Carringtons to their knees. It is an advantage to the both of us."

"How so?"

"If we destroy them, then the Moriat house rises to the top. I can take over the Council, which would leave an opening in our family business. I'd be willing to step aside and relinquish those duties to you." My empty promise slipped like oil from my lips.

"That is quite the offer. It surprises me to hear you so willing to give up your position as head of this family…"

"Do not mistake me, brother, *I* will still be head of the family. I am only offering you the position of president of our company…Still a very prestigious position, and I might say a generous offer from yours truly."

Malikai bowed his head. "Indeed, brother, you are most generous when it comes to me. However, this seems like a lot of effort for such a small gain."

"Taking Victoria Starling from that arrogant fool is no small gain." *That bastard has her guarded wherever she goes.*

"I hear she is quite beautiful, but there are plenty of other beautiful women… and men…out in the world." He growled at my suggestion. "Why risk your life and the status of our family trying to take this one? The Starling line has fallen from grace over the years. Her parents were disreputable humans. How can she be anything worth fighting for?"

"I want to taste her."

"And once you've done that…?"

My laughter filled the office. "I'll savor the look on Caleb's face as he watches me drain her dry."

Chapter Twenty-Five

A t the manor, we had finished dinner and were in the living area having tea and cake. Talin and Galia were there as well. I asked them if they wanted to join in the wait for Caleb to come home and they gladly accepted.

"Collin, what does Caleb hope will come of this meeting?" I asked.

"I think he's hoping to get permission to deal with Malcolm as he sees fit without worrying about retaliation from the Moriat family," Collin answered honestly.

"Can Malikai guarantee that?"

"If he replaces Malcolm as head of the family, then he will be calling the shots, so in a way, yes."

"And Caleb trusts this Malikai?"

Collin shrugged. "I don't know if trust is the right word. Our families used to be close, a long time ago. Malcolm has always been, well…Malcolm. There were many times Caleb saved Malikai from his brother's torturous games. They have an understanding, but Malikai will always do what's best for his family over anything Caleb asks of him. We just have to hope that they both agree on what is best for the Moriat bloodline."

I stared into my cup, a shiver running through me.

"Besides, if Maikai turns on us in the end, he'll meet the same fate as his brother," Blake added. "One way or another, the Moriat family will be reminded of their place in line."

"Victoria, Caleb has been dealing with the other vampire families for a long time. He learned from his father, who was the best at keeping the peace." Serena squeezed my hand.

"It's true. Our father could negotiate like no one I've ever seen. He maintained order for centuries through mediation and intimidation." Collin chuckled. "And Caleb is a carbon copy of our father."

Blake nodded. "That's the truth. Your old man was not one to mess around."

Talin leaned forward in his chair and placed a comforting hand on my knee. "Do not worry, mistress. I've been serving the Carrington house since their grandfather was born. Trust Master Caleb. He never gets into a situation where he wasn't fully aware of what he was facing, and he never fails once he sets his mind on achieving something. He will come home safely."

"Thank you, Talin. Such words of confidence hold great meaning coming from you." Caleb chuckled.

"Caleb!" I jumped from my seat on the couch and flew across the room into his open arms. "You're home." I kissed him soundly on the lips, making him blush.

"Were you really that worried, sweetness?"

I nodded. "It may have been silly, but my imagination was out of control."

He laughed and squeezed me tight. "I'm safe—and starving. Talin, would you mind bringing me a decanter? And if Blake and my brother haven't devoured everything Victoria made this evening, I'll take a warmed-up plate as well."

"Right away, master. Would you like to eat in the dining room?"

"No, I'll eat in here if there are no objections."

"None," I answered for everyone. "Now tell us everything!" Caleb hesitated. "Oh no you don't, old man. You are not leaving me out of this, not for one second. Now start talking." I sat him down in the high back leather chair and placed a dinner tray beside him for when Talin brought his meal.

"I don't see you getting out of it, my friend, so you may as well tell all of us." Greggory grinned.

Caleb sighed and recounted his conversation with Malikai Moriat.

*

I asked to meet Malikai at a bar on the outskirts of our community. Vampires rarely left our little town except for business or travel, and very few would venture into a place like this. I apologized instantly to my old comrade when we settled into a booth in the back of the building.

"I'm sorry for asking you to meet in a place like this, but I felt it would afford us the most privacy."

"Do not concern yourself, Caleb. I am not as egocentric as my brother. I see you brought Bastian with you this evening."

"And you brought Austin."

"Yes, I rarely go anywhere without him by my side." Malikai looked over at the two bodyguards standing not too far off. Though engaged in conversation, their eyes were alert, scanning the surroundings.

"He's been with you a long time, hasn't he?"

"Yes, you could say that we are...*inseparable*."

I nodded and smiled. "I'm glad to hear you have someone in your life that brings you joy."

Malikai's eyes twinkled. "I could never hide anything from you, Caleb."

"And why hide this, Malikai? I see no reason for you to feel ashamed."

"Thank you, but I fear my family disagrees with you, especially my brother."

"I'm sorry to hear that, my friend."

"Are we friends, Caleb?"

"We were once...I see no reason for us not to be now. I know our families have had their challenges. It's never easy doing business with friends, something our grandfathers should have known better than to try. I do not hold you and your brother responsible for the mistakes made before our time. This feuding serves no purpose and only hurts our families and our community. It's time for it to end."

Malikai nodded. "I agree with you. I wish my brother saw things this way. But he…"

"I know there is no love between you and your brother, and believe me, I didn't ask you here to choose sides. I'm merely here because your brother is stepping into territory where he doesn't belong. He may force my hand soon. As much as it pains me, I want to make sure that any actions I am forced to take against him will not result in retaliation from the Moriat house. There has been peace for a long time. The last thing our community needs is a clan war."

"I appreciate your concerns." Malikai steepled his fingers in thought. "I must do what is best for my family. My brother is not thinking clearly and has ambitions beyond reason. He is obsessed with the Starling girl, and I'm afraid that nothing short of death is going to prevent him from going after her."

I growled, "That is not what I was hoping to hear."

"You were hoping there was a way to dissuade him from continuing in his foolish enterprise?"

I nodded. "It was a long shot, but yes, I had hoped there would be a way to change his course. I don't want to kill him, but make no mistake. If he lays a finger on my mate, I will take his life without hesitation."

"So you have marked her? Perhaps once Malcolm learns of this, he will lose interest and move on to the next unfortunate victim of his…affections."

"Malikai, I realize my next question may put you on the spot and you are free to decline to answer, but do you know if he has any set plans at this time toward Victoria?"

"You want to know if he's serious or merely baiting you?" He frowned. "All I know is that he intends to take her…and when he's done with whatever games he wants to play, he will kill her. I'm sorry, Caleb. I do not know your mate, but I would not wish my brother's attention on anyone. He is cruel and holds no value on anyone's life but his own. He was born with that darkness, and that unnatural predilection for pain and suffering was fostered and molded by our father. He is an abomination. If I were not his brother, I would not let him walk another day on this earth, but since he is blood, there is little I can do. He desires taking over the Council as well."

I nodded. "Malcolm has always wanted Collin and I out of the way—that isn't news. It's his fixation on Victoria that is forcing my hand."

"I understand. There's nothing I wouldn't do to protect what is mine." Malikai once again glanced over at his bodyguard.

"Will you tell him of our meeting?" I asked.

"No, it would not be in my best interest or Austin's. My brother is aware of our relationship and will use him to get back at me if I displease him."

"Malikai, I do not wish to bring you or your family harm, but I must deal with your brother."

"I understand. You have my word. Should something tragic happen to end his life and I ascend to the head of the Moriat house, you will not need to fear retaliation. The peace between the Moriat and Carrington houses will stand."

"Thank you."

"Good luck, Caleb. For your sake and Victoria's, I hope you are able to resolve this situation quickly and permanently."

His words were not lost on me.

*

"So, he's on our side, in a sense." Blake sighed once Caleb had finished speaking. Now done, he devoured the plate before him.

"You're going to choke if you keep eating like that, Caleb," I scolded, my tone sharper than I intended. My nerves were on edge, and his story left me feeling tense.

"I'm sorry, sweetness. I'm famished and it's so good."

I frowned. "How can you taste it when you're shoveling it in your mouth?"

"It's good to know that he's on the same page as we are about his brother, even though he can't assist us. At least any action we take won't jeopardize the peace between our two houses," Collin interjected. "But this whole situation still disturbs me." I noticed how all of them were looking at me.

"I'll simply stay in the manor until you've dealt with him. He can't get me here, right?"

The silence was deafening. *I think I might be sick.*

Needing a distraction, I grabbed Caleb's plate and headed for the kitchen.

"Wait...I wasn't done," Caleb pouted.

*

In moments, we could all hear the clang of dishes and silverware as Victoria began cleaning.

"She's terrified." Serena sighed, tears welling in her eyes. "Is she safe here?"

"Yes," I answered, "although I know being confined to the manor will drive her insane."

"What are we going to do?" Collin asked.

"Tonight, nothing. Collin, you're welcome to stay in one of the guest rooms if you'd like. I'm going to go calm my mate down and make sure she doesn't break every dish in the house."

"Master, should I assist?" Talin jumped at every crash from the kitchen.

"Let me handle her. Once she's upstairs, you can see if she's done any damage. Don't worry, Talin. Plates can be replaced."

"Yes, master, as you wish." He sighed. Galia rubbed her mate's back.

"We'll head home." Serena kissed my cheek as they headed out. "Call us if you need anything."

"Good luck." Blake winked.

"I think I'll take you up on that offer, brother. Talin, while he deals with the crazy going on in the kitchen, why don't you show me which room you'd prefer I take?" Collin wrapped an arm around Talin's shoulders, trying to distract the distraught demon. Galia whispered comforting words in his ear as they led him to the guest room.

I entered the kitchen. Victoria was washing dishes by hand, drying them, and placing them in the cabinets with a *bit* too much force. Nothing seemed to be broken, but it was only a matter of time.

"Sweetness, you're going to drive Talin into an insane asylum if you keep slamming everything." I picked up a towel and offered to dry the dish she was rinsing off.

Victoria sighed. "I'm sorry, Caleb. I guess my nerves are all in knots. I've been so worried about you all night and now hearing that even Malcolm's own brother fears for my life…It's too much."

"I know, but I promise I won't let him harm you."

"Can you really make that promise, Caleb?" she snipped. I growled, my fangs elongating. "I'm sorry. I know how strong you are and the twins and everyone else but…he's evil, Caleb, and evil always finds a way. Trust me, I know."

Thoughts of her parents filled her mind. They weren't the same evil as Malcolm, but they were evil in their own way. No one acknowledged how they treated her, nor did anyone stop them. They found a way to continue meeting their own selfish needs—and it still haunted her.

"Your parents were different, sweetness."

She frowned. "You were in my head again."

"You were thinking very loudly, my love." I tucked a loose strand of hair behind her ear and took another dish to dry.

"I lost focus."

"It's okay. You never have to hide your thoughts from me."

Victoria paused as she rinsed off the last dish. "Caleb, what do I do? Staying in the manor will drive me crazy. I'll do it if I must, but am I safe? Can he get me here?"

I sighed. "He would be a fool to try, but I would be lying if I said that I didn't have a small doubt. As you say, evil always finds a way, but it would be extremely hard. I'm thinking of having Bastian and Darin move into the manor for a while. They've been wanting to do some updates to the house they just bought. They can start those projects and use it as an excuse for living here. It won't raise any suspicions, and it will give us the extra security we need here at the manor."

Victoria wrapped her arms around my waist and hugged me tight. Her scent drifted up, filling my senses. It was laced with fear and fatigue. "I'm scared, Caleb."

"I know, sweetness, but you're safe now. I can tell you're tired. Let's go to bed. Talin will be back down, and he can take care of the rest. It will do his nerves good to see that the kitchen isn't in shambles."

Victoria laughed at herself. "I guess I was making a lot of noise."

As we left the kitchen, we ran into the distraught demon. Victoria immediately hugged him. "I'm so sorry for worrying you, Talin. Nothing was broken, I promise. I've done all the dishes except for the pans I used. I'm sorry to leave them for you."

"Please, mistress, it is no trouble. I understand how you're feeling. Galia and I are here for you." He hugged her back before heading into the kitchen to finish tidying up.

"He's very fond of you," I assured her.

Victoria nodded. "The feeling is mutual."

"You're a very odd human, my love."

"Odd?" she pouted.

I laughed. "Unique, exquisite, kind…"

"Keep going, old man."

I chuckled as I scooped her into my arms and bounded up the stairs to our bedchamber.

*

Caleb ran a bath and insisted I take a moment to let the warm water ease my tension. He was right. I was exhausted. Worrying had strained me more than I realized, and now that he was home, the release of that stress brought with it a deep fatigue. I stepped out of the bath, dried off, and put on a short nightgown. Caleb was already in bed waiting for me.

"Come, my sweetness." He held his arms open for me.

I crawled into bed, resting my head on his chest. He enfolded me in his muscular embrace, rubbing small circles along my back.

"Mmm…that feels good."

"Sleep now, my love." He pressed a kiss to my lips and snuggled us deeper under the covers.

The warmth of his arms, the softness of the sheets, and that glorious scent of his all lulled me to sleep within minutes.

Chapter Twenty-Six

"Serena, what a nice surprise." I hugged my friend as I let her in the front door.

"How are you doing, Victoria?"

"Going a little stir crazy, to be honest. I feel like I'm on house arrest even though Caleb keeps telling me to go out. Let's sit in the kitchen. I'll make tea."

"You can't stay cooped up in this house forever, little one. He's right, we should go out for lunch."

I was about to decline when Caleb entered. "Yes, you should, and I'll drive you. Bastian and Darin are already at headquarters. I'll have Bastian meet you at the restaurant."

"But…"

"I'm not listening." Caleb covered his ears.

I laughed at his childish gesture. "And how old are we?" I teased him.

"Hey, respect your elders."

Serena looked at us with an amused expression on her face.

"What are you laughing at, Serena?" Caleb asked, arching an eyebrow at her.

"I never thought I'd see the day when the grumpy, overly serious Caleb Carrington would be joking and laughing like you are right now.

Congratulations Victoria, you may have made the most stoic vampire to ever exist a tad bit human." She winked.

Caleb scoffed. "I can be fun."

"Now, now, my love, don't pout…even though you look absolutely adorable when you do." I kissed his cheek.

Caleb changed the subject. "So, what brings you by, Serena? Surely not to antagonize me?"

"No. As much fun as that is, I came to share this with you and Victoria." She indicated a file in her hands. "I met with Stuart over in archives and he gave me some information regarding the strange experiences Victoria has had with human men."

I leaned forward. "What did he learn?"

"There's only one similar case in our records." Serena handed the file to Caleb, who began flipping through its contents. "The woman was also a seer and had an incredibly unique and strong pheromone output, much higher than the average human. Reports say she experienced similar reactions until she was matched with her human mate. After their union, the problem stopped."

Caleb frowned. "He also reported that this is a common reaction of human males to Fae females."

Serena shrugged. "I didn't think it was worth mentioning since we know that's not possible."

Caleb continued, "I also recognize the name in this file. She was from one of the original human families. Victoria is her direct descendent on her mother's side."

"Really?" I stood and peered into the file.

"She was your great-grandmother. I never knew her, but I recognize her name from the Book of Family Trees."

"The Book of Family Trees?"

"The head of the Council is responsible for updating it with any changes that occur in the human families that have contracts with us. It's a way to ensure that bloodlines don't get too close and helps us determine if we need to recruit additional human bloodlines." I crinkled my nose. "I agree, sweetness, it wasn't my favorite part of the job but it's necessary if our plan is going to continue. If it makes you feel any better, we also track changes in the vampire families too."

"I guess it makes sense, but in that way, everything sounds so deliberate. Love should be spontaneous and natural."

"Vampires are sort of known for being meticulous." Serena giggled.

"Now that Caleb has marked me as his mate, I shouldn't have any issues?"

Serena nodded. I frowned as I chewed my bottom lip. I wasn't convinced.

"Sweetness, you don't look satisfied. What's wrong?"

"There were instances before where someone wasn't affected, like when I first met Greggory. He showed no signs of lustful intent toward me."

"He was already mated to me at the time."

"Okay, that makes sense. What about you, or Collin and the boys? There was another chef I worked with at Tangi's before Collin found me. He was my apprentice and we spent a lot of time with each other, but he never tried anything. As a matter of fact, neither did Nicholas, the owner. Although Thomas wasn't interested in girls. Could that have been a reason?"

"Vampires don't react to human pheromones in the same way, so it's not surprising they weren't impacted by this. As for the other humans..." Serena shrugged. "Those reasons are plausible. I could ask Stuart what he thinks, or even Felix in human studies. Were either of them in a serious relationship? Perhaps they had already found their true mate."

"Nicholas had lost his wife years before I met him, so that's possible. Thomas was single but he had a huge crush on one of the other employees."

"I'm sure you no longer need to worry about this, sweetness." Caleb kissed the top of my head, but his eyes still held their own concern. I decided not to press him. "All right ladies, I'm ready to leave when you are. Bastian can bring you home."

"Will you be working late again tonight?"

"Not tonight, my love. Tonight, I plan to have dinner with my beautiful mate and take a walk in the gardens. The moon will be full, and it's supposed to be clear and warm."

I beamed. It felt like ages since we had dinner and walked together. A menu was already taking shape in my mind. "I'll have to prepare something special then."

Caleb grinned. "I'm looking forward to it."

*

Lunch that afternoon was exactly what I needed. It was so nice to be out of the house, and it lifted the dark cloud in my mind. Serena and I enjoyed each other's company and even ran into Celeste and Danica, two of my newest friends. As we were finishing our meals, a serious expression overtook Serena's face.

"Serena, is everything okay?"

She blushed. "Yes, everything is fantastic."

"You're scaring me. First you looked like you were about to vomit and now you're glowing. Spill it!"

Serena leaned in closer and whispered, "Greggory and I are expecting."

"*What*? Seriously?" I nearly jumped out of my chair.

Serena and Greggory had been trying for years to have a child. They weren't sure it was possible after all the treatments he went through, but they had never lost hope.

"Sshh…Victoria, not so loud." She blushed even harder as all eyes in the restaurant turned on us.

"Serena, really…when are you due?"

"I just finished my first trimester. We were waiting before we told anyone."

"I'm thrilled beyond words for the both of you." I hugged her tightly. "I can't believe we are going to have a little one in the family. Does anyone else know?"

"No, you're the first person we've told."

I gasped. "I'm honored. Can I tell Caleb tonight at dinner?"

"Of course. Greggory is going to tell everyone during tomorrow's weekly meeting, so make sure Caleb doesn't spoil the surprise for the others."

"This is amazing. We need to plan your baby shower and get you registered. Have you decided on names?"

"Not yet. We aren't going to find out the gender until the baby arrives."

"Why don't we have Bastian bring us into town? We can start your baby registry and get ideas for the nursery." I paused. "Oh, I'm sorry, am I overstepping? Greggory probably wants to do all of this with you."

"Actually, he told me to take you. He's not fond of shopping, and I think he's secretly hoping it will rub off on you."

I blushed. "Serena, Caleb and I only recently confessed to each other, and he just marked me. I don't think children are on the list for our near future."

"I'm sorry, you're right. I didn't mean to pressure you. Things are so new for the two of you."

"Right now, it's all about you and your little bundle of joy. Let's go shopping!"

*

Serena and I spent the afternoon browsing a local store, picking out the crib and bedding she would need and completing her registry. I even bought a few yellow and green outfits that I couldn't resist.

"Now you have something to hang in the baby's closet."

"Victoria, you're going to spoil this child before they are even born."

"That's what aunties do." I winked.

"Well, this baby has the best auntie ever!"

"You hear that, little one? Auntie Victoria is the best!" I whispered to Serena's belly.

Bastian followed behind us with an amused expression on his face. After dropping Serena off at home, we headed to the market.

"Bastian, thank you for today. I'm sorry if it hasn't been fun for you."

"Actually, I found it rather entertaining to watch the two of you cooing over every little thing."

I giggled. "Maybe Frosty wasn't an accurate nickname for you. Should I change it to Softy?"

"Do that and no one will ever find your body." He did his best to look menacing.

I gasped in feigned fright, then laughed. "Don't worry, Frosty. Your secret is safe with me."

Bastian smiled and wrapped his arm around my shoulders, giving me a quick hug. "What are you making for dinner tonight?"

"I'm thinking of starting off with potato and leek soup followed by a roasted beet salad, and for the main dish, ginger sesame chicken with jasmine rice and steamed broccoli. What do you think?" As if on cue, Bastian's stomach growled. "I guess that's my answer."

He blushed. "Sorry, I skipped lunch."

"You're more than welcome to join us."

"Oh no! I don't think Caleb would appreciate it if I did. He was so happy yesterday, going on all day about how he doesn't have to work late tonight." He winked. "I'm not going to get in the way of him spending time with his mate."

"Oh!" It was my turn to blush. "Well, at least stay until I've finished cooking. I'll make enough for you and Darin to have together."

"He'll be thrilled."

"Tell him to give any thanks he has to you." I winked.

His face reddened even further. "Once we get packed up and are staying in the manor, you're going to fatten us up, aren't you?"

I laughed. "It won't be my fault if you eat too much."

"Really? Maybe I'll just have Talin restrict you from entering the kitchen."

"He would never. Besides, Darin would be miserable if I can't make him lasagna while you're with us."

"Ah, hitting me in my soft spot. Only you can do that."

I linked my arm through his and we laughed.

"I know it was hard for you in the beginning, Victoria, but I'm really glad you're here with us now." He bent and planted a quick kiss on the top of my head and ruffled my hair.

I smiled up at him. "Me too."

Chapter Twenty-Seven

I wrapped up my business calls early and was heading out of headquarters when I ran into Malcolm.

"Good evening, Caleb. What a fortuitous surprise running into you this evening."

"Malcolm." I greeted him with no emotion.

"How is my beautiful pet? I haven't seen her in quite some time. Hopefully she's not ill. I must say, I miss hearing her voice and seeing her infectious smile."

My eyes glowed and simmered while my fangs descended. "You forget yourself, Malcolm."

"Do I? Indeed, you must forgive me—I meant no disrespect. I only wish to inquire about Miss Starling's wellbeing."

"Miss Starling is no concern of yours."

"On the contrary, my old friend." Malcolm leaned in close. "She is very much my concern. I intend to make her my mate in the very near future."

I smiled, glaring at the vampire before me. "Well ol' boy." I clapped a hand on Malcolm's shoulder, making him wince. "It seems a Moriat once again has been bested by a Carrington. My mark looks resplendent on her flawless skin." I turned my back on him, a wicked grin on my face.

Ah, that felt good.

"It's not often I'm surprised…You'll pay for that, Caleb Carrington. I will take her from you. If I can't have her, then neither will you."

The solid wood door in front of me looked like all the other doors in the Moriat mansion, but this one was special. This door led to my sanctuary, the place I felt most comfortable, most alive. A place where I could be myself.

I turned the key, relishing in the soft click. The familiar tingle of excitement lanced down my spine as I closed the door behind me and headed down the stairs. The basement was dark, silent, and bereft of warmth. Several doors led to smaller rooms, all of which were vacant—except one.

Behind this specific door was my latest treasure, a cute little blonde I had picked up from a local tavern on the outskirts of the community. I couldn't remember her name and, truthfully, it was irrelevant. They were all the same to me…all except Victoria. She was different. She even smelled different. The minute I caught her scent at her *Legătura*, there was nothing I wanted more than to claim her, drive her fear to ultimate heights, and then drink her dry. I shivered at the thrilling thought of her warm, bitter blood trickling down my throat.

I shook my head. Now was not the time. I needed to focus on the girl before me. Her frightened expression when she learned vampires were real was still strong in my memory. The horror on her face now as I entered the room stimulated me more than any drug. I licked at my lips. The air tasted of her fear. The longer I kept her tied up in this tiny room, the stronger it grew. *Oh, how I adore my little haven.*

I had made sure her fear never faded, bringing her pleasure and pain in equal measures. It was the unknown of what she would receive that kept her blood bitter. I had planned on keeping her alive another week, but after running into Carrington, I needed to focus on my plans to capture my true desire: *Victoria.*

This pretty little cupcake would be a distraction, one I didn't need. Today, I would maximize her fear and then drain her fully. Garret, my personal guard, was already preparing to dispose of her body. What he did with them I never asked and didn't care, so long as they were never found, never tied back to me.

I closed the door and approached the table along the side of the room that held all my shiny metallic friends. She whimpered.

"How delightful. Now my little piglet, where shall we begin today?"

*

"I have news to share with you." I practically bounced in my seat. It had been hard to keep quiet about it until now.

"Oh, please do tell." Caleb smiled, taking another bite of his dinner. He had devoured the soup and salad like a man who hadn't eaten in weeks and was draining his second decanter of blood.

"First, may I ask, do you have a tape worm? You're eating like you haven't seen food or blood in weeks."

"I'm really enjoying dinner tonight. I had a very productive day at the office and I'm in a great mood, so I may be overindulging a bit. And I hope to keep overindulging all night long." He winked at me.

A blush warmed my face. "All right." I peered at him closer. His cheeks were bright red, while his eyes had a glassy film. "Can vampires get drunk on blood?"

"Uhm, it's not so much drunk as euphoric. Perhaps I should slow down or you'll be carrying me up to bed tonight."

"Oh I don't think so, darling. You're way too heavy for me to carry. You'll have to lay where you fall."

Caleb pouted and poured himself a glass of water. "So what was this news you were going to tell me?"

"Oh, right. Serena told me something wonderful while we were at lunch today. She and Greggory are expecting!"

"Expecting what?" Caleb shoveled another bite of dinner into his mouth.

"Honestly, Caleb! They are expecting a baby."

"Really? I know they've been trying for years. I wonder why Greggory didn't say anything when I saw him at the office earlier."

"He's waiting until tomorrow's meeting to tell all of you at the same time so you can't say anything before then, got it?"

"Mmhmm."

"Caleb, are you listening to me?"

"Yes sweetness, I heard you. Don't say anything to anyone."

I shook my head and watched Caleb out of the corner of my eye. My curiosity getting the better of me, I asked, "What are your feelings on children?"

"They're necessary."

My fork clattered onto the table, causing him to look up from his plate.

"Well, they are, Victoria. I mean, how else does a race continue to flourish?"

"That's a little cold, don't you think? Have you never wanted children of your own?"

"You're asking me that, knowing I never intended to take a mate?"

"And now that you have?" Silence. "Caleb?"

"What do you want me to say?"

"Nothing." I stood, pushing my chair back so hard it tipped over. "I don't want you to say anything." I threw my napkin down on the table and stormed from the room out onto the terrace.

I crossed my arms. *Why am I so angry? What had I expected him to say?*

Of course he had never intended to take a mate. Caleb most likely didn't want children, had never planned to have them. It was foolish of me to think that simply because he marked me, his feelings would change. *But why wouldn't they? Is it that important to me to have children? Do I want children?*

I had never really thought about it before my conversation with Serena, but we hadn't been careful since our first night together.

What would he think if I were pregnant? Would he be happy, angry... indifferent?

I paced on the terrace until a familiar scent drifted toward me, instantly calming me.

"Sweetness?" Caleb walked up behind me and wrapped his arms around my waist. I didn't answer him, but I also didn't pull away. "I've upset you, haven't I?"

I shrugged.

"Victoria, talk to me."

"What would you like me to say?" I threw his words back at him and felt him wince.

"That came out wrong. It's not what I really wanted to say."

I turned to face him. "Then tell me what you really meant."

He pinched the bridge of his nose. "I guess…I never thought about children. Never considered them to be a part of my future or a possibility since I had never intended to take a mate."

"Other pureblood vampires have children without taking a mate. Why didn't you?"

Caleb sighed. "If I were going to sire children, I wanted a family. When we realized that too many vampires had been killed and we would have to mate with humans to survive, I gave up that dream."

"Why did you hate humans so much? Is it because of all the killings?"

"Yes, and because of my pride. A group of hunters killed my parents when I was young, and I had to take over as head of the Carrington clan and the Council. I did what was best for my race, but I was blindly attached to my convictions. I swore I would never take a human as a mate. Even though I was asking others to do what I couldn't, I never mourned the dreams I was sacrificing. Time passed and I thought about it less and less until there wasn't even a glimmer of that dream left."

"That's incredibly sad, Caleb. Didn't you have relationships with women in the past?"

"Of course, but nothing serious." He blushed. "I never put love as a priority in my life, but that changed."

"What made you change your mind?"

"You." He gazed down into my eyes and ran a long finger along my cheek. "You came along and turned my world and all of my beliefs upside down."

"Are you saying that your dream of a family is coming alive?"

"I'm saying that it's becoming more of a possibility."

I hugged him close. "Caleb, I'm sorry I was angry. To be truthful, I don't know how I feel about having children either. I've been so focused on my career I never really thought about it. I suppose in my own way, like you, I had given up on that dream. While I know I'm not my parents, I spent more time mourning the childhood I never had rather than thinking of bringing someone into this world. When I was on the run, I never knew when I would have to pick up and start over—what kind of life would that have been for a child? Things have moved so fast for us, and I just want to spend time getting to know you."

"Then let's focus on taking things one day at a time and letting nature run its course. There are a few things I'd like to do before we even plan on starting a family."

"Such as?"

"For one, we have a certain pest that must be dealt with...and...I haven't asked you to marry me yet."

I looked up into his eyes, not daring to breathe. *Did he say he wants to marry me?*

Caleb kissed me and held me tightly. "We will be married, sweetness, but I need to take care of Malcolm first."

My eyes grew misty. "Caleb, nothing would make me happier than to be your wife. I'm not in any rush. It's enough to be here with you in your arms every night."

"Victoria, I don't think I can wait until after our walk to take you tonight."

I cupped his cheeks and pulled his face to mine, kissing him soundly. I nipped on his bottom lip with my teeth and flicked it with my tongue, begging for entrance. His lips parted and our tongues met in their familiar dance. We stayed like that until we couldn't breathe, breaking only when he scooped me into his arms and flew up the stairs to our bedchamber.

"I hope you're prepared, sweetness. I'm going to love you until the sun rises," he growled with a burning passion I had never heard in his voice.

"Challenge accepted." I sucked on the soft area behind his ear, leaving the tiniest of marks.

Caleb's eyes glowed as he kicked open the bedroom door and headed straight for our bed.

CHAPTER TWENTY-EIGHT

"Mistress Victoria, I'm going into town today. Is there anything you need?" Talin asked as he washed the dishes from breakfast.

"Actually, would you mind if I tagged along?"

"Not at all. Is there somewhere in particular you wanted to go?"

"Yes, I ordered a book and it should have arrived at Novellas by now."

"You'll need to take Bastian with you." Caleb looked up from his coffee cup. "I have a meeting with Collin this morning."

"Where am I going now?" Bastian asked walking into the kitchen.

"Talin is headed into town and I want to tag along with him."

Bastian poured himself a cup of coffee and leaned against the counter. "Where the princess goes, I go." He winked.

I wrinkled my nose at him.

Caleb chuckled and stood to hand his empty cup to Talin. "I'm entrusting my love with the two of you today." He leaned down and kissed my forehead.

"I'll be fine. I have the best bodyguards in the world." Talin snickered in embarrassment at my compliment. "Will you be late tonight, Caleb?"

"No, actually, I might beat you home."

"That would be a first. I'm glad to hear it."

Caleb waved farewell and headed off to headquarters for his meeting with Collin.

"Let me grab my things and I'll be ready to go when you are." I headed up the stairs to grab my purse and phone. Once I came back down, we piled into Bastian's car and drove into the center of town.

"Talin, where do you need to go?" Bastian asked.

"The cleaners, then the tea shop."

"Oh that's good. The bookstore is right next door to the tea shop. While Talin goes there, I can pop into Novellas to pick up my book."

Bastian chuckled. "Princess, when have you ever just *popped* into the bookstore? You're worse than Caleb."

"If someone weren't with her every time she goes, we'd have to put out a missing person's report." Talin snickered from the back seat.

"Hmph…you two aren't being very nice," I pouted.

"Mistress, we are only teasing you. I hope you aren't offended."

I huffed and turned my nose up. "I'm not talking to either one of you."

Both men looked at each other, then all three of us started laughing.

"Why don't we drop you off at the cleaners? It's a block away, correct?" Bastian suggested.

"Yes. I'm only picking up a few of Master Caleb's shirts, so I can meet you at Novellas."

"Perfect. That way our little one can spend some time in her happy place." Bastian winked at me.

"You're too kind, Frosty." I winked back.

He chuckled.

Bastian parked the car in front of the bookstore after dropping Talin off. As we climbed out, his cell phone rang. He answered it and asked the person on the other end to wait a moment. "Princess, why don't you head in and I'll meet you in there once I'm done. It shouldn't take long."

"Are you sure you don't want me to wait for you?"

"I won't take my eyes off the front door, and it's not a very big shop. The checkout desk is right in front. Ask Mr. Norton if anyone else is in the store.

If he says yes, then come back out here immediately."

"All right."

I headed into the bookstore. It was so quiet and peaceful inside. The smell of books mixed with freshly brewed coffee filled my senses with a calm joy.

"Victoria!" A lively gentleman popped out from behind the front desk.

"Mr. Norton, how are you?" I smiled.

"Victoria, how many times do I need to remind you to call me Nathan?"

I giggled. "It just doesn't seem right, but if you insist. How are you, Nathan?"

Nathan Norton was a pureblood vampire almost twice as old as Caleb and the only remaining member of his bloodline. He deserved to be addressed with more formality, but Nathan was a kindhearted man who had no use for titles.

"I am doing so much better now that I've seen your smile." He gave me a quick hug. "The book you ordered arrived. Shall I go fetch it from the back?"

"Yes please..." I looked around. "Nathan, before you go, is there anyone else in the store at the moment?"

Nathan frowned, clearly confused why I would ask such a question. "No, you have the place to yourself. There are some new arrivals in the fiction section that I stocked yesterday."

"Wonderful. I'll head over and check them out."

The fiction section was in the back corner of the shop. I eased through the long narrow aisles. This wasn't my favorite area of the store. The air seemed stagnant here, which was more eerie than calming. Besides that, the tall shelves, while they could hold many books, blocked out most of the store's light. I had to lean in closer to peruse the new titles. One in particular caught my attention. *Death on the Tundra.*

A chill skittered down my spine. *Don't be childish, Victoria. It's just a book.* A sudden cold breeze enveloped me, and my breath turned to fog. I shivered again.

"Hmm, it's nice to know I have that effect on you, my pet."

I turned around and was face to face with Malcolm. His ice blue eyes shimmered despite the low lighting.

"H-How did you get in here?" I glanced toward the front of the store. The door wasn't visible from this corner, and the shop had no back exit. "Did you hurt Bastian?"

"Your incompetent bodyguard is fine, but he's not the one you should be concerned with, my pet."

"I told you I'm not your pet." I placed two hands on his chest to push him away. It was like trying to move a mountain…damn vampires and their strength.

Malcolm took one of my hands in his and began kissing the tips of my fingers. "Delightful," he purred.

"S-Stop!" Tremors racked my body.

Malcolm sniffed at the air. "Yes, your fear is intoxicating. I can't get enough of it. I really want to know what it tastes like." He leaned in and sniffed at my neck, tracing the finger of his other hand around the shell of my ear, then down my neck and collarbone.

"You're too late, Malcolm. I bear Caleb's mark."

Malcolm hissed in my ear, "I can see that, and Carrington was overly pleased to inform me of that little fact the last time I saw him. No matter, it is a minor inconvenience. Make no mistake, my sweet Victoria, you will be mine. I will have you when the time is right. You aren't quite ready, my pet, but you're close. The fear grows each time I touch you. I suspect the next time we meet, you will be at your most delicious, and I will savor every single drop." He licked the cold sweat beading on my neck and kissed my earlobe.

"Go a-away," I sobbed.

"As my pet commands."

In a flash, he was gone. I sank to the floor, pulling my knees into my chest. My body felt cold. I couldn't stop shaking.

*

I finished my call and headed into the bookstore. Mr. Norton was at the front desk.

"She went back to the fiction section." He pointed to the far corner.

"Thank you, Mr. Norton. Anyone else in here?"

"Only Victoria. And please, Bastian, call me Nathan."

"No can do, Mr. Norton." I winked at the elder vampire. "If my father were alive, he'd box my ears for being disrespectful to my elders."

Nathan chuckled. "Cheeky boy."

I squeezed through the aisles, pulling in my arms to avoid knocking books off the shelves. For a moment, I thought I went to the wrong corner. Then I saw her. Victoria was huddled on the floor, sobbing. The air smelled bitter and strangely of sulfur.

I dropped to her side, kneeling before her. "Victoria, what happened? Are you hurt?" She looked into my eyes. They were filled with fear.

"He was here, Bastian. I don't know how he got in, but he was here and then he... *vanished.*"

"Malcolm?" She nodded. "Did he hurt you?"

"No, I think he was here to try and scare me...It worked."

She was shaking uncontrollably. I held her, rubbing small circles on her back and trying to give her warmth. Her body was freezing, her face pink from cold.

"I'm sorry, Victoria. I should have been in here with you."

"It's not your fault."

"Yes, it is. I never should have let you come in here alone. I promise I will not leave your side again, not until Caleb has dealt with him."

"I want to go home."

I nodded and helped her up. "Do you think you can walk out of here?"

She wiped the tears from her cheeks and smoothed her hair. "Yes, I have to. I don't want Nathan to know what happened in here."

Once she regained her composure, we walked to the front of the store where I collected the book she ordered. We wished Mr. Norton well and headed back to the car. If he suspected anything, he didn't mention it.

Talin was waiting by the car when we stepped outside. He sensed something wrong immediately and flew to Victoria. "Mistress Victoria, are you all right? What happened?"

"Malcolm paid me a visit."

Talin hugged her close. "Did he hurt you?"

"No."

"How did he get in the store?" Talin looked at me.

"I'm not sure. I didn't take my eyes off the front door." The glare the demon shot me made me shiver.

Victoria came to my rescue. "He appeared out of nowhere and vanished just as quickly."

"Did if feel colder after he left?" Talin's brow wrinkled. His focus shifted back to her.

"Yes." She nodded. "It was freezing. And there was a strange smell."

"Sulfur," I added, meeting Talin's gaze.

A low growl rumbled in Talin's throat. "Demon magic."

"That was my thought as well." I opened the car door for her, and we drove home in silence.

*

Caleb was already home when we arrived back at the manor. One look at me and he knew something was wrong.

"Victoria?"

I ran into his arms, sobbing. "Malcolm cornered me in the bookstore."

Caleb looked up at the two men behind me. "What happened?" We all went into the living area and Bastian filled Caleb in on what took place.

"Master, I believe he used demon magic to get inside the bookstore unnoticed," Talin interjected.

Caleb held me closer. "Victoria, did you see him enter or leave?"

I shook my head. "No, I was alone and then suddenly he was there and vanished just as quick."

Caleb frowned.

Bastian knelt before Caleb and I. "This is my fault. Please Victoria, forgive me for not protecting you. Caleb, I vow I will not fail you again. I will not leave Victoria's side until we have rid the community of this monster."

"Bastian, get up." Caleb clapped a hand on his friend's shoulder. "There's no way any of us could have known he would have the resources to use demon magic. It's not an easy task for anyone other than a demon. Talin, do the Moriats have any demons in their employ?"

"Not that I'm aware, master. I will ask around and find out. The spell needed is complicated and would have required the assistance of a very powerful demon. He most likely didn't act alone."

"Look into it and let me know what you learn."

He bowed. "Mistress, I'll make you some chamomile and lavender tea. It will help calm you."

"Thank you, Talin."

Bastian stood. "Caleb, if you're home for the day, I'm going to do some investigating of my own." Caleb nodded his approval.

When we were alone, Caleb leaned back and pulled me into his lap. Covering me with a throw blanket, he kissed the top of my head.

"Victoria, rest for now. You're home and safe. You can tell me what he said later."

My hands fisted the blanket as a fresh onslaught of tears threatened to spill over. "He knows you marked me. He said it doesn't matter..."

"Shh...rest." He covered my eyes with his hand. My eyes fluttered as I tried to fight his power. "Don't resist me, sweetness...*sleep.*"

*

Talin brought in a tray with a teapot and two cups. "I see the mistress is asleep."

"Yes. I thought it was best for her right now."

"Master, you must eliminate this problem." Talin's eyes darkened.

"I know...he won't leave her be until I do. Perhaps I need to reach out to Malikai again. We both wanted to avoid a war between our houses, but we may not have a choice."

His eyes glowed crimson. "There are ways to eliminate him without your involvement."

"Talin, I know you have pledged yourself to this house and I appreciate your offer and how you feel, but I would never ask that of you. It goes against everything you stand for and all you've done to distance yourself from that life."

"I will not let him harm her." A low growl rumbled in his throat.

"I will take care of this matter. There is no need to go to such extreme."

Talin brushed a lock of hair from Victoria's brow with his fingertips. "My loyalty and my life are hers as well, master. I will protect her like family."

I smiled. "Thank you for your vow, Talin. I know Victoria loves you like family as well and would never want you to go against your beliefs, even for her sake. Trust me."

"As you wish, master, but the offer stands…should it be needed."

I nodded, understanding exactly what that would entail. He left the room to attend to other duties. Normally Victoria cooked the household dinner, but tonight I would insist she rest.

*

No one had seen Malcolm since the incident at the bookstore. Malikai told Caleb he left a note that he would be traveling for business. Caleb and the others weren't convinced. Talin hadn't been able to find a possible connection between the Moriat house and a demon, but he still believed Malcolm had somehow contracted with one to help him appear in the bookstore unnoticed, so Bastian remained my companion whenever I left the manor.

I felt bad about Bastian becoming my full-time bodyguard, despite the number of times he assured me it wasn't a problem. It was bringing us closer, something that I sensed was weighing on Darin. They had been living at the manor for a few months, and I think the lack of alone time was starting to make my friend lonely.

"Darin, will you take a walk with me?" I asked him one afternoon.

"Sure." He followed me, Bastian in tow.

"Bastian, I think I'll be safe with Darin. Why don't you take a break?" I winked at him. Bastian nodded and sat back down on the couch to watch television.

"What's up, Victoria?" Darin asked once we left the manor.

I smiled. "Does something need to be up for me to spend some time with you?"

"No, but I can sense your thoughts are racing."

"I've never been able to hide anything from you," I pouted.

Darin chuckled. "I don't know what you're thinking so you're getting better at it, but I can tell something is on your mind."

"Okay...there is something I wanted to ask you. Are you all right?"

"I'm fine, why do you ask?"

"Darin, this is me. Something is bothering you, now out with it." I linked my arm through his so he couldn't run away.

"It's silly."

"Nothing is silly if it's upsetting you." I paused. "It's about Bastian and I, isn't it?"

Darin looked at me in shock. "Victoria, please don't get the wrong idea..."

"It's okay, Darin, I get it. You miss him. We've been spending a lot of time together, so I can understand you being jealous."

"You can?" Darin exhaled. "I don't know why I feel like this. There's nothing to be worried about."

"But you can't help it...You know, Caleb is going through something similar. He and I had to talk about it again last night. Even though he knows there's nothing more happening, he gets jealous of the extra time Bastian spends with me. I imagine that's what you're feeling too." Darin nodded. "He's completely head over heels for you, and he misses you too. So, there's something I want you to help me with tonight."

"Uh-oh, I sense one of your plans. What did you do?"

I grinned. "Yep, and it's a good one. Let's go back to the house."

*

Back in the living room, I flew to Bastian and pulled him to his feet, placing him next to Darin. I then handed him an envelope.

"What's this?" He frowned.

"It's your assignment for tonight." I smiled.

224

Bastian opened it. His eyes widened in surprise. "Victoria?"

At their shock, I practically bounced on my toes and clapped my hands. "Are you excited? Now if you both hurry and change, you should make your reservations with time to spare."

"We can't accept this!" Darin gasped.

"You promised you would help me tonight. That means no arguing and making sure he doesn't argue either." I planted my hands on my hips. "I worked hard to get that reservation for the two of you. You have no idea what I had to promise Celeste, so don't you dare try to back out."

Bastian was still stunned. "Horizons is the most exclusive restaurant in town. It takes months to get a reservation and you have to know someone."

"And you do know someone…me. Now off with you, get changed. You have to wear a jacket and tie." I pushed them toward the stairs. "Go, or you'll be late."

"Victoria?" Darin turned to me, his eyes glistening. "Thank you."

"Thank me by going and having a good time together. You both deserve this date. And don't worry about me. Caleb should be home soon, so I won't be alone. Now shoo!"

Bastian and Darin beamed at each other and headed off to the guest quarters to get ready for their date. I ushered them out of the house quick in case they tried to protest further. While I waited for Caleb, I pulled out my computer. Serena's baby shower had been the week before, and I had put off going through all the photos. My hope was to sort through them and create a keepsake album for her. I also needed to organize the gift list so we could work on getting her thank-you notes completed.

Not only did she and Greggory receive everything they registered for, but they were gifted a special visit from Fiona, the High Priestess of the witches. Fiona had come to bestow a special blessing on Serena so that she would have an easy delivery. It was mostly ceremonial, but I could tell by the way my friend's face lit up that she had been feeling anxious about the process.

Fiona sought me out after the gift exchange. "Victoria dear, it's such a pleasure to meet the woman who was able to capture this petulant ol' vampire's heart."

"So, you noticed how grumpy he is too?" I laughed.

"Tell me, how did you manage it?"

"I used the right bait." I glanced sideways at the subject of our torment. He seemed just as eager to hear the answer as Fiona.

"Really? Do tell."

"Food and moonlit walks."

Fiona laughed. "Oh, many broken-hearted females are going to be sad to learn it was that easy. Good for you, my dear. If he gives you any trouble, let me know. I have a few spells I can teach you."

"I think we are going to be great friends, Fiona."

Caleb huffed.

Unfortunately, my time with the High Priestess was cut short when she received word she was needed for urgent coven business. In the brief time we spent together, I had taken a real liking to her. She was straightforward, honest, and had a devilish sense of humor, which I found delightful.

*

Over the next few weeks, Caleb and I spent more time together. His work often kept him in the office late, but those nights had become rarer. I was getting used to being out of the house more often with Bastian by my side. Occasionally, Blake or Collin would accompany me, but the days I loved most was when Caleb took a full day off and we spent the day together. That morning, I convinced him to help me spruce up the flower boxes on the terrace.

"You really love to get your hands dirty, don't you, my love?" He chuckled.

"I guess so. I find it really relaxing. It's the same with cooking."

"I don't know how you find cooking relaxing. I've never been more stressed than that night you asked me to help you."

I laughed, remembering how flustered he had gotten. "You simply don't like being told what to do."

"Well, you were barking at me," he pouted.

"I wasn't barking…at least, that wasn't my intention. I guess I'm used to issuing orders in a kitchen. I'm sorry if it sounded like I was yelling at you."

"I think I'll stick to clean up."

"You mean eating?"

"That too." He chuckled. "It's my favorite part."

I stood, wiping my forehead. "I think this one is done. What do you think?"

Caleb didn't look at the box. "Beautiful." He tucked a stray hair behind my ear.

"I'm talking about the flowers."

"Hmm…yes, that too." He leaned forward and kissed me warmly, parting my lips with his tongue.

I wrapped my arms around his neck and pulled him close, melting into his embrace as he lowered us onto the ground. The smooth stones warmed my back. He showered me with kisses, stealing my breath and nipping at my bottom lip.

"Don't you have a bedroom for that sort of thing?"

Sighing, we both turned to see Collin standing outside the doorway.

"Your brother has the worst timing," I whispered.

"This better be good, Collin."

"Sorry to interrupt you two love birds, but I thought you would want to know that Serena has gone into labor."

"When?!" I exclaimed, shoving Caleb off me despite his grumbling. We untangled ourselves and pulled each other up to standing.

"Greggory called. He said they are on the way to the hospital now. Her contractions are really close, so they don't expect it will be long before the little tyke is here."

"We have to go!" I turned to Caleb, tearing the gloves from my hands and trying to straighten my hair.

"My car is out front," Collin offered. "After you, my goddess."

Collin drove us to the hospital. The nurse at the front desk informed us that Serena had been wheeled into the delivery room ten minutes prior, and Greggory was with her. They would let him know we were there, and we could expect to see him once the baby was born. Darin and the twins joined us in the waiting room shortly after.

Four hours later, an exhausted Greggory came out. The smile on his face told us both baby and Mom were doing well. I ran up to him, taking his hands in mine.

"It's a boy," he whispered. "I have a son."

I hugged him close, while Caleb and Collin patted him on the shoulders.

"Congratulations, I'm so happy for you. What's the little tiger's name?" Blake asked, shaking his friend's hand.

"We're calling him Victor." He smiled down at me.

I gasped and put a hand to my mouth. "Oh Greggory!"

"Serena is ready. Follow me. You can't stay long, but she wants you to meet him."

We filed silently down the hallway. When we entered the room, I immediately went to Serena's bedside and hugged her.

"Serena, congratulations." She kissed my cheek and showed me the baby. I sighed. "Oh, he's beautiful."

"Do you want to hold him?"

"May I?"

"Of course." Serena gently placed the sleeping boy in my arms. I began rocking him and cooing.

"Welcome, little prince. I'm Auntie Victoria." I felt a warmth behind me and looked to see Caleb staring down at me and the baby, a soft look in his eyes I had never seen before. "Isn't he precious? Look at his pudgy little cheeks and cute nose. He has the longest eyelashes I've ever seen. Serena, how are you feeling?"

"Tired, but it was worth it." She smiled at her husband, who was fussing over her pillows and blankets.

"Do you need anything, my dear? More pillows, another blanket, some water?"

"I'm good for now." She took his hand. He brought it to his lips and kissed her fingers.

One by one, the guys came over to see the new addition to our little family. When he started to fuss, I gave him back to his mom so she could feed him.

"We should go," I whispered to everyone. I kissed Serena's cheek. "I'll come back tomorrow to check in on you. Try to let Greggory hold him so you can rest."

Serena smiled at me. "I won't make any promises."

I waved to the new parents as we left.

*

Later that night as Caleb and I were getting ready for bed, I asked, "Serena looked good, didn't she?"

"She was practically glowing. Greggory too. I'm glad that all went well and everyone is healthy." As I stared out at the gardens from our balcony, he walked up behind me and wrapped his arms around my waist. "You looked quite comfortable holding Victor in your arms."

"He felt so tiny. He looks like Greggory."

"I agree." He frowned at my sigh. "Victoria, are you okay?"

I turned and laced my fingers around the back of his neck. "Yes, I find new life so amazing. To think that two people can create such a little miracle. They've wanted this for so long, and I'm grateful they've been given this blessing of a healthy baby boy...one that wouldn't have happened if you hadn't stepped in all those years ago and did what was needed to save your kind. Do you feel a sense of delight each time a child is born?"

"I don't know I've ever thought of it that way before." He looked at me in wonder. "The plan I put in place, while it achieved its goal of keeping vampire bloodlines from going extinct, removed some of the joy of two people finding love spontaneously and creating life. I guess love found a way to survive."

"You've carried a heavy burden all these years, haven't you?"

"In a manner of speaking, I suppose. Although thinking on it now, most of the unions from the *Legăturas* have had happy endings. Even the humans that used them to find work in our community are happy and free to find love in their own way."

I frowned, remembering what my mother had told me. "Caleb, have any of the humans been used as blood slaves?"

"What? Where did you ever hear such a term?"

"From my mother. She said that the vampires at the *Legăturas* could claim the humans presented and use them in any way they wished…including as food."

Caleb's eyes darkened. "I know they were your parents, Victoria, but they were truly horrible people. One of these days, we need to sit down and go over everything they taught you. The short answer is no. While humans who do not make a mate connection can accept positions within some of the prominent vampire houses, none, and I repeat *none* of them, are slaves or used as a food source."

"I didn't mean to upset you."

"You didn't, sweetness." He kissed the top of my head. "I'm sorry I growled. It just makes me angry when I learn of the lies they told you. There are human families that have willingly contracted with the Council to be blood donors. That's how we get our food."

"Yes, Talin explained it to me once when I first arrived at the manor."

"Your parents must have been bitter at not being chosen at their initial *Legăturas* and held a resentment toward vampires to tell you such things."

"I don't really know what they felt. My father never acknowledged my existence, and my mother only told me what she wanted to control me."

Caleb caressed my cheek and kissed me. "If I could erase those memories, I would take them from you."

I shook my head. "I wouldn't let you. As painful as they are, I am who I am today because of them."

Caleb smiled. "You're always so optimistic. It's one of the many things I love most about you."

"I prefer to look on the brighter side of life. In fact, I seem to have another positive prediction…" Caleb raised an eyebrow. My grin turned wicked. "I predict that a certain vampire is going to have a high success rate at getting lucky tonight, especially if he keeps rubbing those decadent circles along my back."

"Oh really?" Caleb bent his head and pressed his lips against mine, flicking them open with his tongue. He drew me closer, deepening the kiss.

"Nghh…Caleb," I panted.

Before I could say more, he picked me up in his arms and carried me to our bed.

"I want to feel my arms around you, Victoria. I want you to give yourself to me in every way."

"Caleb…" I moaned his name as he showered kisses along my jawline and down my neck.

"I'm going to kiss you all over your body. I want to indulge in you with each bite, tasting you."

"Yes…please." I dug my fingers into his shoulders, begging him.

We surrendered to our passion, our bare skin hot to the touch as our fingers desperately explored each other's bodies until first light.

Chapter Twenty-Nine

"Caleb? Are you in here?" I stuck my head into his study, expecting it to be dark as usual. I was shocked to find the curtains fully open, streams of sunlight filtering into the room. The walls of books towered above me. I could understand why this was his happy place.

"Victoria? I'm up here," Caleb called from the top level.

I craned my neck to find him. "What are you doing up there?"

"Cleaning."

"What? You?"

"Hey, don't be shocked. I clean."

His pout made me chuckle. "Why isn't Talin helping you?"

"He had an errand to run and I didn't want to wait. Besides, I'm finding all sorts of treasures I forgot I had."

"I can see. Is that stack of books on the floor them?"

Caleb nodded. "It is. I think you might enjoy some of them as well."

"I look forward to reading them. There's a farmers market I would like to go to today. I was going to ask you, but since you seem engrossed in your new project, would you mind if Bastian takes me?"

"Not at all. Where is it?"

"About an hour outside of town at that farm stand we've gone to a couple of times. Apparently, there will be several local farmers with their produce, and I'd like to take advantage of it. I hear there might be stands from some of the local honey farmers and jam makers too."

"You sound very excited for a farmers market. As long as Bastian goes with you. Enjoy, and please be careful."

"Always. Love you."

"Love you too."

I closed the study door behind me and pulled out my phone, shooting a message to Bastian.

Hey, are you free?

For you? Yes. What's up?

I need a ride.

I'll meet you at the front door in five minutes.

Thanks, Frosty.

I could picture his faux irritation at the nickname on the other end of the line. I laughed and went to grab some produce bags.

*

The farmers market was bigger than I expected. All the stands had different goods to sell. *Maybe I should have brought more bags.*

"Remember, princess, we can't buy everything," Bastian teased me.

"It all looks so wonderful."

"I can only carry so much."

I giggled. "Come on, Frosty, you're stronger than that..."

"Seriously, Victoria, do you even have enough kitchen space to store all of this?"

"Are you kidding? All I need to do is cook one meal for you and your brother and you'll eat up half of what we've already bought."

Bastian chuckled. "We do love to eat, especially when you're cooking."

"Oh no, don't you go blaming me for that bottomless pit you call a stomach. I think the honey farmers are over this way."

"You buying a hive?"

"No silly…although…" I paused, then shook my head. "No, Caleb would kill me. I want to see what they have, and besides, locally farmed honey is better for you than store bought." As we wound our way through the stalls, the area became more packed. I narrowly dodged someone stepping on my foot. "It's really crowded back here, isn't it?" I instinctively edged closer to him.

"Victoria, stay close." Even Bastian seemed tense.

I nodded. We were much more cautious since Malcolm cornered me at Novellas.

"Bastian, let's go to that tent." I pointed to one on the left. "There doesn't seem to be anyone there but the apiarist."

Bastian nodded and followed me to the tent in the corner. Inside, three tables formed a 'U' pattern. The front flap was tied off wide open for customers. He scanned the area. "I'll stand here so I don't knock anything over. Just make sure I can always see you."

"I appreciate your concern, but the tent is empty except for us. I don't think anything will happen here, do you?"

"Let's not take any chances, okay, princess?"

"All right, I'll be quick," I promised.

*

Victoria made her way up to the apiarist. I was amazed at how easily she could strike up a conversation with strangers. Victoria always put everyone around her at ease. I chuckled to myself as I realized it was probably her smile. It had a way of lighting up an entire room.

She selected three jars, handed them to the farmer, then reached into her purse to find her wallet. *Good, this last stop is going quickly.* Something like an itch on the back of my head had been bothering me the last hour, like a prickle someone was following us, but I didn't see anything suspicious. Maybe I was being overcautious, but I didn't like being away from our community, and after what happened at the bookstore, I wasn't letting my guard down.

A large group of teenagers, probably there for a school trip, swarmed into the tent. *Great timing.* I took a step back to avoid them knocking the bags out of my hands.

My skin bristled. I whipped around, looking for the source. My eyes landed on the farmer's face. I recognized that look. It was one I knew well…fear.

Victoria swirled. "Bastia—"

Her voice was cut off. I dropped the bags and pushed my way toward her, but she was…*gone!* I searched the entire tent for her. Panic enveloped my heart. I grabbed the apiarist by the front of his shirt and hoisted him into the air with one hand.

"*WHERE IS SHE?*" I bellowed, my eyes glowing in anger, my fangs fully extended.

His face went white. The kids in the tent fled. Until that moment, they probably hadn't believed vampires existed…I didn't care.

"I-I'm sorry…I-I didn't have a choice."

In one motion, I ripped the tent down, allowing me to see in every direction. I briefly caught sight of a woman's legs as they disappeared into the back of a gray sedan. The sneakers were Victoria's. Her assailant wore black from head to toe, and a baseball cap hid his face. I didn't recognize his form.

I took off running using my enhanced vampire speed, but I wasn't fast enough. The unmarked car sped off. I desperately continued until it turned down a side road and disappeared. I landed on my knees in the middle of the road. "*Victoria!*" I punched the ground, leaving a hole four inches deep in the asphalt.

She had been taken and it was all *my* fault.

I sprinted back to the farmers market and floored it back to Carrington Manor, ignoring my split knuckles and the blood covering my hand.

What am I going to say to Caleb? How can I even look him in the eye?

*

I knelt on the floor of Caleb's study.

"How? How in the hell was she taken?" He paced before me, his eyes glowing with rage and fear. His fangs gleamed from below his upper lip.

"I'm sorry, Caleb." My voice broke. "I'll find her, I promise."

"I should kill you right here!" His low growl was enough to make a weaker man's heart stop in fear. "You swore to protect her!"

I hung my head. "I failed. My life is yours to take. I deserve it."

"Don't say that, brother." Blake stood to my left side with Darin, who was looking about ready to vomit. Greggory and Collin had hurried over too. "Caleb, obviously Bastian would give his life for Victoria. It could have been any of us with her today and we wouldn't have done anything different," he pleaded.

Caleb stood back and sighed. "Bastian, get up."

I rose to my feet but kept my head hung in submission. *You have every right to take my life.* My fists were still clenched and bleeding.

"Darin, take Bastian to the kitchen and clean up his hands," Caleb ordered.

"I'm fine," I argued.

"You're bleeding on my carpet. Now go!"

Darin took my arm. "It's best you come with me. Give Caleb his space." I nodded and let Darin lead me out of the study.

In the kitchen, my mate was silent as he cleaned and bandaged my hands.

"It's not your fault you know," he finally spoke.

"It was my job to keep her safe and he took her."

Darin pursed his lips. "I know there's nothing I can say to alleviate the guilt you're feeling right now…any of us would feel the same if we had been the one on watch. I only ask that you not do anything stupid or rash…"

"I won't…"

"Bastian," he warned. "You may be able to fool the others, but I know you too well. The minute you get one clue on her location, you're going to be off running full tilt without thinking about your safety. I know what Victoria means to you. You've never let anyone into your heart like you've let her in… Sometimes I'm jealous, but then I remember it's Victoria and how she's wiggled her way into all our hearts."

I cupped Darin's face in my bandaged hands. "Darin, there is no one more important to me than you. You alone bare my mark. I love you, but she was depending on me to keep her safe…and I've let her down. I have to make this right. If she gets killed…"

Darin brushed his lips against mine. "Then be smart, and for me, don't go running off without a plan."

I sighed. He was right, but I couldn't promise him I wouldn't take off the minute we learned anything of Victoria's whereabouts. *I will try, though.*

As we left the kitchen, the doorbell rang. Darin opened the door. We both gasped at the visitor standing on the other side of the threshold.

Chapter Thirty

My head was pounding.

I opened my eyes, but all I could see was the inside of a dark cloth wrapped around my eyes. My arms were stretched straight up. Something cold and hard dug into my wrists. *Shackles? This isn't good… Stay calm, Victoria.*

I was lifted high enough that only the balls of my feet touched the damp earth beneath me. *Why am I barefoot?* The air was cool and musty, as if the room had been closed off for a long time. A sweet metallic scent filled my nose. The scent of iron and blood. My heart thumped in my chest. I took a deep breath, trying to calm myself. *What happened?*

I was with the honey farmer, about to pay for my purchase when he looked over my shoulder and started to shake. I had turned and peered into the steely gaze of a man I didn't know. When I turned to yell for Bastian, a sweet aroma filled my nostrils, making my head feel fuzzy. He had put a cloth over my mouth…and everything else after that was darkness.

"No sense in panicking before I know where I am," I whispered to myself.

A soft chuckle reverberated from not far away. Startled, I turned my face toward the direction of the sound. "Who's there?"

Silence.

A chill gripped my body, covering me in goosebumps. I pursed my lips, trying to stop their trembling. The quiet shuffle of footsteps indicated the person had changed their position. I did my best to follow the sound.

"Malcolm?" I asked, trying to remain calm. Another chuckle. "Have you lost your mind?"

He continued moving around the room. Fear tightened my insides.

"Where am I?" *More importantly, what do I do?*

Then something scraped...like tools being arranged on a metal tray. I gasped against my will.

"Yes, perfect..." he purred. "Let it build."

"Caleb is going to kill you." I tried to sound confident.

A whisper in my ear answered, "Perhaps, but not before we have a little fun, my pet." He licked my neck.

How did he cross the room so fast?

My heart raced. I could barely breathe.

*

"Caleb, we have a visitor."

I looked up as Darin opened the study doors. A growl escaped my lips as I stood from my chair.

"Malikai, what has your brother done with my mate?" In seconds, I had the younger Moriat brother pinned against the wall.

"I've come to help, Caleb." Malikai met my steely gaze. Regret shone in his eyes.

"So, Malcolm has her?" Collin asked.

He nodded. "Yes, one of my men has been assigned to watch Malcolm's bodyguard, Garrett. He saw him put her in the back of his car and drive away."

"Where is she? Did your man follow them?" My tone was cold and dangerous.

He sighed. "I'm not sure where he took her. Unfortunately, he didn't follow them."

I nearly strangled him. "Why the hell not?"

"Regrettably, he is new to his role and thought it was best to inform me right away. I have dealt with him, Caleb. We have warehouses by the docks that have been empty for years. It's possible he's holding her there. Our private jet and airstrip are also located there."

Bastian bolted out the door.

"That reckless vampire, he promised me," Darin cursed as he ran after him.

"Boss?" Blake looked to me for direction.

"Go with them. Make sure they stay out of trouble. Case the buildings first and call me if you see anything. We can't storm in without confirming she's there. We have no idea what he'll do to her if he knows we've found him." I pinched the bridge of my nose. *Why can't I sense her? It's as if something is blocking me.*

Being my mate, I should know her location, feel what she feels…but since this afternoon, she'd completely dropped off my radar.

Once Blake was gone, Collin asked, "Do you really believe that's where he's taken her?"

"No. It would be too obvious." Malikai shook his head.

"Could your brother know that you've agreed to help us?" I released him.

"He doesn't know about our meeting and I'm confident no one followed me here, but with my brother, anything is possible. I told you I won't betray my family, but my conscience won't let me sit idly by this time. My brother must be stopped."

"Where else could he be holding her?" Collin asked.

Malikai frowned as he thought. "Would he be that arrogant?" he mused, then shook his head as if dismissing the possibility.

"This is Malcolm we're talking about…" Greggory interjected.

"True." He nodded. "My brother has a very nasty reputation as you're aware. It is the shame of the entire Moriat clan, but none of us are brave enough to stand up against him."

"You'll need to be more specific. There are a lot of rumors surrounding your brother, most of which aren't true, but he still relishes in perpetuating them." I scowled. Malcolm was always a danger to our community. I begged my father to let me rid the world of him, but he had refused my request, telling me that vampires don't kill vampires unless there are no other options. I tried to explain Malcolm would be a danger to everyone in the long run, but he wouldn't hear it. With his passing, only the Council stood in my way. Malcolm was a member and enough of the other families supported him. If I made a move against him without provocation, it would result in all-out war. But now…

"My brother has a habit of *playing* with his food, so to speak." Malikai shivered. "Malcolm prefers to drink straight from the source. In the beginning, it was innocent enough. He would leave the community, pick up a pretty little thing, and under the guise of an amorous tryst, he would bite them. However, over the years, his desires have become darker, more twisted. He's taken a liking to blood laced with fear."

"What?" Collin shuddered. "Are you saying he prefers the taste of bitter blood?"

"Yes, the more bitter, the better. I came home because I was receiving reports that Malcolm has started abducting humans and torturing them before feeding off them."

"Are you telling me that this is what he intends to do with Victoria?" Malikai hung his head, unable to find the words. "And you've known he's been doing this all along?" Collin's fangs slipped below his upper lip. "You will answer for keeping this from us."

"After we get Victoria," I cut in. "Where does he keep these individuals while he's torturing them?"

"He has a special chamber built under the house. She could be there. I can help you get in the house, but not past the front gate. If I'm seen by our guards helping you, even considering what Malcolm has done, I'll never be able to take over the Moriat clan. With no one to guide my family, it will be chaos."

"Collin, call Blake and tell him what we've learned. Have him meet us on the border of the Moriat estate," I instructed. "We'll get past the guards, Malikai, but you get us into the house."

"You have my word. I will do what I can. And Caleb..."

"Yes?"

"You have to kill him. Or there will be no way to stop him."

I was already rushing out, the others following close behind.

Chapter Thirty-One

"Malcolm," I hissed. "Let me go. You're out of your mind."

"Ah, my pet, indeed…"

A light clanking of metal echoed off the walls. *What is he doing?* Each vibration brought a new wave of shivers down my spine.

"Very good, my pet. Let your fear grow. Mmm…I can almost taste it."

"Please stop." My voice trembled.

"Your fear smells delicious…but it's not quite ready yet, is it?"

Something cold and smooth trailed down the inside of my arm. Malcolm's sweet cologne filled my nostrils. It made me retch. I wriggled and pulled against my restraints, wincing at the sting as the metal cut into the soft skin of my wrists. Thick liquid trickled down my arm.

"Oh, my little morsel…a gift, for me? You are ever so thoughtful." A warm, wet tongue glided up my arm, catching the blood dripping from my wounds. "Hmmm…still too sweet, but nonetheless delicious. I knew I wouldn't regret tasting you. What is this sensation I'm getting? It's no mystery why Carrington wants you all for himself." Malcolm placed a kiss on my cheek before walking away.

"You need to let me go, Malcolm. Caleb will kill you when he finds me." *How am I going to get out of here?* I knew what Malcolm wanted. What I didn't know was how long I could hold out before my fear took over and he killed me.

An arrogant laugh filled the room. The sound bouncing off the walls hurt my ears. "Your oblivious lover will never think to look for you here. My stupid brother will make sure of that. I imagine he has them on a wild chase at this very moment combing the family warehouses at the docks. When they learn that my personal jet took off with my bodyguard on board, they'll think I whisked you away and go running after him." Malcolm laughed again, seemingly proud of his plan.

"When they catch him, they will torture him until he tells them where we really are. They'll kill him," I warned.

"Yes, I surmise they will. It's a shame, really. I am rather fond of Garrett, but getting you, my pet, is worth the sacrifice."

"You're disgusting," I spat.

A cold hand with long fingers wrapped around my neck, squeezing enough to make breathing difficult. I twisted and gasped.

"My patience has limits Victoria. I want something from you, but do not think that means you cannot anger me to the point where I don't simply rip your throat out and feed you to my dogs."

The venom in his voice combined with the lack of oxygen caused a new wave of fear to crash over me. Tears slipped down my cheeks. Malcolm licked up each one as it fell.

"Hmm, delightful."

"Where are we, Malcolm?"

"In the basement of my mansion," Malcolm said so casually I thought I misheard him.

"Your mansion?"

"I have a special area custom built for my *pleasures* here. It makes things so much more convenient than having to maintain two locations. All the driving back and forth…it can be so tiresome."

"Why blindfold me if you were just going to tell me where we are?"

"It heightens the experience, don't you think?" He teased the fabric. "Why, do you wish to look lovingly into my eyes?"

"Go to hell."

"Probably."

He is infuriating. "You're insane."

"Tsk, tsk…such an ugly word. I prefer to be called eccentric."

"Call it what you want, you're crazy."

"Ah, 'A rose by any other name would smell as sweet'—isn't that what Shakespeare wrote in his lovers' tale?"

"We are not star-crossed lovers."

He grabbed my chin. "Not yet."

I wrenched my face from his grasp. *C'mon Victoria, think of something… Oh!* "There's one small flaw with your plan, Malcolm. Caleb can sense me with his mark, and if we are in your mansion, we aren't far from his manor. He won't fall for your little trick. He'll be here in no time."

"You're smarter than you look, my pet. Fortunately for me, I happen to have several witch friends, and with a little *persuasion*, they were happy to teach me a useful incantation that guards against that pesky little tracking beacon Carrington left on your neck." Again, something smooth and cold touched the mate mark. *Is that a knife?* "I could cut it out, but it's right over a major artery. While his fangs were able to pierce it, my blades don't have the same healing properties and you would bleed out, ruining all the fun I have in store for us."

"What are you going to do?" As hard as I tried, I couldn't keep the fear from my voice.

Malcolm chuckled. "First, we need to cut this off." Cold metal scraped against my stomach. I gasped, waiting to feel the pain of the blade, but it never came. I shivered as my shirt fluttered to the ground in pieces at my feet. "And now this…" He cut the skirt I was wearing, letting it fall.

I swayed there in my underwear. The room was silent. Shivers racked my body, followed by the sting of little bumps rising on my skin. I could feel his eyes on me.

"You truly are a vision, my pet." Malcolm's voice came out in a soft sigh. His cold fingers traced from the hollow of my neck, between my breasts, and down to my belly button.

"Don't touch me!" I whimpered.

"Oh, don't worry, I have no need for carnal delights. I'm not interested in your body other than the sweet substance coursing through your veins. Your body is nothing more than a chalice that holds the nectar of life. Once it's ready to harvest, I will hold you close as I drain every single delectable drop. When you are empty, I will toss away your worthless shell. Know that the last thing you'll feel is the touch of my skin on yours, the last scent you inhale mine. My voice will be the last to grace your ears."

My mind snapped at that moment and I lost control. I kicked out wildly, screaming incoherently at the top of my lungs. Malcolm made no move to stop me. I didn't know how long I thrashed against my restraints, ignoring the searing pain in my wrists.

Let the cuffs cut off my hands. I don't care.

I wanted to be free, to lunge at the lunatic in the room and rip him to pieces with my teeth if necessary.

I want to go home…home to Caleb.

After thrashing for so long, my limbs became sore, my throat hoarse. Behind the blindfold, my eyelids drooped.

No, I have to stay awake. Can't…close my eyes.

It was a losing battle. I passed out.

*

Outside the Moriat estate, Collin and I watched as Malikai drove through the front gates and up to the mansion. Although he protested, I sent Greggory home to be with Serena and the baby. He was still human and vulnerable.

Collin hung up his phone call.

"Are they almost here?" I whispered to him impatiently.

"Darin said they're five minutes out. Blake called one of his buddies who works at the warehouses. He told him that Garrett took the Moriat corporate jet, but he was alone. Their guess is Malcolm wants us to think he fled with Victoria."

"An elaborate plan."

"How can you be sure she's in there?" Collin nodded toward the mansion.

"I'm not—it's just a feeling."

"You still can't sense her?" When I shook my head, Collin sighed. "Darin says Bastian is wound up tight. He looks like a tiger in a cage."

"I think we're all feeling that way."

Collin nodded. "Father should have let you kill Malcolm years ago."

"If he were here now, I'm sure he'd agree."

"He would've loved Victoria."

"You think so?" I asked. My father was worse than me with humans. Outside of needing them to survive, he didn't see any value in interacting with them. There were the rare humans he enjoyed conversing with, mostly scholars, but beyond that, he avoided them.

"She's unique. He liked humans that were unique. I think she would've broken through his walls like she broke through yours."

I chuckled. "I can imagine she would've been just as relentless with him."

"You got lucky, my brother."

"You'll find your mate soon enough, Collin."

"Hush your mouth…we've already had that discussion. There are too many lovelies out there in need of my tender loving care for me to settle down."

"Keep telling yourself that." I chuckled. "You're hopeless."

A car pulled up, turning its lights off and coming to a stop. Darin and the twins climbed out and joined us.

"She's in there?" Bastian asked.

"Malikai said his brother has some special room in the basement. We think that's where he's holding her."

"Then what are we waiting for? Let's go." Bastian stood.

I grabbed his arm and pulled him back down into a crouch. "Bastian, I'm equally as anxious as you are to bust in there and save Victoria, but we have to be smart. If we rush in without a plan, he could kill her before we can even break down the door."

Bastian growled.

"What do we know?" Blake changed the subject, glancing at his twin.

Collin proceeded to catch them up on what Malikai had told them, the location of the door that led down to the basement, and what he believed was down there.

"He's never been down there?" Blake asked.

"No. He seemed quite disgusted with his brother's habit. Malikai is almost as proud as his brother and wouldn't deign to step foot in such a vile place. He did say that his bodyguard heard Garrett talking about it once and believes there is a main chamber with several smaller rooms off to one side where he would keep his…*victims* locked up." *And that sick bastard has Victoria.*

"How did we not know about all this?" Collin growled.

"I don't know but it all ends tonight," I hissed. "Once Victoria is safe, I'm ending Malcolm Moriat. The Council can deal with Malikai keeping this a secret after he takes over as head of his family."

"How do you want to do this, Caleb?" Blake rolled his shoulders. "It's your mate in there. Are we going in quiet or loud?"

"Where's Bastian?" Darin looked around in a state of panic.

"Damn it!" Blake cursed. "That stupid, impulsive hothead."

We all followed Blake's gaze and watched as a dark shadow charged across the estate grounds, heading directly toward the mansion.

Darin swore. "He's going to get himself killed."

"Or worse, Victoria." Collin sighed. "Now what do we do?"

"We go after that idiot." I stood and easily vaulted the wrought iron gate, then sprinted toward the mansion.

*

"Time to wake up, my pet. No sleeping through the party. You'll miss all the fun." Malcolm raised my chin with his long fingers. There was no warmth in him.

My eyes were no longer covered. I blinked, trying to focus. The chamber was smaller than I imagined. The stone walls were the same color as the dirt floor. Several doors lined one wall. Each had a small, barred window, and no sound came from them.

Malcolm stood before me, a serene look on his face, but it was what lay behind him that caught my eye. From end to end, silver tools covered a long stainless steel table, each gleaming menacingly in the low light. I could make out knives of different sizes and serrations. I didn't recognize most of the other items, but none of them looked friendly. I bit back a scream as fear bubbled up inside me again.

Caleb, where are you? Will you find me before he kills me?

"No."

"W-What?"

"The answer to your question. No, he will not find you before I'm done with you." Malcolm turned and started surveying the items on the table.

"Please Malcolm, don't do this." Tears filled my eyes. *What can I say to him? I need to stall...* "Why are you like this?"

Malcolm chuckled. "Trying to get inside my head, my pet? All right, I see no harm in it. You'll be dead soon anyway. Would you like me to tell you a story?"

"Y-Yes." If I could keep him talking, it would buy time—time I desperately needed.

"It will be a quick one, my pet, but I'm sure you'll enjoy it."

Malcolm pulled out a chair and set it before me. Sitting and crossing his legs, he looked up at me with his cold blue eyes. I shivered. He smiled. "My parents weren't suited to have offspring. I suppose in that way, you and I have something in common. While your parents pretended you didn't exist, my father taught me the finer points of torment...and he was a very hands-on teacher. He believed the best way for me to learn his *craft* was to experience it firsthand. He insisted that it was essential I understand the emotions of my future victims, felt the results of each tool, experienced what it was like when the master had established his technique and when he hadn't."

I cringed. "Th-That's horrible."

"Don't cry for me, my love. It took me years to understand the gift my father was giving me. Once he taught me everything he knew, I was able to branch out and learn from others through trial and error, honing my special gift. Then I became the master. I took pride in showing my father precisely how skilled I had become."

"You tortured him?"

"Of course! I think it was only fair, don't you? He had taken all that time out of his busy schedule to show me what a skilled sadist he was, making sure I understood the purpose of each cut and the response it was meant to elicit. It seemed fitting that he experience how the fruits of his labor had grown and taken root in his beloved firstborn son."

I shivered at the menacing tone and residual anger in his voice. He still harbored resentment toward his father. I couldn't say that I blamed him.

"Alas," Malcolm continued, "the old man wasn't strong enough and died before I was able to share all of my talents."

A gasp escaped my lips. "You have no soul."

Malcolm calmly stood and tucked the chair back under the table. "What need would I have for one? Now, my pet, story time is over. We really must get started."

The sound of wood splintering echoed from the upper floor. Malcolm's eyes widened in panic a moment before grabbing a long serrated knife and flattening himself against the wall beside the door. Heavy footsteps bounded down what I assumed was a stairwell, each thud bringing the intruder closer. There was a moment of quiet before someone kicked the door in.

"Victoria!" Bastian yelled.

"Look out behind you!"

Bastian turned in time to deflect Malcolm's attack.

"As subtle as ever, I see. I'm surprised you figured out my little stunt with the jet. I have to say, you're more clever than I anticipated, Boylston."

Bastian growled, "Any last words before I rip your heart out, Moriat?"

Malcolm sneered, his fangs descending, almost cutting into his bottom lip. He cracked his fingers and talon-sharp claws grew from his fingertips. Bastian's muscles flexed as his own fangs and claws revealed themselves.

I had never seen this side of them before. My breath hitched in my throat.

These two vampires were now lethal weapons and were going to fight in this small room where I hung defenseless.

Eyes glowing, they glared at each other. Neither moved as they took each other's measure, waiting to see who would make the first attack.

Malcolm glanced at me. "Very good, my pet, let that fear grow. I promise this won't take but a moment." He sniffed the air. "Aahhh, perfect…isn't she divine, Boylston? I'm sure you've stroked yourself to sleep thinking about her soft skin, those supple breasts, the sweet smell of her intoxicating blood. Can you smell it now? Does your precious Darin know of the lust in your groin for our pretty little human?"

Malcolm was trying to bait him into losing control. Bastian growled and shifted his weight.

"Come now, Boylston, do you deny your carnal desires for such a sweet fruit? Look the other way and I'll let you bury your shaft deep within her folds and taste her sweet nectar before you leave. It's truly exquisite." Malcolm licked his lips.

With unnatural speed, Bastian lunged for Malcolm. His claws caught the other vampire's cheeks, leaving deep wounds. Malcolm howled in rage and thrust the knife in his clawed hand forward, aiming for Bastian's neck. Bastian was too quick. He pivoted and swung his leg up, landing a kick to Malcolm's stomach. Malcolm doubled over, but recovered quickly. He swiped at Bastian with his free hand, catching him across the shoulder. Bastian barely acknowledged the deep wounds, though blood oozed through his shirt.

The two vampires traded more blows. Neither seemed to be tiring or giving ground. Their movements became a blur of claws, fangs, and blood.

As fast as a lightning strike, Malcolm landed a kick to Bastian's back, sending him lurching forward. I gasped. It was the opening he needed.

"Bastian, get up! He's coming…" I screamed, but I was too late.

Malcolm lunged forward and stabbed Bastian in the side with the knife. It slid between his ribs easier than I thought possible. Bastian fell to his knees. The look of defeat in his eyes was more than I could bare.

"NO!" I screamed, twisting and wrenching against the metal cuffs. I kicked my legs out in frustration, tears blurring my vision. "Stay away from him!"

Malcolm looked to me. His eyes were wild and dark as he turned in my direction.

"Get away! Don't come near me!" I thrashed, swinging like a pendulum in the air.

"Unfortunately, our time has come to an end, my pet. I'm heartbroken that we weren't able to have the terrifying experience I had planned, but *c'est la vie*."

As he came closer and reached for me, I was overcome with a sense of warmth. My body became still, my heart no longer thumping in my chest. I felt abnormally calm. Everything around me seemed to freeze as if time itself had stopped.

Staring into Malcolm's eyes, I could see the small boy tortured by his father, sense his fear, the feeling of inadequacy—the longing for love in his heart.

He froze mid-step, confusion filling his eyes. "How?"

I pressed deeper, pulling his fears, wants, and desires from his mind with ease. Images of his childhood played in my mind. It was horrifying, but I felt nothing. I replayed those images over and over, adding whispers of his father's words. *Unworthy, weak, useless.*

"Stop!" Malcolm scowled at me, stepping back. "How are you doing this?"

I pulled more images, whispered more haunting words. *Shame, inferior.*

Pressure was building in Malcolm's mind. My intrusion was causing him physical pain. He covered his ears and sank to his knees. "STOP! Make them stop!"

I was vaguely aware that others were in the room now, watching the scene before them in stunned silence. A blue aura surrounded me. Thin tendrils reached out, connecting me to Malcolm. I forced the images and words into his mind over and over again until he lay twitching on the ground, blood leaking from his eyes and ears. He whimpered. Someone in the distance called my name.

A large body suddenly blocked my view of Malcolm. The aura, images, and whispers faded. I shook my head as normal sound returned to my ears. Darin was telling someone that they were going to be okay. Blake and Collin were there too, somewhere. I could hear them, but I couldn't see them.

I focused on the body before me, glancing up at their very handsome face. *I know that face.*

"Victoria? Can you hear me?"

I stared blankly at the man, recognition slowly coming to me. I blinked again, trying to remember his name.

"Caleb?" My voice was barely a whisper. I wasn't even sure I said anything.

"Sweetness, hold still. I'm going to get you out of these."

"What?" I looked up, confused.

"I'm here now. You're going to be okay. Are you hurt?"

I shook my head. "What...what happened?" Malcolm was twitching on the floor. Another vampire that looked like a smaller version of him stood over his body. "Caleb! Who's that?" I started twisting in fear.

"Hold still, sweetness. I've almost got these. You'll only hurt yourself. That's Malikai, Malcolm's brother. He's not a threat."

Then I was falling.

"Oh no you don't. Hold on." Caleb wrapped an arm around my waist to support me, but my legs weren't cooperating. I clung to him, wrapping my arms around his neck.

"I don't think I can walk."

Caleb scooped me up and headed for the door. "Is he okay?" he asked Blake, looking down at Bastian.

"He's lost some blood and his wounds are deep, but they've already started to heal. He'll survive."

"Don't let Malcolm get to his feet. I'll be back to take care of him myself as soon as Victoria is out of this house."

Blake nodded.

"Victoria?" Bastian looked up at me, his hand reaching out.

"Bastian..." I smiled. Our fingers entwined briefly—it was enough to assure him I was all right. I would have words with him later, as it seemed he came rushing in without the others. I was glad he came, but how could he put his life in danger like that?

A bloody figure sprang from the floor and leapt toward us as we approached the doorway. "She's *mine!*" Malcolm dove at Caleb and I, grabbing a knife from the table.

Before anyone could react, two large hands encased Malcolm's head. With one quick twist, it was ripped clean. His headless carcass fell to the ground, blood pooling beneath his lifeless body.

Bastian stood tall, holding Malcolm's head in his hands. He tossed it to the side before swaying on his feet. Blake and Darin steadied him, pulling an arm over each of their shoulders to hold him up. The grin on his face as he met my eyes was ridiculously proud.

Chapter Thirty-Two

Outside, Blake pulled his SUV in front of the Moriat mansion. Caleb removed his shirt and pulled it over my head before tucking me safely into the back seat next to Bastian. We were both bloody messes. He then turned to talk with the new head of the Moriat family.

"I'm sorry it came to this, Malikai."

"I am too. My brother's actions have brought his own demise. The fault lies with him alone. You need not fear retribution for what happened here today. You have my word."

"You will have to face the Council for keeping his activities secret. I've asked Collin to wait until you've secured your place as head of the family, but he won't wait long."

"I understand. Thank you, Caleb."

Caleb shook his hand and climbed into the passenger seat next to Blake. Collin was already in his car with Darin, who hadn't uttered a word since leaving the mansion. We followed their car down the drive.

"Bastian?" I asked once we took off.

"Yes, Victoria?"

I scooted over, and he tucked me under his arm. "This wasn't your fault." He smiled weakly, but I barged forward. "And before you give me some speech about how it was your job to keep me safe, let me say…you did! You have been by my side for months making sure nothing happened to me. We both knew there was always a chance when I left the house that something could happen."

"Victoria, you say that but…"

"No Bastian, you did everything right, except one thing." I sat up and looked into his eyes. "You did everything right to protect me, but you did everything wrong when it came to protecting yourself."

"What?" He looked surprised.

I locked him with my hard gaze. "You stormed in that room without back-up, didn't you?"

"I…yes." Bastian gave up without a fight.

"You could have died! Did you think about where that would leave Darin? Leave Blake, me, or any of us?"

Bastian turned away from Blake's stare in the rearview mirror. "No."

"*No*, you didn't. You rushed in because you felt guilty. Don't you dare do anything like that ever again. My heart couldn't take it if something happened to you."

"How do you have the energy to lecture me after what you went through?"

"Shut up." I hugged the large vampire.

"Ugh, Victoria, that hurts."

"You deserve it."

"I guess I do."

"Consider it your punishment. Besides, I doubt anything I could come up with will compare to what Darin most likely has in store for you."

He groaned. "Oh, just let me die now."

Everyone in the car laughed.

I leaned back against Bastian's chest and met Caleb's eyes. I could tell he wasn't all too happy about me sitting next to another man, but since it was Bastian, he was doing his best to control his jealousy.

I winked at him. "Don't worry, old man. My heart still belongs to you."

*

Finally arriving back at the manor, Blake dropped Victoria and I off and then drove to the small hospital in our community, Collin and Darin following after them. The doctor was there waiting to patch Bastian's wounds. Victoria refused to go, saying she could care for her wounds at home.

"I want a bath and to sleep in our bed."

I couldn't bring myself to deny her request since I wanted to hold her and never let her go. Carrying Victoria into the house and up the stairs to our bedchamber, I didn't set her down until we were in our large bathroom. I put her on the stool before her vanity mirror and turned to run a bath.

"I didn't see Talin or Galia. Are they home?"

"Yes, I messaged ahead and told them we were coming home and to go to bed for the night. They're dying to see you, but I want you to rest this evening. They can see you in the morning."

Victoria nodded. She was fighting it, but I could tell she was exhausted, using what little energy she had left to lecture Bastian. It had been amusing to see her manipulate the deadly vampire that most feared to even look at, never mind speak to.

I knelt before her, looking at her wrists. The cuts were shallow and had already stopped bleeding, though her delicate skin was red and starting to bruise. "Are there any other wounds?"

"No, only my wrists—and maybe my sanity." She tried to chuckle. "My shoulders and back are sore from hanging..." Victoria's voice hitched as tears filled her eyes and fell down her cheeks. "Caleb, I was so scared." Her shoulders shook as she sobbed into her hands.

I pulled her into my chest. "I know, sweetness. It's over now. He's gone and can't hurt you anymore. You're home and safe. I'm sorry I took so long to get to you."

"I wasn't sure you would find me."

"I was scared too."

Victoria sat up. "You were?"

"Yes." I nodded. "I couldn't sense you. If it weren't for Malikai, I'm not sure we would have found you before Malcolm was able to carry out his plans. I owe him everything."

"Malcolm said he used an incantation he learned from a witch to hide me."

I frowned. "A witch? Really?"

"Is that surprising?"

"Witches don't help vampires, or anyone really, cause harm to another person. I'll have to talk to Fiona." I stood and checked the temperature of the water in the tub, then added a few soaking salts and bubble mix that Victoria always used and returned to her. "Come here." I helped her remove her undergarments. Knowing Malcolm exposed her in such a way made me wish I could revive him only to kill him myself. It was all my heart could take seeing her in Bastian's arms half naked. My shirt hadn't covered her nearly enough for my satisfaction. If it had been any other vampire, I would've ripped their hands off for touching her. My jealousy still lingered even though I had her home.

I eased Victoria into the large tub and striped off my clothes. I stepped into the tub, lowering myself behind her, and pulled her against my chest.

She chuckled.

"What is it, sweetness?" I rubbed a sponge down her arms, washing away the dirt and dried blood.

"I always thought this tub was ridiculously huge. I never understood why you would have picked it, but right now, I'm grateful you did."

"Are you enjoying yourself?" I smiled and kissed the top of her head.

"Immensely." She sighed. "Can we do this more often and not only when my life is in danger?"

"You have a very strange sense of humor, Victoria. I don't know any human who could go through what you did and joke about it."

She shrugged. "Finding the humor in bad situations is how I cope with them."

After washing her body, I had Victoria scoot forward and lean her head back so I could wash her hair, erasing all physical traces of her ordeal. I cursed I couldn't take the memories from her mind too. *I have never felt so weak.*

"I'm sorry sweetness. I failed to protect you."

"Stop! You didn't fail me. You didn't fall for Malcolm's trick. Despite not being able to sense me, you found me and brought me home...alive." She kissed me lightly.

"Victoria?"

"Hmm?"

"What did you do to Malcolm?"

Victoria's body stiffened. "I'm not really sure."

"Were you inside his head? The same way you showed me what happened the night of the annual ball?"

"It wasn't the same. With you, I was projecting my thoughts and memories. With Malcolm, I was pulling his memories from a story he told me about his father."

"I thought you had to touch the person to make the connection."

"It was different this time. A blue aura connected me to him. I was angry at what he did to Bastian and afraid. It's a bit fuzzy, but I could see his worst fears and insecurities, and I played them repeatedly in his mind. It was...horrible." Victoria sighed and absently rubbed her temples.

"A blue aura?"

"Yes, didn't you see it when you came into the room?"

I shook my head. "Let's not talk about it anymore." After drying her off, I scooped her up and carried her to bed.

"I'm so tired."

I pulled her into my arms, resting her head on my chest and tucking the covers around her shoulders. She shivered.

"Are you cold?"

"A little...Is it really over, Caleb?"

"Yes, my love. Sleep now. I'm here and you're safe."

Victoria snuggled up into the crook of my arm. Resting her nose into my neck, she breathed deeply, a sigh of content escaping her lips. The sound threatened my self-control. Heat rose in my chest. I wanted to reclaim her, smother her in my scent. It was a primal need...and one that would have to wait.

As if sensing my feelings, Victoria whispered, "Tomorrow, my lustful vampire. I'll be better tomorrow, and you can mark me all over again."

I smiled and squeezed her to me. "I love you, sweetness."

She purred, sleep already overtaking her. Kissing her forehead, I closed my eyes.

Chapter Thirty-Three

I woke early the next morning. In the kitchen, I found Darin already seated at the table drinking a hot cup of coffee, under-eye bags prominent on his sullen face.

"Morning, Darin. What are you doing up this early?"

"Morning Caleb, I couldn't sleep."

"Problems with Bastian?" I poured myself a cup and smiled at Talin who was busy cooking breakfast.

Darin nodded. "I hope we weren't loud coming in last night. The doctor gave him a sedative to bring his adrenaline down so he could rest." He rubbed his forehead. "You know how he gets."

"I didn't hear a thing. Was he that bad?"

"He wasn't singing at the top of his lungs this time, but he wouldn't stop giggling the entire drive home. He kept wanting to check on Victoria. It took all my tricks to get him to head straight to bed. He finally fell asleep around midnight, but he's snoring louder than a jet engine."

"Why didn't you go into one of the other guest rooms?"

"I was worried he'd wake up and disturb you in the middle of the night."

I laughed. "Probably a smart move. I wouldn't have been too happy if he woke Victoria."

"How is she?"

"Still sleeping when I left her. She fell asleep quickly after she took a bath. How bad were Bastian's wounds?"

"They were deep, but he heals so quickly that it shouldn't be long before he's back to full health." Darin's eyes glistened. "Did Malcolm hurt Victoria?"

I shook my head. "Not physically, beyond her wrists. They were tender and bruised last night, but she'll heal. I'm more worried about her mental wellbeing."

"She's a strong woman, master. I'm sure she will be back to her usual self in no time. Now you both need to eat." Talin set full plates before each of us.

"Thank you, Talin. This looks wonderful."

"It's my pleasure, Master Darin. You both have a big job before you in the next few days. Those two are going to need all the support you can give them." The demon then turned to clean up.

"Caleb?"

"Hmm?"

Darin hesitated, taking a deep breath. I looked at him. "What is it? I can tell something is bothering you."

"What did Victoria do to Malcolm?"

"I'm not entirely sure. She spoke briefly about it last night. Apparently, he told her an unpleasant story from his childhood and somehow she was able to access those memories and use them against him."

"How is that possible?"

"It shouldn't be...not for a human. I've known only a few seers in my time, but not one of them could pull memories from another. Especially not without physical contact."

"Are you concerned?"

"A little, more because I don't know what it means for Victoria. She always gets a headache after a vision. She was fine last night, other than being tired..." I sighed. "We need to know the full extent of her gift."

Before Darin could say anything, the door to the kitchen opened and a sleepy Victoria walked in. "Good morning, gentlemen."

"Good morning, mistress." Talin turned with a wide smile. "What can I get for you this morning?"

"Coffee, please...very strong coffee."

"And what would you like to eat?"

She frowned. "I don't think my stomach can handle anything."

"You must eat something, mistress. I'm afraid I'll insist, even if it's broth."

"I can see from the look on your face you aren't going to back down." Talin chuckled. "Fine, I'll have toast with jam. Thank you."

Talin nodded with a smile and turned toward the toaster. "Please sit. I'll bring it to you shortly."

She smiled and joined Darin and I at the table.

"Shouldn't you be in bed, sweetness?" I leaned over and kissed her forehead.

"I tried to go back to sleep but I couldn't."

"I want you to take it easy today," I told her as I brought my empty plate to the sink.

"Caleb, we need to go to my parents' house."

"What?" Both Darin and I gasped in unison.

"Why?" Darin asked.

"I need answers about what happened yesterday, and I can't think of any place better to find them than at the house. Caleb, you said it's been empty all this time. Has it been vandalized?"

"No." I shook my head. "The Council has been tending to it since we learned you weren't living there. It should look exactly like you remember it."

She flinched. "I'd like to go this afternoon, if your schedule allows for it."

"Victoria, are you sure about this?" I sat back down next to her. "There's no rush..."

"I never wanted to step foot in that house again, but I don't have a choice, and it will drive me crazy sitting around here all day. I won't waste time dwelling on what he did to me. What's done is done. I need to figure this out."

"All right, we'll go this afternoon. I'll need to stop by the office to get the keys. It won't take me long."

"I'd like to go with you if that's all right," Darin interjected. "I'm not sure what you'll be looking for, but if I can help and minimize the time you're there, I'd like to."

"Thank you Darin, I appreciate it, but you should stay here and take care of Bastian."

"Why? I'm fine, and I'll be going with you too." Bastian walked into the kitchen, freshly showered and looking like he hadn't been in a deadly battle the day before.

"It's nice to see you up and about Frosty, but you need to rest more than I do."

"Nonsense, Victoria. I'm a pureblood vampire and right as rain." Bastian beamed, leaning against the counter.

"There's no stopping him when he gets that look, Victoria, so you might as well give in." Darin winked.

"All right, the four of us can go. Caleb, you should probably tell Greggory while you're at the office in case he wants to crash our little party."

I chuckled. "I will, but I'm going to tell him to stay home with Serena and the baby."

"Good luck," she called after me as I headed out the door.

*

That afternoon, we piled into Caleb's car and drove to my childhood home. I couldn't identify all the feelings that were coursing through me, except one—a strong urge to run again.

Caleb took my hand and pressed it to his lips. "If you change your mind when we get there, say the word and we'll leave."

I smiled and nodded, not trusting my voice.

Pulling onto the street, I noticed a few young children playing in one of the front yards and several homeowners out watering their flowerbeds. Otherwise, not much had changed since the day I left.

Caleb pulled into the driveway. Besides a few touch-ups, the two-story white house looked exactly as it did over ten years ago when I left and never looked back. The black shutters on the windows looked freshly painted, as did the tall white columns on either side of the front door. The grass and hedges had been maintained.

The guys piled out of the car and stood silently, waiting for me. I stared out the window. *Can I do this? Can I walk into that house again after all this time?*

I took a deep breath. I needed to know what was going on with me, and I hoped those answers were somewhere in that house. My gift was becoming more than just glimpsing people's futures.

I opened the car door. Caleb gave me a reassuring smile and joined me, offering his hand. I took it and found comfort in its warmth.

"Oh my, are you the new owners?" a shrill voice called from the neighbor's side of the low fence. "It's such a lovely house and it's been empty for so long. It will be nice to see it lived in again." A short jovial woman walked around and joined us, her hand extended. "How rude of me. My name is Shirley Stafford. I live next door with my husband Sam."

I shook her hand. "Hello, my name is Victoria."

"Oh, what a delightful name. You know, it's such a shame about the previous owners, the Starlings. They were good people. Such a tragic way to go…a car crash. I don't know why the house has stood empty for so long, but I guess without anyone to inherit it…I heard the Council bought it. Is that how you came to buy it?"

I shook my head at a loss for words. "No, the Starlings were my parents. It's my house."

Shirley gasped. "Oh, my dear, I'm so sorry. I didn't realize they had a daughter."

"No one did." I turned and walked away. I wasn't angry. It wasn't her fault, but I needed to stop the voice in my mind screaming at me to run. Behind me, Caleb apologized on my behalf, making up some excuse that my parents passing was still traumatic for me.

I took the keys from my pocket as I approached the front door. My hands shook as I turned the lock. Stepping inside, I expected the house to smell musty with neglect, but the scent of fresh flowers greeted me. The others joined me.

"Thank you, Caleb," I whispered.

He rubbed my back.

"Where should we start, Victoria?" Darin asked at my side.

I pointed to the left. "The living room is over there and has a few curio cabinets and a desk. If you and Bastian want to start there, Caleb and I can go to the library." I gestured to the right.

"Any idea of what we might be looking for?" Bastian asked.

"Not a clue," I answered. "Anything that might contain a history of my family, I guess."

"Okay, we'll meet you in the library when we're done."

The two of them headed off to the living area. I stood in the entry, staring at the grand staircase before me.

"Shall we go?" Caleb asked.

"Not yet." I laid my hand on the banister and took one step, hesitating a moment before climbing the rest. Caleb followed close behind. At the top, I turned toward a door at the end of the hallway. My hand shook as it hovered over the doorknob. I took a deep breath before entering.

The room was much smaller than I remembered. The white walls were blank. The twin-sized bed still had the same floral pattern bedcover, and a purple fluffy bean bag sat in the corner. A few books and a table lamp sat on the small desk. No dust to be found. My bedroom was the only place in the entire house I felt calm, the only place where I didn't want to run.

Caleb stepped over to the nightstand and picked up the only framed photo in the room. "Is this you?" he asked.

I walked over. The picture was of me holding a stuffed animal. "I was ten, and that was my favorite toy." I reached around him and picked up the white floppy unicorn from my bed. "His name is Ulysses."

"After the book?"

I nodded. "Don't ask me why, but I thought it was the most fantastic name for a unicorn." I laughed and hugged the stuffed animal to my chest and turned to open the closet door.

"Wait...you actually read *Ulysses* when you were ten?" Caleb was staring at me.

"Mmhmm."

"I don't know if I should be impressed or scared."

I chuckled. "Both. We really should have this house cleaned out and donate all this stuff." I ran my hand over the clothes hanging neatly in a row, none that would fit me anymore.

"Can I keep this?" Caleb held out the photo.

"Sure, but why do you want it?"

"It's the only picture of you as a child. Someday our children will want to see how adorable their mother was as a little girl." He smiled.

My chest bloomed with warmth. "Our children?"

Caleb nodded and looked around. "Is there anything in here you want now that we're here?"

"I always regretted leaving Ulysses behind. He's all I want." I headed out the door and down the hallway.

"What's down there?" Caleb gestured toward the double doorway at the other end.

"That's my parents' room." I turned to go down the stairs.

"Do you think we would find anything in there?"

"Caleb...I...."

"Why don't I take a quick look and meet you in the library?"

"All right."

I hurried downstairs, not looking back at their bedroom. Once in the library, I looked around. Memories of the parties, my parents' arrogant friends laughing and clamoring around me, flooded my mind. I put my hands over my ears to block the imaginary sounds. Someone touched my shoulder.

"Are you all right, princess?" Bastian asked.

I turned and leaned my forehead against his chest. His strong hands rubbed the sides of my arms.

"You don't have to do this, Victoria. We can go through everything," Darin offered from my side.

I turned and straightened my shoulders. "No, I need to be here. I need to get past all of the memories."

Caleb joined us, a look of concern on his face as he stared down at me. I went into his embrace and held him close, breathing in his scent. Warm cedar and cinnamon filled my senses and calmed me as he rubbed my back.

"There wasn't anything in your parents' room. Did either of you find anything in the living area?"

Bastian held up a leather-bound notebook. "It seems to be a journal Edgar kept. I didn't see anything important in the first few pages, but it might be worth going through."

I nodded. "Father was always writing in it."

"Let's see if there's anything in here, shall we? The sooner we finish, the sooner we can leave." Caleb pulled away, searching my eyes. "Are you sure you're up for this? You're vibrating with tension."

I nodded, set Ulysses down on top of my father's journal, and got to work starting with the large desk in the far corner.

*

After searching for several hours, we didn't find anything that referenced my family history. I was about to tell everyone we should go when a soft buzzing noise, coming from the front corner of the room, nagged at me. I followed it and found a loose panel in the wall. *Was this always here?* When I pressed it, the panel clicked and swung open. Inside the secret cubby was a small ornate box, trimmed in silver foil with pedestal legs. Standing no more than six inches high, it was the size of an everyday notebook. The lid and sides were enameled with what appeared to be lapis.

The buzzing noise in the back of my mind grew louder when I picked it up. I couldn't look away from the box. I turned it in my hands, looking for a way to open it, but there didn't seem to be a latch or keyhole.

"Bastian?" I called.

"Yes, princess?"

"Can you break this open?"

Bastian took the box in his hands, but before he could pry it open, Caleb yelled from the other side of the library, "Bastian, *stop!*"

We both gasped and stared at him in shock.

"What's wrong?" I asked.

Caleb strode over quickly, taking the small chest from Bastian. "It's a witch's box."

"A what?" we asked in unison.

"A witch's box. Witches keep their most treasured items stored in boxes like these, such as their grimoire, pendulums, sacred stones…whatever they don't want others to get their hands on. It can only be opened by saying the incantation the witch cast when she made it. If anyone tries to break into it, the box and its contents will be destroyed."

I stared at the box and then at Caleb. "Why would my parents have this?"

"I don't know, sweetness. Your mother wasn't a witch"—Darin snorted and muttered something under his breath while Bastian shushed him—"but it's possible they knew a witch and asked her to make this for them."

"How are we going to open it?" I asked.

"We'll have to ask Fiona. As the High Priestess, she's the only one powerful enough to break the spell without destroying the box itself."

"Won't she be here in a few months for the Tribunal meeting?" Bastian asked.

Caleb nodded. "Victoria, do you think you can wait until then? I'm sure she'd come early if I asked her to, but she'll be preparing for her trip and it could be difficult."

"I can wait." I closed my eyes and shook my head.

"What's wrong?"

"You can't hear that humming sound?" I asked, rubbing at my ears.

Caleb exchanged concerned glances with Bastian and Darin. They shook their heads. "No, sweetness, we don't hear anything."

"It's coming from the box. I know it is."

Bastian frowned. "Caleb, maybe we shouldn't wait."

"I'll send a message to Fiona. In the meantime, I'll ask Talin to lock this up in his room. It will be safe there and far enough away from Victoria that it shouldn't bother her."

"Caleb, can we go home now?" I swayed on my feet. "I'm not feeling well."

"Yes sweetness, let's go." Caleb handed the box to Darin so he could help me back to the car.

*

Talin cooked dinner for all of us that night. As we finished eating and the plates were cleared away, Bastian turned to Darin. "I think it's time for us to retire for the night."

Not missing his hint, Darin smiled. "I believe you're right. I'm a little tired this evening."

"You two aren't fooling anyone." I winked at them. "Go on, have some alone time. Thank you again for today."

"Good night, Victoria, Caleb." They both nodded and headed off to their guest room.

"It's nice having them here, isn't it?" I asked Caleb.

"Yes. I've enjoyed their company these past few months."

"How's their house coming along?"

"The renovations have been complete for a while now. I have a feeling they extended their stay for you. Neither one seems to be satisfied knowing I'm here."

I laughed. "I'm sure that's not the only reason."

"Maybe not, but now that this business with Malcolm is over, I expect they'll be going home soon."

"It's going to be very quiet around here when they do."

Caleb nodded. "Are you up for a walk this evening, my love?"

"Would you mind if we had tea on the terrace tonight?"

"Not at all. Why don't you go on ahead and I'll let Talin know."

I rose and kissed him on the cheek before heading outside. Caleb joined me shortly after and pulled his chair next to mine. Taking my hand in his, he kissed my fingertips.

"It's warmer out this evening than I expected," he mused.

"Yes. The sky is so clear. You can see every star, especially without the moon." I hesitated, sighing. "Caleb, what do you think is in that box?"

"I don't know, Victoria. With all we know about your family, I can't imagine what they could have, why they felt they needed that level of protection. While you and Bastian examined the box, I found a journal on one of the shelves that looks like it was your great-grandmother's. I brought it back to the house with us. Maybe something in it will shed some light."

"What do you think I am?"

Caleb frowned. "What do you mean?"

"I'm a human with incredibly strong seer abilities, and I projected a blue aura only I could see that was powerful enough to incapacitate a pureblood vampire. It doesn't make sense. Have you ever met a human like me?"

"Not in all my four hundred and fifty years. That's why I love you." He winked.

"I'm serious, Caleb."

"I know, sweetness. Honestly, I've never known a human with your level of abilities. I've only seen this power to this extent in a…" Caleb paused.

"In a what?" I pressed.

"In a Fae."

"A Fae? But they've been extinct for over a century. How could I be a faerie?"

"You can't."

"We need to read that journal and talk to Fiona." A slight panic filled my voice.

"Sweetness, don't worry, we will figure this out. You're still you. This doesn't change anything."

"Are you sure?" I asked.

"What could it possibly change?" I pointedly glanced between us. Caleb shook his head. "Nothing will change my feelings for you, Victoria. You are mine and I am yours. We are mated and bound together for eternity."

I smiled weakly.

Talin walked out with a tray holding a teapot and a plate of cookies. He set down the tray and poured our tea for us. "If there's nothing else you require, I'll retire for the evening."

"Thank you, we can manage from here." Caleb smiled at his old friend.

"Good night, Talin, and thank you."

"My pleasure, mistress. Have a pleasant evening." He bowed and left us alone again, but I lost the will to talk any further about faeries and my strange powers.

*

The next morning, I went to see Serena and the baby. As I held Victor in my arms, swaying him to sleep, Serena poured us both a cup of coffee.

"Serena, he's absolutely beautiful. Is he sleeping through the night yet?"

"We're close. He'll stay down for about five hours before waking up hungry. I'm not sure I'll ever be able to catch up on the sleep I lost." She sighed.

"You'll probably be playing catch up until he's grown and out of the house."

"Oh please don't say that, Victoria."

I laughed. "Any time you want a break, call me. We can even keep him overnight if you and Greggory need time to yourselves."

"I might take you up on the offer, my friend."

"Please do. I would love to have this little angel all to myself for a night." I cooed at the sleeping babe in my arms.

"All right now tell me, Victoria, what's new with you? I heard you went back to the house."

"Yes. Did Greggory tell you what happened with Malcolm?"

Serena nodded. "He did. I'm sorry I wasn't there that night. Do you want to talk about it?" I filled Serena in on all the details of the past few days. "That is peculiar. You're a much stronger seer than me, but I've never heard of anyone being able to pull someone's memories and play them like a movie in their mind. Were you even aware of what you were doing?"

"Not exactly. I was seeing it all happen, but I wasn't consciously thinking about it. I was on some sort of autopilot."

"Have you read through the journal Caleb found?" she asked.

"Not yet. I can't seem to bring myself to open it...Honestly, I'm afraid of what I'll find. Part of me wants to wait to see what's in the witch's box, but then there might be something about it in the journal."

"Has Caleb spoken with Fiona yet?"

"She's going to try to come a few days before the Tribunal, but she has so much going on with the covens that she's not sure she can break away. Caleb said she wasn't too concerned with the buzzing sound I hear when I'm close to the box. She said that's normal since it was my great-grandmother's. Being a seer, it could also be I'm sensitive to the magic that's keeping it closed."

Serena nodded. "Given what little I know of their magic, it's not surprising you can sense it."

Victor's eyes opened and he started to scrunch his nose and fuss.

"It looks like someone woke up hungry." I handed him back to his mother.

"He's always hungry." She laughed and tossed a blanket over her shoulder and started feeding him.

We spent the next few hours catching up and talking about the upcoming Tribunal.

Serena sighed. "I'm sorry I haven't been much help lately. I'm usually planning all the nightly events."

"Don't apologize. I can handle it and I'm happy to fill in for you. Oh, that reminds me. Galia and Talin said they would love to watch Victor if you wanted to attend the dinner party the first night. Since it's the biggest event out of the three days, they thought you wouldn't want to miss going."

"Are they sure? That would be wonderful. It will be good for Greggory and I to do something as a couple." Tension visibly dropped from her shoulders.

"They would be thrilled, especially Galia. She's looking forward to spending time with him. It'll be good for you to get out of the house. You're still a couple and need to have time together, even if it's only for a few hours."

"All right, please tell them thank you and we would be thrilled to accept their offer."

I smiled. "Perfect. Why don't you and Greggory come to the house an hour before we need to be there and set everything up with Galia? Then we can all ride over together."

"It's a date." Serena laughed.

Chapter Thirty-Four

"Collin, are you in here?" I knocked on the office door.

"Yep, over here. What's up, bro?"

"Do you think you can arrange a reservation at Horizons for this Friday night?"

"I'm flattered, but don't you think you should be taking Victoria to such a romantic place?"

I clenched my hands so they didn't wrap around his neck. "Collin…yes or no?"

"You're no fun. I'm sure it won't be a problem. I'll call Celeste now and make it happen."

"Great. I'll wait."

Collin grinned. "Why the rush? You seem particularly anxious, brother. What's going on?"

"Nothing, I simply want to make sure you can do it, before…"

"Before what?"

I gritted my teeth. "Just call her, please."

"All right." Collin held up his hands and picked up the phone. After a brief conversation, he hung up and smiled at me.

"Well?"

"I'm not telling you until you tell me what's going on." Collin leaned back in his chair.

I sighed. "You're exasperating. I managed to get tickets to see the new opera at the Starry Night Theater and I want to make a night of it with Victoria. She's been through a lot lately, and I want to treat her to a special romantic evening."

"Is that all?"

"What do you mean?"

"You don't have any other plans that night except a show and dinner...say to maybe pop a certain *question* to our beloved goddess...hmm?"

"Collin, do you stay awake at night thinking up ways to annoy me?"

"Yes actually, it's become a habit over the years." Collin shrugged. "But that doesn't answer my question."

"The thought has crossed my mind, yes."

"And?"

"And what?"

"Are you prepared?"

I rolled my eyes. "What do you think?"

"HA! I knew it. You already have the ring, don't you?"

"Of course...it's Mother's ring." I paused. "If you don't have any objections."

Collin smiled. "Of course I don't, brother. It's perfect for Victoria. I'm happy for you."

"Thank you. I suppose I should thank you too for not giving up on me. It's because of you that I found her."

"Let's just say you owe me one."

I grimaced. "I'm not sure I like how that sounds."

"It's too late now. Besides, I like the new mellow brother. He's not such a grumpy old curmudgeon."

I stood and turned before leaving. "Don't say anything to anyone, and tell Celeste not to do anything cute at dinner either. I don't want her finding out before I ask her."

Collin pretended to zip his lips. "Secret is safe with me. By the way, reservations for two are at five. Does that work?"

"It does. Thank you."

"You owe me another one."

I waved him off. "Put it on my tab!"

*

At the manor, I found Victoria setting the table. The house smelled fantastic. I wondered what feast she was preparing for us that evening.

"Good evening, my love." I walked up behind her and wrapped my arms around her waist, kissing the top of her head.

"Hello, I hope you're hungry because dinner is ready."

"I am, but I'm not sure if it's food I'm really craving right now." I pushed aside her long hair and nibbled her neck.

"No dessert before dinner," she teased.

"Aww...can't I indulge a little?" I licked at the vein in her neck and felt her shiver.

"No, because then I'll never get dinner out of the oven and you know it." She turned to face me, breaking the connection. Propping herself on her tiptoes, she kissed me softly. "After we eat, you can have all the dessert you want."

"What can I do to help?"

She laughed. "You can help me carry in the food."

As I followed her to the kitchen, I told her, "Don't make any plans for this Friday."

"Why, is something happening?" She handed me a platter with sliced beef and roasted potatoes.

"Hmm, this smells wonderful." I inhaled deeply. "But not as wonderful as you."

"No drooling in the food," she chided. "But back to this Friday."

"Oh yes, we are going out."

"We are? Where are we going?"

"That, my sweetness, is a surprise."

"No fair, you're such a tease."

I winked and headed to the dining room.

She followed. "Can I have a hint?"

"Nope."

"Meanie."

"Yep."

Her lips formed into the most delectable pout. I wanted to nibble them. "Maybe you won't get dessert after all."

She met my gaze. I didn't respond. Sitting in my chair, I did my best to imitate her pout.

"Don't give me those glowing sad vampire eyes." I kept staring at her, trying to look pathetic. "All right, you win," she admonished. "I won't press for details."

"And dessert?"

"Eat your veggies and you can have your dessert."

"Done." I dug into my plate like my life depended on it.

Victoria's laughter filled the room and my heart.

*

After dinner, Caleb wasted little time clearing the table and carrying me upstairs to our bathroom. He turned the water on and stripped off his clothes. I barely had time to get towels out of the closet and hang them on the rack before he started pulling my shirt over my head.

"Hey, down boy. What's the rush?"

"I need to feel you against me." His eyes were glowing bright with lust.

"Slow down a little. I'd like to enjoy this too."

"I'm sorry, sweetness."

Caleb slowed his actions. Tossing my shirt into the laundry basket by the door, he unhooked my bra. I unzipped my skirt and let it fall to the floor. Caleb's gaze lingered on my breasts before he pressed his lips to mine. I shimmied out of my underwear and let him lead me into the shower. The warm water soothed the tightness in my back. Mixed with Caleb's fingers tracing my curves, all the tension in my body melted away.

He turned us so the warm water flowed down his chest, making his muscles glisten. I traced the defined outline on his abs. His physique amazed me, the well-formed biceps and strong shoulders.

"Enjoying the view, sweetness?"

"Hmm, you look like you were chiseled out of stone." My fingers glided along his shoulders, then down his chest to his hips. "I want to bite you." I blushed.

Caleb chuckled. "Funny, I was just thinking the same thing."

His eyes glowed as he pressed my back against the slick tile, leaning his body weight into me. I tilted my head, giving him full access. He smiled and nuzzled his nose into the hollow of my neck and inhaled. "So sweet."

My body grinded against him, anticipating the feelings that came with every bite.

"Now who's in a hurry?" he teased, licking his way across my collar bone, nipping softly. The tips of his fangs grazed my skin.

"Caleb." My hand drifted up to entangle my fingers in his hair. I pressed closer. "Bite me," I pleaded.

"With pleasure, my love." His fangs pierced my hot skin. A gasp escaped my lips followed by a moan of delight. My heart rate quickened as an ecstasy like none other tightened my core.

Caleb drank from me, moaning as the hot liquid trickled down his throat. Pulling away but not breaking contact, he lapped at my neck, clearing away the few drops of blood that escaped. The puncture marks began to close.

I pulled his mouth to mine, forcing my tongue between his lips. The metallic taste of my blood mixed with the sweetness of his lips. He groaned as his tongue found mine and they began their heated dance.

Caleb's hands slid down my sides. Grasping my bottom, he lifted me. I wrapped my legs around his waist just as he entered me.

He grunted, "So tight…"

I threw my head back as he stretched my inner walls with his girth. He thrusted with urgency. "Caleb, don't stop!" I gripped his back, my heels digging into his legs to pull him into me.

"Victoria!"

"Nngh…deeper, Caleb."

Our breath came fast, pants of pleasure escaping our lips as we reached our climax together.

Turning off the water and wrapping a towel around me, Caleb carried me to our bed. His kisses trailed down the center of my body. He nipped the spot between my breasts, licked at the sweet spot over each hip, until he settled at my core. The kisses on my inner thighs made me wriggle. He pinned me down before licking at the sensitive nub begging for his attention.

"Beg for me, sweetness."

I buried my hands in his hair. "More..." I moaned.

His fingers slid in, filling my insides, adding to the sensation of his tongue as it danced, bringing me to a new height. My hips bucked once as I called out his name. "Caleb!"

He didn't stop. His fingers continued their onslaught, moving in thought-stopping circles, his tongue persistently massaging my sensitive core. The feeling building inside me was almost more than I could bear. I rose onto my elbows, one hand pressed to the back of his head. My hips moved in rhythm with his tongue. The tightness that had been building inside me released with such force I screamed before collapsing back onto the bed, breathless.

Caleb trailed kisses up my sides to my breasts, nipping and sucking on my taut nipples. His mouth claimed mine just as I was regaining my composure. With a wicked grin and mischief glittering in my eyes, I flipped him onto his back. "My turn, old man." Before he could object, I ran my tongue down his abdomen and bit at his hip bones, making him jerk in surprise.

"Victoria?"

I lowered myself down and took him in my mouth. One hand wrapped around the base of his erection. I relaxed my throat further and pulled him in deep.

"Fuck...Victoria..." Caleb threw his head back.

I continued pleasuring him until his breathing became short and caught in his throat.

"Victoria, I'm going to..."

Ignoring his warning, I took him deep inside me again, wrapping my lips around him and stroking him with my tongue. I hummed as he strained, his hand gripping the back of my head. The sensation of the vibration sent him over the edge and he climaxed. I swallowed all he had to give me before trailing kisses up his body.

"You're evil." He grinned.

"Are you complaining?"

"Not in the least." He kissed at my neck, nibbled on my ear lobe. "Shall we continue?"

I purred as he entered me again. Our bodies rocked in perfect rhythm. We held onto each other, our lips pressed together. I teetered on the edge of a bottomless pit of pleasure, the familiar tightness building again.

"Caleb, bite me again. I want to feel your fangs..." The sentence died in my mouth as the heat swelling in my core threatened to explode. A whimper escaped my lips.

*

Victoria was testing my control. That little sigh nearly undid me. "If you keep making those beautiful sounds, I fear I might break you."

Her eyes met mine. "Caleb...please," she pleaded, exposing her neck to me.

It was hard enough to contain my passion for her, especially now with her entire body flushing a rosy pink. Now she was begging me to bite her as she climaxed. The carnal lust rose inside of me, threatening to break lose. I had to remind myself to let her breathe between kisses. Tension gathered in my core. I wouldn't be able to hold back much longer.

My fangs descended as if they had a will of their own. I lowered my lips to her neck, licking my chosen spot before sinking them deep into her soft skin. I loved the taste of her blood. It was sweet and warm, and it filled me completely.

Overflowing passion clouded my vision as my body shook, my pleasure reaching its peak and exploding like a geyser. Her body tremored underneath me, and she moaned as she reached her pinnacle. I pulled back, licking at the two small wounds on her neck, helping them heal.

Her hands cupped the sides of my face. I could get lost in those deep blue-violet pools. My lips claimed hers softly, lovingly.

"You are my everything," I whispered between kisses.

A single tear fell from the corner of her eyes as she gazed at me. "You are my beginning, my now, and my end. I love you, Caleb, with all that I am."

I pulled her to me, lifting her into my lap so I could place us under the covers. I held her there until she fell asleep in my arms before joining her.

Chapter Thirty-Five

I sat on the terrace, enjoying the warmth of the mid-afternoon sun. I was surprisingly calm considering the leather-bound journals that sat on the table before me, one belonging to my father, the other to a great-grandmother I never knew. Her name was Corrina, and she had been the only daughter of one of the original human families to contract with the Council. During the Council's review of those presented ninety years ago, she met Christophe Chalifoux. He was from one of the other human families. They had an immediate connection. The members of the Council could also see their attraction and paired them together. Their children would go on to the *Legăturas*.

My mother never spoke of her family. Once she married my father, her world was all about being a Starling. The Chalifoux name ceased to exist. Thanks to Caleb, I learned my mother wasn't an only child as I had believed. She had a sister, Collette, but she passed away while giving birth to her first child when I was still a babe. I had so many questions that a part of me didn't want answered.

I chose to read through my father's journal first and finish it along with my cup of coffee. It was full of financial figures and notes on his hobbies, nothing that would shed light on the box we found. He did have one entry about me.

When I first saw it, I had a glimmer of hope that perhaps he had cared for me. I was mistaken.

We took the girl to the doctors again. Her migraines have increased in frequency. She will need special medications to control the pain—another unwanted expense. However, if this 'gift' she seems to have persists, perhaps she will bring in enough revenue to pay for this additional level of care. Personally, I think she's faking the pain to get Cynthia's attention…She's such a fool to think her mother will ever have anything but contempt for her.

Tears fell as I closed his journal. I wanted to toss it across the terrace. My eyes rested on my great-grandmother's journal. *Will the words it contains be just as cold? Was love foreign to my family on both sides?* I flipped open the cover and began to read.

Recipes and dates of friends and family members' birthdays filled the pages. She had even made notes about their favorite things, mostly what they liked to eat. I wondered if she baked for them when they had birthdays or special events.

As I neared the end of the journal, I had lost hope that there would be any reference to the box until I reached the last couple of pages. Corrina wrote about her family contracting with the Vampire Council and meeting Christophe. She spoke of their instant love, his kind eyes, and gentle touch. He was a soft-spoken man full of intense emotions. After that, the writings were faded in many places and appeared to be random thoughts.

Husband is not the father.

Firstborn, always girls…eyes of blue-violet…seers.

The box should never be opened—but it is all I have left of him.

Not of this world.

There were even notes about my mother and grandmother. *Catherine's daughter, Cynthia, was not chosen, just like Catherine. She was paired instead with a human, that Starling boy…bad match. Unlike her mother, she is miserable and cruel. Daughter will be the one.*

I paused on the last sentence. *What? Was that referencing me? I will be the one? The one what?*

The last entry on the page was written in Gaelic. My parents had taunted me when I asked to learn, but something about the fluid lilt of the language brought me comfort. I begged them to hire a tutor to teach me, something I was grateful for now as I read the next entries.

Bosca Cailleach. Nochtfaidh an stór istigh an solas. An té a bheirtear ar dtús iompróidh sí sciatháin Cinniúint.

I worked out the translations in my head. 'Witch Box.' 'The treasure inside shall reveal the light. She that is firstborn will bear the wings of Fate.' *What does this mean?*

I read the words again until I was pulled from my thoughts by a familiar voice. "There's my beloved."

Caleb was home from work sporting the widest grin I had ever seen on his face. I smiled up at him. "I didn't hear you come in."

The smile on his face faded as he realized what I held in my hands. He sat down in the chair next to me. "Everything all right?"

I cupped his cheek. "Yes, everything is fine. I finished going through them." I gestured to the two books.

"Find anything?"

"There wasn't anything of importance in my father's journal. We can burn it." Caleb sensed my disdain and didn't press. "As for Corrina's journal, it mostly contains recipes and special dates. It seems she liked to cook for others."

Caleb chuckled. "Sounds familiar."

I laughed. "Take a look at these last two pages." I handed the open book to him. "It's in—"

"Gaelic." Caleb frowned, finishing my sentence. "Witch box…"

"Yes, 'The treasure inside shall reveal the light. She that is firstborn will bear the wings of Fate.'" We recited it together.

Caleb turned to me. "You can read Gaelic?"

"Yes. I learned when I was young. I thought I'd be a little rusty since it's been so long, but my translation must be correct if you interpreted it the same way. Although I don't know what it means."

"The box obviously contains some sort of treasure. Maybe a family heirloom? It seems that the box is supposed to pass to the firstborn daughter through your mother's line."

I nodded. "That was my thought as well, but what could 'the wings of Fate' mean?"

"I don't know, sweetness. Based on the other entries, it seems that firstborn daughters have always been seers. Perhaps it means the gift that runs in your family is only passed from first daughter to first daughter."

"But my mother was the second born of her family."

"Then maybe it refers more to the timing. If your mother had you before her sister had a daughter, that would make you the firstborn, wouldn't it?"

"I guess so." I frowned. "I'm curious what she means by something not of this world. Caleb, do you know if my aunt's child survived? Do you think she saw the child's death?"

"I can check the Book of Family Trees again tomorrow, unless you want to go to the office with me tonight."

I shook my head. "We have plans, and I've been looking forward to this surprise of yours all week long. Now we should put these away and get ready. You still haven't told me what to wear." We stood, gathering up the books and heading into the house.

"You'll find a dress laid out on the bed for you."

"Caleb? What are you up to?"

He leaned down, kissing me deeply. "You'll see." He winked.

"You kiss me like that again and I guarantee you we won't make it out of the house tonight."

"Don't tempt me, my love."

*

The dress Caleb bought me was beyond perfect. The black sheath gown trailed all the way to the floor, while its halter cut left my entire back exposed. The neckline plunged deep, stopping at the point between my breasts. A high slit in the side stopped mid-thigh.

I showered and styled my hair and makeup before slipping the gown on.

I chose a simple black heel and silver hoop earrings decorated with inset diamonds. They sparkled in the full-length mirror as I turned before it, making sure everything was falling in place before joining Caleb in the sitting area of our bedchamber. He was already dressed in a black suit, navy vest, and matching tie. *If I hadn't spent the last hour getting everything perfect, I would drag that man to bed and pin him there until morning.*

"Thoughts like that are going to make us late, sweetness."

I smiled wickedly. "You're reading my mind again, my love."

"Wasn't that your intention?" He stood and stalked over to me.

Guilty.

"You are too sexy for my own good, Caleb Carrington. You are going to give this girl a heart attack looking that fine."

He smiled. "I'm surprised you can't feel my heartbeat from there. It's taking all my willpower not to rip that dress from your body and ravish you until you no longer have control over your limbs."

I leaned into his strong chest. "Caleb," I whispered.

He captured my lips with his, nipping longingly at my bottom lip. I wrapped a hand around the back of his neck and pulled him into me, kissing him hard as our tongues fought for dominance. When we finally broke from each other, we were breathless.

"Caleb, I'm afraid if we don't go now, we are not going to make it to whatever you have planned."

He growled low in his chest. "We will continue this later."

"Promise?"

"Promise."

*

I reclined in my seat, watching the river glisten beneath the rising moon. I couldn't decide on my favorite: the breathtaking nighttime view from the restaurant or the superb dinner. I sighed. "I've been wanting to come here for months."

"I know." He winked.

Caleb reached across the table and entwined his fingers in mine. "Are you enjoying our special evening, my love?"

"I am. As much as I love to cook, it's nice to be on the receiving end and not have to worry about something burning."

He lifted my hand to his lips and kissed my fingertips, sending little waves of pleasure through my body. My eyelids fluttered, a purr escaping my lips.

Caleb's eyes lit up with that familiar glow. "Sweetness, you're tempting me again."

"You started it." I grinned back at him.

He chuckled. "I suppose I did." He took a sip of his wine. "We have some time before my next surprise. I thought we could stroll by the river."

"There's more?"

"Of course, my love, the night is only beginning."

"You're going to spoil me."

"That's my plan." He winked.

After Caleb paid the tab, we walked hand in hand to the river boardwalk, enjoying the cool night air. Caleb led us to a lookout point. The outlet jutted out over the river, and judging by the number of ducks still floating around, it appeared to be a popular feeding spot during the day. He turned me to face him, holding both my hands in his.

"Victoria…" He paused.

"Yes, Caleb?" I gazed up into his eyes, noting he seemed nervous. "Are you all right?"

"I'm perfect." He took a deep breath and then chuckled. "I had this whole thing planned out, and now that we're here, I seem to be at a loss for words." I waited while he collected his thoughts. "I know that our relationship didn't start off in the most ideal way and we've had some challenges to overcome, but I'd like to think that we've reached a point where we are confident in how we feel about each other." He sighed. "This isn't coming out the way I wanted it to."

I reached up and cupped his cheek. "Caleb, take a deep breath and speak from your heart…You're trying too hard." I smiled at him, though silently admitted it was nice to see him flustered for once.

The knowing look in my eye must have given him the confidence he needed. Caleb took a deep breath and met my gaze. "Victoria, before you came into my life, I thought I had everything I would ever need. I thought I knew happiness, but I was incomplete. You have brought a light into my heart that I never knew was missing. I believe it was you I've been waiting for all these years. I love you with all that I am. You are my joy, my light, my mate, and I would be honored if you would also agree to be my wife." He stooped to one knee. "Victoria Starling, will you marry me?"

"Oh Caleb..." Tears filled my eyes. "Yes, *yes*, I will marry you. I never dreamed I would ever find someone that would love me so completely, so unconditionally as you. I would be honored to be your wife and stand by your side for all eternity. I love you, Caleb."

Caleb slipped the most beautiful ring on my finger. It was a perfect fit. An intricate design that resembled a rose framed the single round diamond in the center.

"It was my mother's ring. I hope you like it."

"It's...beautiful, Caleb. I'll treasure it always."

He pressed his lips to mine, wrapping his arms around my waist. We stood there silently holding on to one another. When I glanced at him, he was already staring down at me. "You make me so happy, Caleb. I only hope that I can make you feel a fraction of the joy you give me."

"My love, if I felt any more joy at having you in my life, I would explode."

"This night has been perfect." I smiled up at him.

"And it's not over yet."

"What? There's more? Caleb Carrington, where are we going now?"

"It's a secret."

I laughed as he grabbed my hand and gently tugged me down the boardwalk back to the car.

CHAPTER THIRTY-SIX

"Sweetness, what do you think about getting married on the last day of the Tribunal meetings?"

She dropped the wedding magazine she'd been rifling through into her lap. "So soon?" Her voice held a note of panic.

"I don't see any reason to wait, do you? I'd like Kaan to perform the ceremony."

Victoria's eyes glazed for a moment. It was amusing to see every emotion show in her expressions as she gathered her thoughts. I couldn't help but chuckle.

"Caleb, don't laugh at me," she pouted.

"I'm sorry, my love. You're so cute when you're thinking."

"Hmph. The last day of the meetings…that doesn't really give me a lot of time to plan." I could see the wheels in her mind turning as she ran through her mental to-do list. "Kaan. He's the dragon on the Tribunal, right?"

"Yes, sweetness. He's the oldest living being in the world and a very dear friend of mine."

"There's someone older than you?" She winked.

"Very funny. And you know, I'm not the oldest vampire living either. Mr. Norton is nearly twice my age." I frowned.

Victoria rose from the library's couch and meandered over to my desk, settling herself into my lap. "Don't be cross with me. I'm only teasing you." She wrapped her arms around me. Her scent filled my nose, her touch sending waves of pleasure through me.

I remained silent.

Victoria kissed my neck, then turned my face and brushed her lips across mine. "If it's important to you that he marry us, then we will make it work."

Her smile was infectious, and I found myself grinning back. "Thank you, my love."

"We will have to make it a small affair then. I don't see how Celeste can get Horizons ready with so little time."

"You'd be surprised. Celeste has pulled together elaborate events on last-minute notice so many times I'm sure even she's lost count. She can handle it."

"I'll give her a call now and see what she says. I'm not going to ask her to cancel a full night of reservations for us." Victoria rose and kissed me before heading toward the door. Her hand paused on the knob. "Caleb, she asked me if I wanted to work for her."

I raised my eyebrow. "What did you say?"

"I would think about it and talk to you." A nervous expression crossed her face.

"Do you miss working?"

"Sometimes, but cooking here every night for us and the staff leaves me feeling fulfilled."

"I will support you with whatever you decide, Victoria."

"Really? You wouldn't mind?"

"Of course not, as long as it means you can still cook for us. I would miss our nightly dinners too much."

"I would too." She smiled. "But right now, I have a wedding to plan, so I won't be making a decision until after the Tribunal."

I nodded. "That's fine."

"Caleb?"

"Yes, sweetness?"

"I love you."

"I know." I winked at her as she turned to leave.

*

First order of business: call Celeste. I took a seat at the kitchen table armed with my planner and updated her on the change to the wedding date. To my surprise, she had no reservations about hosting our reception on the last day of the Tribunal.

"Are you sure, Celeste? It doesn't give you a lot of time."

"Victoria, don't you worry about a thing. I have this covered. Everything will be perfect. Leave it to me."

"You really are the best. Thank you."

"Have you thought any more about my request?" she asked.

"I have, and I'm still considering it. I can't decide until after the wedding."

"Fair enough. It doesn't have to be full-time, you know. We can work out the details when you've made your decision."

"Thank you, Celeste. I'll talk with you soon."

"*Ciao*, my friend. Call me if anything changes."

After hanging up with Celeste, I sent a message to Serena.

> *Are you available to go dress shopping?*
>
> > *Victoria, you should know by now that I'm always available to go dress shopping. Or any other kind of shopping.*
>
> *Of course.*
>
> > *I know the perfect shops. Pick me up around lunch time.*
>
> *You got it.*

*

We had lunch at a small café in town, then headed off to the nearest boutique.

"Why is dress shopping so hard? Maybe I should wear something I already have in my closet." I sighed.

She fixed me with a hard stare. "Over. My. Dead. Body."

"What's the big deal? It's not like I've worn them every day. I bet no one will notice."

"Victoria, this is your wedding day. As your matron of honor, I forbid you to wear anything that has been seen by anyone in this town. Am I clear?"

"Yes...*Mom*." She stuck her tongue at me, making me laugh. I turned back to the racks. "I can't believe I have to find three separate gowns. This is impossible."

Serena chuckled. "Maybe if you focus on one at a time, it will be easier. You said you liked that pink one. I think it's perfect for your going-away dress after the reception."

"I think I will get that one. Caleb still hasn't told me where we are going for our honeymoon, but I suppose it will be the most comfortable one to wear if we are flying."

"Okay, that's one down. Now, what about the Tribunal gala? This crimson dress is stunning."

"Do you think it's a good color for me?"

She held up the dress to my frame. "Honey, you can wear anything. You're so gorgeous even a burlap sack would look fantastic on you."

"I still think it would look better on you."

"Oh no, I'm not wearing anything that tight. Not until I finish losing all this baby weight."

I stared at my friend. "What baby weight? You don't look like you even had a baby recently."

Serena sighed. "Please, this belly is not to be seen."

"Serena, stop, you're gorgeous! Go try this one on. It gathers across the middle and will hide that invisible belly of yours." I giggled.

"You think so?" Serena rubbed a hand over her lower abdomen.

"Dressing room, now!" I ushered her off.

A moment later, Serena stepped out in the deep purple dress looking like she belonged on the front cover of a fashion magazine.

"You're buying that, it's perfect. You look like a model—absolutely stunning."

"I don't know." She turned around, looking at her body from every angle in the large mirror.

"Well, I do. For once, trust me."

"If you say so, but you have to try on that crimson gown or no deal."

As I expected, Serena's pick for me was perfect. Besides the divine color accentuating my eyes and skin, the dress hugged my curves.

I sighed. "Now just the wedding dress."

"Let's go over to Belphor. Danica owns that shop, and she has the most stunning wedding gowns."

"And the most expensive. I don't really want to pay too much for a dress I'll only wear once."

"Psh…It's because you only wear it once that you shouldn't put a price tag on it. Besides, Caleb can afford it and he told you not to worry about the cost, didn't he?"

"Yes, but that doesn't mean I shouldn't."

She wagged her finger at me. "Actually, it does, little one. Now let's go see what beautiful creations she has for you."

*

"Serena, I'm exhausted." I must have tried on fifty gowns at Belphor. All the lace and tulle were starting to make my skin itchy.

"Trust me, this one is it." She shoved another dress into my hands and pushed me toward the dressing room.

"You and Danica have been saying that for the last twenty gowns," I groaned.

She tsked and closed the curtains. Sighing, I unraveled the heavy champagne gown. The lace and beadwork made it sparkle with every movement. The bodice had a sweetheart strapless neckline and a laced corset in the back, which dipped into an A-line skirt. A short three-foot train brushed the floor. I had little hope this would be the gown as I stepped into it, but after pulling it up, I gasped—it was *perfect*.

I stepped from the dressing room. Both Serena and Danica screamed when they saw me. Danica quickly turned me and laced up the back of the dress, then situated me on the pedestal before the tri-fold mirror.

"This. Is. It." She beamed. "It even fits you perfectly. I'll need to take it in a little in the waist but not much." She whipped out her measuring tape.

"Well, Victoria?" Serena asked from beside me.

Tears filled my eyes. I couldn't speak.

"I think that's a yes," Danica whispered.

The three of us giggled as we stared at the image in the mirror.

*

"Sweetness, how did shopping go earlier today?" Caleb asked as he filled his plate with a second helping of dinner.

"It was exhausting, but overall successful."

"Really?" Caleb raised an eyebrow as he gazed at my goofy grin.

"What? I'm grinning, aren't I? I can't help it."

He laughed. "It's okay, sweetness. I love seeing you this happy."

"Promise me you'll still feel that way when you see the receipts."

"I told you not to worry about what everything cost, didn't I?" He took a seat at the table. "So what colors am I wearing?"

"For the Tribunal gala, you'll need to wear crimson, and for the wedding, I was thinking a black tux with a champagne vest and tie."

"Not white?"

"No."

Caleb nodded and smiled. "As my love commands."

"Are you taking lessons from your brother?"

"What's this, you're talking about me?" Collin waltzed into the dining room, a cheeky grin on his face.

"What are you doing here?" Caleb asked.

"I was working late and got hungry. I didn't feel like cooking or going out, so I thought I'd stop by and join you." Collin sat at the table and scanned the dishes full of food.

I laughed. "Let me get you a plate."

"Thank you, princess." Collin smiled from ear to ear at his brother. "See, our beautiful goddess is happy to see me."

"There you go with that *our* business again," Caleb growled.

"And when did I say I was happy to see you?" I teased as I put a plate full of food before him.

"You don't have to, my goddess. I can see it in your eyes." He winked.

"Just eat your dinner."

"How are things coming with the wedding plans?" Collin asked before shoveling a huge forkful of potatoes in his mouth.

"Very well. Celeste is great. She's making this too easy for me."

"She really knows how to plan a party. Have you found your dress yet, princess?" When I nodded, his eyes gleaned with mischief. "What's it look like?"

I chuckled. "You'll have to wait and see."

"Come on, I'm not the groom. It's not bad luck for me to know about it."

"Nope, sorry. No one sees the dress until that day."

"What color is it?" Collin pressed.

I rolled my eyes. "I'm not telling you."

"Caleb, do you know what color it is?"

"Yep." He nodded at his brother, this time flashing his own grin.

"Tell me," Collin begged.

"Nope." Caleb winked at me as he took a bite of his chicken.

"You two are no fun."

To save me from more of Collin's pestering about the wedding, Caleb changed the subject. "How are things going with the preparations for the Tribunal?"

"Everything is all set. We'll hold the gala at the clubhouse like always, and the new table for the conference room arrived today. As long as you don't go anywhere near it, you and the other members can meet there."

Caleb scowled. "I only broke it once."

"Twice, actually. I had to replace it after you cracked it the first time."

"Serena says everything has been ordered for the gala and the caterers have the final menu, so there shouldn't be much left to do," I added.

Caleb nodded. "I'm sure she appreciates your help. I also spoke with Fiona, and it looks like she'll be able to come the morning of the first day. It will give us plenty of time to talk with her about the box before the gala that evening." I took a deep drink from my wine glass. Caleb paused. "Are you nervous, sweetness?"

"A little…When we first found it, I really wanted to know what was inside, but now, I'm worried about what it might contain."

"Hopefully it holds information that explains your gift. You need answers so you can put all of this behind you," Collin interjected. "I'm worried about you, princess."

"I hope so too. Even though I asked Caleb not to tell you everything"—I smiled as he winced—"I'm feeling fine, I promise."

Caleb reached over and covered my shaking hand with his. "We'll find the answers you need, Victoria."

Collin perked up. "Caleb, do you think Kaan would know anything?"

"He might. I intend to ask him when he arrives."

"Being around as long as he has, I would be surprised if he didn't. Of course, getting a straight answer out of a dragon is like winning a drinking contest with a werewolf."

"And how's that?" I asked innocently.

"*Impossible,*" they said in unison.

"Since you brought them up, what is Angus like?" I asked.

Collin let out a deep breath. "Wow, how do you describe Angus?" He scratched his head. "He's…well, he's a werewolf."

"That doesn't help me, Collin. I've never met a werewolf."

"As Fiona puts it, 'He's more beast than man.' He can be abrasive and brutal." Caleb thought more. "He likes to drink…oh, and he's *huge.*"

"So scariest beast imaginable…That's all you needed to say."

Caleb laughed. "He's not that bad. Just think of him as a large, cranky dog. He barks—a lot—but he rarely bites."

"Keep his stein full of ale and he's as calm as a kitten," Collin added.

"You're not painting a very positive image of him."

"It's kind of hard to do with Angus. He's an acquired flavor." Collin chuckled.

"Great." I sighed. They would be staying in the elaborate guest house near the Council headquarters, but the night after the gala, Caleb and I would be arranging a dinner for them at the manor. I already had the menu planned to accommodate everyone's preferences. With Talin and Galia's help in the kitchen, I wasn't worried. I was more concerned about how to speak with these individuals and making a good first impression, both as Caleb's mate and as the hostess for the meeting this year. What could I have to say that would interest immortals who had been around for centuries?

"Be yourself, sweetness. That's all you need to do." Caleb smiled at me, reading my thoughts.

I nodded and took another sip of my wine.

Chapter Thirty-Seven

The day of the Tribunal gala arrived, along with several last-minute details to finalize. I was at the clubhouse making sure everything was in place for that night. Serena had been here earlier in the morning but left to get Victor ready to go to the manor for the evening.

As I passed through the clubhouse again to check on the preparations, I noticed one of the sconces on the wall was flickering. I grabbed a ladder and was changing out the lightbulb when I heard what sounded like a grizzly bear enter the hall.

"I know I'm early, but what difference does it make?" a deep voice rumbled, shaking the walls.

"Sir, wouldn't you be more comfortable in your quarters at the guest house? We are still setting things up in here."

"No, now out of my way." He grumbled and pushed past the attendant.

Up until that moment, Collin and the twins were the largest men I had ever seen, but they didn't compare to the burly man who stomped into the main room. He stood seven feet tall. His broad shoulders were wider than the doorway, and bulging muscles threatened the seams of his shirt. If he lifted his arms, it might tear away the fabric like tissue.

His thick, chestnut hair fell over his shoulders in waves. Day-old growth covered his face, and his yellow gold eyes were so bright they seemed to glow. He was gorgeous in a terrifying way. Power emanated off his body. The ladder swayed beneath me. Before I knew it, I was toppling over, but instead of hitting the ground, I landed into the well-muscled arms of this stranger.

He must be the Alpha King.

"Girly, if you can't manage to stay on the ladder, maybe you should have someone more skilled working on that," he chuffed, his eyes taking me in.

"Thank you for catching me, but I can handle it. You just startled me."

He grinned mischievously. "Really now? I've been known to sweep a few women off their feet, but I will say this is the first time I've made one fall for me."

"You can put me down now." I pushed on his rock-solid chest.

"Let's not rush things, darling. I'm starting to take a liking to you. Perhaps I can carry you off to a quiet little corner and we can get to know one another. What do you say?"

"She said to put her down if I'm not mistaken." Caleb walked into the hall, his arms crossed. His eyes glowed deep blue in warning.

"Aw, come now, Caleb. Haven't you found your mate? Can't I have this little beauty all to myself? You know how I like the tiny ones."

Caleb's eyes glowed brighter. His fangs poked from between his lips. I leaned in toward the stranger's ear and whispered, "I am his mate."

I'd never been set on my feet so fast. I had to grab on to the burly man to keep from falling.

"Pardon me, Caleb. I didn't know she was yours." He shifted, shaking me off.

"You must be Alpha Angus. I'm Victoria." I held my hand out to the Alpha King.

Angus looked to Caleb and waited for his nod of approval before taking my hand in his and pressing it to his lips. "It's a pleasure to meet you, Victoria. Please call me Angus. I'm not fond of formalities outside of my pack."

"Welcome Angus, I've been looking forward to meeting you. Is there anything I can get you? We made sure to have several barrels of your favorite ale on hand."

Angus's eyes lit up. "I knew there was a reason I liked you. I would love some."

"I'll be right back. Caleb, would you mind finishing changing out that bulb for me?"

"Sure thing, sweetness." He leaned over and kissed my forehead.

"Can I get you anything?"

"No, I'm good for now."

*

Both of us watched Victoria leave the room.

"Angus, make yourself useful and pick up the ladder for me."

"Sure thing." Angus seemed distracted. "She's a pretty little thing."

"She's mine," I growled, fangs elongating.

"Oh, I know. I'm just admiring from afar." He grinned.

"Well don't."

"You vampires are too possessive."

"Are you saying you'd share Sheila?" I asked.

Angus growled at the thought. "Never, and she would rip off the head of any male that tried to touch her anyway."

"How is she?"

"She's expecting a pup any day now, and you know how *delightful* that makes her. She wasn't thrilled I left without her, with the wedding and all, but she told me I didn't have a choice."

"You can skip it if you need to get back. Victoria and I will understand. There isn't much going on anyway. I expect we can wrap up the Tribunal early this year."

"Honestly, I'd rather be here. All that screaming and swearing, and that's before she goes into labor." Angus shivered. "The birth stuff isn't really my thing. I'd rather be here drinking all your ale."

"Is that why you're here so early?" Angus nodded, and I chuckled. "For a creature as fierce as you, you're really a coward."

Angus snarled.

"Did you boys get that light fixed?" Victoria asked, reentering the hall with a large stein of beer filled to the brim with ale.

"Ah, darling, you're my savior." Angus took the stein from her and drained it in one gulp.

She planted her hands on her hips. "Maybe I should have them roll the barrel out here."

"Might save your feet the trip going back and forth all day." Angus winked.

"Ooh no, first one is courtesy. If you think I'm going to be fetching your drinks all evening, you have another thing coming. The barrel is tapped and behind the bar." Victoria pointed toward the back of the room.

"She's feisty, isn't she?" He grinned, bearing his thick canines.

"You have no idea."

*

Before I could respond, a melodious voice sounded from the doorway. "She would have to be to put up with you, Caleb."

We all turned toward Fiona striding into the hall. She was wearing a flowing gown of light blue which matched her eyes, and her golden blonde hair was lose and curled down her back.

"Fiona!" I chimed and met her halfway across the room.

"Victoria, it's always a pleasure to see you." I pulled her into an embrace.

"Why does everyone keep inferring I'm problematic?" Caleb pouted.

"Because you are, my love." I winked. "At least, you used to be."

"Are these two grouches giving you any trouble?" Fiona asked.

"Not at all, I can handle them. I've had a lot of practice with Caleb, and Angus seems like an overgrown puppy."

"Puppy?" Angus growled. "Let me tell you something, kitten, this puppy has fangs."

I chuckled. "Fangs don't scare me. Shall I get you a refill?" I took the empty stein from his hand.

Angus looked to Caleb and then to Fiona and sighed. "Is it always impossible to stay mad at her?"

"Yep." Caleb laughed. "Once she gets into your heart, you've already lost the war."

"Be nice, gentlemen. Victoria is an absolute angel."

I rushed over to the bar, returning with another stein of ale for Angus and a glass of strawberry juice for Fiona, her favorite.

"See, didn't I tell you she was an angel? Thank you, Victoria. You're a life saver." After taking a few sips of her juice, Fiona looked to Caleb and I. "Now, shall we see to this box you found?"

Caleb ran out to the car to get it while I cleared off one of the tables.

"Victoria, you have no idea why your family might be in possession of a witch's box?"

"No, my mother never mentioned it, and as far as I know, there aren't any witches in my family."

"That's true, I checked our records as well. No one in your family ever joined a coven or showed any inclination toward magic, other than your great-grandmother being a seer. I also don't have any record of a witch's box being commissioned for your family. On the rare occasion where a human family asks for one, we keep an account of it, what it was made for, and the incantation to open it, but there's no such…" Fiona's voice dropped away as Caleb returned and set the box down on the table. Her eyes widened as she gazed between us. "Wh-Where did you get this?"

"Fiona, do you recognize it?" Caleb asked, concern showing in his eyes.

"It's not possible…"

*

The minute I saw the box, my mind was flooded with memories. How could this box be here, and why had it been hidden in the Starling home?

"Taniel, what need does a Fae have for a witch's box?"

"The truth will be revealed in time."

I sighed. *"Must your kind always be so enigmatic?"*

Taniel laughed. "I suppose not, but I find it enjoyable. In all seriousness, it's best you know as little as possible this time."

I peered at my friend. "What did you do?"

"Fiona, the Fae will fade from this world very soon. Humans are destroying our forest, and what remains is not enough to sustain us. Our elders are blinded by their arrogance, and they refuse to acknowledge that Lanithal is dying, the Fae along with it. Some part of us must remain behind to keep the balance."

"Surely Tharaat and the others will see reason. You haven't given up trying to convince them, have you?"

"They will not listen to me." Taniel hung his head, a deep sadness darkening his eyes.

"Will the world survive the passing of the Fae? What will you put in this box, Taniel?"

"The world will survive. I have ensured that we will not fade completely. Please Fiona, for all the years we've known each other, do not question me further. Help me complete my destiny."

I held his hand, haunted by the feeling this would be the last time I'd see him. "I will do as you ask, Taniel."

"Fiona." Victoria placed a hand over mine, the same way I'd held Taniel's. "If you know something about this box, please tell me."

I gazed at Victoria. My eyes brimmed with tears. "I made this box a long time ago for a very special friend. He never told me what he needed it for or what he was going to do with it, only that it was necessary if they were to live on in this world."

"They?" Caleb asked.

I inspected the box again. "I can't believe this is here."

"Oh for goodness' sake Fiona, get to the point." Angus was starting to lose patience.

"You always were one to rush into everything," I hissed. "I made this box for Taniel!"

"The Fae council member?" Caleb asked.

"Why would my family have a witch's box that was requested by a Fae?"

Victoria's voice held a note of panic. Caleb placed a calming hand on her shoulder.

"That would be because you are part Fae, little one."

*

A tall lean man, with hair as white as snow and eyes as black as coal, entered the room.

"Kaan," Fiona greeted him warmly. "What do you mean she's part Fae?"

"That's not possible," Caleb started.

"Can't any of you smell it? Or have you been away from them for so long that you've forgotten?"

"Is that what I've been smelling?" Angus twitched his nose. "Never could stand the smell of faeries. Always too sweet, made me sick to my stomach."

"Well I'm sorry to offend your delicate constitution," I quipped at him.

"Sweet darling, for you, I can put up with it." Angus winked. "Caleb, I like this one—she's fun."

"She's still *mine*."

Angus snickered and took a drink from his stein. "For now."

"Making friends with the beast already, Victoria?" Kaan approached me, his hand out. "I am Kaan, the last of the dragons. It is a pleasure to finally meet you." He raised my hand to his lips.

"It's nice to meet you as well." I looked to Caleb, who was staring at me like I was the newest wonder of the world. "Kaan, are you sure I'm part Fae? I mean, how is that possible?"

"You'll need to open the box to find out."

"I don't know how to open it."

He smiled. "I think you do."

I looked to the box and then at Corrina's journal Caleb had placed beside it. *Could it be?* Taking a seat at the table, I pulled the ornate box before me, then closed my eyes and whispered, "*Nochtfaidh an stór istigh an solas. An té a bheirtear ar dtús iompróidh si sciatháin Cinniúint.*" 'The treasure inside shall reveal the light. She that is firstborn will bear the wings of Fate.'

The top of the box popped open with a soft click. I lifted the lid. The inside was lined with black velvet. The box contained only three items—a creased letter, an untouched sealed letter, and a necklace. The pendant was a lotus carved out of lapis and hung on a black cord.

I opened the worn letter first. The writing was faded but still legible. "It's from Taniel to my great-grandmother, Corrina…" I gasped.

"What does it say, sweetness?" Caleb looked over my shoulder.

"It appears that Taniel was the father of her child. He mentions that the box would call to the one destined to receive it. Caleb?"

Fiona answered my unspoken question. "That's why you hear a buzzing sound when you are near the box, Victoria. It was calling to you."

"Why me?"

"Open the other letter, little one." Kaan smiled.

I cracked the seal and swayed in my seat as a wave of power coursed through me.

"Victoria?" Caleb held my shoulders to steady me.

"I'm all right. Did you feel that?"

He shook his head.

Unfolding the letter, I recognized the handwriting and gasped. "It's another letter from Taniel." I read it out loud for all to hear. "*My dearest great-granddaughter, the time has come for the light of the Fae to return to your world. If you are reading this, it means that you have been made whole, and the box has called to you. I am sorry for any hardships you had to endure on your path to finding the one that would make your life complete. I know not what trials you've encountered as a result of the spell Shatale placed on me to ensure the continuance of our kind, but finding your mate will eliminate any curse the spell has set on you. Fulfill your destiny and bring forth the light. The talisman will show you our way. Wear it, and your fate will be revealed. All my affection, Taniel.*"

I took out the necklace. "The treasure inside…" I looked to Caleb.

"The choice is yours, sweetness. I'll be right here." He gently squeezed my shoulder.

Kaan nodded at me, while Fiona smiled. When my gaze met Angus's, I paused.

"I was never one to trust the Fae, darling, so don't look to me." He took a deep swig from his stein, but I could see the worry in his eyes.

"Caleb, don't let go, okay?"

"Never, my love." He winked.

I pulled the black cord over my head. The world around me swirled, but I didn't feel dizzy. My surroundings were blurry, but I could still feel the solid warmth of Caleb's hand on my shoulder, and it brought me comfort.

When my vision cleared, I was watching a group of men argue around a table. One stood out among them, his face scrunched in anger.

"The Fae have never mixed with another race and we will not start now... even if it means our extinction."

"That's Tharaat."

I jumped at Caleb's voice. "You can see this?" I didn't remember moving, but we now stood side by side, his hand still grasping my shoulder.

Caleb nodded. "It must be because we are connected."

"Don't let go."

The scene before us faded, transporting us to a small cottage with Taniel and an older woman.

"If I'm right, her Fae blood will act much like a pheromone, drawing unmated men to her until she finds the one meant for her."

"That explains that mystery," I remarked dryly. Caleb only smiled.

The scene swirled away again. This time, we were standing on the edge of a forest, watching Taniel with a dark-haired woman.

"You are with child, Corrina. My child...our child. She will be the start in ensuring we do not disappear forever. Her children will carry the fate of the Fae, but she must never know of her true lineage. You must keep our affair secret."

Something strong pulled us from the scene and whisked us into the forest. Dark trees surrounded us. We stopped at a small clearing shrouded in shadow except for an ethereal form standing in the middle. That form came closer. Taniel.

The ghostly image smiled at me. He didn't speak, and I wasn't afraid.

"I don't know what to do," I whispered.

You will. The words echoed in my mind.

I gazed into Taniel's clear eyes and felt a warm love, a love of family, wash through me. He raised his hand and pressed his finger to my forehead. White light blinded me, so bright it blocked everything from my sight. I could no longer see Taniel, or Caleb, or the clearing. I heard nothing, felt nothing at first, then memories enveloped my mind—Taniel's memories. His knowledge of the Fae took root inside of me.

"See who we truly are…who you truly are. You are Fae, the bringer of light. Your fate is to return the power of the Fae to the world. Absorbing my magic, my knowledge, will change the balance within. The shift will be painless, but you will no longer be merely human—YOU ARE FAE!"

*

I watched as Taniel touched his finger to Victoria's forehead. Her eyes closed and her head tilted back. I caught her in my arms before she fell to the ground.

"She will wake knowing she is Fae. All the knowledge of my lifetime has been bestowed to her. My kind will live on and return to this world through your children. Take care of them well, Caleb Carrington, for I am entrusting you with the wings of Fate that will maintain the balance of this world."

I nodded as Taniel's form vanished. Our surroundings shifted once again, bringing us back to the clubhouse.

*

"Well, that was a waste," Angus grunted.

When I blinked open my eyes, I was still sitting in the chair, Fiona and Kaan staring at me in anticipation. Caleb stood behind me with his hand on my shoulder. "Caleb, did that really happen?"

"Yes, sweetness."

"Did what happen?" Angus drained his stein. "You put the necklace on and nothing."

307

Kaan chuckled. "I have a feeling we were not witness to their journey."

Fiona frowned. Reaching her hand out to me, she brushed my hair behind my ear and gasped. "Oh my."

"What?" I raised my hand to my face.

"Your...your ears. They're Fae." She smiled.

I ran my fingers along the outer edge of my ears. There was nothing round about them anymore. They were longer and came to an elegant point. Speechless, I glanced at those around me and met Caleb's gaze. He was smiling.

Kaan laid a gentle hand on my shoulder. "You'll have to share your journey with us over a round of drinks."

Chapter Thirty-Eight

C aleb and I recounted everything we saw during our shared vision.

"Well, my dear, it seems that all the pieces of the puzzle have finally fallen into place for you." Fiona smiled and patted my hand.

"All except I still don't have the first idea what it means to be Fae. What do I do? Do I do anything? Should I *feel* different?"

"I don't know what a Fae feels like," Angus replied and laughed, "but it looks like we have to make a seat for you on the Tribunal."

I paled at his comment. "What? Why?"

"Now Angus darling, don't scare the poor girl on her first day. She's been through enough already," Fiona chided.

"True, just meeting Angus must have been enough of a shock." Kaan nodded his head at the werewolf king by his side.

"I'll ignore that, Kaan."

"Since you know you don't stand a chance in a fight with me?" He egged the cantankerous werewolf on. Angus growled in frustration.

Fiona clapped her hands and changed the subject. "I, for one, am glad you'll be joining us. There's been way too much testosterone in these meetings. Women rule the world anyway, so it's about time I have another of my kind by my side to keep you lot in line."

Angus snorted. "Women rule the world, that'll be the day."

"I'll be sure to let Sheila know you said that the next time I see her," Fiona threatened.

Angus cowered like a scolded puppy, causing all at the table to laugh. "What? She's scary," he admitted.

"She's your mate," Caleb noted.

"Yes, but I didn't choose her. That was the Moon Goddess's plan. I was happy being a carefree bachelor. There are so many beauties out there to love." He looked at me and wiggled his bushy eyebrows.

"Down boy." Fiona looked sideways at Caleb, whose eyes were glowing again. "You'd be lost without Sheila and you know it."

"Now I definitely can't wait to meet her." I chuckled.

"I'm going for a run and then take a nap before tonight." Angus left the hall in a huff.

"We didn't really upset him, did we?" I asked.

"Don't worry about him. He'll be as happy as a pig in mud after his run," Kaan assured me. "He puts on a good show, but he's head over heels for his mate. They can't help it—the Moon Goddess rules over werewolves, and she's never wrong."

"We should all retire and get some rest before tonight's gala." Caleb rose and held his hand out to me.

"Victoria." Fiona caught my attention. "If you need anything, please don't hesitate to ask me. Over the next few days, you're going to be learning more about who you are, and it can be scary when your personal magic reveals itself—I've been there. I'll support you in any way that I can."

"Thank you, Fiona, I truly appreciate your kindness. I'm sure I'll have many questions for you. Please rest and I'll see you later this evening."

She winked and blew Caleb and I a kiss before heading out to the guest house.

"Kaan?" I placed my hand on his arm, preventing him from leaving.

"Yes, Victoria?"

I paused, looking intently into his dark eyes. "You don't seem surprised by any of this. Would I be correct in saying you knew?"

Caleb looked from me to his old friend. "Did you know that Taniel had mated with a human?"

Kaan smiled and chuckled softly. "You are very observant, little one. Yes, I knew. Taniel came to see me first. He told me of his relationship with Corrina and his plan for the necklace you are wearing. For the sake of his descendants, he made me swear an oath, an unbreakable vow, that I wouldn't reveal anything to anyone. However, until I arrived here today, I had no idea that the bringer of the light was you, Victoria. I'm sorry, Caleb. for keeping this from you. I admit it has not been as easy a vow to keep as I thought."

"Do you know what this means for Victoria? Fae magic is beyond my comprehension but turning a human into a Fae...I never knew such a thing was possible."

"Victoria is still herself. The difference now is she carries within her a piece of Taniel's life force. I cannot say what part of himself he infused in that talisman. His letter refers to his memories and his knowledge, but he imbued enough to trigger a change in her physical appearance. Only time will show us the true extent of this shared existence." When I sighed, Kaan smiled. "Do not fear, little one. Taniel would never do anything to cause you harm. Shatale's magic was the purest I have ever encountered. I have no concerns for your wellbeing, if that brings you comfort."

"It does. Thank you, Kaan."

The dragon rose. "I will take my leave for now. Until this evening." He bowed and left the hall.

*

Caleb and I drove back to the manor in silence, lost in our own thoughts about the events of that afternoon. The ornate witch's box sat in my lap, Taniel's letters safely tucked inside, but his talisman remained around my neck. I traced the patterns on the box with a finger. The buzzing noise had stopped once it had been opened.

As we entered our room, I put it on the top shelf of our closet and turned to

Caleb. "Will you lay down with me for a little bit?"

He nodded.

As we settled in each other's arms, I laid my head on Caleb's chest, feeling the rise and fall of each breath, the beating of his heart. "You've been awfully quiet." I played with the buttons on his shirt, afraid to look into his eyes. *Will this change things between us?*

Caleb's fingers glided up and down my spine, but he remained silent.

"Do you want me to leave?" I asked.

Caleb flinched and hooked a finger under my chin, forcing me to meet his gaze. "Why would you think something like that Victoria? I never want to be without you. Knowing you are part Fae doesn't change my love for you."

I breathed a sigh of relief. "You haven't said anything since we finished telling them what we saw. I can't tell if you're happy, worried, or angry right now."

Caleb chuckled. "Actually I'm stunned...and slightly amused." I leaned up on my elbow, trying to read his expression. "Victoria, I knew Taniel, not well mind you, but we had many conversations during Tribunal meetings in the forest of Lanithal. He shared my opinion on the need to mate with humans for survival. He didn't see a way the Fae could survive...but I never would have guessed he had it in him to go against his fellow council members or even Tharaat. He idolized the man."

I smiled. "You're finding this humorous."

"Yes, if I'm being honest. However, I am also very worried about you. You've had quite the morning. Between your encounter with Angus, which alone would have been a shock to anyone, meeting Kaan, and then everything with Taniel and learning you are part Fae..." He trailed off.

"My head should be exploding, but surprisingly, I don't feel any different. Do you think it's going to hit me all at once?"

Caleb frowned. "I don't know, sweetness. I thought you would feel something, but perhaps Taniel's magic is protecting you."

I sighed. "Maybe. All I know is I'm tired and need a nap if I'm going to make the gala this evening."

"You've been complaining of fatigue frequently these past few days. You've been pushing yourself too hard getting this gala ready." He scolded me with a tap on my nose. "I'm going to insist you relax while we are away on our honeymoon."

"Really? I never expected you would let me rest on our honeymoon." I winked.

"Well, I've heard that intimate relations can be very good for releasing stress." He nuzzled my neck.

"Then you may be just what the doctor ordered." I giggled and then sighed. "Caleb, we will have to tell the others tonight. Unless I wear my hair down, I won't be able to hide…" I paused.

"Your ears?" I nodded. Caleb brushed my hair back to reveal them. "Sweetness, are you sure you want to tell them tonight?"

"I think it's best. They are going to find out sooner or later, and if I keep this from Serena, she'll never forgive me. Besides, if we invite them to the manor early tonight and tell them, it won't cause a scene during tonight's event."

Caleb nodded, still entranced by my ears. "You're probably right. I'll let them know." He reached up and traced his fingertip along the outer edge, making me shiver. He smiled wickedly. "Sensitive?"

"Apparently…" I purred. He leaned in closer and gently nipped the tips with his teeth. I couldn't hold back a gasp from the little thrill. "That's certainly a surprise."

"A good one I hope." He continued to trace the edge with his tongue.

I shivered. "Caleb, as much as I'm enjoying this new…sensation, I'm really, really tired."

"All right, sweetness. I will save exploring this new delicacy for later." He pulled me in close. "Why don't you wear your hair down tonight at the gala? We can tell everyone else when the opportunity arises."

"Whatever you think is best." I yawned.

Snuggling into his embrace, the feel of his long muscular arms around me, I drifted off to sleep.

*

Serena and Greggory arrived at the manor first with little Victor and what looked like his entire nursery.

"Serena, is Victor moving in?" I teased as I took two bags from her shoulders.

"The blue one needs to go in the fridge."

"All right, I'll put it away while you haul your entire house into the living room. Galia and Talin are waiting for you." I winked. "By the way, you look absolutely stunning in that gown."

Serena's eyes narrowed on me. "Thank you, and you look as gorgeous as ever, but something's different."

I smiled. I knew I wouldn't be able to hide anything from her. "Go on, I'll be there in a minute."

I put away the bottles from the bag and headed into the living room.

"Victoria, you're wearing your hair down," Greggory commented.

"That's what's different!" Serena exclaimed, then frowned. "Why?"

"What do you mean? Am I not allowed to wear it down?" I was evading her question and she knew it.

Serena's eyes locked with mine, nearly melting me with her piercing gaze. "You *never* wear your hair down."

"Stop being such a mother hen and please don't glare at me. I promise I'll tell you everything once the others get here."

"You opened the box earlier today and found something out, didn't you?"

I nodded. "We did, but we want to tell everyone at the same time. No sense in repeating it."

"All right, I'll wait." Serena sighed and went back to sit next to Galia, who was rocking little Victor in her arms and singing him a lullaby.

Once Collin, Darin and the twins arrived, Caleb and I recounted the events from earlier in the day.

"You're fully Fae now?" I could see Collin's mind reeling from all the information we dumped on them.

"How is that possible?" Serena asked.

"Kaan doesn't believe I'm fully Fae, but I certainly have some of the physical characteristics now." I lifted my hair so they all could see my elongated, pointed ears. "I don't feel any different, as he said a part of me is still human."

Collin stared at my ears in amazement. "Can I touch them?" He raised his hand, but Caleb quickly slapped it away.

"You may NOT!" he growled.

"Spoil sport," Collin pouted, rubbing his hand.

"How is this possible?" Serena shook her head, repeating her question.

"Taniel imbued the talisman he left in the box with his life force, as well as all his knowledge of the Fae. When Victoria put it on and we encountered his memory, for lack of a better word, whatever enchantment he and his mother used caused his life force to fuse with hers."

"And the Fae are reborn?" Bastian questioned.

"Essentially, yes." Caleb nodded. "Their magic was always much too powerful for this world. It doesn't surprise me that they had this capability."

"What does this mean for Victoria?" Bastian and Serena still had concerned looks in their eyes.

"I have always been part Fae. Taniel is my great-grandfather, after all. While I don't fully understand what this means for my future, I'm still me. Other than my ears, nothing else has changed physically, although I guess I'll be wearing my hair down more now."

"I'm not going to complain about that." Caleb smiled and draped his arm around my shoulders. "I think we need to give it time. Taniel was a good man, and I doubt he would have done anything to harm his descendants. My suspicions are that whatever magic he used will reveal the truth to Victoria slowly and over time so she has the chance to adjust."

"We just have to be patient?" Bastian scoffed.

"Not your strong suit, we know, Frosty." Collin clapped him on the shoulder. "But unless our little goddess here has sprouted hidden wings, I don't see anything different in her, do you?" Everyone shook their heads. "Then I suggest we all head out and enjoy tonight's festivities. I'm sure there are some beauties anxiously awaiting my arrival." Collin smiled.

"You're delusional, my friend. You know they're all waiting for me." Blake winked.

"You two are incorrigible. I can't wait for the day you get snared by your mates," Serena teased.

"Hush your mouth, Serena." Collin shivered. "Never going to happen."

"Never say never," I added.

"Aw, my goddess, you know my heart belongs to you." He hugged me into his side.

"That's enough of that." Caleb pulled me away. "Hands to yourself, brother."

Laughing, we all headed out to our cars.

Chapter Thirty-Nine

The Tribunal gala was the opposite of the annual ball. Where the ball gathered everyone in our community together for a night of celebration, the gala was open only to the members of the Vampire and Tribunal councils and their immediate family members. A much smaller and more diplomatic affair. Conversations that night were a mix of socializing and political positioning. A long dining table had been placed on one side of the room, the seating arrangements carefully coordinated by Serena and I with some of Caleb's guidance. A modest dance floor sat on the opposite side of the room to allow for less formal socializing.

Serena and I mingled to ensure everyone was having a good time. We couldn't help but chuckle at the group of single women who flocked around Collin and Blake.

"They are having way too much fun. We should do something about that, don't you think?" I winked at her.

"I agree, let's find Bastian and Darin."

"I want in too," Fiona whispered from behind us. "I'm absolutely bored with council ramblings. Let's have some fun."

I giggled as the three of us went off to find our accomplices. When we met up with Darin and Bastian, they didn't need any convincing to join our ruse.

"I have to say, Victoria, I'm not sure what to think of this devilish side." Darin smiled.

"Me? Devilish?" I feigned innocence.

"They may never forgive you for this," Bastian warned.

"Oh, come now Frosty, it's just a bit of fun. Besides, they wouldn't hesitate if the roles were reversed."

"Are you sure this is a good idea? It is the Tribunal gala. Won't Caleb be angry?" Darin asked, having second thoughts.

"We aren't blowing up the clubhouse, Darin. Victoria can handle Caleb anyway." Fiona chuckled, waving off his concerns.

"Which one should we target?" I asked.

"My brother is overdue for some payback," Bastian immediately offered.

"Do you have a plan?"

Bastian winked with a devilish smile.

"What are you all up to?" Caleb walked over, a disapproving scowl on his face.

I smiled sheepishly. "Nothing…just having a bit of fun."

"Mmhmm…why do I get the feeling that you're up to your tricks, my love?"

"Wait, are you having fun without us?" Angus joined in, canines visible beneath his wide grin.

"Seems that Victoria is causing a bit of mischief tonight. Could her spritely side be coming out?" Kaan raised his eyebrow as he looked over at me.

"Oh, well…" I found myself at a loss for words before the Dragon Lord.

He smiled. "How can we be of assistance?"

I blushed. "Maybe we shouldn't…"

"Oh no, we are not letting my brother off the hook that easily." Bastian shook his head.

Angus's eyes gleamed with excitement. "Wait, are we going to disrupt that little gaggle of geese he has flocked around him?"

Bastian smiled. "That's the plan. I was going to see if you were interested in helping us." He leaned forward and whispered his idea.

"Ha! I love it! Count me in. I've been itching to get him back for that prank he pulled three years ago." Angus drained his stein of ale and rubbed his hands together.

"Shush, not so loud. Blake can smell a plot a mile away." Bastian glanced around to see if anyone noticed.

Caleb crossed his arms. "You all do realize this is the gala we are at right now. It's a time-honored traditional affair, not some backyard cookout."

"Blah, blah, blah...don't be a killjoy, Caleb." Angus slapped a large hand on his friend's back. "It's about time something livened up this stuffy event. Victoria, you are a breath of fresh air, my darling. If you ever get tired of this old crusty curmudgeon, give me a call."

Sensing the tension wafting off Caleb, I wrapped my arms around him. "Sorry, Angus, but I have no plans of leaving this old man, grumpy or not. I'm all his."

Caleb huffed but wrapped his arms around me and kissed my forehead.

"Alright, enough of that lovey-dovey stuff. It's show time." Angus straightened and cracked his knuckles, then headed toward his target. "Blake, a quick word?"

The dark-haired Boylston twin bowed to his admirers. "Ladies, please don't go anywhere. It will only be a brief moment before I am back in your loving care." A chorus of giggles floated through the air. I clapped a hand over my mouth to stop my bark of laughter. Blake shifted to look at the Alpha King, but not enough to turn his back on the women surrounding him. "Angus my old friend, what can I do for you?"

"It's not anything you can do for me. I only came to give you fair warning that your mate is on her way. You may wish to disperse these lovely gentlewomen from your presence before she arrives."

"My mate?" Blake cocked his head. "But I don't..."

"You have a mate, Blake?" one of the women asked.

"A werewolf mate?" Another gasped in shock.

Angus solemnly nodded. "Yes. I don't know if you know much about our kind, ladies, and forgive me my bluntness, but she-wolves don't share their mates or take kindly to other females around them. It leaves a scent behind. If she catches even the smallest whiff of another woman on her mate, she will hunt them down and, well…let's just say it's a messy affair to clean up."

The women quickly gathered their belongings and made their excuses to leave. Blake glared at the Alpha King.

Angus met his steely gaze and clapped him on the shoulder. "As much as I enjoyed that ol' boy, I can't take all the credit." He smiled and gestured my way. Blake's eyes softened, but only slightly, when he looked over at me. I couldn't help but laugh, despite knowing he was going to pay me back one day.

"I think you're in trouble, princess," Bastian whispered in my ear.

"Caleb, protect me."

"Oh no, sweetness." He laughed. "You're on your own with this one."

"Come with me, you little imp." Blake grabbed my hand and led me to the dance floor. "So, you're the mastermind behind this little ruse?"

"I guess I'm the one that started the ball rolling. I'm sorry, Blake. It was only a bit of fun."

Blake stared at me for a few moments looking like he was about to lecture me, then he burst into laughter. "I'm impressed, princess. Remind me the next time I want to pull a prank to make sure you're on my side."

"You're not mad?"

"No, I was getting bored with them anyway." A darkness clouded his eyes. I could sense his longing for someone special. My vision blurred, and a feeling of deep connection and love overcame me for a moment. "Are you all right, Victoria?" We had stopped dancing.

"Y-yes, sorry. I think I was getting a vision, but it's gone now." I looked at the vampire holding me up as we started dancing again. "You'll find her, Blake… and soon. I promise."

"Did you…?" His words trailed off, as if he dared not hope.

"I didn't see anything. It was more of a feeling. You will find the one intended for you." I smiled as the light returned to his eyes. We finished the dance and joined our friends.

"It appears our little Victoria has been forgiven." Kaan chuckled.

"I don't know how I'm being saddled with all the blame. It's not like I acted alone," I pouted.

"Those at the top always shoulder the burden of blame for the actions of their cohorts," Caleb teased.

I elbowed him in his ribs. "You're supposed to be on my side."

"Always, my love." He kissed the top of my head.

*

"Why don't you two stay with us tonight? It's late, and with everything you brought over for Victor, it would be easier to pack it all up in the morning," I suggested as we drove back to the manor.

Serena sighed. "Caleb, you're an angel. That would be wonderful. I'm not sure I have the energy to load everything back up anyway."

After checking in with Galia and Talin and wishing everyone good night, Victoria and I readied for bed.

"I think tonight was a success, don't you, sweetness?"

"I do."

"You and Serena put a lot of work into this gala and it shows. Thank you."

Victoria smiled. "You're not mad about the shenanigans with Blake?"

I wrapped my arms around her. "No, it was amusing seeing him on the receiving end for once."

"I have to admit, I was impressed with Angus's improvisations. I'm not sure I could have come up with antics like that without planning ahead." Victoria giggled. "The look on their faces was priceless."

"How are you feeling, sweetness? You seem tired again."

She laid her head on my chest and hummed. "Yes, I am. Taking a nap earlier helped, but now I feel like I'm crashing again, and my back hurts for some reason."

I rubbed her back and noticed it felt warm. I touched my lips to her forehead. "Your back is warm, but you don't seem to be running a fever. Why don't you take a quick shower and head to bed? It's been a long day."

"Will you join me?"

I smiled. "As if I would ever refuse such a request."

CHAPTER FORTY

T he following day passed by in a blur. I never expected Angus was serious when he mentioned me joining the Tribunal, but it seemed that the others agreed with him.

"What did you think of your first Tribunal meeting, sweetness?" Caleb asked as we returned to the manor.

"It was interesting, although I'm not sure what value I added to today's discussion." I frowned.

"Are you still worried about what will happen when we let our communities know that the Fae have returned?"

"Aren't you?"

"Not really."

"I don't know how you can be so calm." I bit at my nails as I paced in our bedroom.

Caleb walked over and took my hands in his. "Victoria, it will all be all right. We've been through worse. We can handle this, and I will be by your side always. You don't need to worry."

"When Taniel's life force joined with mine, do you think it changed my mortality?"

Caleb paused. "I don't know, sweetness. It's possible. The Fae have very long lifespans, much like vampires, if not longer. I'm more worried about the demon that helped Malcolm. No one is able to identify them."

"Do you think Fiona will be able to restore that witch's memories?"

"It's unlikely. She's lucky her mind wasn't completely erased by the demon. Whoever it is, they're extremely powerful."

"But why would this demon leave her alive? If they were working with Malcolm, they can't be a nice demon."

Caleb laughed. "Nice demon?"

"What would you call it?"

"I think it's a perfect term, sweetness, especially coming from you." He chuckled. "I'm surprised she's alive too. Thankful…but surprised."

I sighed and rubbed at my forehead. There were so many questions left unanswered.

"You're going to make yourself sick with worry. You're tired again, aren't you?" Caleb asked. *Can't fool him.* He gestured to the bed. "Take a nap."

I shook my head. "I can't. I need to make sure everything is ready for tonight's dinner."

"Let Talin and Galia handle that. You need to rest." Caleb frowned.

"No. I need to take care of this myself. I'll go down and get things started. If I have time before tonight, then I'll lie down. I promise."

"And I'm sure there's nothing I can say that will stop you," Caleb mused. I nodded. "What can I do to help?"

"If you can make sure we have enough ale for Angus tonight, I would appreciate it. And bring up a few bottles of the wine that Kaan prefers from the cellar. That will save me the trip."

"As my love commands." Caleb kissed my forehead and headed off to his tasks. I smiled and sat down in one of the chairs by the fireplace after he left.

I'm so tired. Maybe Caleb's right. I should take a quick nap. I'll go make sure Talin is all set in the kitchen and then come back up. I sighed and leaned back in the chair. *First, I'll just rest my eyes for a minute.*

*

"Victoria, sweetness…" I gently shook her shoulders.

"Hmm, what is it, Caleb?" She sat up and rubbed her eyes.

"You fell asleep in the chair. It's time to wake up."

"What time is it? How long have I been asleep?" Her eyes widened as panic took over. "Oh no, dinner. I need to get downstairs."

"Victoria, relax, dinner is coming along just fine. Talin has everything under control. Take a shower and get dressed. It will make you feel better. Everyone will be here in an hour."

"An hour?" She plopped back into the chair. "How could I have fallen asleep?"

I took her hands and pulled her to her feet. "You were tired. A nice hot shower will wake you up."

Maybe she'll feel better after relaxing during our honeymoon.

*

"Talin, Galia, I'm so sorry for leaving all the work to you. Everything looks and smells wonderful."

"We are glad to help, mistress. Master Caleb said you were feeling tired, so I'm glad you decided to rest." Galia smiled. "With the wedding tomorrow, you need to make sure you are in bed early tonight. I'll make you a special tea that will help you sleep and ensure you wake up feeling refreshed."

"Galia, what would I ever do without you?" I hugged her close.

"Oh, now, mistress…" She blushed and hugged me back. "Go join Master Caleb as you wait for your guests. They will be arriving soon."

"All right but if you need me, don't hesitate to come get me."

*

As the night wore on, Collin finally stood. "Well, brother, are you ready?"

"Ready?" Caleb raised an eyebrow.

"Yes, ready to head over to my place."

"And why would I be going to your place this late at night?"

"Because it's the night before your wedding and you cannot stay here.

Besides, I insist we throw you a bachelor party."

Caleb pinched the bridge of his nose. "Collin, I have no desire to have a bachelor party."

"Come on you grumpy curmudgeon, don't be a party pooper. It's just the guys hanging out at Collin's having a few drinks and laughs." Greggory glanced sideways at his wife and I. "I'm under strict instructions to make sure things don't get out of control."

Caleb looked to me. I had been staring between the two of them with a frown on my face. "Sweetness, say the word and I won't go."

"You can go. The girls can stay here with me." I then looked at Collin, aiming a finger in his direction while he did his best to look innocent. "But if he shows up tomorrow looking like he hasn't slept for a month, I'm coming for you."

"My sweet goddess," he purred, taking my tiny hand in his and pressing it to his lips. "If my brother so much as looks like he didn't get a full night's sleep, I will gladly stand in his place."

"How come he's allowed to touch her?" Angus pouted. Kaan chuckled.

"He's not. That's enough of that." Caleb slapped his brother's hand away. "I'll be fine, sweetness. Will you walk me to the door?"

I smiled, then glared at his brother. "I'm serious, Collin." He chuckled as he crossed his finger over his heart.

"Victoria, are you sure you're okay? I don't want you to feel any stress over this." Caleb brushed a lock of hair behind my ear.

"I'm fine. Go have fun."

Caleb wrapped an arm around my waist and brought my hand to his lips. "Tomorrow will be one of the happiest days of my life. By this time, you will be Mrs. Victoria Carrington." He kissed each finger, then pressed his lips to mine.

My arms twined around his neck, pulling him close. "Maybe I should insist you stay home," I purred, a strong desire building in my chest.

Caleb's eyes glowed. "Don't tempt me, sweetness."

"All right you two, you'll have plenty of time for that when you're on your trip." Collin pulled his brother from my arms. Caleb growled but followed his brother and friends out of the house.

I turned and looked to Serena, Fiona, and Galia. "I guess it's just us tonight."

"Not quite." Serena giggled.

Moments later, the doorbell rang and Danica and Celeste crashed through the entryway carrying all sorts of goodies.

"It's party time!" Celeste whooped.

"What in the world?" I gasped. "Did you two raid the bakery and liquor store?"

"Not exactly." Danica smiled. "Well, we did ransack the bakery, but tonight is going to be alcohol-free. We bought all kinds of stuff to make different punches."

"No alcohol?" Celeste pouted.

"It dries out your skin and leaves you dehydrated. We can't have anyone looking like a zombie or fainting tomorrow." Danica looked pointedly at the pouting party animal.

Celeste held her hands up in resignation. "All right, guess we can all make up for it tomorrow at the reception."

"Celeste, you're hopeless," I teased. She winked and smiled at me.

We spent the next few hours relaxing and enjoying the delectable pastries Danica brought. When it was time for bed, Galia brought me a cup of tea as promised and sent me up to my room.

"Make sure you drink all of it, mistress. It will help you sleep." She winked.

"All right, I promise." I wished everyone good night and headed up to my room. After undressing and finishing off the tea, it didn't take me long to fall into a peaceful sleep.

*

The next morning, I woke to the sun shining through the curtains, the sky a bright blue and clear of any clouds. I stretched as I threw off the covers, not remembering the last time I slept so deeply. "I'm not sure I even moved during the night." I chuckled to myself.

There was a light knock on the door. "Victoria? Are you awake?"

"Yes, come in." Serena opened the door and filed in along with Fiona, Danica, and Celeste.

"How did you sleep?" Fiona asked.

"Wonderfully. The tea Galia gave me really worked. I feel so refreshed."

"Galia is in the kitchen now making breakfast. She's going to bring it up for us and then we'll have to start getting ready. We need to be at Horizons by noon."

"What time is it now?" I asked, standing and putting on my robe.

"Just a little past nine. We have plenty of time."

"Hmm…" I pulled aside the curtains and opened the double doors leading to the balcony. The girls exchanged glances as Galia came in with a tray of food and coffee.

After breakfast, I hummed to myself as I applied the last touches to my makeup at my vanity while Serena brushed and curled my hair.

She met my eyes in the mirror. "You're awfully calm, little one. Everything all right?"

"Yes, I feel fine. Remind me to thank Galia for the tea. I don't think its effect has worn off yet."

"Greggory mentioned that Caleb's been worried about you lately, saying that you're always tired. How are you feeling today?"

"There's been so much to do between the gala, the Tribunal, and the wedding. I haven't been sleeping very well. Between the long nap I took yesterday and getting such a good night's rest, I'm feeling much better."

"That's good. You must promise me that you'll relax while you and Caleb are away on your honeymoon."

"Yes, *Mom*," I teased.

Serena smiled and bopped my shoulder. "Has he told you where you are going yet?"

I shook my head. "Not a word. Sneaky vampire says it's a secret. Although I did catch him talking on the phone the other day about making sure that the location was well-provisioned and the kitchen was stocked. He might be taking me somewhere remote and reclusive."

"I wouldn't put that past him. He's never been one for crowded places, so I'm sure he wants to whisk you off to a place where you two can be alone."

"I won't mind if that's the case. Laying in a hammock on a private beach sounds really good right now."

Serena chuckled. "I definitely have to get some of that tea from Galia."

"It really is amazing."

"All right ladies, are you ready?" Fiona poked her head into my changing room. "It's time to put on the dress and get going."

I looked at myself in the mirror. My makeup was done, and Serena did a fantastic job curling my hair. It tumbled in loose waves over my shoulders and down my back.

"I'm ready." I nodded.

*

"Where in the world are my cuff links?" I paced in the guest room.

"Right here, master." Talin handed me the silver ornaments.

"And the ring?"

"Right here in my pocket." Collin patted his chest. "Brother, you need to calm down. The ceremony isn't for another two hours. You're going to have a heart attack at this rate."

I stopped pacing and blinked at him.

"Sit down and drink this." Greggory shoved me into a chair and handed me a shot.

"No, I don't want a drink." I pushed it away.

"It's one shot to calm your nerves." He glanced at Collin.

"Brother, drink it before we tie you down and force it down your throat."

I relented and shot the strong whiskey down in one gulp, wincing at the burn.

"Master, take deep breaths. All will be well." Talin placed a hand on my knee. "I've known you all your life, and while you tried to deny it for far too long, this is something you've wanted since you were a young child. Mistress

Victoria completes you. She loves you with all that she is, and you feel the same for her. There is nothing for you to be nervous about."

I smiled and let out a soft sigh. "Talin, you always see through me…Thank you, my friend."

*

In the garden at Horizons, I stood at the alter with Collin and Kaan. Wisteria draped the lattice archway, while small bouquets of lilies and roses were tied to every other chair lining the aisle.

"Breathe, my friend," Kaan whispered. "Your love will be arriving shortly."
I shifted.

"Brother, you're putting my teeth on edge with all that fidgeting."

"I can't help it. When is she going to get here?" I glanced down the aisle, watching as the guests filed in and found seats among the rows of chairs.

"Are you worried she's going to change her mind?" Collin laughed until he noticed the look on my face. "Caleb Carrington, I didn't think I'd ever see the day where you worried about getting dumped." At my growl, Collin's expression turned serious, and he placed a calming hand on my shoulder. "She's not going to stand you up. You have nothing to fear."

I took a deep breath. "You're right. I'm being silly."

"Yes, you are, and it's progress to see that you can admit it."

"Collin, I swear…"

"Relax, just trying to lighten the mood."

A hush descended among the guests as the piano started playing.

"She's here," Collin whispered. "Last chance to run, bro. Say the word and I'll jet you out of here."

I shooed him away and anxiously gazed down the long aisle. In moments, Serena appeared carrying a bouquet of off-white roses and lilies. She winked at me, then took her place at the altar.

The melody shifted. Our guests stood and turned toward the entrance. They blocked my view, and a growl rumbled low in my throat.

"Easy, brother," Collin whispered.

Everyone sighed, and I knew Victoria had entered. I could feel her presence and heavens help me I could smell her—that soft scent of rain and jasmine. It calmed me instantly.

Victoria came into view. My breath hitched in my throat. She was stunning, simply perfection.

Her champagne lace gown accentuated every beautiful curve, and her long dark hair hung loosely around her shoulders. The tips of her ears peeked through the tresses just below her thin floral crown. The memory of how sensitive they were to my touch filled my mind. Blushing at the wicked thoughts, I met her gaze.

*

We should have banned everyone from standing. Stepping slowly through the entrance, I looked to the altar where I knew Caleb would be, but I couldn't see him. His scent called to me, cedar and cinnamon pulling me forward.

Keeping a steady pace down the aisle, I smiled at our guests. Everyone looked so happy. One of the guests shifted, and I caught sight of him. He was so handsome in his tux, taking my breath away. Using every ounce of strength, I reminded my feet not to run down the aisle. Only three more feet and I would be at his side.

I smiled as I approached my groom and took his outstretched hand. Leaning close, I whispered, "And what is my lustful vampire thinking about right now?"

"Only how beautiful his bride is and how he can't wait to get her home and out of that dress."

"Caleb Carrington, you're hopeless."

"When it comes to you, sweetness, yes I am."

Standing before Kaan and all our family and friends, we recited our vows and exchanged rings.

"By the power vested in me...by me"—Kaan chuckled—"I now pronounce you husband and wife. Caleb, you may kiss your bride."

Caleb didn't hesitate to wrap his arms around my waist. He spun and dipped me while pressing his lips to mine. Lost in the warmth they provided, I held onto him, our tongues entwining in their familiar dance.

Placing me back on my feet, he grinned from ear to ear and pressed my hand to his lips. "You're truly mine now." His chest puffed out.

I smiled. "Deeply, always and forever."

Kaan's deep voice boomed as he announced, "I present to you Mr. and Mrs. Caleb Carrington. Please join us inside the restaurant for the reception."

We headed down the aisle, smiling and hugging our guests.

*

The reception was full of laughter, good food, and lots of dancing. By the end of the night, my feet were aching, and I collapsed back at the head table under a whole new level of exhaustion.

Kaan sat next to me. "How are you feeling, little one?"

"Tired, actually." I sighed, taking a large sip of water from the glass he handed me.

He nodded. "That is to be expected."

"Yes, I suppose so. It's been a busy few days."

"Ah, yes, that too."

I looked at him sideways. "Kaan, are you keeping secrets again?"

"Not at all, little one. I simply mean that you are going through a lot of changes right now and that surely is influencing you."

"Mmm." I narrowed my eyes at him. "When will you be returning home?" I asked.

"I will leave tomorrow after seeing you and Caleb off. It's a tradition for the family and close friends to send the happy couple off on their honeymoon. Once you and Caleb leave, I will return to my forest."

I placed a hand on his arm. "Will you make me a promise?"

"If it is within my power."

"I think you can manage this one. Promise not to be a stranger and come visit us even when it's not time for the Tribunal. I was nervous about meeting you, but now that I have, I don't think I would be happy only seeing you every five years."

Kaan smiled and raised my hand to his lips. "If that is what you wish, then I will make it a point to come and visit you more often."

"It would make me most happy."

"What is my love scheming now?" Caleb joined us along with the twins.

"Your beautiful bride has confessed that she longs to see me more often and wishes for me to visit you more frequently," Kaan teased his friend.

Caleb's eyes glowed. "Really now?" His brow arched. Bastian and Blake chuckled.

"Kaan, don't tease Caleb tonight. I merely asked that he visit us and not wait every five years." I reached over and grabbed Caleb's hand.

"Yes, old friend, it would be good to see you more often." Caleb wrapped an arm around my waist and pulled me close, still showing his possessiveness. I smiled. "My sweetness, it is time for us to bid everyone good night and head home. We are leaving early tomorrow."

"Where are we going?" I asked in another futile attempt to learn our destination.

"Ah, that is a secret." He tapped my nose with his fingertip.

I crossed my arms. "How will I pack if you won't tell me where we are going?"

"Don't you worry about a thing. I have that all taken care of...Galia has already packed your suitcase for you."

"That's cheating!" I exclaimed.

"Yep." He smiled as he drained his glass of wine. "Now gentlemen, if you will excuse us, my *wife* and I have someplace to be."

"Leaving already?" Collin asked, joining us. "Where do you need to be that's more important than here?"

I blushed as Caleb responded, "Our bedchamber."

"Caleb Carrington!"

He hoisted me into his arms and carried me all the way out to the car, smiling at all the guests that waved us off.

*

Once at the manor, I whisked Victoria into my arms and carried her up the stairs to our bedchamber.

"Caleb, what's the rush?"

"I need to feel you, Victoria. I need to touch every inch of you."

"Oh." She gasped as I kicked open our bedroom door and headed straight for the bathroom. I pulled at the lacing on her gown as soon as I set her down, kissing her firmly as I did so. She fumbled with the buttons of my shirt only a moment before gripping the collar and tearing it open.

My chest rumbled with a low growl of desire. "Sweetness if you keep up with this aggressiveness, I don't think I can be responsible for how I respond."

She answered with a wicked grin as she ripped my belt from around my waist.

Her dress fell to the floor, revealing her breasts. I kneaded them in my hands as I nipped my way down her slender neck.

"Victoria, I can't wait."

She tilted her head to the side. Sweeping her hair away, I plunged my fangs into the tender flesh. She gasped. I gulped down the warm sweet liquid as my fangs plunged deeper. She moaned in my arms, leaning into my embrace. My head swirled as I drank from her. Lifting my head, I licked at the wounds, healing them. She was gorgeous standing before me in her natural state. I shed my pants and boxers and led her to the shower. Turning on the warm water, I pulled her close.

Her fingers traced my muscles in their familiar patterns, each swipe of her fingertips inciting waves of pleasure. She reached over and grabbed her loofah, filling it with liquid soap, and then began to massage my tense muscles with it. The sensation of her washing my body was arousing and relaxing. She covered every inch of me.

When she reached my hips, her delicate, sudsy hands gripped my hardened erection. I tossed my head back at her irresistible touch. Her fingers wrapped around me and began pumping my length, building the tension in my groin. Turning me away from her, she continued her ministrations, washing the lather from me. My back suddenly felt cold, and I realized she was kneeling before me.

"Victoria?"

Without a word, she gripped the base of my erection and took me deep inside her mouth, her lips encasing my girth, her warm tongue massaging my length. I shuddered and moaned when she teasingly flicked the tip.

"Victoria, I'm..." She hummed. "Fuck, it feels so good...I'm going to..."

She continued, her motions quickening. No longer able to hold back, I placed a hand on the back of her head and thrust forward as I climaxed. She sucked and licked every drop from me.

Bringing her to her feet, I ran my thumb over her swollen lips and took the sponge from her. "My turn," I whispered.

I didn't leave one spot untouched as I washed her. My fingers pinched her taut nipple, making her back arch, while my other hand relentlessly thrusted into her core, bringing her to her peak several times. I pulled them out to rub at the sensitive nub bursting for attention. Victoria cried out my name, writhed in my arms, her body flush from her arousal and the warm water flowing over us.

I pressed her against the cool tiles and knelt before her, nipping at her hips before plunging my tongue deep inside her. The cry that escaped her lips urged me on in my assault. Tasting her put me in a state of euphoria.

Relentless in my affections, I lost count of the number of times I brought her to the peak of pleasure. Rising to my feet and placing my hands under her buttocks, I pinned her to the tiled wall and thrust into her. She bucked and moaned.

"Caleb..."

I slammed my mouth to hers, pushing my tongue between her lips. She entwined her fingers in my hair, pulling me closer.

"My love..." I huffed, quickening my pace. I was close.

She rocked her hips against me as we reached our pinnacle together.

Still holding her in my arms, I turned off the shower and carried her to our bed. I hovered above her.

"Victoria, I never thought I could be this happy. I love you."

She surprised me by flipping me over and straddling me. Victoria raised her hips, and as she leaned back, I felt myself enter her fully. I closed my eyes momentarily in pleasure, my hands gripping her hips. As she slowly rose up and down, the tension built again. I squeezed her harder, begging her to move faster. She tightened in response. Her body vibrating with anticipation, she tossed her head back.

"Don't hold back my love," I urged.

She placed her hands on my thighs, rocking her hips faster until she shuddered in release. Still aroused, I placed her on her knees. Kneeling behind her, I grabbed her hips and thrust hard, sheathing myself completely. I enfolded her body in my arms, one hand gripping her breast in my long fingers, the other fondling with her sex, holding her open so she could take all of me. I rubbed the taut nub that always brought her so much body-shivering pleasure.

"Caleb," she gasped. "I want you...to...bite me again."

Without a word, my fangs descended, waiting for the right time. Sensing our peaking tension, she tilted her head to the side, granting me full access to her neck. Her fingers entwined in my hair, she pulled my mouth to her soft supple skin.

I licked her neck, prompting goosebumps to pop out over her body. I plunged my fangs into her, moaning as I tasted her lifeforce. She sighed in pleasure. Rocking her hips in perfect unison with mine, we both cried out.

Collapsing to the bed in pure exhaustion, we fell asleep.

Chapter Forty-One

"Victoria, are you almost ready to go? Everyone is downstairs waiting for us," I called, entering our bedchamber. When there was no answer, I called again, "Victoria?"

"In the bathroom. Almost done."

I jingled the doorknob and found it locked. She was retching on the other side.

"Victoria, are you all right?" Silence. I knocked. "Sweetness?"

"Yes, I'll be fine, just an upset stomach. I'll be down in a minute."

The water started running, then shuffling and more retching. Was she ill? "Victoria, open this door right now. What's wrong?"

"Caleb, it's nothing…I'll meet you downstairs."

I didn't press but decided to wait for her to exit the bathroom. When she came out, she looked paler than usual.

"What's going on?" I approached her, rubbing her arms.

"I'm fine. My stomach is just upset. I think it was too much bacon at breakfast."

"Are you sure? Do we need to postpone our trip?"

"We most certainly will not. I've been looking forward to going away with you and having you all to myself."

I smiled. "If you're sure you're up for it."

"I am. Now let's get going. I'm excited to learn what you have planned for us."

"Want me to tell you?" I teased.

"Really?"

"Really."

"Tell me, tell me! I want to know." She gripped the edges of my collar and pulled me close, pecking me on the lips.

"All right, calm down. I rented an island for us in the Caribbean. We have a house and a private beach all to ourselves for two weeks."

"Seriously? A whole island?" Her eyes glittered with delight. "What a dream come true. We can walk the beach at night...Think of all the stars we will be able to see!"

I nodded. "The house even has a high-powered telescope we can use."

Victoria giggled with excitement. "I can't wait."

"It has a fully stocked kitchen so you can cook, or we can have a personal chef come out and cook dinners. You can decide when we get there. There's a pool that overlooks the ocean, and we can even schedule massages for us on the beach."

"Oh, Caleb, it sounds like a dream. I can't wait."

I kissed her. "I'm glad you're happy, but we really need to get going or we will miss our flight."

"Then let's go." She grabbed my hand and pulled me from our bedroom and down the stairs.

*

In the entryway, Serena, Greggory, Collin, Fiona, and Kaan all waited for us. Angus had to go home early because his mate had given birth. He promised to invite us to his castle soon so we could meet Sheila and his children.

"Have a wonderful time, little one, and make sure you get plenty of rest." Serena kissed my cheek.

"I will. I'll send you lots of pictures."

"You better." She smiled.

"My dear Victoria, I hate to say goodbye. I promise I will make time to come visit soon, and you can always take a trip to see me if your husband can manage a few days without you." Fiona winked.

"I would love that very much, Fiona. I'm sure I'm going to need your help over the next few months. Let's plan something when I return."

"It's a date." She smiled and embraced me.

Collin sighed in fake despair. "My sweet goddess, now that you're married, I guess I need to face the fact that you'll never be mine."

"You big lug, must you always be so dramatic?" I laughed.

"Giving up on the sharing bit?" Caleb asked suspiciously.

"Just for today." Collin winked. "She's still *our* goddess." He hugged me close, teasing his brother.

"All right, enough of that, Collin. I can't breathe."

He released me and ruffled my hair. "Have a great time and don't give this place another thought. Enjoy yourselves." He patted his brother on the back, then pulled him into a warm embrace. "You both deserve this."

I approached Kaan. "Remember your promise. I expect to see you soon."

"I would never go back on my word, little one, especially not to you." He raised my hand to his lips.

"Thank you, and don't be a stranger." Caleb shook his friend's hand.

Talin and Galia entered through the front door. "Your bags are all packed in the car, master. You're all set to go."

"Mistress, I made sure to pack everything you'll need. Be safe and use this time to rest your body." She smiled. "I've also packed some extra vitamins for you. I want you to take them while you're away. They will help with your energy level."

"Thank you, Galia. I appreciate it, and I promise I will."

As we turned to leave, Collin called out, "Make sure to have several libations in my name, preferably with those little umbrellas in them."

Kaan took my hand, stopping me. "Not for you, little one. I'm afraid you'll have to forgo spirits on this trip."

"What do you mean?" Caleb asked.

Kaan grabbed Caleb's hand and placed it on my belly. "It isn't good for the children."

"Children?" We both asked, looking from each other to Kaan. Collin inhaled a sharp breath, while Serena gasped. Greggory chuckled. Fiona, Galia, and Talin all snickered, sharing knowing looks.

Kaan nodded. "Yes, little one, you are currently expecting. Did you not know?"

I shook my head dumbfounded. Caleb was grinning from ear to ear. "Are you sure?" he asked.

"Without a doubt. Dragons are never wrong."

"Wait…you said children," I stammered as realization struck.

"Why yes, Victoria, you're pregnant with twins."

"*Twins!*"

—

With Thanks

...And A Sneak Peek!

Dear Reader

Thank you for reading *Haunted Fate: Destined Lovers*. I would love to hear from you, so please take a moment to leave a review on Amazon. If you enjoyed this story, please also share with friends and family by posting about it on Facebook or Twitter.

As a special thank you, keep reading for a sneak peek of the next steamy installment of *Haunted Fate: Captured Hearts* continues with Collin and Blake, the two most eligible bachelors in the Vampire Council.

C.A. Cleary
Massachusetts, September 2021

CAPTURED HEARTS

CHAPTER ONE

"COLLIN!" Victoria screamed through gritted teeth.

"I'm driving as fast as I can…"

"Drive *faster!*"

I grimaced. "My sweet goddess, please retract your claws."

"Sorry." Tears streamed down her cheeks.

"We'll be at the hospital soon. Caleb should be on his way."

She sobbed. "Caleb."

You better be there, brother.

I was deeply regretting each decision I had made that morning. The first, stopping by the manor. While Caleb was meeting with one of our larger clients from overseas, he asked me to check on Victoria. Though he had passed on the responsibility of head of the Council to me, he was still overseeing the family business—Carrington Properties, Inc.

"I'm so glad you're here." She hugged me when I came in and handed me a cup of coffee. "Do you want anything else?"

"My sweet goddess, all I need is your company."

"You're incorrigible." She chuckled as she turned and waddled into the kitchen.

Made you smile. "I try."

"Why aren't you at the meeting with Caleb? I'm surprised you're not sitting front and center while they sign this new contract. It's a pretty big win from what Caleb's told me."

"Then I wouldn't be able to spend this quality time with you, princess." She rolled her eyes at me over her cup of tea. "You know I hate that stuff. I'm more about drawing them in, wining and dining them. Caleb's the master when it comes to the fine print." I took a sip of my coffee. "How are the little nippers doing? I have to say, you're glowing right up through the tips of your pointed ears."

"They're quiet for the moment. After the acrobatics they were doing throughout the night, I'm surprised my stomach didn't burst." She rubbed absently at her swollen belly.

"You're still the most beautiful creature to grace these halls."

"Shameless flirt."

"Devilish imp." She stuck her tongue out at me as I rose from the table to place my empty cup in the sink. When I turned back, her face had gone pale. "Victoria, what's wrong?" I rushed back to her.

"Collin?"

"What is it, princess?" I took her hand in mine.

"My water broke…"

"No…no, it couldn't have." My mouth went dry. "You're not due for another two weeks."

"I'm telling you it broke," she repeated.

No. No. No. "Caleb's not here!"

"I know that…"

"It couldn't have broken. It wouldn't break without him here." The blank stare she gave me did nothing to calm the panic rising in my chest. "Put it back…" She punched me in the arm. "Ouch! What do you want me to do about it?" I could barely contain the volume of my voice.

"Collin Carrington, I swear…" She placed her hands on either side of my face and forced me to look her in the eyes. "You need to pull it together. I need you right now."

I shook my head, my cheeks squishing between her palms. *No, you need my stupid brother. Why did he leave you? Why did I come here?*

"I need you to call Caleb and take me to the hospital. When they start, we'll need to time my…." A scream, one I never thought could come out of one so tiny, cut off her last words. Her fingers gripping my face turned from tender to vise-like before I could blink. *Aaagghh…*I'd never felt such excruciating pain. Before I could make a sound, Galia came running into the kitchen.

"Mistress, you need to let go of Master Collin before you pop his eyes out." She gently removed Victoria's hands and placed them on the armrests of her chair. She didn't make a sound, but her face was scrunched up and red. "Grip this instead."

Galia, you're an angel.

"Master Collin, let me see your face." Galia examined the fingernail impressions in my cheeks. "You'll survive, they're already healing. I'll call Master Caleb. You need to focus on getting her into your car and to the hospital."

"She wanted me to time something?" I whispered.

"Her contractions."

"I don't know what that means."

"Count the time between pain episodes and how long they last."

"Ah…and…how do I do that?"

"Oh for the love of the heavens, sweet boy." Galia rolled her eyes. "Give her something to squeeze when she's having one. Time how long she holds it and how long in-between squeezes. Understand, dear?"

I shook my head, but when she fixed me with a serious glare, I nodded. "Yep."

Without another word, I scooped Victoria up in my arms and carried her to my car.

The second thing I regretted that morning was sacrificing my arm for Victoria to squeeze during her contractions, the divots from her fingernails clear evidence of my mistake. *Very bad idea.*

She was a whirlwind of emotions in the passenger seat. Raging one minute, weeping the next, and screaming shortly after the tears dried. *I'm not cut out for this.* I wanted to laugh, scream, and cry right along with her.

Driving through the crowded streets was also grating on my nerves. Victoria howled again.

"Why don't we try the breathing exercises you learned?" I suggested.

Closing her eyes, she began taking slow, measured breaths. Her hand never left my arm but her grip loosened…briefly.

"*Eeee…*" Victoria bit down on her lip.

Here come the claws. Sure enough, the sharp pain shot through my skin moments later. I groaned, my fangs elongating, unbidden.

"Sorry." She sobbed, trying to take quick breaths.

"The contractions are coming faster."

She nodded, leaning back into the headrest.

"We're almost there, princess. Once Caleb arrives, he will be able to soothe your pain."

She furrowed her brow at me.

I chuckled. "Have you forgotten? Vampires have the power to soothe their mates when they're in pain."

"Ah, yes, that's…a useful…power." Victoria huffed.

I took her tiny hand in mine, pressed it to my lips, and winked. She smiled.

When we veered into the hospital's valet, an orderly rushed out with a wheelchair. *Galia must've called ahead.* He opened Victoria's door and helped her out.

I ran around the car, tossing my keys to the attendant. "All yours." Looking at the orderly, I asked, "Mind if I drive?" Taking control of the chair, I wheeled her into the lobby. The nurse behind the counter looked up. One glance at

Victoria's face had her running around the desk.

"Mrs. Carrington?" Victoria nodded.

"According to your records your due date isn't for another two weeks."

"Surprise." Victoria hissed through clenched teeth.

"Are you having contractions?"

"She is," I answered for her. "Her water broke too." The nurse turned to me for the first time.

"Are you the father?" she asked.

"Oh no! No kids for me. That honor is my brother's. I thought he would be here already." I looked around the waiting area. *Where is he?*

"And you are?"

I frowned slightly. *Ouch!* "Collin Carrington."

"Oh! My apologies, sir. I didn't recognize you." She returned her attention to Victoria. "Dr. Hansing is away on vacation this week. Dr. Downing is covering in delivery. We paged her as soon as we received the call you were coming. Let's get you checked in."

"I can help you with that. I'm not sure she'll be able to answer between the screams." The nurse nodded and beckoned me over to the desk.

Victoria grabbed my hand before I could walk away. Fear shone in her eyes. I patted her hand. "I'll be right here, princess."

As I gave the nurse Victoria's information, I pulled out my phone and called my brother. "Where the hell are you?"

"I'm almost there," Caleb answered on the other end. He sounded almost as panicked as Victoria. "There was an accident on the main road. I should've ran there. How is she?"

"Terrified and in pain. She needs you, Caleb. Do what you need to do but get here...now!" I hung up, following after the nurse who wheeled Victoria behind the delivery room doors. I knelt down so we were eye to eye. "Caleb's almost here. You're all checked in, and the doctor should be here any minute."

Victoria nodded, tears filling her eyes. "Collin, I don't know if I can do this."

"It's a little late for doubts, darling. Besides, when have you ever shied away from a challenge?"

"It...*hurts*," she cried.

Before I could respond, we were interrupted.

"Mrs. Carrington, I'm Dr. Downing." A tall chestnut-haired woman approached. My heart thumped and pounded in my chest.

Wow.

"Hello...doctor." Victoria answered weakly.

"Please call me Gianna. Is this your husband...?" Her voice hitched when her winter-gray eyes locked with mine.

"No. He's my brother-in-law." She looked between us.

"Uh...yes...that...I'm her..." I couldn't think. "Collin!" I shoved my hand out to her.

"What is wrong with you?" Victoria hissed. "And what is that smell?"

Gianna breathed in deeply. "Clove and amber."

"I think I'm going to be sick." Victoria covered her mouth, heaving in the back of her throat. Neither of us turned to her until she smacked my arm. "Get me a..."

"What?" I looked to her.

"Bucket," was all she managed before vomiting on the floor.

Gianna's attention returned to Victoria. "Oh! Mrs. Carrington, let's get you into a room and changed."

"No need for formalities. Please call me Victoria."

"How far apart are your contractions?"

"Five minutes!" I barked.

Gianna jumped at my voice. "And how long are they?"

I held up one finger.

"One minute?"

I nodded.

She smiled. "Are you always this articulate?"

"No...yes...um...what?" I scratched at the back of my head. *What is wrong with me?*

She laughed. "Is the father on the way?"

"He better be, or I'm going to drive a stake through his heart," Victoria growled.

She's really scary right now.

The doors opened, and Caleb came charging in. "Victoria!" He ran to her side, taking her hand in his and kissing it. "I'm so sorry I wasn't home with you. You aren't due for a couple of more weeks. I thought you'd be…"

"What the hell took you so long? This is your fault! You were seconds away from being staked. How dare you leave me…*Aaahh!*" A contraction hit her. Her face scrunched up as she squeezed Caleb's hand.

Caleb's eyes, full of pain and confusion and *tears*, met mine. His ears, cheeks, and neck flushed from the tension. His fangs poked out from between his lips.

"Welcome to my world, brother. This bundle of crazy is all yours."

I watched as the doctor wheeled Victoria further into the delivery area, Caleb being dragged along like a lost puppy. My eyes instinctively lingered over the curve of Gianna's hips. My world seemed to sway, matching their rhythmic swish—left, right, left…I shook my head to clear my thoughts and took out my phone.

Maybe I should follow them…No. I like my heart stake-free.

"Hey Collin, what's up?" Blake answered on the first ring.

"Victoria's in labor."

"*What?*"

"They just took her back. Can you call everyone and let them know?"

"Sure thing, boss. What are you going to do?"

"See if I need stitches."

"She beat you up?"

"That's putting it mildly. I think I've permanently lost feeling in my right arm." I shook out the numbness, then carefully inspected the fingernail indents, some of which had drawn blood.

"Ha, she's tougher than she looks. I'll call everyone and see you there."

"Make it quick. I expect the youngsters will be here shortly."

"You got it."

I hung up. Sitting in a chair, I leaned back and closed my eyes, the image of Dr. Downing immediately filling my mind. *Why am I so flustered?* She was a beautiful woman, but I'd been around beautiful women before. What was it about her that made me so tongue tied? Her warm chocolate hair? Or her eyes, the color of the sky before a thunderstorm? Perhaps her scent...citrus and gardenia. It was intoxicating.

Gianna.

—

Acknowledgements

There are so many people I want to thank for helping this dream come true. Those that inspired and encouraged me and those that were the source of life trials that led me to create these stories in my mind…you all played a part.

I want to thank my parents, for always pushing me to excel and be the best I can be. For loving me through it all and teaching me that anything is possible if you put your mind to it.

My best friend, Carol, for urging me to pursue my dream. For being the whisper in my ear saying, "You can do this." Your words of encouragement never let me give up.

My soul sister, Lori, your unwavering faith in my ability was the light in a tunnel of doubt. Thank you for always being there.

My beta readers, Amanda and Kim, thank you for being my guinea pigs and for helping me bring Victoria and Caleb to life. Your input was invaluable.

My cover designer, Mark, thanks for being able to get into my head and bring my cover visions to reality. I'm looking forward to the next cover design.

And finally, my editor Makenna, what would I have done without you? You took a process I was terrified to face and made it exciting. Without you, *Destined Lovers* would not be the book it is today. Your love for these characters almost surpasses mine. I look forward to working with you on the next installments of the *Haunted Fate* series.

Thank you everyone!

About the Author

C.A. Cleary was born in northern California, currently residing in Massachusetts, and is a single mom to her vivacious son. Since she was a young girl, she's been fascinated with the mythical and supernatural. Growing up in the 1980s, she spent her Saturdays watching horror films and writing short stories about the mythical creatures, especially vampires, werewolves, and dragons. Today, she recognizes that dream through her debut paranormal series. When she's not writing, she spends most of her time traveling with family and friends, or relaxing in the back yard with their two dogs.

Discover more about C.A. Cleary via her website:
www.clearypublishing.com

You can also connect with her via social media:

www.facebook.com/clearypublishing
Twitter.com/CACleary1
Instagram.com/cacleary527